"Effervescently funny and stealthily heartbreaking . . . An extraordinarily humane book that only Jonathan Ames could have written."

—Peter Cameron, author of *Andorra*

"The most hilarious book we've read all summer."

—*Bay Area Reporter*

"Brilliant . . . a coming-of-age tale that explores the labyrinth of our sexual selves."

—*St. Petersburg Times*

"An utterly charming—and never saccharine—tale of friendship between two peculiar people. Henry and Louis are so beautifully drawn that it's easy to get caught up in their drama."

—*New York Post*

"Ames's second novel is outrageous, yet his characters evoke sympathy and interest."

—*Library Journal*

"In Henry and Louis, Ames has created . . . two of the most startlingly human characters in recent fiction. . . . Beguiling, quietly disturbing."

—*Seattle Post-Intelligencer*

"Jonathan Ames has always been one of my favorite contemporary writers, both for his limpid and elegant Lost Generation prose style and for his utterly fearless commitment to the most demanding psychosexual comedies. *THE EXTRA MAN* extends his accomplishments considerably. This is one of the most charming and alarming books of recent years."

—Rick Moody, author of *Right Livelihoods*

AN IMPRINT OF PUSHKIN PRESS

Acclaim for Jonathan Ames
and *The Extra Man*

"*THE EXTRA MAN* wins us over with its sheer energy and good will, its confidence in the ability of its own humor and intelligence to widen our ideas about the possibilities of love, and about the permissible range of inner and outer lives to which today's young gentleman may properly aspire."

—Francine Prose, *New York Observer*

"By updating the moral education of a young gentleman, Ames has written a *Bildungsroman* for the end of our century."

—*Washington Post*

"Not since *Harold and Maude* has there been such a lovable odd couple as Louis Ives and Henry Harrison. Told in a lucid, diverting prose style, *THE EXTRA MAN* is a picaresque tale of a young man's sentimental education (in subjects ranging from tuxedo studs to transsexuals). In Henry Harrison, Jonathan Ames has created a truly memorable character."

—Jeffrey Eugenides, author of *The Virgin Suicides*

"The Louis and Henry show is honest, funny, and original, making the meaning of 'human' deep and strange in the best way."

—*Village Voice*

"Wonderfully odd and charming, at times riotously funny, Jonathan Ames's *THE EXTRA MAN* strikes a perfect balance between sympathy and comedy, drawing upon deep reserves of compassion for the strange and unnamable urges that infiltrate the lives of his two remarkable characters."

—Martha McPhee, author of *Bright Angel Time*

"A miracle . . . This novel is not to be missed."

—*Booklist* (starred review)

"Ames makes it clear that his protagonist's sexual tentativeness and anxiety are really just flimsy covers for his passion and warmth. That's what makes *THE EXTRA MAN* work so well. Louis may feel as awkward as Milton Berle in drag, but inside he's really Fred Astaire—he just doesn't know it yet."

—*New York Times*

"If you thought the mix of Jewish and sexual comedy in *Portnoy's Complaint* was unpredictable and wild, Ames's second novel almost has it beat."

—*Jerusalem Report*

"An endearing, entertaining story."

—*San Francisco Chronicle*

"[A] blissfully funny, brilliantly written novel."

—*Paper* magazine

"Funny, delightfully odd and surprisingly sweet . . . With Ames, the sensational is oddly charming. So is the mundane."

—Long Island *Newsday*

"A gentle account of a burgeoning friendship between two likable oddballs . . . It's just plain fun to watch these quasi-misfits fall for each other."

—*Kirkus Reviews*

"Written with almost embarrassing candor, *THE EXTRA MAN* is a novel of exceptional control about the uncontrollable passions that shape our lives . . . bittersweet . . . boldly vulnerable and touching."

—*San Diego Union-Tribune*

"An *Odd Couple* for the sweetly naive and the cautiously dissolute . . . Here is a confection to be devoured on the loneliest of nights."

—J. D. Landis, author of *Lying in Bed*

"Makes verbal high jinks look almost as easy as pie in the face . . . An urban confection."

—*The New Yorker*

THE
EXTRA MAN

JONATHAN AMES

AN IMPRINT OF PUSHKIN PRESS

Pushkin Press
71–75 Shelton Street
London WC2H 9JQ

Original text © 1998 Jonathan Ames

The Extra Man was first published in 1998 by Scribner
Published by ONE, an imprint of Pushkin Press in 2018

1 3 5 7 9 8 6 4 2

ISBN 13: 978-1-78227-468-1

Designed and typeset by Tetragon, London
Printed in Great Britain by the CPI Group, UK

www.pushkinpress.com

For my parents

Acknowledgments

The author would like to thank and acknowledge the following individuals and institutions: Rosalie Siegel, Peter Cameron, Blair Clark, Joanna Clark, Leigh Haber, Greer Kessel, Doris Klein, Elizabeth Thayer, Larry Wolhandler, The New Jersey State Council on the Arts, Runt Farm, and the Corporation of Yaddo.

My story is much too sad to be told,
But practically everything leaves me totally cold.
The only exception I know is the case
When I'm out on a quiet spree,
Fighting vainly the old ennui,
And I suddenly turn and see your fabulous face.

—COLE PORTER,
"I GET A KICK OUT OF YOU"

Who will teach me what I must shun?
Or must I go where the impulse drives?

—GOETHE

CHAPTER I

The Brassiere

I came to New York to find myself and get a fresh start. I was also, to be honest, running away from some messy business that occurred at the Pretty Brook Country Day School in Princeton, New Jersey. I had been a respected English teacher there for four years, ever since graduating from college. My downfall was a brassiere.

I came upon it in the deserted teacher's lounge after school one day late in the spring of 1992. Its white strap was hanging out of the large gym bag of one of my colleagues, a Ms. Jefferies, whom I found attractive, though that's more or less incidental to the case. She was the assistant tennis coach, and I imagined that she must have changed into a sports bra of some type and that she was out practicing with the girls.

So I saw that strap dangling out of the bag like a snake and I was alarmed. I decided to be virtuous and ignore the strap. To show my strength, I sat at my little desk to grade some essays, which had been my original intention. We all had our own little desks in the lounge for doing work and after laboring over three or four poor samples of seventh-grade grammar, I forgot entirely about the brassiere. I did become thirsty though, and I walked over to the watercooler to get a drink. Without realizing it, my path took me right alongside Ms. Jefferies' gym bag and there, miraculously, the strap of that bra hooked itself into the cuff of my khaki pants and the bra was yanked out like a magician's handkerchief.

I felt only a slight tug, like a bite, saw a flash of white out of the corner of my eye, realized it was the bra, and my first impulse was to look to the door. No one was coming! Then I stared down at the bra. I saw the barely visible etchings of flowers in the white material. I saw the sturdily lined, ample cups, whose very shape implied so much. I saw the white loops for lovely shoulders. "Oh, God, it's beautiful," I thought. I wanted to steal it and take it home.

Again, like a sinner, I looked to the door. I became rational. I was in Pretty Brook! I kicked my leg out and the bra dislodged. I then kicked at the bra like a soccer player, aiming to get it back in the bag, but it only skidded a few inches and stopped. It just lay there, still, on the low-cut brown carpeting.

My weakness prevailed. I bent down quickly and scooped the bra up. The touch of it aroused me immediately. I felt the stitched-in wire supports of the cups. The weight they held! Why couldn't I have such weight? Then I pressed a cup to my nose and I smelled perfume. It was intoxicating. Then I did something mad. I put the bra on over my spring-weight tweed coat and gazed at myself in the mirror above the watercooler. I looked absurd, I was wearing a tie, but I had a wonderful, fleeting sensation of femininity, and then at that very moment the head of the Lower School, kindergarten through fifth grade, came in. A Mrs. Marsh, who was married to Mr. Marsh, the principal of Pretty Brook. I faced my executioner with her brown skirt, yellow blouse, and bullet-gray hair, and she said, baffled, yet accusingly, "Mr. Ives?"

"It was in Ms. Jefferies' bag!" I blurted out, which was of course an incriminating and ridiculous thing to say. I could have escaped by passing it off as a joke, a silly gag. I could have kicked out my leg this time like a Rockette, but she had heard my guilty exclamation, she saw my guilty eyes, and then she looked down—how could she fail to notice—and saw my protuberance pressing up and to the left (pointing north to New York? to my heart?) which proclaimed the guilt of my action even more profoundly than the wild look of sex that must have been in my eyes.

To Mrs. Marsh's credit she discreetly left the room without saying another word. I took the bra off and I wondered if it was sturdy enough to act as a noose. I could take it to the men's room and hang myself. I knew my career at Pretty Brook was over. The publicity of my erection had sealed my fate.

I bravely stayed on for the remainder of the spring term, but I wasn't asked back for the fall. I was let go supposedly because of budget cuts and declining enrollment, but I knew the real reason why the budget could no longer sustain me.

I spent most of the summer depressed and ashamed. I had liked teaching. I had enjoyed pretending that I was a professor and dressing like one, even though I only taught the seventh grade. But I was afraid to apply for other teaching jobs. I feared that Pretty Brook would give me a terrible reference: "He's very good with the children, but we suspect that he's a transvestite."

I had a little money saved up, but it wasn't going to last me long as I had my college loans to pay. I was eligible for unemployment, but that wasn't going to start until the fall, nor was it a solution. In my nervousness about my future, I took to walking the beautiful and elegant tree-lined streets of Princeton. I often marched up and down Nassau Street, the main drag, though I made sure to avoid the window of Edith's Lingerie Shop.

I frequently saw former students during my walks and their happy greetings would initially cheer me up and then further depress me. But overall, walking in Princeton was a very good thing—it's quite a civilized and genteel community. There's nothing else like it in New Jersey, or even perhaps the rest of the United States. It has both an English feeling to it and a Southern feeling. There are grand colonial mansions; middle-class houses with wraparound porches; a poor black neighborhood with clotheslines waving like international flags; and then, of course, Princeton University, peering down upon everything from its eerie Gothic towers, and resting regally behind its gates like Buckingham Palace.

In the center of town, off Nassau Street, there's a charming grassy lawn with old trees and flowers and many benches. It's called Palmer Square and it rests between the attractive art deco post office and the century-old hotel, the Nassau Inn. The benches of Palmer Square were often my destination when I would exhaust myself from my daily marches.

Because of my act of spontaneous, self-destructive bra-wearing, which had cost me a beloved position, I thought of myself as unwell and imbalanced. Also I had started reading Thomas Mann's *The Magic Mountain* and I overidentified with the main character, a profoundly confused young man, Hans Castorp, who takes a seven-year tubercular cure in the Swiss Alps even though he's perfectly healthy.

So I began to think of my walks as a form of cure and I took to wearing a light coat because Hans always wore a coat. And I started to view all of Princeton as a gigantic sanitarium and considered the other Palmer Square bench-sitters to be fellow patients, which in fact was true. For some reason, Princeton has attracted a number of halfway houses that cater to various mental disorders, and many of the residents gravitate towards Palmer Square.

So we all sat on the benches, holding on, in differing states of desperation. Two of the regulars on the benches were old professors who had lost their minds, but I admired how elegantly they still managed to dress. And along with those of us who were having mental problems there were quite a few pensioners, men and women, and they weren't crazy, but they were mad with loneliness. A few of them were dangerous to speak with: the only way to disengage was to suddenly stand up, say good-bye politely, and then walk away while they were in mid-sentence.

As a result, I only had passing acquaintances with these bench colleagues—I had no close friends. The only person who could have fallen into that category was a student at the Princeton Theological Seminary, Paul, who had left town a few months before to take up a Presbyterian ministry in Adelaide, Australia. So my only solace, besides walking, was drinking iced coffee and reading as much as possible.

Then one day in late August I was sitting on my favorite bench in front of the post office and I was stupefied by the central Jersey heat and atmosphere, whose degree of moisture in summertime can be Amazonian in content. I had made matters worse by parading around like a vain fool in my gray-striped seersucker jacket, which you can wear in summer in most climates, like in the Swiss Alps or even the South of France, but not in Mercer County. I had sadly finished *The Magic Mountain* and I was now carrying around Henry James's *Washington Square*, but I was too devastated to do any reading. My copy was an old paperback and on the cover was a watercolor painting of the Washington Arch viewed from Fifth Avenue. And I was simply staring at the cover in a state of depression and dehydration, when I suddenly had an inspiration as to what I should do: Move to New York City and live!

A simple plan unfolded: Find a cheap room and gain employment. Since I had been an English major at Rutgers, in the honors program, I thought I'd look into the magazine and publishing worlds for a job. But the first step was to find a room, a base of operations.

I thought that the romantic thing to do was to live in a hotel. I liked to imagine that I was a young gentleman, and so the idea of having a friendly hotel clerk who took messages for me, and said good-bye to me every morning as I headed out in my jacket and tie, appealed to me.

The next day I took the train into New York. I used *The Village Voice* classified section as my guide and I sought out the hotels that advertised under the heading "Furnished Rooms for Rent." It was easy for me to find the hotels, as I was quite capable of making my way around Manhattan. I grew up in northern New Jersey, just fifty miles from the George Washington Bridge, and I had been coming to the city for museums and plays and odd quests my whole life. But until that moment when I looked at the Henry James cover, I had never really thought of living in New York.

My earliest memories of the city are of how it appeared from the top of the Ramapo Mountains, at whose base my hometown, Ramapo, is located. The Ramapos aren't a very impressive mountain range—in other states they would be considered large hills—but as a child I thought they were beautiful, and from them you could see New York. During the day, only the tops of the buildings were visible: they rose out of gray mist and pollution. And at night, my father sometimes took my mother and me to a peak of one of the Ramapos, on a road called Skyline Drive, and he exclaimed every time, "Look! There's the city!"

He was proud that he had moved from Brooklyn to a place with such a view, almost as if he himself had discovered it. And it was spectacular. You could see the buildings as they were defined by the light around them. They looked like rocket ships to me, and the whole city shone like a crown, like a faraway Oz.

So in some ways I had never let go of my initial awe and fear of New York, this feeling that it wasn't a real place where a person, where I, could live. But having lost my job at Pretty Brook, and armed with a pleasant fantasy about being a young-gentleman-about-town, I put my old fear away and I went to hotels all over Manhattan.

I unfortunately discovered that a young-gentleman-of-limited-means no longer stays in hotels. Even the least expensive places cost five hundred dollars a month and the rooms they offered were squalid and depressing. The beds were collapsing and stained, all the windows looked on to air shafts, and you had to share a bathroom with everyone else on your hall. And the other residents, whom I caught glimpses of, looked like crack or heroin addicts.

I spoke to only one person, a young woman. She was leaving the Riverview Hotel on Jane Street in the Village just as I was climbing the stairs. She was carrying a guitar case, and I thought to myself, "Maybe this is where artists live. This could be good." I decided to be gregarious and I said to her, with a smile, "Excuse me, I'm from out of town, and I was wondering, is this an all right place?" She gave me the most frightened look and upon closer inspection I saw that her hair was filthy and clotted and that there were violet pools beneath her eyes. She fled past me down the stairs and I imagined, in that brief moment, that she was a folksinger who had fallen upon hard times. I watched her walk quickly up the sidewalk and I realized that her guitar case was burst open on its side and that it carried no instrument.

I hadn't expected beautiful accommodations, but the environments in these hotels were much worse than what I had imagined, and the clerks were not at all what I had hoped for. There was no chance that they would take an interest in my life and wish me well in the mornings when I left for work. They all dealt with me from behind bullet-proof sheets of glass, and even with the speaking holes I found it difficult to understand what they were saying.

At the finish of this first day of starting a new life, I ended up in a Greek diner. I had a cup of coffee and I felt the despair return that had been with me all summer. My life was obviously a mess and I thought myself a fool for having pursued a clearly outdated notion of how one might live in New York. I wanted to give up, but I didn't have many options left in Princeton, so I reopened my crumpled *Village Voice*. I looked in the "Apartments for Rent" section, but everything seemed far too expensive. And then under "Roommates Wanted" there was an ad that caught my eye. It read as follows: "Writer looking for responsible male to share apartment. Don't call before noon. Can call after midnight. $210/month. 555-3264."

It was odd, it gave an old-fashioned phone exchange, but it was also the cheapest listing in the whole *Village Voice*, and the idea of a writer was romantic to me. I was enthused again and immediately called the number from a pay phone in the diner.

"H. Harrison," answered an older man's voice.

"I'm calling about the room—"

"Can you pay the rent?"

"Yes, I think so."

"What type of work do you do?"

"I teach—"

"Can you come right now? I don't want to talk on the phone. I can't stand all these calls."

His phone manner was abrupt, but that was understandable considering how many people must have been inquiring about the room. I told him I'd come see him immediately. He gave me the address and I jotted it on a napkin. It seemed like incredibly good luck that I should have caught him in. He lived on the Upper East Side and his full name was Henry Harrison. I told him that I was Louis Ives. We said good-bye, I paid for my coffee, and I rushed out of the diner with a feeling of great expectation. This Henry Harrison had sounded very promising.

There's to Be No Fornication

I took a Number 6 uptown and I looked at myself in the train's darkened window. My hair, which had begun to thin, looked thick in the window's black reflection, and this buoyed my confidence and added to my good feeling.

I got off at the Ninety-sixth Street station and I walked down the hill from Lexington to Second Avenue. It was early evening, still light out, and the air was pleasant. The city felt calm.

Mr. Harrison's building was on Ninety-third, between Second and First avenues. It was an old five-story brick walk-up—there were about a dozen walk-ups on the street—and in the little vestibule I buzzed the appropriate buzzer. Out of the intercom came his voice; he was obviously shouting: "YOU'RE THE TEACHER?" I shouted back into the speaker, "Yes, it's me!" He then buzzed the door open and even as I climbed the first set of stairs the sound of the lock clicking followed me. He was making sure that I was able to get in.

The apartment was on the fourth floor and despite all my walking in Princeton I was a little winded. But I was also energized. I was nervous and my heart was pounding. I felt like an actor going on an audition. I wanted that room! It had to be the cheapest in New York. I knocked at the door. I heard some shuffling.

Then the door opened and with a small breeze of air coming from inside, I smelled Henry Harrison before I saw him. It was a strong, mixed odor: unwashed shirts and sweet cologne; a smell of salt and a smell of sugar.

Then I saw him. There was the immediate impression of both beauty and decay, like an elegant room whose high ceiling is yellowed and chipping off. He was old, somewhere in his late sixties was my immediate guess, but his face was still strikingly handsome. He had a good-looking nose. It was straight and appealing and the tip was in fine shape—no mottling or holes. His hair was dark brown, too dark it seemed, but it was thick, thicker than mine, and it was swept straight back like a 1930s movie star. He had a confident chin and he was clean-shaven, but he had missed an obvious portion of grayish moustache directly under the nose. And there was something about the deep lines around his mouth and the wild, curious look in his dark eyes that was reminiscent of an old street bum lit up with drink, though I smelled no alcohol.

"Come in, come in," he said, and he closed the door behind me. He offered me his hand and we shook and we reintroduced ourselves to get through those first awkward moments. "Harrison, Henry. Henry Harrison," he said.

"Louis. Louis Ives," I answered and our hands let go.

He wasn't a tall man. He stood around five feet nine inches, and he was wearing a frayed blue blazer, a pair of stained tan pants, and a button-down red shirt. The collar of the shirt, on the left-hand side, had escaped the lapel of the blazer and was pointing out like a red dart.

I was in practically the same outfit, blazer and khaki pants, except all my clothing was in much better shape. But I didn't judge him for the rattiness of his attire: I immediately deferred to his age, and I was more concerned, and pleased, that he see that I was dressed in a similar proper way.

"This is it," he said, waving his hand before us. "It's horrible, but it has a certain ambience and mad gaiety."

We were standing in the apartment's small kitchen. It was cluttered and dusty and poorly lit by a flower-shaped ceiling fixture. The kitchen table was actually a door resting on two filing cabinets. To my right, protruding from the wall, was a very large dish cabinet. On top of the cabinet was an old steamer trunk, and on top of that were several valises piled to the ceiling. I liked the trunk; it made me think of ocean crossings. And in the corner of the kitchen was a silver New Year's Eve balloon. It was wrinkled like an old fruit, but it was still floating and must have been considered the source of the mad gaiety.

The kitchen's left wall had a large picture window and through this window the apartment's living room was visible.

"Let me show you the room," he said. "And if you can't stand it, then we don't have to bother with the interview."

There was a serpentine little path that one could walk along amidst the clutter of the kitchen (wine bottles, kitchen chairs held together by wire, a stationary bicycle, a metal golf-bag carrier, books, and newspapers), and Mr. Harrison took this path and led me to a doorway on the right.

The path was made from strips of stained orange carpet of at least two different shades. The floor underneath was an old dark wood, which I thought was attractive for a New York City apartment, though the wood did appear to be rotting. As I followed Mr. Harrison, I picked up his salty, sweet odor—it pervaded the whole apartment actually—and I liked it. It smelled alive.

In about four paces we crossed the kitchen and entered the next room.

"These would be your chambers," he said. "I'm afraid it's not very beautiful." His voice lowered, he seemed momentarily embarrassed by the shabbiness of it all, but then he regained his confidence, and said, "But it's difficult to find good staff to keep things in shape."

"I think it's perfectly fine," I said, which wasn't the truth, but was the polite thing to say. It was a tiny, narrow room and the bed was a gray mattress on a metal frame with wheels. One of the back wheels was missing and so the shortened leg was propped up on the indented cover of an old book. The bed took up almost the whole length of the room; there was just enough space for the orange path which I could see led to the bathroom. Beside the bed was a little night table with a reading lamp and next to that was a standing closet whose plywood sides were split open.

"You can keep your clothes in that armoire," he said. "And anything else can go into the file cabinets in the kitchen."

There was a window in the room, but it looked onto an air shaft. The moaning of pigeons was quite loud.

"You can really hear the pigeons," I said.

"Yes," he said, "it's nice to have access to nature."

We followed the orange path and went into the narrow bathroom. It was filthy and off-putting. There was a patch of worn blue carpet on the floor, and a set of shelves painted blue to match the carpet. On the shelves were dozens of ointments and toiletries. Most of them were squeezed out and ancient. On the top shelf there was an artistic arrangement, like the seating of a Greek theater, of tiny, dust-covered shampoo bottles bearing the crests and imprints of various hotels.

The bathroom was lacking a sink; there was only a shower and a toilet. Above the toilet was a framed ink drawing of a Victorian woman holding a fan in front of her face.

"Do you brush your teeth in the kitchen sink?" I asked.

"Yes," he said. "When I remember to."

He gave the toilet a quick flush to demonstrate that it functioned and it made a great enginelike noise. He apologized for it by saying, "It works, but I think there is an outboard motor in there. It likes to pretend that it is a yacht heading out to sea. The plumber may have stolen it from a boat in Long Island—that's where he lives."

He then led me out of the bathroom through the bedroom, across the kitchen, and into the living room, all in about ten paces. It was the largest room in the apartment and it was here that the orange path came to a glorious end—the floor was covered with two layers of light orange and brown-orange carpet. This was the ocean of orange which the path, like a river, bled into, and above this ocean were two big windows facing north with thick, dirty curtains. The view was a look into the back windows of the buildings on Ninety-fourth Street, and above the rooftops was the darkening blue of the early evening sky.

"This is where I sleep," said Mr. Harrison, indicating a narrow couch underneath the wall with the interior window. "But this is also the communal area for communal relaxation. It is barracks-style living here, but it can be done."

Next to his couch-bed was a coffee table that was like a microcosm of the whole apartment—it was layered with hundreds of pennies, unopened bills, loose aspirin, a glass wine goblet, and a bowl filled with Christmas balls which managed to gleam through their dust.

There were two matching wooden chairs with cushioned seats. He sat on the one in the right-hand corner and I sat on the chair near his bed.

"Now we're supposed to talk," he said. "See if we're compatible . . . What's your name again? It was something with a *V*. Eaves?"

"Ives," I said. "Louis Ives."

"Sounds English. But you look German. Are you German?"

"No . . . well my father's side is Austrian," I said, and it wasn't a lie, but it was sort of a lie. It is one of the peculiarities of my life that while I am one hundred percent Jewish and feel very Jewish on the inside, my outer appearance is very Aryan. I have blond hair, blue eyes, I am almost six feet tall, and my build is slender, but reasonably athletic. My nose comes close to giving me away, but most people look at my hair and naturally assume that my nose is aquiline or Roman, when really it's Jewish.

I was afraid that Mr. Harrison might not like Jews and so that's why I misled him about Austria. The truth is my father's side did come from the pre-World War I Austro-Hungarian empire, though that doesn't account for my blondness. My father's family, and my father, were extremely dark. My lightness comes from my mother and my mother's side, which was Russian-Jewish, specifically from a shtetl near Odessa where light-eyed Jews must not have been uncommon. I didn't mention Russia to Mr. Harrison, because claiming Austrian heritage was a better cover, I thought, and I felt more desirable as a roommate if I were viewed as an Aryan. It is a weakness of my character that I always think to hide my Jewish identity.

"They must have changed the names to Ives at Ellis Island," he said.

"The usual immigrant story," I said, though I didn't tell him that the original name had been Ivetsky.

"Austrian," he mused, and then he smiled at me and said, "You may be a lost Hapsburg prince."

"I don't think so," I said, though I took his remark as a compliment.

"One can always hope," he said. "You may have royal blood and a vast fortune you are not even aware of," and then he slipped out of his usual accent, which sounded almost English but was actually a well-enunciated, clipped American, a Mid-Atlantic accent, and from that he went into a peasant's Irish, and said, "But until then you are forced to look for shelter with the likes of me."

I smiled at him shyly. He was a great eccentric and I felt cowed in his presence. I wanted to amuse and impress him, but I could only think of polite and pleasant things to say.

"Where are you living now?" he asked.

"New Jersey," I said.

"Why are you coming to New York?"

"I was teaching for several years, but I'm hoping to do something new . . . I'm sort of looking for myself." I thought he might appreciate such a sentiment since his ad said he was a writer.

"You won't find yourself in New York. New Jersey is much better for things like that. Much less depraved."

I wasn't sure how to respond to this remark about depravity, and then I noticed that above Mr. Harrison's head there was a painting of the Virgin Mary on a piece of wood. I mumbled, "I was only joking, I'm not really looking for myself. I just want a new career."

"Why don't you want to teach anymore?" he asked.

"There were budget problems at my school and I was junior faculty and so they let me go." I was lying as honestly as I could. "I see it as a chance to try something new."

"Where were you teaching?"

"In Princeton."

"Princeton?!?"

"Not at the university, at a private school called Pretty Brook. I only taught seventh grade. Though I did go for walks at the university and I used the library."

"How is Princeton these days? My uncle went there. It was great once. But then they let women in. That's destroyed it, I'm sure, turned it into a Midwestern U."

"It's still an excellent university," I argued. "There's no reason why women shouldn't go."

"I'm against the education of women!" he proclaimed. "It numbs their senses, their instinctual drives. It affects their performance in the boudoir and hampers their cooking ability."

"Do you really believe that?" He was too eccentric, I thought, too crazy. How could I live with him? But despite myself, I found him charming and I wanted him to like me.

"Yes," he answered. "Women shouldn't be educated. They're becoming a nuisance. Taking jobs, thinking they're equal. They are clearly inferior in all respects . . . They do make good mothers and good cooks. The women I like best are the ones in Williamsburg.

The Hasidic women. They seem to have the right touch. They wear gingham gowns like Mary Pickford. But I don't like the men's costumes at all. It's not very attractive to wear your hair in pigtails, and the black hats aren't very good. They should get rid of the hats."

I was relieved that he had said something positive about Jews. It didn't seem likely that he could be an anti-Semite *and* like Hasidic women. It made me feel that I perhaps could move in after all. I wouldn't have to hide my identity and that would make things a lot easier. Still, the place was a filthy mess, even at its low price, and I had been raised in an overly hygienic way by my mother. I kept our conversation going, but I steered it back to more neutral territory, away from the Hasids, should he suddenly say something disparaging and anti-Semitic and make me feel uncomfortable. I said, "Well, the Princeton University campus is still very beautiful."

"I remember my uncle took me there during one of his reunions," he said. "He was in Fitzgerald's class. He said he could have written *This Side of Paradise* just because he was there at the same time. My uncle was an idiot."

"Do you like Fitzgerald?" I asked. Fitzgerald had always been one of my favorite writers, and it was because of his short stories that I thought a young gentleman should live in a hotel.

"Of course," he said. "His prose is like cocktail music. But there won't be any more Fitzgeralds. You need an all-male environment . . . the Muslims might produce a Fitzgerald. They're good at separating the sexes."

I imagined for a moment a new type of *The Great Gatsby*, written in Arabic, and being translated, and making a great sensation over here. I said to Mr. Harrison, "I love Fitzgerald's writing. In fact, what caught my eye about your ad was that it said you're a writer. What type of writing do you do?"

"I'm a playwright."

"Are you working on anything now?"

"I am trying to finish my *chef d'oeuvre*. It is a sexual comedy about the Shakers. Do you know who the Shakers are?"

"I'm familiar with the Quakers. And I think I've heard of the Shakers."

"They died out because they didn't believe in sex. They believed in shaking. Though every now and then they are revived, only to die out again. They're like a play. They die out and then they come back. It will be a comic *Hamlet*. A play within a play."

Since sex was brought up I thought I should ask an obvious question. I had the hope that if I moved to New York that I might fall in love, another Fitzgerald notion, and that could mean sleeping with a woman. I said somewhat bashfully, and as discreetly as possible, "If I did move in here, could I have guests?"

"You mean overnight guests?"

"Yes."

"No! Absolutely not. The place is too small. There's to be no fornication! I wouldn't even conceive of having sex in here," and then his voice trailed off, and his eyes looked down, away from mine, "I'm retired from all that anyways."

"I'm sorry," I said. "I didn't mean to be rude." I was ashamed and I glanced at the Virgin above his head. Also hanging on the walls were antique picture frames. They held no paintings; they only framed the off-pink color of the walls.

"The Church, you know, is trying very hard to stop people from having sex," he said. "If *they* gave up all hell would break loose. Some resistance is needed. People need to be told not to have sex. If you make it difficult most people will just quit and develop other interests. Like mah-jongg. You'll find I'm to the right of the pope on most of these issues."

I kept thinking that he was perhaps of a state of mind beyond eccentric, but there was also this constant underpinning of irony to everything he said which seemed to clearly indicate intelligence and sanity. He was conscious that he was outrageous, but he was also stating his honest beliefs.

I wanted to make up for my remark about guests and win back his favor, so after he mentioned the pope, I said, "I like that painting of the Virgin Mary very much."

"Oh, yes, I found it in a garage sale in New Jersey. The people of New Jersey are virtuous. All the good people went there and all the lost ones went to Long Island. The government of New Jersey is a mess, but the people are good. You used to be able to go over there and register a car without having insurance. New Jersey was a godsend. You could do anything. We need a state like that again."

"I've been in New Jersey almost all my life. I was raised there," I said.

"That's the best reference you could possibly give."

Two of my usual insecurities were soothed: he was attracted to Hasidic women and he was fond of New Jersey. I'm always afraid people won't like me because I'm Jewish, especially people like Mr. Harrison, who despite the poor condition of his clothes and strange apartment, had the air of the upper class and of England. And regarding my New Jersey heritage, my fear of state bias is almost worse than my fear of anti-Semitism. People of all social classes tend to look down upon you when you mention that you are from the Garden State. But on both these fronts I felt very good about how our interview was going. I decided to repay Mr. Harrison for his liberal feelings about Jews and New Jersey with another compliment. "I like your empty picture frames," I said. "It's very interesting."

"Most frames are more beautiful than their pictures," he said. "And less expensive."

After that we briefly discussed money. As advertised, he was renting the room for two hundred and ten dollars a month, plus an additional forty for electricity, the basic phone charge, and for cable television. It was perfectly reasonable and was actually one hundred dollars less than what I was paying in Princeton. I had enough money saved for a month or two of frugal living and for making loan payments, while I looked for a job. So the money was perfect, but I didn't know if I could really live in such close, dirty quarters. My feeling was that I probably couldn't. We ended our interview with both of us playing our cards close to the chest. He said, "Let's both think about it and talk tomorrow."

"Yes, that sounds good," I said, and I gave him my number. While he wrote it down I asked, "Have you seen many other people?"

"Dozens. But you are the only one from New Jersey, and you speak English."

We both stood up. My eye, for a moment, caught hold of the Christmas balls on the coffee table and I remarked, making my final compliment, "I like your Christmas balls."

"I love them," he said. "Don't you think they're beautiful? I love the colors, the way they catch the light. If you ever want to give me something you can give me Christmas balls. Of course what I'd really like is a bowl of jewels. The Queen has jewels."

He showed me to the door; we walked along the orange path. He opened the door and I stepped into the hall.

"Good-bye," I said, and I reached out my hand to shake his. I wasn't sure if I'd ever see him again.

His eyes suddenly grew more intense and alive. He had been tiring a little by the end of our talk, or was getting bored, but now he seemed almost passionate. He took my forearm in both his hands, squeezed it, and said in German, "*Auf Wiedersehen!*" It startled me and he smiled and closed the door.

The Young Gentleman

I left Mr. Harrison and went to Penn Station. His embrace of my arm was how I imagined German soldiers might have bid farewell to each other at the front. I was a little worried that I had overconvinced him of my Aryan status.

I took the train back to Princeton and as usual I enjoyed the trip. I love train travel of any kind. Sitting on those vinyl seats with my fellow Jerseyans, I imagined that I was in Europe, leaving Paris late in the evening for an overnight journey to Rome. I transformed my fluorescently lit New Jersey Transit car into a small French berth. The ruined land between New York and Newark became the farms outside of Paris. It wasn't 1992, it was 1922. I stared out the window. I was a reflective young gentleman traveling alone; my emotions were still damaged by the War. I was a romantic figure.

Then the conductor came along in his dark blue uniform and his standard-issue black shoes, and my fantasy changed. He had a nice, blushing Irish face and it wasn't Europe anymore, it was New

York in the 1930s. He asked me for my ticket and as I handed it to him I said, "Thank you." And then I asked, with great civility, "What time will we be arriving in Princeton?" He smiled and said, "Nine-fifty," and moved on to the next passenger. I imagined and hoped that he was thinking, "There's a young gentleman headed back to Princeton after a long day in New York. He probably had dinner at his club."

I did in fact have a long day and I fell asleep with my head leaning against the plastic window. My last vision was of a brilliant orange flame emanating from the tip of an Edison refinery that looked like the Eiffel Tower, even though I hadn't switched back my fantasy.

I awoke with a start, afraid that I had missed my stop and would land in Trenton. But some interior alarm had gone off and I had come to just outside of Princeton Junction.

I then took the Dinky, the small train that connects Princeton Junction to Princeton Borough. It's only a five-minute passage and has the feeling of a ferry ride, as if Princeton was an island separate from the mainland of New Jersey.

The Dinky lets you off at the base of the Princeton University campus, which is situated on the top of a long, sloping hill. One has to walk up through the campus to get to Nassau Street and the center of town. As I stepped off the Dinky I was struck by the beautiful quiet of Princeton. In New York there is a constant throb and grinding that you don't fully hear until you remember it when you are somewhere silent.

I started across the campus and I appreciated anew the cultivated order of the university: the sloping lawns, the rows of dark old trees, the ruled, slate paths, the sculptures of tigers, and the Gothic dormitories made from Italian granite. It had a cold beauty.

I stopped and sat on a bench. There was a tiny bit of moon casting a diffused silver light. It was late August and there was no one around; I had the whole school to myself. There was a slight breeze of warm air and the campus seemed to breathe shallow breaths. It was preserving itself, sleeping, until it woke up for the arrival of the students. I felt a great, peaceful remove.

I thought of Mr. Harrison and our discussion of Fitzgerald. *This is paradise*, I thought. And was it like paradise, I wondered, because when you are expelled you always want to return? I thought of how Fitzgerald died in Los Angeles reading the Princeton football scores. It made me think I shouldn't leave Princeton. I wondered if I should get a job in the library. I could pretend I was an undergraduate for the rest of my life.

I left the bench and climbed the stairs of Blair Arch and I saw a gargoyle in the stones, which I had never noticed before, though I had tried to be very observant of all the hundreds of Princeton gargoyles. But gargoyles are like that, you see them when they have meaning for you, and this one's face was contorted with lust. Sex. It was always my problem. It was driving me out of Princeton. I thought of my erection at Pretty Brook. I thought of the brassiere. I still wanted to wear it. I wished I had stolen it and taken it home with me.

I reached my little studio apartment on my quiet street, Park Place, and I washed my hands and face to comfort myself. I looked around my neat little room. I wasn't the most disciplined housekeeper, but the surfaces were clean. "This is my home," I thought, "this is where I belong."

It struck me as almost perverse that I had been let into a stranger's dirty apartment that day, that I had looked at a gray mattress and had even considered for a moment making that bed my new home. Mr. Harrison was certainly eccentric and interesting, but the thought of living with him was crazy, irrational.

I then thought of all the dirty hotels I had looked at, the people standing in the shadows of the hallways like wraiths. I thought of the subways I had taken, the crowds which had mangled me. The whole day felt like a hallucination.

I sat in my favorite chair. New York was receding from my mind as a possibility for my new life. It was too dirty, too difficult. I was too soft; Princeton had spoiled me with its quiet streets. I was at the starting point all over again. I thought of the train conductor who had so nicely taken my ticket—should I try and join New Jersey Transit? The post office? The police department? I liked jobs with costumes, but I knew that I was unfit for any of those trades. My thoughts were ridiculous and desperate. I was a young man without much hope. Then the phone rang.

"Hello," I answered with a defeated voice.

"Hello. Hello. H. Harrison." It was him. I couldn't believe he was calling. He and New York had already started feeling like a dream.

"Oh, hello," I managed to say.

"I was thinking," he said, "I think we should do it. I didn't want to bother waiting until tomorrow. We should settle it now. We can take it a week at a time. Sixty-two dollars a week. And then if you don't like it you won't have lost a whole month's rent." There was a rush to his voice, a desperation.

"I'm not sure," I said. I was caught off-guard. But I didn't want to say no immediately and hurt him, reject him.

"I think we'd get along fine, and you only have to try it for a week," he said. "We can even make it per diem. Nine. No, eight dollars a day—"

"I'll do it," I blurted out suddenly. "I'll give it a try." What moments before had been out of the question was now the path I had leaped upon. I changed my life without a moment's consideration. It was lunacy. And mostly it was because he wanted me. I was responding to that. I was flattered. I wanted to be wanted.

"This will be very good for you," he said, and he sounded happy. "There's much I can teach you about New York, you know. I can advance you socially." His voice was confident again, regal.

"That would be very nice of you," I said. My heart was pounding. I think we both felt giddy. His wanting me and my accepting of his wanting had both of us rejoicing. I gushed to him, perhaps revealing too much, "It's really very strange that I'll be moving to New York. It's all because I was looking at the cover of Henry James's *Washington Square* and I thought I should be in New York."

"I can't stand James!" he proclaimed. "He's unreadable."

"I know what you mean." I was worried that I had said the wrong thing, but then I stood up for myself and James a little bit by saying, "But the earlier books are quite good, like *Daisy Miller*, or *Washington Square*."

"Yes, that's true, his style did change. I wonder why. He burned himself, you know. Sat on a stove and shriveled his testicles. That may account for the change in style."

He laughed and I laughed with him. But it was hard to know what to expect from him. The issue of sex was unclear. I wasn't sure if he was heterosexual, homosexual, or if he was some kind of bawdy puritan. But this uncertainty didn't bother me. I found it intriguing and familiar.

I told him that I would need a little time to tie things up in Princeton and that I'd move in as close to the first of September as possible. This was suitable to him and we rang off.

I didn't give my Park Place landlord sufficient notice, but he returned to me my security deposit. I was doing things hastily, but I felt drawn to New York and to Henry Harrison. It was my perception that Mr. Harrison was a gentleman and that I was a fledgling gentleman, and so we would be well-suited for one another. I had been acting like a novice gentleman for almost six years. It started in my sophomore year at Rutgers when I began to address myself in my thoughts as the "young gentleman." And I think its precise beginning was after I read W. Somerset Maugham's *The Razor's Edge* and Evelyn Waugh's *Brideshead Revisited* in too close a succession.

Then there followed Fitzgerald and Wodehouse and Wilde and Mann, and I came to only want to read books about young gentlemen. For me they were like Don Quixote's books of chivalry. I tried to live as the young gentlemen lived. I wrote thank you notes and I enjoyed train travel. I shaved daily, ate solitary meals, and dressed neatly.

I used the authors themselves as models: I attempted to dress like them after studying photographs in their biographies. I never wore sneakers, favored pants with texture—linen, wool, or corduroy—and went to Italian barbers for short haircuts.

So I developed a style, a manner of living. It was a fantasy that I wore like armor to get me through the day and to enjoy the day. It made loneliness feel like a movie.

A typical Saturday in Princeton sounded like this in my mind: "*The young gentleman strolls up Nassau Street. He wears his blue blazer. He goes to his favorite restaurant, the Annex, for his luncheon. He sits at his bachelor table and reads the paper while he eats. He is kindly to the ancient waitresses. For his digestion the young gentleman strolls some more.*

He stops at Micawber's Bookstore, greets the hardworking proprietor, and browses. He is one of the legions who browse and rarely buy, but the proprietor appreciates the young gentleman—his dignified manner, his wearing of a tie.

The young gentleman walks to Palmer Square and sits on a bench. The other bench-sitters wink at him and desire his company. The young gentleman smiles, but remains aloof.

He watches the packs of young girls get ice cream at Thomas Sweet's. He sniffs the air as they walk past him, hoping to catch a hint of young perspiration. He looks at their sugary mouths, their thin legs and arms, their ice-cream cones. He wants to run home and hide in bed. . . . He's nothing but an onanist!"

Unfortunately, I was always dissolving into overly lonesome thoughts, which turned sexual out of desperation, but that sample day illustrates very well the young gentleman's life. The idea was to establish a routine; routines were romantic. Young and old gentlemen had them. You went about your routines quietly, but people took notice and admired you. I wanted them to be able to count on me appearing at the Annex on Saturdays. It was like being a force of nature: a robin redbreast who returns to the same tree every spring; a young gentleman in a blue blazer at the same restaurant every Saturday.

I felt that I had done a good tour of duty in Princeton: people didn't know me, but they would miss me. And now I wanted to go live with Henry Harrison. He was a fellow gentleman. He wanted to advance me socially. I didn't really think he could advance me, but the fact that he said such a thing inspired me. I had been living as a gentleman all by myself, but now I could do it in the company of someone who understood. As I packed up my life in Princeton, I began to think of him as some future vision of myself. And I wasn't repelled by the future—I wanted to know more.

CHAPTER II

Arrival

On the second of September 1992, I drove to Manhattan in my dark blue Pontiac Parisienne. It was a big-boned, handsome car with a cushioned velour interior. It was like driving a living room, and I felt capable of crushing most other cars. It had one hundred and fifty thousand miles and was dear to me. I had inherited it from my father when he died in 1984.

I arrived at Ninety-third Street around noon and I was able to park in front of the building. I buzzed Mr. Harrison from the vestibule, but there was no response. I felt a cold panic. I had called him the night before. He had said he would be home. I was frightened that he was up there and had changed his mind. I had been lured into New York; a horrible trick had been played.

I took several deep breaths and calmed myself. I hoped that he was out or that the buzzer was broken, and I went to the corner and called him from the pay phone. After several rings, he answered, "H. Harrison." I could hear loud music—a show tune—in the background.

"It's Louis. I'm at the corner, Mr. Harrison," I said.

"Who?"

"Louis—"

"Let me turn off the music . . . I'm in the middle of my dance." The music stopped. He hadn't heard the buzzer. "Who's calling?"

"Louis, your new roommate—"

"Where are you? Broken down on the New Jersey Turnpike?"

"I'm at the corner."

"Oh, you're here. Good. I thought you might not show up . . . Do you need help with your bags? I can get Gershon downstairs to help you."

"Gershon?"

"He's someone who carries heavy things for me."

"Oh . . . I don't need any help," I said.

I unloaded my car—I had very little with me—and in just a few trips I carried up my belongings. I was struck again by the strong smell of sweat and cologne in the apartment. I had liked it when I interviewed for the room, but now my mind was registering doubts and fears. Would I take on this smell, like living with a smoker? And the apartment seemed even smaller and more cluttered than I remembered. And for the second time that late morning my heart fluttered with panic. Was I making a terrible error?

But there was no turning back. I unpacked my sheets and blanket and made my bed. And this little bit of order in all the disorder was comforting. Then Mr. Harrison and I sat down in his room to discuss some of the ground rules of our living together. He sat in his chair in the corner and I sat in my interview chair. He was wearing a green blazer and his tan pants, and bright sunlight was coming in through the two windows and it seemed to bring out the oranges of the carpeting.

"Don't think of me as your landlord or roommate. Consider me your host," he said. "And you are my houseguest."

"Thank you," I said. It was a nice welcome, but I felt shy in his presence.

Then Mr. Harrison explained to me that it was actually against the rules of the lease for him to rent the room. "So never answer the door if you should hear someone knocking," he said. "It could be the landlord or a bill collector. If anyone should ever question you on the staircase—though it is unlikely—tell them you are my illegitimate son and that we have only been recently reunited. I'm allowed to have relatives and heirs staying with me."

I was secretly touched by this notion of illegitimacy, and then Mr. Harrison said, "And you should think of your rent as a gift to me."

I told him that I wanted to pay for the first week right away and I went to my room and got my wallet. I handed him the sixty-two dollars and he feigned surprise, but he quickly put the money in his pocket and he said, "So kind of you, so unexpected!" And I realized he was saying this in a very loud voice in case anyone, like the landlord, was listening through the door.

Then Mr. Harrison had to leave for a lunch date and I was left alone in my new home. I went to my room and finished unpacking.

All my shirts and coats and pants fit into the armoire, and my underclothing went into the filing cabinets beneath the kitchen table. I had sold many of my books to Micawber's, but had kept a box of my young gentleman books and I piled these on the floor and along the windowsill.

And having my books around me, seeing their familiar spines and covers, like family pictures, was very good and reassuring: I had all of Fitzgerald's short stories and novels; Waugh's *Brideshead* and *A Handful of Dust*; Maugham's *Razor*, and three volumes of his short stories, the reading of which are a great substitute for travel if you can't afford to go anywhere; a collected works of Wilde; several of Wodehouse's *Jeeves*; and Mann's *Magic*, and a volume of his diaries with photographs of the Swiss clinic that had been the inspiration for *The Magic Mountain*. I also had Turgenev's *Fathers and Sons*, a Russian young gentlemen story; and Cervantes' masterpiece on the most famous *older* gentleman, *The Ingenious Gentleman Don Quixote de la Mancha*.

I also brought—not for reasons of gentlemanhood—a well-worn copy of Richard von Krafft-Ebing's *Psychopathia sexualis*, the famous nineteenth-century study (219 case histories) of aberrant human sexuality (pre-Freud) that I had been secretly holding on to for over ten years. I didn't read from it anymore, but it was very important to me and I couldn't part with it. I put it with my underwear in the filing cabinet.

That first night, I lay in bed and I was homesick for Princeton. I was almost twenty-six years old, but I felt like a little boy. I actually turned my face to my pillow and I smothered a few tears, but then I stopped. I was afraid that Mr. Harrison would discover me. Our rooms had no doors. So I listened to the pigeons moan and I tried to read Mann's diaries.

Mr. Harrison had come home from his luncheon in the late afternoon, napped, and then had gone back out for a dinner. His engagements were mysterious to me. He returned around eleven and put on the television. He invited me to join him, but I declined out of shyness and stayed in my room trying to read and not to cry.

After an hour of television, he shut it off, and I listened to him prepare his bed and then brush his teeth in the kitchen sink. Then he passed through my room on his way to the bathroom. He was wearing a tuxedo shirt and a blue bathing suit with white tubing along the edges. A black eye-mask was propped on his forehead. It was a remarkable sleeping costume. I was only in T-shirt and boxer shorts. He closed the door to the bathroom and I listened to him urinate and then prematurely flush while still urinating, which I found puzzling.

He came out, the Long Island motor was still churning in the toilet, and he stood at the end of my bed and said, "Do you have earplugs for sleeping?"

"No, I don't. But I am a sound sleeper."

"Well, in New York you should have them. They're quite wonderful. They'll change your life."

"I'll see how it goes," I said, and then I tried to make a joke with him. "That mask makes you look like the Lone Ranger."

"I need it for sleeping," he responded quite seriously. "I prefer to think that I resemble the Phantom of the Opera."

He took a step to head out and then looked at my book. "What are you reading?" he asked.

"Thomas Mann's diaries," I said.

He raised his eyebrows in a suspicious way. I had a feeling he was thinking about *Death in Venice.* He then said in a friendly tone, "If you like we can have readings at night to help us fall asleep . . . I think a chapter of *Winnie-the-Pooh* would be very good, followed by some Rabelais."

"Sure," I said, laughing a little, my homesickness leaving me.

"Well, *gute Nacht*," he said and strode out of my room, reminding me that he still thought I was Aryan, a lie whose revelation I wanted to postpone.

42

The Next Event

One of the first things I had to learn about New York was how to park my car without getting tickets. Mr. Harrison, who also had a car (a Buick Skylark, he said), told me that the "*polizei*" would certainly be after my Parisienne, that tickets generated money for the city, and I would have to accept this as a fact of life. "It's entirely unjust, but think of it as a duty to the King," he said.

I found that if I read the signs carefully I could avoid tickets, but I was worried that my car, though it was old, might be vandalized. It was a 1982, but I kept it in good shape. My father had always lectured me on the importance of changing the oil, and never letting the gas go below half a tank, so as not to run dirt through the engine. He took care of his cars because they were his livelihood; he was a traveling salesman.

He sold furniture to schools and nursing homes and prisons. His territory was New Jersey and Pennsylvania. It was a difficult business; institutions held on to their old furniture for as long as they could.

He died a week before I was to go to college. He was killed by a massive heart attack. He was only fifty-seven. He wasn't overweight, but he never exercised and he smoked cigars. It happened in a hotel room in Scranton, Pennsylvania. He died "on the road" as my mother and I called the many nights that my father wasn't with us.

My father was very aware of *Death of a Salesman* and he often referred to himself, in a derogatory manner, as Willy Loman. And sometimes he used to say, "I'll solve all my problems: I'll drop dead." But I never knew if he got that from Arthur Miller, or came up with it on his own. I do think it disgusted my father that his life as a salesman had been so accurately depicted for the stage, as if his own existence had been turned into a cliché.

After he died, I sat *shivah* and then I began classes. I was supposed to live on campus, but my mother needed me, so I drove to Rutgers three days a week in the Parisienne. For several years, until it finally faded, I could always smell the ash of my father's cigars when I first entered the car. I didn't like the smell, but I missed it when it finally disappeared.

My mother was never right after my father's death, and her depression turned into ovarian cancer, at least that's my theory, and three years after my father died, my mother died, almost to the day.

My father, because he was a commissioned salesman, had very poor insurance, and this affected my mother, who was unemployed when he died, and she never went back to work. Her cancer treatments used up almost all of our money and the mortgage, and I was left with very little.

So I treasured the Parisienne as a remnant of my family and I asked Mr. Harrison if he thought that my car was likely to be damaged or stolen. He didn't think so, but he recommended that I buy a Club for the steering wheel. He didn't have a Club, he said, but he had found a red pipe and he put this through his steering wheel because it looked like a Club and would most likely fool any potential thieves.

After a few days, I stopped calling my host Mr. Harrison and began to address him as Henry. He, on the other hand, didn't use my name very much. He was struggling to remember it. A few times he called me Otto, the name of the previous tenant, which I had learned when some mail had come for an Otto Bellman. Henry had taken the mail from me and put it in a bin in the refrigerator so as not to lose it. And I didn't correct him when he called me Otto. I didn't want to embarrass him.

I started looking for a job and every day I took *The New York Times* and *The Village Voice* to the Greek diner on Second Avenue. I circled ads and then I mailed résumés and letters. I used Henry's old typewriter, and the keys were a bit gummed, but this gave my correspondence an old-fashioned look that I liked. I also visited numerous temporary agencies and took typing tests, always averaging a measly twenty-eight words per minute. Twelve words per minute too slow to get a job. I thought that with each test my speed would increase, but it didn't. I was quickly growing discouraged, but kept trying.

Henry was very impressed with my diligence. He wanted to help and so he said, "I'll play military music for you in the mornings to keep you in the right frame of mind."

He had many records, including one for marches, but he never woke up early enough to play it for me. He slept until eleven or noon every day, and went to bed around midnight. He said he needed twelve to fourteen hours of sleep, like Katharine Hepburn.

Though Henry had suggested it, we also didn't begin any nightly readings of *Winnie-the-Pooh* and Rabelais. This, like playing military music in the mornings, was one of several regimens that Henry would conceive for my self-improvement or our mutual self-improvement, but they never went beyond the proposal stage.

Still, we could have used some improvements. Despite our gentlemanly appearances we lived like two bums shacked up together: Henry kept a bottle under his bed for peeing in the middle of the night. I had been with him for about ten days when he told me about the bottle, which was embarrassing for him. I had spent that particular day failing typing tests at temp agencies and I was sitting dejectedly on Henry's couch watching television. I had loosened up by this time and felt free to come into his room, and he had thoughtfully put down a brown coverlet on his couch so that I wouldn't have direct contact with his bedding.

Beneath his couch were a few pairs of his devastated shoes and several bottles with their labels still on: prune juice, apple juice, and spring water. Some of the bottles still had liquids in them. I happened to nudge one of them with my foot and Henry saw this and misinterpreted my motive.

"Don't ever drink from one of those bottles!" he said to me with great alarm. "A great mistake could be made! It is one of the sacrifices I make for communal living that in the middle of the night I use a bottle rather than pass through your room and wake you from your Freudian dreams. It's not that I don't want to share if you are thirsty, but even I don't know what's what anymore. It all may be a mixture by now. So everything beneath that couch should be considered poisonous!"

45

Even though he didn't say so directly, I knew immediately that he was talking about peeing, and I appreciated the sacrifice he made. "Thank you, that's very nice of you," I said. "I hope it isn't too difficult."

"No, it's more difficult to get out of bed."

He had mentioned my Freudian dreams because two nights before I had woken up screaming for my mother. It was probably caused by the anxiety of starting a new life. I dreamt that she was running away from me and that I desperately needed her help. I had just moved to New York after all and was full of fears and I missed her, but I also had the sensation that my need for my mother was sexual. The next day I had been worried that I might have disturbed Henry's sleep and I asked him, "Did I wake you with my screaming in the night?"

"I didn't hear a thing," he said. "The plugs were in very deep."

"Oh, good," I said, and then asked, "Do they ever get stuck?"

"Sometimes. Hot water dislodges them. Once I had to go to the emergency room. There may be still one in there . . . Why were you screaming?"

"A dream," I said.

"About what?"

I hesitated to tell him the truth. Henry hadn't asked many questions about my life, and I hadn't told him about my parents. And I didn't want to bring up my mother, but I couldn't think quickly enough to produce a good lie and so I said, "I was calling for my mother."

"Why were you calling her?"

"It was quasi-sexual," I said.

"Well, you are in your twenties," Henry said, "that's par for the course. If it continues until your forties go to an analyst." He paused, contemplating what he had just advised and then recanted it. "But so what? You find out what it means and then what? Change something? No. It doesn't matter. Just move on to the next event."

Moving on to the next event seemed to be the guiding principle in Henry's life. Each domestic task was viewed as the next event or the next problem to be solved. The greatest problem of his that I observed was the finding of keys. Several times a day he would say something like, "Now the next step is the keys. Where are they? I found my socks, now the keys are gone. It's all madness!" His keys were an endless source of frustration.

The domestic event of laundry took place in the shower. I noticed that Henry took exceptionally long showers—up to thirty or forty minutes. I found out that during these showers he was not only bathing, but also washing his clothes. He would walk on his shirts, while the water beat down, to simulate the rinse cycle.

The first few times, though, when he was in there, before I knew about his laundering, I was concerned that he might have slipped in the tub. I would be in a state of anxiety, wondering if I should knock at the bathroom door, but I didn't want to commit a faux pas. Then one night as he emerged from the bathroom with a green towel wrapped around his waist, his beautiful, thick hair slicked back, I needed to expel my anxiety about his slipping and so I discreetly remarked, "Did you enjoy your toilet? You were in there for quite some time."

"I did my shirts," he said. "I walk on them. I think of wine."

Besides always trying to move on to the next domestic event, Henry also had a full calendar of social events. I thought it was unusual. He had at least five ladies calling several times a day inviting him to various functions. He was very popular. I answered the phone for many of these calls and the women sounded old and shaky, but they were obviously still spry enough to go out in the evenings.

So there existed in New York a mysterious, vibrant elderly social crowd of which Henry was a vital cog. And they weren't getting together for bridge playing and lunches of tuna-fish salad; Henry had engagements at the Russian Tea Room, dances at the Waldorf, dinner parties at the Supper Club.

One of the ladies who called frequently was Marjorie Mallard, his ex-fiancée. When he told me that they had been engaged for ten years and had only recently broken up, I asked, "You were engaged for so long, why don't you marry her?"

"I can't marry her now," he said. "She's dying. It wouldn't look very good to marry her just before she died. Also she's always been too managerial, I would never see the money. That's what nobody knows, when you marry money you never see it. The hardest way to make money is to marry it. I like the Victorian idea: the man gets the money no matter what."

One night during my second week in the apartment, Henry was getting ready to go to a dinner party. He placed his legless ironing board across the kitchen table and prepared his shirt, which had been hanging in the shower. The shirt wasn't fully dry and he was using the iron to warm it up.

When the shirt was done he selected a tie from his thick collection. The ties were draped around the neck of an old orange vacuum cleaner, which didn't work. The vacuum cleaner was kept hidden in the kitchen in a tiny closet, which used a red curtain for its door. The closet was next to the china cabinet. When I had one day opened the cabinet's doors, I discovered that Henry had long ago removed the shelves, installed a bar, and had hung up his one suit, one black-tie outfit, two blue blazers, and many sport coats. And the cabinet, once opened, was like an enormous scent box: it expelled Henry's smell of sweat and cologne—like flowers dipped in a locker room—and I realized that this cabinet was the primary source of the apartment's odor and why it was most strong in the kitchen.

So after taking a tie from the vacuum cleaner's neck, Henry opened the china cabinet and removed his gray suit coat (our few plates were stored on top of the refrigerator) and when he was fully dressed, I said, "You look very nice tonight."

"I'm not wearing my vest," he said. "I wore my vest last week. This way they don't know that I only have one suit. But Marjorie Mallard will be there, my ex-fiancée, you know, and she notices everything about clothes. One night she liked my shoes very much. She said she had a shoe fetish. So I kept my feet entwined in the legs of my chair all evening hiding them. It's best not to encourage these people with shoe fetishes."

The Opera

In the third week of my job search, I went for an interview at an environmental journal called *Terra* that was looking for someone to do phone sales. There was also the potential for some light copyediting. The editor of the magazine was a thin, dark-haired man named George Cummings. He conducted my interview and it turned out that he went to Princeton. I talked of the campus as if I too was an alumnus and this impressed him. Also, he looked like he had just walked out of Brooks Brothers, and I think he appreciated my neat, young gentleman appearance.

I was worried, though, that he would notice that my hair was thinning. He was in his late thirties and had all his hair. My balding was occurring behind my hedgelike front hairline. It was an odd way to go bald, like a forest whose outer trees are healthy, but peer farther in and you see that there's been a fire.

But George either didn't care or didn't notice—my blondness made it difficult for some people to recognize what was going on—and he was so taken with me that he said, "I'd like you to start this week, if possible."

"I can start tomorrow," I said, and perhaps I should have been more aloof, but he was the kind of person you didn't have to play games with.

I returned to the apartment around five-thirty and gave Henry the good news. He was sitting in his chair in the corner, and I sat on his bed. He was very pleased that I had found employment, but he was also cautious.

"What type of magazine is it?"

"An environmental journal. A quarterly."

"It might be a front for pornography."

"I don't think so. It's in a very nice building." *Terra* was on Sixty-second, near Lexington.

"That means nothing . . . but you have a job. I knew you were someone who could pay the rent. You should call your parents and let them know that you're making your way in the big city."

I was silent a moment. I needed to tell him. It would be grotesque to deceive him. I was bold and direct and I said, "I'm sorry I haven't said anything sooner. I always find it sort of difficult . . . But both my parents had illnesses and died a few years ago."

My heart pounded and Henry seemed to take true notice of me for the first time since I had met him. I didn't look at him directly, but I felt the intensity of his eyes on me. Previously, he had always seemed somewhat distracted in his manner towards me, as if I was getting in the way of the next event. He said one word in a somber, quiet voice: "Yes."

It was odd. He was simply confirming what I had said, and yet there was empathy in that one syllable. I was about to make a poor joke about dropping a personal bomb, but mercifully the phone rang. It was one of Henry's ladies and I was able to retreat to my room. I sat on my bed and I listened to his end of the phone conversation, and apparently his plans for the evening were being canceled.

When he hung up, he called out to me, "We should celebrate your finding a job. Let's go to the opera tonight."

"All right," I said, "but isn't the opera expensive?"

"Don't be so middle class," he said. "We don't pay. The aristocracy never pays. You'll see how it works when we get there."

I was thrilled that Henry wanted to do something with me and around eight o'clock we were both dressed and ready in our blazers and thin Barracuda raincoats. Henry's raincoat had several black grease marks, but they didn't seem to bother him at all.

We left the apartment and headed for Henry's car, which I had yet to see in our three weeks of living together. I offered to take us in the Parisienne, but he wanted to go in his Skylark.

Henry and I were an atypical household in that we had two cars, but we weren't unusual as individual car-owners. The myth that Manhattanites didn't own cars, I had learned, was simply untrue. The number of vehicles parked nightly on the streets of the Upper East Side was astounding. And these automobiles didn't lead lives of their own—there was a secret, massive population of car owners who obeyed the immutable laws of alternate-side-of-the-street parking. And so these unseen people snuck out each night or early morning and moved their cars like diligent farmers plowing one side of the field one day and the other side the next. I was one of these car farmers, and so was Henry.

As we walked up Ninety-third, a light rain began to fall. His car was on Ninety-fifth, and I wasn't surprised to see that the Skylark was an automobile version of the apartment. It was dirty and bruised. There were tears in the vinyl roof and I could see garbage along the shelves beneath the back and front windshields.

It was only drizzling so we weren't getting too wet, but Henry was frantically searching for his keys which had somehow disappeared on his person in the few blocks we had walked from the apartment.

"It's the curse of the House of Harrison," he said. "Keys lifted by spirits."

While Henry felt in his pockets, I saw that the car's tires were bald and low on air. And the back license plate was from Florida.

"Why does your car have Florida license plates?"

"They only test for emissions down there and the insurance is inexpensive. I could never be on the road in New York. They're much more sympathetic to us poor in Florida."

Then he found his keys and opened the passenger-side door. He got in and slid across the front seat, groaning and grunting dramatically the whole way, until he was behind the wheel. I then got in the car and Henry explained to me, "I can only afford to have one working door."

He removed his red pipe from the steering wheel and turned the ignition and the car failed to start. He pumped the pedal and tried again, but without success.

"We have to give it a moment to find the courage to press on," he said. We sat there quiet and patient, the light rain trickling on the windshield, then Henry asked, "How are the New Jersey insurance rates these days?"

"Very high, I think. But it's not too bad for me—my car is old and I have a clean driving record."

"Yes, you're very neat, like a pharmacist. You make your bed every day. It's an inspiration. I feel I have to keep up with you."

"Well, it's good that you can get cheap insurance from Florida and not even live there."

"I do live there, part-time. I go to Florida, to Palm Beach, every winter. I'll be gone from mid-December until the first of March. I didn't tell you, but now that you have a job I know that you can be trusted with the apartment . . . If our arrangement continues."

I was shocked by the news that Henry would leave me alone in the apartment. "Why do you go to Florida?" I asked. I was hurt by his announcement, especially since we were about to have our first evening together.

"That's where the social life is in the winter—I must follow the circus."

"Do you drive down?" I asked. The Skylark didn't seem capable.

"Yes. This car has made it four years in a row."

"You stay in hotels along the way?"

"Only the first night. Then when I am far enough south I camp out."

"You camp out?"

"Yes. I have a tent. I love to be in contact with nature. Ideally, I'd like to spend every day lying by the sea looking at the sky and water, doing nothing else." Henry paused, reflecting on his ideal existence, then he continued, "Yes, contact with nature during the day. But at night . . . when night comes I want to go to a masked ball."

He turned the key again and the Skylark came alive.

"Where do you stay in Palm Beach?" I asked. I was disappointed, but already resigned to the idea that he would leave.

"I have a few lady friends down there," he said, and his tone indicated that he didn't want to go into specific details, and then he swung out into the road a little wildly. As he accelerated there was the immediate smell of gas.

"The mechanic told me that these fumes are killing my brain cells," he said. "I think this is a good thing. Wise people know that it's best not to think. And people with dead brain cells can't think and so the result is the same."

We both opened our windows and we raced up Ninety-fifth Street and then careened down Fifth Avenue. Henry was impervious to the needs of the other cars. He took up two lanes. The rain suddenly grew heavier and the road was slick. Henry had his wipers on, but only the wiper on my side of the windshield worked. He leaned against me gruffly to peer out. I dug my right foot nervously into the pile of spent coffee cups and newspapers in front of me, pushing reflexively at an imaginary brake pedal. I fastened my seat belt. I said, "Henry, don't you think you should put on your seat belt?"

"I'm no Mr. Milquetoast like you young-generation types."

I was feeling a little scared with the way he was weaving and the lack of visibility. We began to cross the park at Seventy-ninth Street. I said, "Is it safe to be driving with bald tires?"

"Listen," said Henry, annoyed with my lack of courage, "as Napoleon said, 'If rape is imminent, relax and enjoy it.'"

I did relax a little, and it was beautiful to be cutting through Central Park with the wet, dark trees on both sides of the road forming a tunnel above the stone walls. It was like plunging into a forest. "It's wonderful going through the park," I said.

"That's what's nice about having children," Henry replied, "you get to reexperience things."

We made it to Lincoln Center without an accident and we even found a parking space. Henry had timed it so that we would arrive just before the end of the first act. There was an umbrella on the backseat which we shared as we walked to the Center's plaza. Conspiring under the umbrella, Henry revealed to me how the operation would work.

"When someone leaves you say to them, 'Excuse me, are you leaving the opera?' If they say yes, you say, 'May I have your ticket?' And make sure to get their reentry stub—if you don't get that the ticket is worth nothing. Do you understand? *Reentry stub is everything.*"

"Why do people leave in the first place? Isn't it a waste of money?"

Henry explained to me that our targets were people who didn't like the opera and so they left after one act, regardless of the money spent; or Midwestern tourists who simply couldn't take it; or a certain type of sophisticate who thought it was stylish to take in a little opera and then go for dinner. And even when people were planning to leave the opera, they would take their reentry stubs out of habit or because they didn't want to embarrass themselves with the ushers.

We entered the theater's lobby with its high glass fronts and Henry set up our positions. He would stay inside and guard the escalator that led to the indoor parking garage. I was to wait outside and stop the people who were exiting onto the plaza.

"I hope you don't mind my pulling rank," Henry said. "But you are the junior officer and you're young, so you go outside. Here's the umbrella. I will man the fort here."

We had some competition. Henry pointed out a group of five old men and one old lady. "Look at them. Vultures! Opera addicts. That one old woman has been at it for years. She should be in a rest home. We must distance ourselves from them, the security has memorized their faces. They usually don't get in until after the second act."

I went outside and then the first act ended and people began to come out. I addressed people just as Henry told me, but I wasn't having any luck. All the people I was encountering were simply getting fresh air or smoking while standing under the awning which protected them from the rain. No one was leaving the opera. Growing discouraged, I went to see how Henry was doing. The lobby was thick with people.

"Get back to your post, you're not following orders," he whispered at me angrily. "You might miss someone."

Chastened, I went back outside, and then sure enough two women started walking away from the protection of the awning. I followed after them with my umbrella; they were sharing one umbrella and moving quickly across the plaza, but I caught up with them.

It turned out they didn't like the opera at all and gladly gave me their tickets, but they only had one reentry ticket. One of the ladies hadn't bothered to take a reentry ticket from the usher because she knew they were leaving, and she very sweetly apologized to me about this. I still thought I had done very well. I brought Henry my trophies, hoping to be praised, but he wasn't pleased. I was sent back outside to get another reentry ticket, but I had no luck and then the lights inside were dimmed in warning. I went back to Henry and he was also empty-handed. The reentry ticket system was designed purposely to foil people like us. I saw that none of the opera addicts were successful either. But Henry came up with a plan.

"You go and give your ticket and reentry ticket and I'll follow right behind," he said. "I'll act like I can't find mine and then you ask me what I did with it. They'll probably believe our ruse and let me in so as not to hold up the line."

The entrance to the theater was cordoned off with red velvet ropes except for two openings where women ushers, in their official blue uniforms, were collecting tickets. We stood in one of the lines and when it was my turn I gave the usher my reentry ticket and showed her my seat ticket. Henry came right after me and began searching his pockets. "Did I give you my reentry ticket?" he asked me with realistic concern, and he kept fumbling for the nonexistent stub as if it was a set of keys.

"I don't know," I said, "did you give it to me?" And I started patting and searching my pockets. Both of us were patting and fumbling and holding up the line. The lights dimmed again. The usher grew a little exasperated and said, "Go ahead, it's O.K." And we walked in together, shoulder to shoulder, and we both started snickering. Chagall's angels were looking over us. We walked up the glorious red staircase amidst the beautifully dressed people and we both felt very happy. Our seats were rather high, but I didn't mind. I had been to Broadway shows, but I had never been to the opera before. That night it was *Tosca* and it was fantastic. Pavarotti was singing!

After the second act Henry, not satisfied with our seats, went back out, but told me to stay and mingle in the splendour of the people and the atmosphere. I felt very much like the young gentleman.

When Henry came back in he had two new tickets for us. A couple had abandoned their one-hundred-and-thirty-dollar seats in the orchestra, and so Henry and I had the great privilege to be just a few rows away from the marvelous performance. Tosca was played by a Russian woman with a beautiful and explosive voice. She even outshone Pavarotti. Henry whispered to me admiringly, "Only Russia can still produce women like that!"

When it was over we drove home safely. It had stopped raining, and Henry seemed to career less. In very little time we found a parking space; it was truly our evening.

We silently climbed the four flights of stairs to our apartment. We undressed and crawled into our beds. The opera had made us feel quite content.

Henry called out to me from his bed, "I am about to put my plugs in. Is there anything I need to know before I can no longer hear the world?"

"I just have a question. Can we go again soon to the opera?"

"Why not?" Henry said. "We can afford it!"

The Extra Man

I started working at *Terra* and after I got over my initial anxiety that I couldn't handle the job, I settled in all right. And I was free to go back to the opera, but Henry was too busy. In addition to his full social calendar, he also taught English Composition two nights a week, from six to ten, at Queensborough Community College in Bayside. He would drive the Skylark out there, and at least once a week he would break down or get a flat tire. This explained why his raincoat had so many grease stains.

One day he told me that he had held up traffic illegally on the Fifty-ninth Street Bridge when he got a flat and jacked up his car to put on the spare. The law requires that you wait for a tow truck, but he didn't want to miss his class, and he was able to put on a fresh tire before the police arrived.

I didn't think he earned enough at Queensborough to live on, and I had noticed an official-looking piece of mail from the federal government which I held up to the light in the kitchen: it was a social security check. I wondered how old you had to be to qualify. I wasn't sure if Henry was in his sixties or his seventies.

I had many questions about him. I wondered what he was like at Queensborough. I imagined that his students had never met anyone quite like him. He didn't seem to prepare very much for his classes, though some afternoons he sat on his chair in the corner and graded papers. His chief concern and occupation, as far as I could see, was keeping up with his lady friends, though at first I didn't fully understand the nature of his social life.

The woman who called even more frequently than his ex-fiancée was apparently the most wealthy of Henry's ladies. She was a billionairess, a Mrs. Vivian Cudlip. Henry told me that she was ninety-two years old and I said, "Your lady friends seem quite old. Don't you like younger women?"

"I can't afford younger women. They expect you to pay. It's only the older ones who pay. And they weren't so old twenty years ago when I met them—when they were seventy!" he said, and he laughed at the geriatric nature of his love life.

Mrs. Cudlip's money, Henry told me, dated back to the railroads. She was originally from Philadelphia, she still had a house there, and her whole family was anxiously anticipating her death. "Everybody in Philadelphia is waiting for someone to die," Henry said. "That's what they live for."

But Henry told me that Mrs. Cudlip was very durable despite many illnesses. Cancer of the jaw from too much smoking had horribly disfigured her (most of her chin had been removed), and she had terrible osteoporosis, but none of this kept her from doing something every night of the week in New York or Philadelphia or Palm Beach or Southampton—her four main residences.

"She has an incredible constitution," Henry said. "Broke her ankle in Philadelphia at four a.m. in a discotheque. Lay on the floor for half an hour waiting for an ambulance. Bounced back in record time. Got pneumonia in Newport visiting friends, recovered immediately. Now she's been told she has anemia and a leaking heart, but nothing fazes her. She presses on to the next event!"

When Mrs. Cudlip would call Henry to invite him out, it was actually her secretary who called. On my second day at *Terra* she called very early in the morning, around eight. I was just getting dressed and Henry didn't hear the phone ring because of his earplugs, so I came running out of my room into Henry's dark room to answer it. He had asked me never to wake him before eleven, so I told Mrs. Cudlip's secretary that Henry was out. I hung up the phone with the secretary and almost immediately, as I tiptoed away, not wanting to disturb Henry, the phone rang again. He didn't move at all, his eye mask still stared at the wall, and I again answered the phone.

"Hello," I whispered, not fully confident in Henry's earplugs for blocking all sound.

"This is Vivian Cudlip," a voice rasped. "Wake Henry up."

I knew that Mrs. Cudlip was important to Henry. He had shown me a photograph in which he was standing next to her on her yacht. He was wearing a red blazer and a white shirt open at the collar. They were holding drinks and he looked very handsome, but she was stooped over and tiny. Her head was even with Henry's elbow, and she was wearing a curly red wig and she had on enormous sunglasses which covered almost her whole face, obscuring her loss of chin. Remembering her image in the photograph and responding immediately to her commanding tone, I put the phone down and I roused Henry, tapping him politely on the shoulder.

He first lifted up his eye mask, then removed his earplugs. He looked at me and said, "What is it? What catastrophe has occurred?"

"It's Mrs. Cudlip on the phone, she sounds angry," I said, still whispering so that she wouldn't hear my voice through the receiver.

He motioned for the phone with urgency and I handed it to him.

"Hello, Vivian . . . I will wake at any hour for you . . . That was the second lieutenant. He's my aide-de-camp in the mornings. I will instruct him that when you call I am to be awakened . . . Yes, I can come. I believe that I am free, if not I'll call you . . . Very good, tomorrow, six o'clock at Turtle Bay . . . Right . . . Right . . . Very good, 'bye."

I inwardly beamed when he referred to me as the second lieutenant. I felt it to be a term of slight affection, though I was uncertain if Henry felt really close or affectionate to anyone. He hung up the phone and said, "My sleep is destroyed. Calling at dawn for dinner tomorrow. But the Queen must be obeyed . . . I don't like you standing there in the shadows. Can you please open the curtain? You'd make an excellent valet or squire."

I opened the curtain and some dusty sunlight gave the room, with its orange carpet, a citrusy glow. Henry sat up straight in bed and said to me, "I always let them think I might not come. You don't want to seem too available, then they don't want you."

"Mrs. Cudlip seems to want you a lot," I said.

"Yes, I guess Vivian is my best friend, but she has too many court flatterers. I'm just one of fifty sycophants, really, and the whole thing could blow up at any minute and I'd be out. Of course there are people who try to destroy your friendships. Barry Barbarash is always seeking Vivian's favor. He's hoping to be installed permanently as the resident rosen knight. He's a dedicated pederast, but Vivian likes to have him around because he's always introducing her to new people. She likes that . . . But Barbarash wants me out. He's waiting to strike. If I'm removed, less chance of him being kicked out of the court. But I'm a man of such depth that I can foresee his attacks."

"What's a rosen knight?" I asked.

"A knight who brings roses. Or a Rosenkavalier. An escort."

I felt that I suddenly understood the true nature of Henry's popularity with women. He was an elderly gigolo. "Are you an escort?" I asked.

"Yes."

"Are you paid?"

"Of course not. Except in pleasure—a free meal, good champagne, and a good orchestra. There's nothing wrong with receiving those three things, especially when you can't get them otherwise."

"Do you ever pay for the ladies?" I asked, thinking that things should be reciprocal.

"That's not the way it works!" he shouted at me. He was annoyed with my obvious lack of knowledge, and it was early in the morning for him, but then he cooled down to instruct me.

"We all inherit something," he said. "I inherited a mind. They inherited money. I inherited a certain charm . . . and a *joie de vivre*, which is nice to have. I give them wit and conversation and they give me food. It's a fair exchange."

"What about their husbands?"

"Dead. All dead. Women outlive men, so there's more of them, that's why sometimes you simply need an extra man at the table. It maintains a good seating arrangement. Boy-girl, boy-girl. I am an extra man."

"Are there extra women?"

"You never need an extra woman. Such a thing is never heard of."

"Why do these rich women need escorts?"

"To show that they can still get a man. And if you go on a trip a man is good to have. A man is good for carrying the luggage and counting all the pieces."

"What about the women without money? What happens to them?"

"They are abandoned. Lost. Men without money can still hang on. They don't lose their looks. They didn't have any to begin with."

"Do you think I could escort someone or be an extra man at a table?" I asked. I liked the idea of getting dressed up and eating a fancy meal. It was a very young gentleman thing to do.

"You're young," Henry said. "Do you know how to dance?"

"No."

"Your generation is hopeless . . . but we might fit you in somewhere. Vivian has a granddaughter, she might like you."

"That would be incredible," I said.

"But I don't think you're cut out for escorting," Henry said, and he saw the smile leave my face, so he quickly added, "but you might have potential. If you deal with very old women you have to be careful that they don't fall. I was dancing with Vivian at Doubles and suddenly she just slipped out of my arms and went right to the floor. You have to pay attention every second. It's hard work.

Constant vigilance. That's why escorts are often called walkers. The women have to hold on to your arm when they walk into lunch or the Artillery Ball, otherwise they collapse. But I am not a walker."

"Why aren't you a walker?"

"Because I have a job. No real walker has a job. They are one hundred percent freeloader."

Then Henry looked at me blankly. "Are we having a discussion?" he asked.

"Yes, I think so," I said.

"Well, it has to stop. I never speak this early in the morning until after I read the newspaper. I have to get my blood going with the latest atrocities."

He stood up and looked at himself in the long mirror that hung on the wall between the two windows. He smiled. His hair was standing straight up and was grayish-brown, which it often was in the mornings. Then later in the day it would be dark brown, and sometimes there were smudges and odd little crumbs near the hairline. His method of hair dyeing was a mystery to me, as there were no coloring products in the bathroom and yet it was always from the bathroom that he would emerge with darkened hair. He lifted his arms above his head to stretch and I went to the refrigerator for some juice. He walked towards me and with his hands he smoothed down the front of his tuxedo shirt.

"I have the most elegant sleeping clothes, don't you think?" asked Henry, already lifting his ban on conversation.

"You certainly do," I said.

When I returned home from work that day in the late afternoon, Henry was on the phone with yet another one of his women. I stood in the kitchen, peering into the refrigerator, and discreetly listened while Henry talked to her.

"Doris, you have to give yourself at least an hour where you refuse to think about your problems. It's bad enough when you have to face them. This is good to do before you sleep. Never think of problems before sleeping . . . If that nurse is rude again, tell your doctor . . . I'll visit you tomorrow, room two-fifteen, Beth Israel,

I won't forget . . . We'll be in constant contact. Get some rest . . . Right . . . 'Bye."

He hung up the phone and I closed the refrigerator. He said to me sadly, "All my old lady friends are dying."

"I'm sorry," I said.

"I'd be falling apart too if I didn't dance," he said.

And then Henry put a record on his portable record player. It was an album of old Cole Porter show tunes. Henry usually danced every afternoon and when I first moved in he had warned me one afternoon, "I am going to dance now, but I can't be seen. I'll try to do it when you are not here, but sometimes the need is too great. If you could stay in your room I would greatly appreciate it."

But this time after his conversation with the ailing Doris he began to dance right in front of me. He shuffled his feet, extended his arms into the air, contorted his neck, and grimaced his facial muscles, all to the beat of the orchestra. The dance was part waltz and part Isadora Duncan. He shouted to me over the music, "I MOVE WHATEVER I THINK IS ROTTING!"

Otto Bellman and His Gang of Swiss Yodelers

I had watched Henry dance before, but always I had done it surreptitiously. From the end of my bed there was just enough angle so that I could peer into the kitchen where a mirror hung on the far wall, and this mirror, through the window in the wall on the left, was able to reflect the long mirror in the living room, and so using the two mirrors like a spy I was able to watch Henry dance.

And I loved the way he moved. He often threw in vaudevillian flourishes and choreographed stumbles, and of course the music was wonderful. It was usually Cole Porter or Gershwin.

His dance would last about ten minutes, and he was often in a sport coat to help him build up more of a sweat. And this dancing kept him relatively fit. He had a little bit of a paunch, but other than that he was in good shape, and he wasn't prudish about his body. He was discreet, but if he needed to change, to drop his pants, he didn't hesitate if I was around, though he made sure to turn his back. More than once in those first weeks of living together I saw the soft white flesh of his buttocks. In stark contrast to his tanned, lined face, his rear seemed almost young and preserved.

So it was difficult to judge Henry's age. And as I stood there in the kitchen, watching him dance after his conversation with the ailing Doris, I was more impressed than ever with Henry's vitality. I wondered if maybe he was only in his late fifties.

After about ten minutes he slumped into his chair. And the vantage point of this chair, in the corner, with the whole apartment and me before it, always made me think of it as Henry's throne. I never sat on it.

"Wine," he said to me, feigning a greater exhaustion than he really felt. I got the bottle of cheap red wine which he kept next to the refrigerator. He held out to me his stained red goblet and I poured for him.

"You may have a glass too," he said. "Free of charge."

I retrieved the one glass I used (all the other glasses were too deeply fogged and stained) and I poured myself a small amount. I sat on the couch and I said, "Henry, how old are you?"

He looked at me with anger and indignation as if I had just insulted him, which was the opposite of my intention. I thought he was incredible: teaching two nights a week, going out with ladies, sneaking into operas, changing flat tires, dancing. It was a question asked out of admiration and awe, but he took it as an affront. He drew himself erect and said, "Women and we of the theater must never reveal our age! We must be prepared to play an eighteen-year-old at a moment's notice!"

"I'm sorry," I said.

"I forgive you. It was an indiscretion of youth." And he seemed to genuinely pardon me, as we ended up having a lengthy conversation about his career in the theater. I discovered that in addition to writing plays and teaching English and drama, Henry had done quite a bit of acting, both off Broadway and summer stock. He had also toured college campuses, giving staged readings of his own works.

His plays were historical dramas about great figures from the nineteenth century: George Eliot (*The Dead Hand*), Tchaikovsky (*The Pathetic Beauty*), Nellie Bly (*The Mad House*), and Lord Alfred Tennyson (*Queen Victoria's Poet*); and from the seventeenth century, Anne Hutchinson (*Anne Hutchinson Fights the Church*).

The dialogue of his plays, he explained, was adapted from these great figures' letters and writings. This academic quality of his work appealed to universities, and Henry showed me the promotional flyer he sent out to schools. It featured a picture of him in jacket and tie looking very young and handsome, with dark penetrating eyes.

The flyer also had excerpted sentences from reviews of his performances. They were from obscure papers like *The Kansas Star* and *Rochester Reporter*. An excerpt from *The Sacramento Bee* described him, in the role of Tennyson, in this way: "Harrison is a real Victorian swinger!"

Henry still mailed his flyer out, but he hadn't actually given a reading for some time: "I'm between engagements," he said. "Unfortunately, two years between engagements."

He wasn't very proud of these historical works. "It's really a matter of collage," he explained, "turning their correspondence into dialogue. Anyone can do it. And there are hundreds of letters to choose from. In London in the nineteenth century they had seven mail deliveries a day. It was like talking on the phone. It was a great age . . . They were so concerned about sex, the Victorians, that the legs of the Queen Anne chairs were covered with panties, lest they give rise to desire."

Henry was proud of his one work of complete fiction, which he considered to be his greatest play, though it had never been performed. It was titled *Henry and Mary Are Always Late.*

He actually hadn't started his sexual comedy about the Shakers and he didn't really think of it as his *chef d'oeuvre*, as he said during our first meeting. But it was a play that he wanted to write. "I'm too disorganized to get started on the Shakers," he said. "To write I need to be on a hill in my car, looking at something beautiful. There are some wonderful peaks in Harlem from which you can see the cliffs of New Jersey. The Palisades. I'll have to go to Harlem to write about the Shakers."

I asked Henry if I could read one of his plays and he said the historical works were buried deep in the trunk of his car and that *Henry and Mary Are Always Late* was simply missing. "Every few months," he said, "I make a sighting of it. Something gets displaced, a piece of furniture is moved, a pair of trousers are washed, and then suddenly there it is—my *chef d'oeuvre*. It made a brief appearance last spring. The next time it floats to the surface I will make sure to quickly grab it and put it in a safe place. It's around here some-where, but to try to find it would kill me. It's depressing to live in a mess, but to clean it up is more depressing."

Henry then conjectured that the previous tenant, Otto Bellman, who was an illegal alien from Switzerland, had stolen the play.

"Why would he steal it?" I asked.

"Revenge. I threw him out."

This information alarmed me. It was the first real information I had received about my Swiss predecessor, besides periodically being called by his name. "Why did you throw him out?" I asked.

"He was chasing Negress prostitutes on the Lower East Side. I won't be a part in any way in the spreading of the AIDS virus!"

"How do you know what he was doing?"

"He told me. He was attracted to them because they were so different from the lumpenproletariat he had grown up with. I'm sure he took *Henry and Mary*. He's probably having it produced in Yugoslavia and living off the proceeds."

"Why did he come to New York?"

"He wants to be an actor, claims to know martial arts. He thinks that's the way to become a movie star. He *could* play villains. He was hoping I would give him contacts."

"How long did he live here?"

"Six months. He wasn't bad at first. He has a good profile. He looks like Brigitte Bardot, except he has a slight hunchback . . . I like good posture. But I did a terrible thing. I couldn't just throw him out—he had no money, gone through it all. So I asked my friend Virginia if he could stay on her couch. She's the daughter of my closest friends in Greenwich. I thought he'd only be there a few days, but he hasn't left! She's forty-five and never been married. She might be desperate enough to fall under his spell. I may have set in motion an evil seduction."

I didn't want to end up like Otto Bellman, thrown out for suspicious sexual behavior, so I was very glad that I had prudently hidden my copy of Krafft-Ebing's *Psychopathia sexualis.*

That night, after our talk about his plays and Otto Bellman, the lights were out and we were both in bed. He called out to me from his room, "Can you check the door to see if it is properly locked? I'm too exhausted."

"All right," I said, and I was glad to help out in some way. It made me feel trusted and close to Henry. I made sure that the chain, the police lock, and the door lock were all secure.

"It's all set," I said, and I stood in the kitchen peering into the darkness of his room. I could see the top of his head at the end of his couch.

"Thank you for locking us in," he said. "We don't want Otto Bellman and his gang of Swiss yodelers to break in and rob us of our virtue!"

"Certainly not," I said. "He may have already stolen your play."

"That's right. We may have to lure him here by offering schnapps, and then tie him up and threaten to hand him over to immigration if he doesn't return the play. And leave Virginia. We must think of her as well. Of course he might be very strong. Hunchbacks often are. And he might know a few kicks. Well, this is no time to think of anything, it's bad to think before sleeping . . . I'm putting my plugs in . . . Did you let the cat in?"

"The cat?"

"That's what people say to each other before going to sleep."

"Oh . . . yes, the cat is in."

"Good. Now both my plugs are in. I've lost radio contact. *Gute Nacht!*"

"Good night," I said, but he didn't hear me, and I tiptoed on the orange path back to my bed.

CHAPTER III

I Felt Connected to Women All Over America

I liked my job at *Terra*. I enjoyed getting dressed for it each day and putting on a different tie. I had ten ties for a two-week rotation.

In Princeton, I only had seven, but I had increased my number when one Saturday afternoon, Henry had taken me to a charity thrift shop on Second Avenue, and I had picked up three neckties, two blue oxford shirts with Paul Stuart labels, and a rust-colored sport coat. The quality of everything was high since it was the Upper East Side, and it all cost me about fifteen dollars.

Henry had taken me to the thrift store because he needed a clean shirt. He was feeling too lazy to walk on one in the shower. He said, "Some people go to the laundromat. I go to the thrift store."

Each day when I left for work in the mornings, Henry was asleep and so the apartment was pitch-black. My air-shaft window let in no direct sunlight, so I never knew what it was like outside until I emerged on the street. And whether it was gray or clear, the daylight was always a shock, but a pleasant one after the close darkness of our rooms.

I would walk up to Ninety-sixth Street for the subway, and when I would stand on the platform, waiting for the train, I hoped that the other people thought, "There goes a young gentleman to his office."

On Lexington Avenue, before I went into *Terra*, I stopped every day at a deli and ordered a coffee and a whole-wheat roll with butter. I wanted to be thought of as a regular. I was trying to set up a routine.

At the deli I developed an acquaintanceship with the young cashier, Roberto, whose hair was the deep black color of oil and very thick. Every day when he tilted his head and recovered my change from the till, I secretly examined his hair, and not without feelings of awe and envy. There was no weakness anywhere in the scalp. It was my diagnosis that his hair would never abandon him.

He was always talking about the Knicks to the deli men behind the counter, and since I am a Knicks fan, I managed to throw in a few remarks. It was not in keeping with my notion of the young gentleman to be a basketball follower, but when I was nine years old I briefly worshipped an older cousin who came and stayed with us for a few weeks and he was a Knicks fan. So from that time forward I have always rooted for them.

It was the pre-season when I first started going to the deli, and Roberto and I had high hopes for our team. We were always exchanging the same bits of information that we picked up in the papers, but saying them in different ways, so that we would appear knowledgeable. I looked forward to seeing him in the morning and was disappointed on the odd occasion when he wasn't there.

After the deli, I'd go to my office, where I had been assigned my own little cubicle. We were a small staff of eight: George, the editor; four women; two men; and myself. Two of the women were in their late fifties and married, and the other two were single. One of the single girls, Mary, was extremely attractive and she caused me anguish the way pretty, clean-looking blond girls with thin arms always have—in their presence I feel a physical pain as if I've been punched in the stomach. Also, around these pretty girls I suffer a vacuuming of all personality. I am unable to say a single interesting thing.

And Mary provoked in me all these symptoms. I felt attacked by her beauty. I would notice acutely the way her thin figure would move underneath her loose blouses, her light wool pants. I would smell the air when she would walk past me and then try to hold the scent of her perfume in my nostrils for as long as possible. It was all very painful, so I avoided her as best I could, and I also kept a low, shy profile with my other colleagues as well.

But on the phone, doing my job, I was gregarious. My assignment was to contact all the natural history museums and nature centers in the country and try to get them to buy bulk subscriptions of the magazine for their memberships. There were thousands of such places.

The best part of my job was that almost everyone I spoke to on the phone was a woman. And over the phone, they really liked me. After I made my pitch, we often had little conversations. They were glad for the break from their jobs, and they would unburden themselves to me. They would tell me how hectic things were in their office, how overworked they were—a new dinosaur exhibit had gone up; a disorganized new director had come on; the budget was being cut. After a few weeks and numerous calls to follow up, to check on the progress of my proposal, I came to be on a first-name basis with many of these women and they would talk to me even more.

While the ladies spoke, I would start to imagine what their day was like. I would picture them rushing in the morning to get ready for work, thinking about the struggles to come, putting on their bras and panties and stockings. Then I'd see them in simple dresses, standing in their kitchens, drinking coffee. Then they would be driving to work. There was traffic. I imagined traffic throughout the United States. I'd picture myself in the car with them and I'd look out the window. I'd glance at the Mississippi in St. Louis, the rain in Seattle, the desert in Tucson.

Then I'd see the women at their offices. They'd have another cup of coffee. They'd go to the bathroom. I'd get to be in the women's room. I'd see them readjust their bras and panties. The nonchalance of it all would excite me. And then the phone would ring on their desk. It was me calling from *Terra*, and they'd smile happily. *Louis Ives from New York City*, they'd think. It was my hope that they thought I was a sophisticated Manhattan gentleman.

Even with all this fantasizing while they talked, I was a good listener and I would try to counsel them with the same platitudes that I heard Henry use with his ladies: "Try not to think about your problems before sleeping," I'd say, or another one of Henry's, "It never was easy and it only gets harder."

My ladies would laugh at my remarks; I would make them feel better. And I didn't care if they were old or married or flabby, it was the enormous femininity of it all, and it was happening everywhere. I felt connected to women all over America.

Porky Pig Fell Off a Cliff

I was on the job for about two weeks when I used the phone for an unusual personal call. I was taking a break, sitting in my cubicle, and I was reading the *New York Press.* I discovered in the back pages that there was an extensive listing of "Adult Services." One ad caught my eye: "Transvestite Makeovers." The number it gave had a 718 area code.

I trembled. I dialed. A woman answered: "Hello."

"I saw your ad," I whispered.

"In what magazine?"

She was checking up on the effectiveness of her advertising. "The *New York Press*," I said.

"We're located in Bay Ridge. Where are you?"

"Manhattan."

"Can you come to Brooklyn?"

"Yes," I said, white-lying. I had no idea how to drive to Brooklyn.

"Well, we perform a complete makeover. Two hours for eighty-five dollars. Makeup. Wigs. Lingerie. Dresses. Heels. Femininity lessons. We can take you shopping, go to a movie. Whatever you like. But no sex. Do you want to make an appointment?"

"Maybe . . ."

"If you want we can take pictures. Bring thirty-five millimeter, or Polaroid."

"What speed film?" I asked, to show that I was a serious caller.

"Two hundred."

"Thank you," I said, and I hung up. My heart was pounding, but I wasn't ready for such a service, even though I thought the price was extremely fair. I figured that it was probably so low because of the Brooklyn location. But I didn't want to do it. What if I really did love being dressed as a woman when it was done properly? I'd have to do it all the time. I had read enough transvestite-oriented pornography to know what happens to men. It takes you over: I'd have to shop, spend money. I imagined myself hiding my women's clothing from Henry in the apartment. The whole thing would be a lot of work.

But I didn't rule out trying that service in the future. I copied the phone number onto a little piece of paper and put it in my wallet. I knew that I had a powerful curiosity that at some point I was going to have to address. But I was still too scared to take that step: What if I crossed some invisible line of femaleness and couldn't come back? I didn't want to give up being the young gentleman.

But I had a bipolar condition. It wasn't mood-related, it was sex-related. On one pole there was a desire for femininity and beauty, to appear like a pretty girl, and on the other pole I wanted to be a young gentleman who wore a tie and went to hear *Tosca* at Lincoln Center. How was I to reconcile this? I wished that the girl thoughts would go away, just disappear, but they wouldn't.

I first became aware of this longing to be a girl when I was quite young. I was only four or five years old and I was watching cartoons on the television. One of the characters, it was Porky Pig I believe, was pushed off a high cliff and as he fell endlessly through the air his clothes were whipped about him and somehow through the miracle of cartooning he was transformed into a girl. His fluttering pants became a dress, his face became pretty, his eyelashes curled upward, his hair grew long, and little breasts bloomed beneath his shirt. He smiled happily. And as I watched this, something I had never felt before came alive inside me—it was a tingling, erotic longing. And somehow as Porky Pig became a girl, I thought that I was also becoming a girl, and I liked it. I liked it better than being a boy.

But then all too soon Porky Pig slammed into the ground. There was a cloud of dust and then it cleared. He was alive, but he was a boy again, and so was I.

I wanted to cry. I thought we had been changed back too soon.

After I saw that cartoon, I started saying to myself and to God: "I wish I could be a girl for ten minutes and look at myself in the mirror." I just wanted to know what it was like, and I had come up with the time limit of ten minutes because I thought that made it a more reasonable request. But I knew that God only did things for you if he liked you, and it seemed terribly frustrating to me that I might never be a girl. So I hoped that one day God would decide that he liked me and he'd just do it. And I'd go look in the mirror and instead of seeing me, I'd see a pretty girl in a dress, smiling.

And this wish or prayer to be a girl, which I never told anyone about, stayed with me for a number of years, but then, in the way that childhood works, I simply forgot about it.

But the wish came back when I was nearly sixteen. I was just starting a very late puberty and was beginning to experiment with masturbation. I found in the basement of our house a hidden stash of my father's pornographic magazines and a single book: *Psychopathia sexualis.*

I looked at the pictures of the naked women in the magazines and I liked them, but what really excited me was when I discovered the chapter and the case histories in *Psychopathia* that dealt with men who thought they were women. And it was then that I remembered the Porky Pig cartoon and my childhood wish to be a girl, and the wish came back.

Dr. Richard von Krafft-Ebing, who was Freud's superior when Freud was first starting out in Vienna, was the author of *Psychopathia*, and the case histories are his records of the people he treated. And the men who dressed as women and thought they were women were suffering from a "delusion of sexual change." I wanted such a delusion and so every night I'd read and reread the same case histories and I'd masturbate and try to time my release with a sentence that excited me.

So there I was, a young Jewish boy in New Jersey reading about nineteenth-century German-speaking men who were losing their minds and their male identities, and I saw them as erotic role models.

Krafft-Ebing also provided some anthropological data and phenomena on the subject, including my favorite passages about the Pueblo Indians who purposely cultivated feminized men.

It described how the Pueblos every few years took one of their strongest warriors and made him ride a horse excessively and masturbate excessively, and this had the combined effect of destroying the man's testicles. His skin would then become soft and his breasts would enlarge. He would take on the role of a woman in the tribe. He would dress as a woman and would be used sexually as one in religious ceremonies. Such men were called *mujerados* and were held in high esteem.

This struck a nerve with me and I often fantasized that I was a tribe member chosen for transformation. Once I got so carried away with the idea of it all that I masturbated as much as I could and I rode my ten-speed bicycle, bouncing up and down on the seat, as if I was cantering on a horse. But the experiment only lasted for a few days.

In a separate experiment, I also tried putting on my mother's clothing. One day I had the house to myself for a few hours and I started out completely nude and when I slipped on a pair of my mother's panties it was like receiving a shot of pure adrenaline. I could have sprinted a hundred yards. The panties also gave me a powerful erection, but I felt very feminine. My buttocks looked girlish and I caressed myself.

The feeling of the panties was certainly exquisite, but then when I awkwardly slipped on the bra, and felt the strap against my back, and looked down upon two white cups, cups for breasts, I felt beautiful. I felt like a girl. I was high. I had breasts. I was flying. My two bra cups were wings.

I then put on a light cotton skirt and I walked about my parents' room. The unfamiliar feeling of air moving between my legs made me feel vulnerable and sexy. I wanted to be a girl! And most of all I wanted to be pretty. I thought of all the pretty girls in school parading down the hall in their skirts, how lovely they were, how aroused they must feel with the air secretly caressing them.

I put some tissues in my bra and I put on a blouse. I paused frequently to touch myself and to feel the materials against me. The fluffiness of the skirt hid my erection a little. And then I looked in the mirror. I had purposely saved that for last. I was going to make my old wish come true: to look in the mirror and see a beautiful girl.

But when I saw myself it was like cutting one's finger with a knife by accident. For a moment there's simply dullness, then recognition, and then repulsion and pain when you realize you've opened up your own flesh. So it took me a few seconds to focus, but when I clearly saw myself in my mother's clothes, I was ashamed and disgusted. Coming out of that blouse and skirt was my lifelong face, no pretty girl smiling, just me looking lost and morbid, and yet pathetically hopeful at the same time.

I lay down on my parents' bed and I was on fire with humiliation. "What is the matter with me?" I screamed in my mind. I didn't move for several minutes; my eyes were closed.

I calmed down a little, and the sensations of the bra and panties against my skin were still pleasurable to me. I was free from the image in the mirror and I wanted my experiment to work in some way, and so very careful not to soil anything, I masturbated, and right after my orgasm I was even more ashamed. The clothes, which just moments before had felt beautiful, now held me like ropes. I wanted them off of me: *What am I doing in my mother's clothes?*

I carefully put everything away, afraid that my mother, so neat, would notice the slightest wrinkle, but as far as I know she never did. And if she did notice that something was out of place, she must have thought that it was simply a mystery of the household.

Despite the bad feelings, I actually tried dressing up a few more times. I wanted it to make me feel good. My last attempt, when I was almost seventeen, I applied lipstick and attempted to fix my hair, but the result was the same: when I looked into the mirror I was still there, unbeautiful, a boy.

An International Agreement on the Virtues of Chastity

After I called the Brooklyn makeover service, I perused the rest of the dozens and dozens of sex listings in the *Press*. It was mostly people offering S&M and role-play and massage, and I loved reading all of the ads. I felt less alone—the whole city had sex problems.

THE EXTRA MAN

But also the listings were like Pandora's box. Too much was out there. Too much was available if you were feeling weak. So I put the *Press* away and got back to work, calling my ladies at their nature centers and museums.

That night, Henry came rushing home around eleven, back from teaching, just in time to watch *Are You Being Served?*, which was a British comedy about the staff of a department store. We had fallen into the pattern of watching it together most nights after Henry returned from his evening classes in Queens or from a dinner with one of his lady friends. He had been watching the show for years; it came over a cable channel, and he said that there were hundreds of episodes, many of which he still had not seen.

"Has it started?" he asked breathlessly, while removing his raincoat.

"Just began," I said.

"Thank God. It was only the thought of *Are You Being Served?* that got me through my last class . . . Any messages?"

"No."

"It's the end of an era! I will have to withdraw into myself."

He sat down on his couch to watch our program and I was in my chair. We each had a glass of wine.

We both loved the character of Mrs. Slocombe. She was a widow and the head of ladies' lingerie in the department store. She had a matronly figure, a sour and puffy face, long false eyelashes, and hair that was dyed either purple, red, or orange. The high point of every show came when Mrs. Slocombe, in her earnest attempt at an upper-class accent, would fret about the well-being of her cat.

"My pussy was out all night in the cold. I had to warm it by the fire," she'd say, and Captain Peacock, the floor manager, would raise a discreet eyebrow, the canned British laughter would be let loose, and Henry and I would snicker into our wineglasses.

It was one of Henry's generosities that every night he gave me a glass of red wine, free of charge, as he liked to say, for our television watching. Though for anything else, Henry made a strict point that all transactions between us should have a cash reimbursement or something should be provided in trade. For example, if he borrowed my shampoo for one washing of his hair, I was to take an equivalent portion of toothpaste—one brushing. One night he needed a pair of socks to go out to dinner and he was despairing. "I will have to paint my ankles black!" So I lent him a pair of black socks, and, despite my protests, he gave me one dollar. He said that we should feel no obligations towards each other, which secretly wounded me.

After *Are You Being Served?* was over that evening (Captain Peacock was passed over for a promotion), Henry began to scan the channels, clicking the remote control with fury. "The culture is dying," he said angrily. "There must be something still out there." He chanced upon the Court Channel and announced, "We should do away with trials in this country. They're too expensive."

"What should we replace them with?" I asked.

"A single tyrant," he said.

He finished off the bottle of wine and then he took a plastic bottle of spring water from beneath his couch—somehow he knew that it was a safe one—and he drained it. Then he put the wine bottle and the plastic bottle in the garbage in the kitchen.

"Henry, we really should recycle those bottles," I said. "We can have a garbage bag just for recyclables."

"They've brainwashed you. Environmentalists. Nothing is recycled. It all goes to the same place," he said, and he stood in the doorway between the kitchen and the living room.

"It doesn't, and we really should try. It won't be difficult. I'll carry everything down. Recycling is important."

"Recycling is the most insidious idea of this generation," he said. "And helping the homeless, most of whom deserve the position. The only problem they should be looking at is sex. If we can get that under control then we can take care of these other problems. We need to have an international agreement on the virtues of chastity. Yes. It will require a lot of work . . . a lot of exercise, folk dancing, long walks, seven- and eight-course meals, mah-jongg, and what else? . . . War! That will get their minds off sex."

Henry paused, weighing his solutions, how chastity might be achieved on an international level, and then he said, with resignation, "Then of course there's the homosexual problem. No one has been able to solve that. Not enough research."

So he sat back down on his couch and resumed his flipping through the forty-odd cable channels. Cable was Henry's one extravagance. It was over twenty dollars a month, but I also covered half the expense. (At the beginning of October we had dropped the weekly "gifts," and I had begun the first of my monthly rent-donations. Henry liked to receive it in cash.)

He stopped his channel flipping when he came to the New Jersey public station, which was advertising a documentary about the royal family that it was going to air. Henry was an avid follower of the family, and more than once had expressed his great respect for the Queen and her jewels. Brief clips of the documentary were being shown and we saw some black-and-white footage of the Duke of Windsor and Wallis Simpson holding hands and walking together in a garden. Then the preview of the documentary ended, and Henry, unable to find anything else to watch, clicked off the TV.

"You should read about Wally Simpson," he said. "She's one of the most interesting people of our time. Perhaps the greatest woman of the twentieth century."

"The greatest? Why?"

"She was an American who almost became Queen of England! Almost brought down the whole royal family single-handedly. A fascinating woman . . . Marlene Dietrich tried to get Edward away from her to save him. Dietrich also had experience with homosexual boyfriends."

"Are you saying the Duke of Windsor was homosexual?"

"Of course. The English are all homosexual because of public school. They never really get over it."

I was enough of an Anglophile to know the important facts about the Duke of Windsor. I had also been told by the tailor in the English Shoppe in Princeton that the Duke of Windsor had thrown his sport coats to the floor of his closet to give them a worn look, and so I had done the same thing.

"Why did he give up his kingdom for Wally Simpson if he was a homosexual?" I asked.

"Wally was sympathetic," said Henry. "She understood. Also, she had a masculine jaw and very beautiful dark eyes. The shape of her head was masculine and she could procure him boys. She was strong and he was weak, a total mess . . . But it's a fascinating and corrupt era, you should study it . . . They were friends with Jimmy Donahue, the Woolworth heir, and he was a total homosexual. Once in New York he was drunk with his friends and they were shaving the sex organs of a soldier. Then they decided to cut off the soldier's testicles, so they did. They left him at the Brooklyn Bridge. He made it to a hospital. It cost Jimmy's mother two hundred and fifty thousand dollars, which is not enough for having lost your testicles, but in those days it was. So that's the type of people Edward and Wally were running with. Supposedly, though, Jimmy Donahue could be very charming. Unless you were a soldier."

"It seems like everyone interesting is homosexual," I said.

"No. Everyone interesting is trisexual."

"They try anything?"

"No. They have three sexualities. Asexual, homosexual, and heterosexual."

"Are you trisexual?" I asked.

I meant this to be a playful question, indicating that I thought Henry was interesting, and therefore most likely trisexual, but the words came out of my mouth in a greedy way, indicating my very real desire to know Henry's sexuality.

And if I knew he was homosexual, bisexual, or trisexual, then I could imagine that he might be attracted to me; it could be a way of being sure that he liked me. But was trisexual a real option? Was I trisexual? Did the opposing forces of heterosexuality and homosexuality, like Drive and Reverse in a car, knock someone into the neutrality of asexuality?

"I am a follower of the Church of Rome," he said, answering my question. "I only have sex when married."

"But you've never been married," I said, unable to control myself, wanting to know the truth.

"Yes."

"You've never had sex?"

"You won't get anything out of me."

"I apologize for prying." I had really gone too far with my curiosity, but it had been building up for the six weeks I had known him; I didn't dare look Henry in the eye.

"You have to understand that if we are going to share this apartment," said Henry, "that it's best to know as little about one another as possible—the best relationships have this as a foundation . . . All I ask of my houseguests is that they don't stab me in the back in the middle of the night."

"You're not really worried about being stabbed, are you?"

"Everyone I let in here is a stranger. It is the risk I take."

"I'm sorry I was rude," I said.

Henry was forgiving of me. His voice was calm, instructive. "Try to think about more important things," he said. "Think about your soul, your character. Think about the freezer. It's a solid block of ice. It needs defrosting. There might be a steak in there. Concentrate on things like that. There could be a meal in it."

Then Henry went to the sink and brushed his teeth and performed his toilet; I followed suit and then we both lay down for the night. Before I fell asleep, he called out from his couch, "If we're feeling brave let's melt the freezer this weekend."

"All right," I said, though I sensed that we would both procrastinate.

"Good . . . Any final thoughts? Comments?"

"No."

"So there we are. Where are we?"

Henry often ended our day with that question, and then invariably the plugs were plugged in and radio contact was lost.

The Recession Spankologist

The next day I was at work and I couldn't help myself and I was looking at the *New York Press* again. I came across an ad that I had somehow missed. It said: recession spankologist. It was too odd and curious to pass up, so I called.

"Hello," answered a woman's voice.

"I saw your ad," I whispered.

"Which one?"

She had more than one? "Recession spankologist," I said.

"What time do you want to come over?"

"I'm not sure . . ."

"I'm a mature brunette with a full figure. I'll spank you. Do you have something special in mind?"

"I'm a beginner . . ."

"You like cross-dressing? I'll put you in some of my things. When can you come over?"

How did she know I was interested in cross-dressing? "I get off work at six."

"Come over at seven. How much can you afford?"

"I . . ." She was listening to my hesitation. She was trying to sense the depth of my wallet. She got it just about right.

"Forty dollars for an hour," she said.

That was cheap. Recession prices. "All right," I said.

"I live at 153 West Ninety-third Street. Tell the doorman Miss Hart. What's your name?"

"David," I said.

"You have the address?"

"Yes," I said.

"Be here at seven," she said and hung up.

It had all happened so fast. I had just wanted to talk to this spankologist. I didn't think I was going to make an appointment, but the price was so low and she had sold me so rapidly. And she lived on my street! It was on the other side of the park, but still it was a huge coincidence and I took this as a good sign.

It was a Friday and I could barely think straight the rest of the afternoon. I was picturing a full-bosomed brunette in her late thirties: she had said she was mature. I wanted to tell my coworkers that I had something exciting planned, but I couldn't do that. I did tell one of my ladies at the Cape Cod Museum of Natural History that I had a date that night and she wished me well.

I got off the cross-town bus at Ninety-sixth Street and then walked over three blocks. It was an old high-rise with a dirty lobby. There was a doorman, but no elevator attendant.

In the elevator I looked at myself in the small mirror in the corner of the ceiling. From that overhead angle, the thinning of my blond hair was revealed. It wasn't fair. I'm too young to go bald, I thought. I hoped that Miss Hart would at least think that I had a handsome face.

She was on the fifteenth floor; her apartment was down a long hall with many apartments. I rang the buzzer. The door opened about a quarter of the way. She stood in the opening, shielding herself behind the door so that her neighbors couldn't see her. She was wearing an all-black outfit of bra, panties, garters, stockings that came to the mid-thigh, high heels, and even black-rimmed glasses.

"Am I too old?" she asked. "If I am, it's all right. You can leave right now."

She was over sixty years old and she looked eerily, at first glance, like my father's mother. She had the same thick black glasses, and the same kind of dyed black hair that you get at a beauty parlor. Her skin, like my grandmother's, was without wrinkles, but there was the looseness of age to it.

"You're not too old," I said gently. Her breasts were milky white and large.

"Come in," she said, and she rapidly closed the door behind me. "What's your name?"

"David."

It was a studio apartment with a kitchen behind little shutter doors, a large bed in the corner near the door, and a living-room arrangement at the other end of the apartment. She led me to a couch and told me to sit down.

"You should call me Mistress Hart, or if you forget, just Miss Hart. I have to go to the bathroom. Take off your clothes. We'll start when I come out."

She was strange, distracted; her eyes were all distorted behind her thick lenses. She had a thin, unhappy pale mouth. But the shape of her face, the strong cheekbones, the fine, straight nose, made me think that she had been very beautiful once.

She left me on the couch. I watched her walk away. She was short, about five foot four—with the heels. Her shoulders were round and drooped down. Her rear in her black panties was very wide. The tops of her legs, above the stockings, were ghostly white, the muscles looked soft, the skin loose. I had said she wasn't too old because I didn't want to hurt her feelings. Also, she didn't look half bad standing there in the doorway. I had never seen a woman that old in her underwear. It was exciting. And also it had been too late to turn back. I had been in a sort of trance since I had spoken to her on the phone and I had to go through with whatever was going to happen, though it had been very fair of her to give me the option to leave.

I undressed down to my underwear and T-shirt and looked around me. The apartment was dreary and stark. There were very few personal objects. The furniture was old, and obviously secondhand since none of it matched. The curtains were heavy and thick, and only two weak lamps were lit, so the place was cavelike and shadowy in its darkness. The carpet was an old faded green.

Miss Hart did have one interesting thing. Across from the couch was a table with two black phones and two answering machines. Above the phones, on the wall, was a piece of paper with large, numbered reminders written in thick black ink with an awkward, slanting script:

1) Find out what they're calling for
2) Give a price
3) Give the address
4) Set a time
5) Repeat address

Then I noticed that on the little end table next to the couch were several books. I was sitting in my underwear, waiting for her, growing a little anxious, and I picked up one of the books, a large blue one, and on its cover it said *Alcoholics Anonymous*. "My God,"

I thought, "she's a recovering alcoholic, but she must have lost her memory to booze and needs written reminders." I was impressed with her. I admired her ingenuity in trying to run her business better; it was Benjamin Franklinesque.

Finally, the toilet flushed and this was a little embarrassing. She came out and said, "What's your name again?"

I was starting to doubt my own memory, since I kept on supplying a false name. Was she trying to trip me up?

"David," I said.

She sat on a chair across from the couch. "What do you want to do?"

"I . . . you did mention cross-dressing."

"All right, we can put some things on you . . . Do you want to be spanked too?"

Thinking that this was her specialty, I figured I should try it. I said, "I've never been spanked—well, once when I was a child—but maybe we could do a little."

"David, right?"

"Yes."

"I'll call you Debbie," she said, and she seemed to suddenly come alive. She had been very matter-of-fact and businesslike, but now she smiled. "You're in very good hands, you know. I'm sorry I'm so old, but you get a lot of experience with me. I used to be very beautiful. I was in Hollywood, you know. They always needed pretty girls. I slept with Ronald Reagan in the fifties. You can find my name in Kitty Kelley's book on Nancy Reagan. I'm in the back, the index. Katherine Hart. Look it up. Nancy hated me; I was much better in bed than she was."

"What was he like?"

"He had a lot of girlfriends, but he was a gentleman."

I believed her about being in Hollywood and sleeping with Reagan. It was a life story that made sense—a young beautiful actress hooks up with a star; maybe she has talent, maybe she doesn't, in the movies it doesn't matter; her beauty starts to fade and she hits the bottle; she gets farther and farther out on the fringe; years later she sobers up, and slightly addled she makes a meager living spanking men. I should have asked her if she had spanked Ronald Reagan.

"Do you have another ad besides 'Recession spankologist'?" I asked, alluding to number one on the list above the phone.

"I also do massage. 'Mature massage,' I call it. Sometimes things get busy. That's why I have two phones, so I don't miss any calls. A lot of men want the spanking, and a lot want the massage. But you're here for the spanking and the cross-dressing, right?"

"Yes," I said, and then I complimented her. "I like your Recession Spankologist ad. It's a funny way to put it, very effective, I think."

"You have to catch people's eyes, and I do offer good prices . . . Let's get started."

She began to fuss in her bureau and took out some things. She put next to me a black bra like her own, a pair of white panties with frilly edges, and a white slip that was gray from age and many washings. She didn't have very nice things, but it was sort of fun to be doing this with someone else. I hadn't dressed up since high school, except for a bra I found at the laundromat in Princeton and put on in the bathroom, and Ms. Jefferies' bra at Pretty Brook.

Miss Hart had me stand up and she said very gently, "Take off your underwear, dear."

I stepped out of my shorts and I took off my T-shirt. I stood in front of her naked and I felt like a little boy. She had called me dear. She cupped my penis in her hand affectionately and she smiled.

"Put the panties on, Debbie."

It was very embarrassing to be called Debbie, but I did think it was funny that she could remember my girl name.

I put the panties on and I got an erection. Panties aren't so dissimilar to male underwear, but they tug the rear a little differently, which is nice, and there's no opening for the penis to come out and so, visually, it's exciting.

After the panties, Miss Hart then scooted behind me to help strap on the bra. She was trying to move with purpose and energy to show me that she was professional, and she made little cooing sounds while the bra was being bandaged around me. Once it was in place I felt great. I don't know what it is about brassieres. My whole inner feeling was changed. I felt pretty and girlish, happy and light. The breast, the bra, for me it's all very potent, though I didn't dare look in the mirror. I just stared down at the black cups and I felt good.

Then we put the slip on, and like my mother's dresses so long ago it gave me that sexy hidden-air feeling between the legs. And I thought that this dressing up was relatively safe compared to what the place in Brooklyn offered; I wasn't being completely transformed.

"I'll teach you how to be feminine," Miss Hart said. "The first thing you have to learn is how to sit. Most men don't know how to sit like women. Sit down."

I did and she said, "A woman just doesn't plop down. That opens the knees. When a lady sits down, she presses her calves against the couch and presses her knees together at the same time. Then she lowers herself slowly."

I stood up and followed her instructions, and the pressing of the knees together felt very ladylike and prim and made sitting down a sexual experience. She made me do it three times to get it right and I was feeling very aroused. Then she had me cross my legs. I did so at the knee, like a woman, and she said, "Your foot is poised like a man's. See how it's pointing up, full of tension and aggression. Men's feet are like that because they're trying to get somewhere. Let your foot relax down. That shows you're a woman, open to a man's advances."

I felt some masculine pride that my foot had on its own behaved aggressively, but nonetheless I released my ankle, let the foot relax, and I pretended I was a pretty girl sitting in a hotel lobby hoping to meet a man.

"Very good, Debbie," she said. "Now you can be spanked. Come over to me."

She was being very commanding and professional, though she did look a little batty with her thick glasses on. She sat on her chair and she had me lie across her legs. My penis, through my panties and slip, pressed against her thigh, and she smacked my rear about a dozen times. It didn't really hurt. Then she drew down the panties and slip and spanked me with little taps and then great big smacks. The phone rang twice during this time, but both times the party calling hung up before the answering machine came on. Miss Hart's strokes grew harder after these hang-ups, consciously or unconsciously punishing me for keeping her from the phone, though she did say, "They'll call back."

Every time she smacked me, I found myself saying, "Ow!" It seemed like a phony response, but it was actually genuine. She kept on saying, "Debbie's a bad girl," which I tried to ignore. It sounded too scripted.

But my naked penis was pressing against her white thigh, that contact was good, and the whole thing was so crazy that I felt happily distracted from the world.

Then she seemed to grow tired of spanking me and looked at her watch, while I lay draped across her knees. The sudden silence was pleasant. It only lasted a second, but it was an intimate moment of sorts. "Oh, dear. You've only been here twenty-five minutes. How long did we say your session was?"

"One hour," I said, and it wasn't easy talking with my belly on her legs. I stared at the back of her high heels.

"For how much?"

"Uh . . ." I thought of lying, but didn't. "Forty."

"Why don't we end early and I'll charge you thirty," she said. She was true to her advertising.

I thought of declining out of chivalry, but I was happy at the chance to save ten dollars. "That's fine," I said, agreeing to her new terms.

"Why don't you lie on the bed and I'll masturbate you with some oil. Is that all right, dear?"

"That sounds good," I said, and I loved it every time she called me dear. It felt like a term of affection.

We walked to the bed and she followed behind me sort of nervously and fretfully, as if I might suddenly disturb something. It was the same way my grandmother would be when she wanted to make sure that you didn't off-set the way she liked things done—that plates were put in the sink just so, that pillows on a couch were put back in place.

I went to lie down, but Miss Hart said insistently, "Not yet."

She got a white bath towel and put it over the coverlet. I then lay on the towel and she sat on the edge of the bed beside me. She removed my slip and panties. She wanted me to take off the bra, but I asked if I could keep it on. This seemed to annoy her, but she acquiesced. She placed several tissues on my belly and on the cups of the bra in exaggerated anticipation, I thought, of my ejaculation's range.

She poured some oil into the palm of her hand and coated my penis. She attended to me like a nurse. She began to stroke me and she seemed to relax, not so worried about me hitting the bra. She looked at me fondly and then she asked, "Are you Jewish?"

The question caught me off guard. Had she felt I had bargained her down? Or was she Jewish? Was Hart a Jewish name? She probably had changed it back in Hollywood anyways. And if she was Jewish, she would think I was a Jewish boy who was all mixed up. That would spoil everything. She was looking like my grandmother again. I lied, "No, I'm not Jewish. Why do you ask?" Then I remembered my false name was the very Jewish David, but she had probably forgotten.

"You look like an old lover of mine," she said sweetly. "He was Jewish."

Now I regretted my lie, but it was too late. If I had told her the truth she would have liked me more, I would have brought back the past. But I relaxed, everything was all right, and the stroking with the oil was wonderful. My head was propped comfortably against a pillow, and her old white breasts were about a foot from my face.

"Can I kiss your breasts?" I asked.

This didn't make her happy. She frowned, but I think she wanted to get me out of there. Maybe she had an AA meeting to go to. She unhooked her bra and scooted up closer to my mouth, all the while still stroking me with the luxurious oil. I took her left breast and it was like a tube of skin. Her flesh was loose-feeling, befitting her age, but it was also soft and her nipple protruded and was fiery pink. I took it hungrily in my mouth.

"Gently," she said. "My nipples are very sensitive."

I closed my eyes in babyish bliss. I was a man with a hard-on, I was wearing a bra, and I was nursing like a child. Every aspect of my being was attended to. I moved my tongue around her nipple and opened my mouth to take in more flesh. "Gently!" she reprimanded me. The insides of my eyelids were crimson. I came in two minutes' time. I felt a little patter on one of the far tissues. She was right to have been prepared.

Then there was the cleaning up and getting out of there. The bra felt terribly silly as I took it off, the spell gone with the flight of my sperm. She threw away the tissues, folded the towel, fluffed pillows, and in general busied herself with removing any evidence of my visit. I dressed by the couch, and then she came with me to the door and I gave her the thirty dollars. On the door there was another piece of paper, like the one above the telephones. It had only one reminder: "Don't forget keys." And there was a little wicker basket nailed to the wall and inside it was her key ring.

"These signs must be very helpful," I said.

"I'm a daydreamer," she said. Then she opened the door and I stepped into the hallway and turned to say good-bye, but she closed the door before I could get the words out. I felt hurt by this unfriendliness. But I realized she was a professional. She didn't want her neighbors peering out peepholes while she said good-bye to the many men she spanked.

Her hallway was very long and I walked past a dozen peepholes on the way to the elevator and it felt like a gauntlet of glass eyes. I held my head with confidence, the way I thought a man would, and I pretended that I had nothing to be ashamed of.

Hot for Cockroach, Cold for Lead

I went home to make myself some dinner. Henry was there, watching television and drinking wine. He was slumped on his couch; his goblet was held to his chest, his chin leaned against its rim. It was Friday night, but, uncharacteristically, he had no plans.

I was shaky after my spanking and cross-dressing, and I wondered if my transgression with Miss Hart was somehow visible on my face, if Henry would perceive a change in me.

I made a plate of spaghetti. I put it on the kitchen table to cool and I went to the bathroom.

When I came back to the kitchen there was a cockroach in the middle of my spaghetti. It was all too much. Miss Hart. My dinner contaminated.

"Oh, God! There's a cockroach on my food!" I bellowed.

"What?"

"A cockroach on top of my spaghetti."

"You forgot the first rule of survival in this apartment," said Henry without sympathy. "Never leave food out!"

"You didn't teach me that rule," I said.

"You should have learned it before coming here. Don't enlist in the military if you're not prepared to fight."

I threw the pasta away, and the cockroach, since I am unable to kill anything directly, even cockroaches, with which our apartment was infested, though none had ever been so brave as to mount my food.

After dumping the pasta, I boiled some more water and started all over. Henry from his couch told me to wash my dish, and added that I should always wash my dishes before eating. He explained to me, teaching me some survival rules after all, that our cockroaches were walking all over our plates while we slept, leaving behind an invisible trail of germs. So we were to wash our dishes before eating, as well as after. He came into the kitchen and rinsed a plate to demonstrate his special two-step method.

"First hot water to get rid of the cockroach germs," he said, "then cold to get rid of the lead from the hot. Otherwise you die. New York has lead in its hot water. *That* you might not have learned in New Jersey."

Henry looked at me intently to make sure that I understood the lesson, and then said, "Hot for cockroach, cold for lead. Hot for cockroach, cold for lead."

"I got it," I said.

"Well, don't catch on too quickly. That's the problem with staff, once they know what to do, they leave."

It was a backhanded compliment, but it made me feel good. He didn't want me to leave.

That night, I was awakened by a cockroach on my cheek. It was daring to trespass my face. It was on the cheekbone moving towards the nose. I could see it. I screamed and slapped it off.

The crisis was over, but I spasmed in my bed. The aftershock of the cockroach on my face had me thrashing my blankets and sheets around like a man attacked.

When I untangled myself, I immediately saw the cockroach on the floor. He was in a beam of silvery light coming from the air-shaft window. He was moving without worries on the path of orange carpet and then he disappeared into the bathroom. I was horrified. I wondered if, like well-trained staff, I should leave Henry and his dirty apartment. Cockroaches on my food and on my face were unbearable.

I had a glass of water and I calmed down. It occurred to me that perhaps the cockroach who had crawled into bed with me was the one whose life I had spared. It had escaped out of the garbage bag and had come looking for me, either to thank me or to seek revenge. If it was revenge, I wondered if I was being plagued in a religious-insect way for having been with Miss Hart. Then I thought of her key basket and reminder signs, and I chastised myself for not proposing this to Henry, but I would tell him in the morning. I fell asleep with the pleasant thought of how I could help him with his key problem, and that he would be appreciative.

I also felt confident that the chance of having a cockroach crawl on my face twice in one night had to be very low. My sins with Miss Hart hadn't been that grievous.

Are You Jewish?

The next morning, Henry and I both woke up around noon. On the weekends, I tended to mimic his sleeping patterns.

When we were both dressed and conscious, I asked him, "Did you hear me scream in the night?"

"No. That's why I have plugs. What happened now?"

"A cockroach crawled across my face. I think we have to do something more effective than boric acid." Henry had previously lined the kitchen sink with boric acid and sugar.

"Did it go in the mouth?"

"No."

"Well, you are going to have to be more brave if you are going to live here in the former Soviet Union. But maybe I'll set a bomb, if that will make you happy. In the meantime, we can feed them more sugar."

Henry took some sugar and boric acid and started making a ring around my bed, and as he sprinkled, he said sadly, "It's too bad this *isn't* Russia."

He was often longing for Russia because that past July he had traveled to several Eastern European countries with a wealthy lady friend, and then he had gone by himself into Russia and the Ukraine for ten days. And it had been the best part of his trip.

"In Riga," he told me as he finished pouring the white trench of poison around my bed, "you can get a hotel room for two dollars a night and a bottle of champagne for three dollars. And the men and women have the most beautiful eyes. None of the things that concern us here in America bother them because the Russians still have souls."

He took the boric acid and the sugar and went into the kitchen. I was touched by his gesture of wanting to secure my bed, and I didn't want to seem ungrateful, but I worried about stepping on the acid and getting it into my sheets. And then it would get into my eyes and mouth: I would blind and poison myself.

Henry started to shave with his electric shaver over the kitchen sink. With this cover of sound, I quickly took my shoe and brushed the acid under my bed as best I could. This relaxed me and then I went into the bathroom to shave with my razor by the edge of the tub. I used the water from the faucet to clear the blade. I wrapped a towel around my neck to protect my shirt.

While we shaved, Henry called out to me, and said, "You and I may have to move to Russia if this Clinton wins the election. He looks like W. C. Fields, but has none of Fields' integrity."

It was the middle of October and the election was just a few weeks away. I was for Clinton but hadn't said anything to Henry. Still, it pleased me immensely, despite his anti-Clinton feelings, that Henry proposed that we move together. The previous night, I was staff that he didn't want to leave, then in the morning he makes the gesture, albeit lethal, of protecting my bed and follows that up with a suggestion that we flee to Russia. I was feeling very much like a favorite son.

Then Henry continued his harangue against Clinton and said an unfortunate thing: "Clinton will destroy what's left of this country, just as Dinkins is destroying New York . . . I should have gone into New York politics years ago, but now I'm too disorganized. And I have no money for a campaign. The Jews wanted Dinkins in and now they see the mistake they've made after the way he handled Crown Heights." Then Henry stopped himself; it had finally happened, and he called out with some hesitation, "Are you Jewish?"

I stopped shaving. First Miss Hart and now Henry. Everyone was on to me. I had been living with Henry for a month and a half, listening to his occasional "*Auf Wiedersehen*'s" and "*Gute Nacht*'s," and letting him think that I was Aryan, hiding myself like Anne Frank, when I knew rationally that there was no reason to conceal my identity.

But I had wanted Henry to think I was like him—a person with aristocratic bloodlines, a gentleman, who nonetheless has no money. He had intimated a few personal details, enough for me to gather that he had come from an old Baltimore family which had lost its money, but not its position, at the end of the nineteenth century. It was probably one of the reasons Henry loved the nineteenth century and wrote about its great figures. People are always nostalgic about a time when their families had wealth.

So to me, Henry, with his regal handsome face and Maryland lineage, and despite his stained clothes and dirty apartment, was a real Mid-Atlantic gentleman, which was the American equivalent of the English gentleman—my ideal. And I, of course, wanted to be a gentleman—the Young Gentleman—but I secretly knew that I couldn't be one and Jewish at the same time. There were no such Jewish characters in any of my books, and to make things worse all my favorite authors, I always found out, were heartbreakingly anti-Semitic. I worshipped them and they wouldn't have even liked me. So their anti-Semitism and my Semitism were the major flaws in my young gentleman fantasy, but I tried not to think about these things most of the time.

And for the most part, I believed my own ruse, but deep down I knew that before anything else I was Jewish, very old-fashioned Jewish in a way: I always expected anti-Semitism from the gentile world. But I didn't disdain non-Jews for their prejudice; it was too old and inherent to eradicate. I just worried that they would see me as ugly and cheap and nervous if they knew I was Jewish, whereas otherwise they wouldn't perceive these qualities. The answer was to be with other Jews, but I was hooked on being the young gentleman.

So I was afraid that Henry wouldn't like me as much if he knew; he wouldn't think I was a fellow gentleman, and I didn't want to lose his affection, especially after he had just invited me to run away to Russia. But if he didn't like me because of my Judaism, I was prepared to not like him, though in my heart I still would.

I said bravely from the bathroom, my face half-shaved, "Yes, I am Jewish. Why do you ask?"

Henry, in the kitchen, turned off his razor, and was quick to reply, to erase the slight atmosphere of anti-Semitism, the implication of Jewish power, that his statement had created. "It's important when you are living with someone to have an idea of their religious training," he said. "I have found that I know more about the Old Testament than most Jews. My friend Howard Shapiro should study the Torah. Instead, he follows gurus. When he was younger he followed con men. There might be a connection . . . His latest guru is Jewish, but preaches Buddhism. He's given the guru thousands of dollars and the guru told him to grow a beard. He looks terrible. For a man who is supposed to be so full of peace, he looks loosed from hell."

Then Henry and I resumed our shaving (no beards for us), and he didn't say anything more about the Jews electing Dinkins. One of my secrets was out and I had survived. I already started imagining that in Henry's eyes I was a proper young Jewish gentleman, not the English kind, which appealed to me romantically, but the well-mannered, cultured, dark-haired, American-Jewish kind, who is always snubbed. It wasn't too bad a role. I had blond hair, but I imagined Henry thinking of me this way.

One of the Greatest Hoaxes of All Time

We completed our toilets and went down to our café, The Salt of the Earth, on Second Avenue and Ninety-sixth Street. Ninety-sixth was something of a dividing line, separating the end of the Upper East Side and the beginning of Spanish Harlem. Henry called it the "fever line."

And Second Avenue, like much of the Upper East Side, was bland and unfriendly, with large high-rises and numerous dry cleaners, but when I walked on it with Henry to our café, I felt like this was our Boulevard, our Montparnasse. And along with watching *Are You Being Served?* this was another routine we had fallen into—going for coffee together on Saturday mornings. On Sunday mornings Henry went to church, and the rest of the week I was at work before he even woke up.

On our way to the café that Saturday, we picked up our newspapers at the twenty-four-hour store. I paid for my *Times* and as Henry paid for his *Post*, he noticed a sticker on the counter that said it was illegal to sell cigarettes to persons under the age of eighteen. To the very overweight but sweet-faced black girl, who was wearing a smock and operating the cash register, he said, "So they can't buy cigarettes if they're under eighteen, but they can buy crack!"

The girl looked at Henry and let out a nervous giggle. She didn't know what to say. She looked at his hair, which hadn't yet received its mystery dye. It was part brown and part dark brown.

The girl continued to giggle and Henry said, "Yes," which was his way of confirming the truth of his own statement. We headed out of the store and Henry was in front of me. He had just opened the door when I heard the girl remark to the teenaged black stock boy, who was also behind the counter, "I'm getting all the characters today. He said they can't buy cigarettes, but they can buy crack."

"Oh, man," said the stock boy.

Henry paused in the door and I don't think he heard her refer to him as a character, the sudden infusion of street noises had blocked that, but he heard the rest of her remark, and said to me in his most royal accent, "Yes. The working class appreciate my understanding of things."

"I think so," I said, and then we went to The Salt of the Earth. When we first went together, Henry liked for us to sit at adjoining tables and act as if we were complete strangers. But he soon realized that this charade wouldn't work, so we were to behave as though we were friendly acquaintances. He didn't want the staff to infer anything about our relationship, even if they correctly presumed that our relationship was landlord and tenant.

He didn't say it, of course, but he was concerned that they might think he was an old homosexual keeping company with a young man. I also knew that he didn't want them to realize that we were roommates, that he needed to rent out his only bedroom. He wanted to be treated with respect by the staff. The place was run by Yugoslavian immigrants and Henry had instructed the girls behind the counter how to address him. He had told them never to say to him, "Enjoy," or "Have a nice day."

He had explained to me why he requested this. "I don't want talking. I want subservient service from a distance . . . The English used to say of the French, 'They have women serving food over there. They're unclean, you know.' I'm not so particular. I don't mind women servers, I just don't want to be told to ENJOY. I might not want to enjoy."

So that Saturday morning, with the staff fully trained as to how to deal with us, we sat down with our coffees and rolls and newspapers. Henry, when we would read our papers, would often comment on some piece of gossip, usually about the royal family, or about an article that was of a political nature. That morning he was outraged to read another pro-choice remark by candidate Clinton's wife.

"She says women own their bodies and can have abortions. There's no ownership! We're all part of an ongoing cosmic process. Yes. Any questions?" When Henry pontificated, he often acknowledged it by asking me if I had any questions.

"No questions," I said, hiding my pro-choice sentiments.

"It's quite possible that she is Clinton and Clinton is she—they're cross-dressers! She has a very strong chin and he has a woman's hips. It could be one of the greatest hoaxes of all time."

I became excited when Henry said cross-dressers. It was a modern term that I didn't think that he would have in his vocabulary. But he did read the paper every day and was familiar with crack and other modern vices, so I shouldn't have been surprised. I didn't let on that I had expert knowledge on the subject, that I had just cross-dressed the night before with Miss Hart, but I did show some awareness. I said, to be playful, "It might be a fair representation of the country if they're elected. I've read that there are a lot of cross-dressers."

"And now they're about to seize control. Cross-dressing is all right for Shakespeare. Most women can't act, except for Garbo, Dietrich, Mary Pickford, Joan Fontaine . . . Well, there are quite a few. But it was bound to happen that cross-dressers would take over. They have been silent too long. But these Clintons are too depressing to think about. We have to try not to think."

We finished our coffees in silence and then left the café. We were walking back to our apartment when I saw a very large man coming out of our building with a bicycle, which he then mounted and rode off. He had a great beard and a stout torso, the kind where chest and belly are all one. I had seen this man a few times before, wheeling his bicycle into his third-floor apartment, which was the one directly below ours. These sightings usually occurred in the morning as I left for work. He was always sweating profusely—it looked like steam was emanating from his enormous body—and once or twice he had glanced at me shyly. I was curious about him and I said to Henry as the man disappeared up the street, "Do you know who that is?"

"Of course, that's Gershon Gruen."

"He's the one who carries heavy things for you?"

"Yes, he's also my mechanic."

"Your mechanic?"

"He repairs all my automobiles free of charge. He's very devoted to me."

"I often see him with his bicycle."

"Yes. He's cycling away his sex drive. He used to bring prostitutes from Eighty-sixth Street into his apartment and they would steal from him. Not to mention the germ factor. But he couldn't stop doing it. I told him he had to develop other interests. I recommended reading the dictionary and bicycle riding. I told him that chastity is easy with the right frame of mind and physical exercise."

"He could also wear a chastity belt," I said, hoping to amuse Henry.

"Yes, chastity belts are good," said Henry. "I'd wear one myself, but I'm always losing my keys, and if Clinton is elected I might have to procreate for patriotic reasons. It's the only thing left that I can do for my country. So I can't be locked up in a chastity belt."

We entered our building and climbed the stairs. At the third-floor landing, we stopped to catch our breath and I said, "That's Gershon's apartment, isn't it?"

"Yes. That's where he used to bring them. I think my advice worked, but he's not talking to me anymore."

"Why isn't he talking to you?"

"He stops calling when he suspects that I only use him as a mechanic and don't want his friendship. But I do want his friendship—one based on auto repair. Then of course there's Otto Bellman. He's turned Gershon against me."

"Bellman who used to be in my room?"

"Yes. All his actions are based on revenge for my throwing him out. I was a father figure to him. He stole my play, he's seducing Virginia—her parents will be very upset with me—and he's robbed me of my mechanic. Well, as the cow said to the bull, if it's not one thing it's an udder."

We climbed the remaining flight of stairs and I was thinking about this Bellman, my predecessor. Could he really be as nefarious as Henry depicted? And even though Henry didn't like Bellman, I felt jealous thinking about him.

At the door to our apartment, Henry couldn't find his keys. So I opened the door for us and as we walked in I remembered Miss Hart's key basket and reminder signs. I said, "Henry, we should put up signs to remind you about your keys. And maybe a little basket where the keys could go."

"What?" he asked indignantly. He was immediately infuriated.

I was taken aback, but said, "Signs to remind you about the keys. And a basket so the keys wouldn't get lost."

"Only a deranged person hangs up signs. And a basket is ugly and would only get lost with the keys in it. That's a ridiculous suggestion."

Henry went off to the bathroom insulted and annoyed, and I was left standing in the kitchen feeling embarrassed. I wanted to recant authorship of the idea, but I couldn't tell Henry its true source. He would kick me out, just as he had Otto Bellman, if he knew I was inclined to visit people like Miss Hart. And I had thought she was almost normal, considering everything. But Henry, without meeting her, had a better understanding of her mental state: they were of the same generation and he knew what it meant when a person had to hang up reminder signs.

CHAPTER IV

We All Wanted to Be That Femme Fatale

When I returned to work after the weekend, I started looking at the *New York Press* again. I read a brief article about a club that catered to transvestites, transsexuals, and cross-dressers. Suddenly transvestism was cropping up everywhere for me. It was that phenomenon where you don't hear about something for a while, or you've never heard of it—a word, the name of a writer, an unusual disease—but then all at once you're confronted with it repeatedly.

The club was called Sally's and it was on West Forty-third Street. I thought that I should go visit this Sally's. I was curious about life and sex, I told myself, and I was living in New York, so why not take advantage of the city's odd possibilities?

After work, I headed home to rest and change before going to Forty-third Street. I wanted to put on something a little more casual than my blazer and tie. I thought I'd wear a turtleneck and a sport coat. I'd still be a young gentleman, but more relaxed.

I arrived at the apartment around six-thirty and there was a note on the door from Henry in his cursive scrawl warning me to not come in if it was before six o'clock, and then in large printed letters: a roach bomb has been set. He hadn't conferred with me about this and I was a little put off that he would bomb the place without telling me. I hadn't taken him seriously when he had mentioned a bomb a few days before. I would have preferred traps; they were a much less poisonous alternative.

I took the note off the door and since it was after the deadline, I entered the apartment. Henry was in the kitchen, right in front of me, and he was bending over, revealing a large split seam. He was plugging in an old rusty fan. The place reeked of poison.

The fan began to blow, and Henry stood up and said to me, "I've opened all the windows. I've done my best. I've probably killed off the weak ones and have created a superior cockroach."

"Where are my bananas?" I asked.

"I put them in the filing cabinet so that the radiation wouldn't seep in. I also turned these cups upside down so that the radiation wouldn't get in them." The cups were on top of the refrigerator, and Henry began turning them right side up and was looking at them carefully and said, "Now there's probably roach excrement on the rims. Well, you have to choose how you go. We never have a secure moment. What a life. It's worse in Yugoslavia, though, we must remember that."

I opened the top drawer of my file cabinet and retrieved my bananas from the underwear file. I was grateful that Krafft-Ebing was buried in the drawer that I used for T-shirts. I put the bananas back on the kitchen table where I always kept them.

I decided to take a shower to freshen up for Sally's and then get out of the apartment right away without lying down—I couldn't stand the smell of the roach bomb. I said to Henry, "The odor in here is terrible."

"Don't be so sensitive," he said. "Everything comes to you through the nose. You lead the life of a dog."

I absorbed his insult. He was annoyed that I wasn't more grateful that he had done something about our cockroaches. And also he had noticed on a few occasions what a keen sense of smell I had—I would always remark when the person across the hall was smoking and I had once or twice complained about cooking odors that would come to me through my air-shaft window.

Still, my good sense of smell didn't warrant comparison to a dog. But I didn't say anything. I was going to Sally's and the secrecy of it made me feel guilty, and undermined by this shame, I didn't have the confidence to defend myself.

I showered and Henry, to be defiant of the bomb's fumes, put on a record and danced. When I came out, dressed and ready to go, he was sitting on his throne-chair, with the window open, grading papers for his class. He was wearing a pair of plastic women's bifocals, which he had bought for twenty-five cents at a garage sale in New Jersey, and since he was in the privacy of our home, Henry didn't care about the feminine shape—the pointed corners—of his reading glasses.

I brushed my teeth in the kitchen sink, and I realized that my heading out was creating a role reversal for Henry and myself. Normally, I was the one sitting at home, while Henry had evening plans or classes to teach.

I had been hoping that he would ask me one night to go to the opera again, or to help with escorting Vivian Cudlip and her granddaughter, but Henry hadn't extended any invitations and I didn't want to annoy him with requests and seem like a hanger-on.

So I felt a little glad that for once I was the one going out on the town and leaving him behind. And as I unlocked the door, Henry asked, "Where are you going?" He sensed from my appearance—well-combed hair, sport coat and turtleneck good for the October coolness—that I had something special to do. Usually, if I went out it was only to go to the Chinese restaurant on Second Avenue. I hadn't expected him, though, to ask me where I was going, to show that much interest in me, so I was caught off guard, but I lied instinctively. "I'm going to visit friends in the Village," I said.

"I don't believe you. 'Friends in the village' sounds like a Bunbury. That's good. Don't tell me the truth . . . Where is Bunbury from?" he suddenly inquired, quizzing me like a professor. Grading papers had inspired him.

"Wilde. *The Importance of Being Earnest.*"

"You know your Wilde. Maybe you did go to college. From now on when we go out let's tell each other that we're visiting Bunbury. The less we reveal of ourselves, the better we'll get along."

"I know, you told me."

"Well, that's the key to education. Repetition."

"All right . . . I'm going to see Bunbury," I said, and I left the apartment. The Bunbury quiz had me feeling both good and bad. On one hand, Henry felt that I was well read and I was happy about this; I wanted his approval. But on the other hand, he was stressing again that we shouldn't really know each other and this saddened me. I didn't want him to know my secrets, and he had immediately sensed that I was hiding something, but at the same time I wanted us to be close, which usually meant revealing one's self.

I went to the Chinese restaurant before going to Sally's and I ate a lonely meal. I was a little somber when I got in my car, but as I drove the Parisienne downtown, its living-room interior and powerful engine boosted my morale. It was emboldening to fly along Park Avenue at night and feel invincible. My expansive blue hood in front of me was like those cow-scoopers at the fronts of locomotives. I was bigger than all the other cars, and I was the equal of the taxis.

Of course the size of my Parisienne did have its drawbacks. It was a hindrance for parking, and each night as I moved the car and searched for and prayed to find a parking spot, I had to make sure that I worded my prayer carefully so as to find an especially large parking spot.

So I raced downtown to Forty-third Street, but I couldn't spot Sally's from my car. I parked the Parisienne on Ninth Avenue (there was plenty of room), and I walked east. I checked the building numbers on Forty-third all the way up to Eighth Avenue, which was lit up and Tokyo-bright with the neon of many peep shows.

I crossed the avenue and as I walked farther east on Forty-third, there were two little peep shows and then there were two inconspicuous glass doors. I looked through the glass and there was an old cardboard sign on a wall and written in a faded pink with glued-on glitter was the name I was looking for—Sally's. I had found it. To the left of the sign there was a dimly lit red-carpeted staircase. My legs felt weak and my stomach was nervous. I wanted to go in and I didn't want to go in. I was scared.

I kept walking east, to build up my courage, and I saw across the street, on the north side, that there were half-a-dozen *New York Times* delivery trucks. I wondered what were they doing there. Then I saw that on the imposing building across from me that there was a small, white neon sign with a digital clock. The sign was in that unmistakable font: 𝕿𝖍𝖊 𝕿𝖎𝖒𝖊𝖘. Sally's was across the street from the most famous newspaper in the world. I had been a reader of its sports pages for most of my life.

THE EXTRA MAN

I was excited, like a tourist, to discover it, but I felt caught. How could I go into my just-found transvestite-transsexual club with the *New York Times* looking at me? I resented its presence. It was getting in the way of my adventure. And what was the *Times* doing in this peep-show neighborhood anyways? Forty-third Street was more fitting for the *Post* or the *News*. I wouldn't have been embarrassed in front of those papers. And then I realized where Times Square got its name.

I had never thought about it before, and I was very pleased with myself for having figured this out. And this little achievement gave me the impetus to go in Sally's. I bravely piloted myself through those double glass doors and up the stairs to the first landing where an orange-haired, light-skinned black woman sat behind a card table. She looked like a worn-out prostitute. She had beautiful cheekbones, but the cheeks below were hollow.

"Ten-dollar cover," she said. I realized somehow, through no real hint, that she once was a man. Her maleness was like something drawn in pencil that had been erased, but you could still see it, the outline of it.

I gave her ten dollars and she gave me a ticket, which I looked at.

"It's for a free drink," she said.

There were three more stairs to climb and at the top stood a large black man in a windbreaker. I went to walk past him and he stepped in front of me.

"Lift your arms," he said.

I did and he frisked me for weapons. Even though I wasn't carrying anything, I thought he might find something. It was not unusual for me to feel guilty without reason. But he didn't discover any weapons and he let me pass. There was a large circular bar right in front of me, and I took the first open stool, which was like a big high chair. Sally's was darkly lit and around the bar in the shadows there were many sexy women and grave-faced men, and the air was smoky, and dance music played.

The bartender approached me. She was a young dyed blonde. Her skin was flawless and olive-colored. She was wearing a tight, buttoned, yellow halter top. A few buttons were undone, revealing small, firm round breasts. She was in jeans and her hips were narrow. She had the figure of a teenager. And it was only her rounded shoulders, just a little too big, that told me what she once was.

I gave her my drink ticket and ordered a beer. She reached above her where the glasses hung, and the lifting of her arms highlighted the shape of her round breasts. And her armpits were bare, smooth, alarmingly sexy. Seeing them felt like something intimate; I thought of her shaving them, how she would feel like a girl doing that, and I fell in love immediately.

She poured my beer for me, then walked away to attend to someone else. And while I watched her swing her narrow hips, a very large black woman in a low-cut, black cocktail dress sat next to me. I gave her a sideways glance and she smiled at me. She had perfect red lips and her teeth flashed white. Her skin was rich looking and shiny, like fine chocolate. Her hair was black and sleek and went to her shoulders. Her eyebrows were thin and curved. She looked at me with bedroom eyes.

"How are you tonight?" she asked.

"Fine," I said.

"I like your blond hair," she said, and she closed her eyes slowly and then opened them slowly.

"Thank you," I said, and I was surprised and pleased by her compliment.

"Is that your natural color, child?" she asked.

"It's natural," I said, and then added, "but I am losing it a little."

I had this bad habit of admitting to everybody that I was balding. In part I was looking for them to deny it and reassure me, and also I confessed it because I thought that they couldn't secretly mock me for losing my hair if I so openly acknowledged it.

"You better not go bald, child. White men look terrible bald. You better get a wig."

I hated it when people recommended wigs to me. When I had confessed to Henry that my hair was thinning, he suggested a hairpiece. When I said to him, "I will never wear a hairpiece," he became annoyed with me and said, "You should worry about building your character, not your hair."

"I hope I won't need a wig," I said to the black woman.

"You look good to me," she said sincerely, and she put her hand on my thigh. "Do you want to buy me a drink?"

"All right," I said. The beautiful bartender came back, and my new friend ordered a rum and coke. I paid for it and I didn't mind. I liked this big black woman, liked the way she complimented me.

"Thank you, child," she said, after taking a sip from her drink. "What's your name?"

I thought of using David, but it had somewhat backfired with Miss Hart. "Louis," I said.

"I'm Pepper," she said and offered me her hand demurely. Her nails were painted red and I put my hand in hers and I felt like a small boy. Pepper was probably six foot two without heels and she had hands to match.

She moved one of those big hands from my thigh to my penis. She found it expertly, immediately, circled it, and caressed it. I was frightened and shocked, but I responded to her touch. Pepper widened her bedroom eyes. "This feels like a nice dick, child," she said. Her frank language embarrassed me, but I was happy. I had been in Sally's only a few minutes and I was already having an escapade.

She stroked me and then she said, "Do you want to go on a date, child?" I was flattered, though I was savvy enough to realize that the word date might mean something different in Sally's.

"What kind of date?" I asked.

"Have you ever been here?"

"No, this is my first time."

"Do you know what kind of bar you are in? What kind of woman I am?"

"Yes, I think so," I said.

"Men come here for dates, child. We're all working girls. You and I go on a date, and you give me a tip, a donation. That's the deal because it costs a lot of money to be a Queen."

"How much of a donation?"

"One twenty-five, but because it's your first time, and you're blond, I'd do it for one hundred."

That was a lot of money, much more than the Recession Spankologist. "I don't think I can afford such a date, but thank you," I said, but she didn't stop massaging my penis, hoping to sway me.

"Have you ever been with a Queen?"

"No, I haven't," I said.

"It's the best of both worlds, child. You don't know what you are missing."

"I don't mean to be rude," I said. "But have most of you had the surgery?"

"A man-made pussy? Child, men don't come in here looking for pussy. They come here for dick," she said, and she gave my penis a little extra squeeze. "All the Queens are still functional. That's where the money is."

"You're not transsexuals?" I asked.

"You're a transsexual if you take hormones or have implants, child. It has nothing to do with pussy . . . I don't have implants, but I take hormones. That's why I have these titties."

Pepper certainly had breasts, but they weren't firm and round like the bartender's; they were a little saggy and flat, like an older woman's, but her nipples poked through the material of her cocktail dress in an attractive way. She appeared to be in her late thirties, but I wasn't going to ask her age; Henry had taught me that lesson.

"Don't any of you get the surgery?" I asked, thinking that surgery was the goal. I was taking a risk being so bold, but she didn't seem to mind my questions and she was touching me intimately.

"We all wanted to be that femme fatale at first, have that pussy, that surgery, but that's a dream, child. You have to do stunts to survive, that's where the money is. And for stunts you need a cock . . . I'll go for eighty," said Pepper suddenly, and then she went from stroking my penis nicely to giving it a threatening squeeze.

I liked Pepper very much. She had a beautiful smile, she was gregarious and talkative, and she kept lowering her prices for me, but I didn't want to have sex with her. And she was hurting my penis right there in the bar. What if I was alone with her? I could really be injured.

"I'm sorry," I said. "I think I just want to sit here and look." I was afraid she could truly damage me if she squeezed any harder. But I didn't want to try to remove her hand and create a scene. It was an unusual dilemma of manners: how to ask someone not to hurt your penis.

"Have you ever had sex with a man?" she asked, and, thankfully, she loosened her grip.

"No," I said, and she again tightened her squeeze. Her grip was like a lie detector.

"See, child, when you're with a Queen, you get the best of both worlds. If you want to try it, I'll be around." Pepper let go of me and got up from her chair regally, and just then three new Queens came in. They all kissed Pepper on the cheek, and one of them called her Miss Pepper. From the way they acted, I could tell that Pepper commanded a lot of respect in Sally's.

I sat there sipping my beer and looked around me. The bar was a big circle with the blonde serving drinks in the middle. Beyond the bar was a dance floor with tables to the left and right, but no one was dancing. The Queens were talking with each other or approaching the men, who all appeared to be solitary. No man had come with a friend.

The Queens were in skimpy dresses or just bikini tops and skirts. A few were in gowns, and some were in jeans and tight T-shirts. They were black or Hispanic or Asian. I didn't see any white girls. And there were lots of mirrors on the walls and the Queens kept checking out their hair, their makeup. They liked to look at themselves. And many of them did have the most beautiful faces. Faces I had never seen anywhere else in the world. Some kind of crazy mixing of man and woman: the arrangement of cheekbones and eyes and lips was all different and yet beautiful.

I loved being there, and I didn't really know why, but something Henry had said seemed to explain it. One night he called out to me from his bed and instead of making his usual final remark, "So there we are. Where are we?" he had said unexpectedly, "There seems to be a curious maladjustment of things." I asked what he meant by this, but he had put in his earplugs and didn't answer me. But that's what I liked about being in Sally's: it was the most curiously maladjusted place I had ever been. Some of the most beautiful women I was ever seeing were really men.

Many of them approached me as Miss Pepper had, but I politely declined all their offers, though I did like the way they touched me and caressed me. And they wore lots of perfume, which I liked. Then around ten o'clock, an alarm went off inside me and I decided that I should go home. A lifetime of being a student and then a teacher made it difficult to stay out too late on a school night.

I Met Someone Jewish

I drove back uptown and I thought of the lie I had told Miss Pepper about not having sex with a man. I had been afraid she would judge me, and even though she told me she had a penis, on some level I didn't really believe her and so I thought of her as a woman, and I didn't want a woman to think I was homosexual. But one time I did have sex with a man.

It happened when I was living in Princeton and I was in my second year of teaching at Pretty Brook. I was coming back from a field trip to Rutgers with my students and I was looking out the school bus window and I spotted an adult bookstore on Route 1, near New Brunswick. I wondered if any of the children saw the place. I pretended that I hadn't, but I made a mental note of it.

So late one night, I went back there. I bought several magazines, all of them dealing with transvestism, and a little paperback book called *Forced to Be a Girl*. The title had attracted me.

I made my purchases, feeling ashamed of my choices, wishing that I had bought something a little more macho, and I fled there quickly. It was a Friday night, no school the next day, and it was around midnight. I had purposely gone very late, hoping to avoid running into any of my students' fathers or a colleague.

As I was heading south on Route 1, I was so anxious to read my magazines that I couldn't wait till I got home. I put on the Parisienne's interior light and tried to read a little while I drove.

I was in the right-hand lane, probably going around fifty miles an hour, and a car pulled alongside me in the left-hand lane. I instinctively looked over with a shudder thinking it might be a policeman who would pull me over and see that I was reading *The Transvestian*, a cross-dressing newsletter.

But it wasn't the police, it was a civilian, a man, and he gave me a come-hither smile. Then he accelerated past me, signaled, and switched into the right-hand lane in front of me. Then he went back into the left-hand lane. I knew instinctively that he was trying to communicate with me. With my heart pounding, I pulled the Parisienne into the left-hand lane behind the man's car. To see if I was actually conversing with him he then pulled back into the right-hand lane to test me. I followed him. His car seemed to increase its speed happily. About a mile down the road he exited. I was in hot, insane pursuit.

I followed this highway-seducer through a few rights and lefts until we were in a condominium development of attached gray, wood-shingled houses aspiring for a Nantucket look. He parked and I parked a few cars away.

"I am going to be killed," I thought, but I didn't drive off. He got out of his car and I got out of the Parisienne. I took a few steps away from my car so that he wouldn't peer in and see my transvestite literature. I was even embarrassed about my perversion with a potential serial killer. He was a big lumbering fellow, about six foot three, with curly brown hair and a drunken smile. His face seemed harmless but also lustful.

"Hi," he said.

"Hello," I said stiffly.

"This is strange, isn't it?" he asked. We were standing about ten feet from each other like cowboys.

"Yes," I said.

"What's your name?" he asked.

"David," I said, lying naturally.

"You want to come in, Dave?" he asked, trying to act calm and intimate, shortening my phony name, and then he said, "I'm Richie."

I didn't say "Yes, I'll come in." I didn't want to take responsibility for my actions. I felt robotic. He walked to his front door and I followed him. We had met on a highway and I was going into his Nantucket condominium. As we passed through the door I saw a mezuzah! He was Jewish! A Jewish murderer? A Jewish homosexual? I felt a little closer to Richie.

We had a drink in the living room. I had thought he followed me from the porno shop, but it turned out he was returning from a gay bar. He was rather drunk and nervous, and he told me his story. He was divorced from his wife for a year, this had been their home, and it was just in the last few months, at the age of thirty-eight, that he was coming out of the closet. I nodded my head sympathetically. I was very formal, barely spoke, and was appalled by the situation. We went up to his bedroom and undressed.

When we were both in our underwear I said, "You're Jewish, aren't you?"

"How'd you know?" he asked, and a look of Jewish insecurity and defensiveness crossed his face. I knew it well.

"I saw the mezuzah," I said, and then to reassure him, "I'm Jewish too."

We lay on his large bed totally nude. I felt shy about my body and I was nervous and my penis was flaccid almost to the point of recession. I wasn't making a very good showing, and he was nervous too, but his penis was enormous. Even if I had been erect I didn't compare to him. I regretted the whole mad thing. I never liked locker-room comparisons.

But Richie was kind, he didn't seem to care that I was tiny. He was breathing heavily and he delighted in gently touching my stomach and chest while I lay very still.

"I'm sorry I'm so small," I said. "I'm nervous."

"You're fine," he said. "Touch *me*."

I put my hand on his penis. It was like a large, older cousin to my own. I was impressed by its width. I didn't mind holding it, and he was encouraged by my touching him and he went to kiss me, but I couldn't do that. I said, "Please don't."

He was a little rejected, but took another course of action. "Do you want a massage?" he asked.

"All right," I said.

I didn't lie on my belly but turned on my side and he began to knead my shoulders. He wasn't a terrible masseur, but he also wasn't very good at it—his hands weren't really sensitive—and I wondered if his wife had seen this as one of his deficiencies.

He quickly tired of the massage and he scooted close to me and he put his arms around me and held me in a spoon position. We stayed like this for a few minutes and then his penis slipped between my thighs and lay between my legs and he just let it rest there. And I felt like I did when I was a little boy and I would cuddle with my father. I think it was inadvertent, but I remember feeling my father's penis against my rear or against the back of my legs when we would lie in his bed and he would sleep.

And I did a lot of lying down with my father because my mother went back to work when I was in the first grade. She had to leave early in the morning and so she put me in bed with my father because he was often depressed and didn't want to be alone. So my mother used me as her substitute, and this helped her feel all right about leaving because my father and I were both taken care of. And about an hour after she left, he would wake up and help me get ready for school.

And it was odd, but as Richie held me I felt exactly the same way as I did with my father so many years before. I felt small and sick and excited. Richie began to rub his penis between my legs, and with my back to him I masturbated and I ejaculated on to his sheets. A moment later I practically leaped out of the bed, wiped myself with a tissue, got dressed, and fled.

At first he looked as if he was going to be enraged as I put my clothes on and I was afraid that I would be hurt after all by this stranger. But then he almost started crying, urged me not to leave, quickly wrote down his number, proposed that we have dinner sometime, and again begged me to stay. But I was too ashamed, too bewildered. I said, "I'm sorry. I'm very confused about sex. You're very nice, but I have to leave."

I ran out of there and drove off quickly. I felt better the farther I got away, and then I thought to myself, "At least I met someone Jewish."

Americans Are Too Concerned with Athletics

I wanted to return to Sally's the next night, but I saw that there were many dangers. What if someone from work saw me go in there? Or what if I weakened out of curiosity and went off with one of the Queens? It was very expensive and I could get a disease. So the following night I stayed home and I was alone in the apartment; Henry was out teaching.

I watched a Toronto Blue Jay–Oakland A's playoff game and the wholesomeness of it made me feel better about myself. All day I had wanted to return to Sally's, but I had also been tormented by thoughts that I was a pervert for having ventured over there in the first place. And even though I hadn't really done anything wrong, I had sat in my cubicle at work with this feeling that I was about to get in trouble.

So I was very happy to observe my enjoyment of baseball. I felt less corrupted if I could derive pleasure from a ball game.

In the eighth inning Henry came home and he asked, as always, "Any messages?"

"No."

"It's the end of an era!"

I assumed that because Henry was in the theater that he liked to repeat good lines. And I didn't mind at all; I appreciated his consistency.

He took off his raincoat and he saw that I was watching baseball and he said, "Americans are too concerned with athletics. Tennis is all right. But even that has become depraved. I won't watch it unless the men wear long pants and the women wear dresses like Helen Wills-Moody."

The Blue Jays were far ahead and I switched the channel and we watched *Are You Being Served?* The episode centered around an Oxford professor who takes a liking to Mrs. Slocombe.

Henry remarked, "I'm going to write a television series about Oxford in the Middle Ages. It was like the Bronx. They carried weapons and stabbed each other in the chest."

"Sounds like a good idea," I said. "People like shows with period costumes. I think it could be successful."

"It will be educational, which is dangerous, but the violence will make it popular. There won't be any sex, of course, but we can show the tops of breasts. The women wore loose garments because they were always nursing each other's children."

"That's kind of sexy."

"Don't be disgusting."

Mrs. Slocombe, as always, didn't get her man, and *Are You Being Served?* came to an end. Henry started flipping through the channels, and we chanced upon the last few minutes of the New Jersey public television station's royal family documentary.

"Oh, God, we missed it!" said Henry.

The ending concerned itself with the family's lack of privacy and the relentless media hounding, and there was a blurry photo of the Duke of Edinburgh, the Queen's husband, in a small black bathing suit on the beach of some tropical island.

"Look at him," said Henry. "He's nothing but a consort! That bikini is vulgar. He probably has syphilis." Then there was another photo of the duke in black tie. He was bald, but he looked elegant, which I found encouraging.

"He looks very presentable there," I said.

"He's nothing but a consort!" Henry repeated.

The documentary came to an end and Henry and I prepared for bed. When I was brushing my teeth, Henry was already tucked in. Previously his head had always been positioned next to the door to the kitchen, but this night his feet were dangling in the opening.

"I notice you've switched positions," I said.

"I'm trying something new. My head may have been in the wrong direction for years, could be the cause of all my problems."

"Why?"

"We're all untethered, flying around because of the constant spinning. We're never really still or resting, it's all an illusion. But

I heard that during sleep you can at least place the head so that you're not going against the wind."

"You heard this today?"

"No, years ago. But I've been too lazy to do anything about it, and now I've forgotten which way they said we should spin. There are always problems. My head has been in the west for years and nothing has been accomplished. Your head is in the west, but you seem to be able to get up for work . . . If you could have made the world, would you have made it like this? Going round and round?"

"I would have had it going up and down like a pogo stick," I said, trying to crack a joke.

"This is very interesting really. It's the root of all philosophy, this going round and round. It's what fatigues us, always being sucked down in the middle. I'm going to sleep with my head in the east and the feet setting in the west, see if there's any improvement. If it works, I'll let you know."

"Thank you," I said.

"Keep the change," he said.

Deep in Queens

I went to work the next day and as I came in to the office, Mary, the beautiful blonde, said, "Hi."

"Hi," I said, and I thought to myself, "Why are you doing this to me?" She was wearing a short-sleeved white blouse that was of light material and so I could see her white bra, which was really too much. I loved her and I hated her. Her hair was in a loose bun, which looked like it could fall apart and spill beautifully. She was in gray slacks, perfectly pressed, and there was only a slight hint of rear, a little sucking in of the pants right where the two halves of the buttocks must have parted. She had me by the throat.

"How are you today?" she asked. She was simply engaging me in early-morning office pleasantries, but then she lifted her right arm above her head and she adjusted one of the barrettes in her blonde bun. I saw the alabaster underside of her perfect arm: the beautiful part of the limb that led to the hidden armpit.

"I'm fine, thank you," I said, and my manner was so cordial and tense that I literally felt as if my head was going to spin off my neck. Some kind of involuntary head loll was starting and out of the near corner of my eye I could see that my nose was moving from the lolling, the trembling. The tension was too much for me. I was so stiff that I was snapping. The lifting of her arm had been too stupendous—I could see the movement of her bra and breast—and I wanted to lick the underside of her arm and then jump off the top of a building.

She smiled at me and said cheerily, "Off to my desk," and then she marched to her labors. I retreated to my cubicle and I let my head finish its loll, and out of her presence some of my strength was restored and I could keep the head attached to the neck. My chin simply fell to my collarbone and then I lifted up my chin and I looked at myself in the gray screen of my computer. I had the sad eyes of a dog.

I actually thought of going into the bathroom and masturbating with the image of her underarm in my mind, but I wasn't that depraved. So I consoled myself with this thought: "I can just go to Sally's tonight." Somehow it lessened the burden of my attraction to Mary.

That night I drove to Forty-third Street. Miss Pepper was at the bar. I said hello to her. She told me to buy her a drink and I did. Then she said, "You know, child, you'd make a good Queen. I'd contour your nose. Get you a blond wig to go with those blond eyelashes. You could make us some good money."

"Don't you think my nose is masculine?" I said.

"That's why I'd contour it."

I was flattered that Miss Pepper would take such an interest in me and think of doing something with me, even if it was to act as my pimp; I liked the attention.

Then she saw a man whom she thought she had a chance to date and she left me and took the drink I had paid for, which she had barely sipped from. I did sort of expect her company for the price of a drink, but I also understood her need to do business.

Left alone, I watched the dyed-blonde bartender reach for glasses above her head and I indulged in secret glances at her armpits. I thought of the underside of Mary's arm. It had driven me to Sally's.

The armpit of a woman is a place of wonder for me. I like the sculpture of it, the hollowness. Also it's very near the bosom. And in spring and summer you can often look right up a woman's sleeve and see the armpit, the beginning of the swelling of the breast, and sometimes a bra strap—you get three of the best things in the world in one momentary glance.

My fascination with armpits has its roots in an experience in the sixth grade. It was late spring and I was sitting crushed against the window on the school bus. A blond-haired girl, Tina Kirchenheimer, stood up near the front of the bus in anticipation of her stop. She was very pretty and she was wearing a yellow cotton dress with shoulder straps and no sleeves. She took hold of the padded green pole next to the driver. Bright late afternoon sunlight, so beautiful because it meant freedom after the oppression of school, came in through the windshield, and the bus swayed as it pulled to the side of the road. Tina's arm extended straight out as she balanced herself, and the sunlight coming through the windshield illuminated in the pit of her arm, for just a few seconds, wisps of yellow hair like tangled gold thread.

I had only seen grown men with armpit hair. I was stunned and I got a boner, as they were called back then. I hadn't started puberty—that wouldn't happen until I was almost a sophomore in high school—but those yellow hairs suffused with sunlight were incredibly beautiful to me, and shocking. She was changing, becoming a woman, and I was in awe, and my tiny penis turned to stone.

The bus came to a stop, her arm went down, and she left the bus. I stared out the window at her—she was beautiful in her yellow dress—and I hoped that she would wave at her girlfriends so that I could see her armpit again. I also had the insane hope that she would wave at me, though I had never really spoken to her. But she turned her back to the bus and started walking home. We pulled away.

I sat at the bar and sipped my drink and Queens approached me and made their offers, but I kept saying no, and it was more out of cheapness than fear of disease.

As with my first visit, I was quite happy sitting at Sally's bar. It was all curiously maladjusted; it was a spectacle in the best sense of the word. The Queens looked alive and the men looked sad, and they all moved around a lot. It was like an adult game of musical chairs. Everyone was looking for a lucky spot. It was frenetic and if you remained still, as I did, it was interesting to watch. But after a while I too decided to move and I went and sat at one of the tables by the large dance floor.

Mirrored columns ran from the dance floor to the ceiling and there were mirrors on the walls, and a few of the girls danced alone and looked at their reflections. They were staring at themselves, just like I would have, just like I had wanted to when I had dressed in my mother's clothes. One girl spontaneously lifted up her shirt and showed her breasts while she danced. They were nice breasts, unusually round, but healthy looking, and then another dancing girl flashed her breasts in response. The girls were smiling and laughing. They were happy to have breasts. I could understand that.

I sat by the dance floor for an hour, and then went back to the bar. I had several beers. I was ignoring the fact that it was a school night. I was rebellious. And the later it got, the more Queens and men arrived. Sally's was quite full. I looked around for Miss Pepper, but she was gone. She had landed a date.

Then a girl approached me and I thought that she was the most beautiful girl in the bar, even more beautiful than the bartender.

Her name was Wendy and she spoke with a Spanish accent. She didn't look like a Wendy, but she must have wanted to feel like an American girl when she renamed herself.

She had dark curly hair to her shoulders, large brown eyes, clear olive skin, and a sexy, slightly hooked nose. Her lips were full and the color of beets. Her cheekbones were very high, which made her look like a young Sophia Loren. She was wearing a tight, black halter top. She had beautifully shaped breasts. I wanted very much to touch her breasts.

She asked me to buy her a drink to test my servility; I ordered one without question.

Her screwdriver came and she asked, "You want to go out, baby? You like me?"

"You're very beautiful."

"We can go to the Carter," she said, "it's only forty-nine dollars," and she pointed to the two glass doors to the left of the bar. I had seen quite a few Queens walk proudly with men on their arms through those doors, and earlier I had asked a Queen where everyone was going and she had told me that Sally's was connected to a hotel, the Carter.

"I don't think I can afford going to a hotel," I said. I didn't want to say, "I can't afford you"; I didn't want to insult her, to make it more obvious that she was a prostitute. But I also wanted to somehow keep the door open for negotiations, to keep her talking to me. When I had told the other Queens that I was there only to look they would more or less give up on me after a few minutes, but I didn't want Wendy to leave me. She put her arm around my shoulders; I could smell her exciting, cheap perfume.

"We can go to my place in Queens," she said. "One hundred dollars. You won't be disappointed."

"I can't drive to Queens," I said. Queens frightened me. It seemed too far away, too complicated.

"My sister has a place on the Lower East Side. A room. We can go there."

I wanted to be with her, and I was drunk, and I looked at her breasts and I said to her, "All right." And I immediately felt this incredible spike of adrenaline. She took a large swig from her drink, and she said, "Let's go."

I was in a sex-trance and I slid off my stool. All caution was trampled. I could hear a little voice saying "Don't go," but it was too late.

When we got outside Wendy proudly put her arm through mine and showcased me as we walked past some Queens who were just arriving. She didn't look at them and they didn't look at her, but they all saw one another.

"Don't you have a coat?" I asked. "It's a little chilly."

"Baby, I'm not cold."

I walked us quickly down to Eighth Avenue, past the two peep shows, and past the crowd of young black men hanging out on the corner. Wendy, who was only an inch or two shorter than me in her stacked platform shoes, walked with grace and confidence, squeezing my arm, playing my girlfriend. I felt myself sobering up with nervousness.

As I started the Parisienne, Wendy stroked my hair and my cheek and she said, "You're nice looking." That sounded sweet in her accent and I smiled. Then she said, "I like your car." This compliment also made me feel good; I was proud of my Parisienne.

We drove to a cash machine; she of course knew where the closest one was, on the corner of Ninth Avenue and Forty-second, and then we drove to the Lower East Side.

When we got there she had me go past her sister's building because her brother was sitting on the stoop with his friends. We went down the block a little, then she got out of the car and told me to wait. She wanted to make sure that the room was available.

I watched her in the rearview mirror and saw that her brother wouldn't let her in the front door. They seemed to be exchanging words. He raised his hand to feign a slap.

She came running back to my car tilting awkwardly in her heels and her brother was following her, walking quickly. I wondered if I was being set up for a mugging. Should I leave? That would be the smart thing to do. I stayed. She burst into the car and said pleadingly, "My brother doesn't like my titties hanging out. We have to go! Go!"

I looked in my rearview mirror. He was practically at my car, looking brotherly and mean, and I pulled away, and Wendy turned around, peered out the back window, and gave her brother the finger. She was beautiful. I had saved her.

"We have to go to Queens where I live," she said. I was afraid to drive to Queens; all the boroughs of New York beyond Manhattan seemed like impossible places to drive to. My father had always carried on about driving to Queens to visit my great-aunt Sadye (my mother's aunt), like it was an overwhelming and complex voyage. But Wendy was too beautiful to resist and I agreed to drive to Queens. And I felt a stab of guilt because my great-aunt was still alive and living there, and I hadn't called her since moving to Manhattan.

Wendy directed me to the Fifty-ninth Street Bridge and as we crossed she took a little brown vial of liquid from her purse, snorted from it, and then lifted up her halter top. Her breasts were revealed! They weren't beautiful. The tops of her breasts and her cleavage had been perfect looking, but the whole bosom was blocky and hung stiffly on her torso, and yet it was very sexy that she was half-naked in my car and the nipples were pretty and dark brown, and the skin was smooth and olive, and I reached over to touch, thinking that's what she wanted, but she pushed my hand away, and said, "Not yet, you like me too much."

It seemed beyond incredible that I was leaving Manhattan and crossing the black, oil-slickish East River with a topless transsexual. I felt proud. I was having an adventure. I was brave. A taxi passed us and I wanted the driver to see Wendy in my car.

Then it occurred to me that maybe her nudity could get us arrested. And then we crossed the bridge and we were officially in Queens and I suddenly had this feeling that my great-aunt was going to lean out a window and see me.

I was filled with guilt and nervousness, but also excitement. Wendy held my free hand as I drove and I liked it, though for all her beauty her hand felt substantial like a man's. A woman's hand is fragile. Their hands give them away, I thought. But I didn't care. I was glad that she wanted to hold my hand.

We drove for a long time under the roof of the el train, which made Queens feel like an indoor city. At one point Wendy said, complimenting me again, "You're nice in the heart. Do you want to be my boyfriend?"

"I'd like to be," I said, especially the way she was praising me.

"You want to live with me? Be my husband?" she asked.

I figured that she was high on what she had snorted and that it was making her feel overly romantic. "I have a very inexpensive room right now," I said, avoiding her proposal. "I don't think I can give it up."

"If you want to be my husband you have to live with me," she said. I didn't know what to say, so I tried to touch her again and again she pushed my hand away, and then covered her breasts with her top. Here she was proposing that we live together, but I still hadn't touched her.

We drove for a good twenty minutes and I asked her when she knew she wanted to be a girl, to see if there was any correlation with my development.

"One day I want to be a woman," she said, "and I go to school in my sister's dress with my little titties. I look like a nice girl and all the boys like me." She smiled when she said this, acknowledging that what had happened had been the right thing, her right path.

I asked her more questions and she told me she had grown up in Puerto Rico and the day she went to school in the dress she was thirteen; I figured that she was probably just starting puberty. From that point on she had always dressed like a girl.

"What about your parents? Do they mind?" I asked.

"My parents they are very nice. They say, 'Whatever you want.' When I was sixteen I moved to New York. That's what I wanted. I started taking the hormones, and hustling. Then when I was seventeen I got my titties. Three thousand dollars. When I was eighteen, three years ago, I got the castration, you know, just the balls. Now I'm saving my money for my pussy. Twenty thousand."

She gave me this whole history of her transformation, along with its expenses, in a very matter-of-fact and prideful way. Then our journey through Queens, after numerous turns, came to an end and we arrived at her building. It was an old three-story, wooden row house that was divided up into small apartments. As soon as we were in her room, she asked for the money. I gave it to her and she counted it.

Her room was small, neat, and narrow. She had a sink, a single bed, a night table, a small refrigerator, and a bureau with a television on top. The room was almost all furniture and no space to move. The bathroom was on the hall, shared by two other rooms. On her night table was a vase with dried roses. There was also a thing made out of plastic with tubes of different colors fanning out from a base. She turned on a switch and the tubes sparkled.

"It's like a fountain, you know, of water," she said. There was also a plastic clamshell and inside the clam was a little white lightbulb which was supposed to be a pearl, but this didn't work anymore. She wanted the place to be feminine and clean, her bed was neatly made, and these ornaments were to make it like a boudoir. There was something heartbreaking about the cheapness of her plastic treasures, her desire for elegance.

She went over to the refrigerator and took out a bottle of water. I saw that inside the refrigerator there was some food—bagels wrapped in plastic and a few apples. I was shocked by the food; it was as if I had forgotten that she was a human being who needed to eat.

"Are you hungry? You want something?" she asked.

"No, thank you," I said, but her offer had been sincere and generous.

She drank some water and then began to undress in front of her closet. "Don't look," she said. I sat on the edge of the bed and took off my shoes and I sneaked glances at her. Her back was to me. The halter top came off, I saw the sides of her breasts, and I was glad that I was in Queens.

Then she struggled out of her tight jeans and she took a short, diaphanous robe from the closet and put it on. She turned to me and smiled. I took off my clothes, except for my underwear, and I made a neat folded pile on top of my shoes. I slipped my college ring and my wallet discreetly inside my shoes.

She brushed her teeth in her little sink. Then she faced me and put her hands in her hair. She removed a large curly wiglike attachment. Her hair was still girlish, but only came to the middle of her neck. The attachment had been incredibly natural; I hadn't noticed it at all.

She put the hair on a nail in her closet. "I'm hanging it up, you know what I mean? I hang *it* up," she said, indicating her hair, and explaining her pun, proud that she had made one in English, which she spoke well, but not with ease. "And now I'm off. You get it? Work is over. How do I look?"

"Still very pretty," I said.

"Nah, I don't look good without the hair," she said. "With the hair I'm a whore, a slut, a tease, sexy," she shook her hips, her breasts moved slightly underneath the robe, "but without the hair I'm just a nice girl and we're normal. You're my husband and you're back from work and now we go to bed."

I didn't mind her defining our roles for us, and she shut off the lights and put on her black-and-white TV without the sound. The television gave the room a romantic light, and the little rainbow fountain of tubes still glowed.

She lay down on the bed and I was shyly sitting on the end. I was staying in my underwear so that everything would be safe. She pulled me up next to her. She slid her panties down part of the way. She had a dark little patch of hair and she raised her hips and put her hand between her legs. She was making sure her penis was tucked back securely; I could see the root of it bending down. She saw me watching her and said, "Don't worry, it's just a little dickie. It won't get hard." She pulled her panties back up.

Then she took off her robe; I figured she had put it on just to use part of her wardrobe for a few minutes. Her breasts were hard balls protruding from her chest. They didn't fall to the sides, or melt away like real breasts, but still she was beautiful. Her brown nipples were large. I wondered if the hormones made the nipples grow. My own nipples were tiny, the size of nickels; hers were half-dollars. She said, "What do you like to do?"

"I just want to hold you," I said.

She opened her arms to me. I lay my chest against hers, my face was in her neck. I inhaled her perfume. She squeezed me tight. I hadn't been held by anyone for a long time.

I'd only had one love affair in my life. My third year at Pretty Brook, the art teacher became fond of me. Her name was Elaine and she was thirty-five years old, and she thought I was unusual in a good way. She thought we were soul mates. "You're pretending to live in another time, aren't you?" she said to me once. "I like to think it's the 1920s. What about you?"

"The twenties are good," I said. "But I also like the end of the nineteenth century." There were a lot of young gentlemen in both eras.

Elaine was a tall woman and I thought that she was beautiful. She had thick chestnut-colored hair to the middle of her back, and she had a long graceful neck. She didn't wear makeup, and her large brown eyes were very loving; she liked to mother me.

Her apartment was on the first floor of a house on a quiet dead end in Princeton (it was called Humbert Street and some people in town believed that Nabokov, whose first American home was in Princeton, must have taken note of this when he would go for his constitutional walks), and Elaine had this fantasy of putting her breasts in her opened bedroom window as if she was just leaning out to get some night air, and her window was on an alley, and I was to come along and suck on her breasts in the darkness, and then go away without saying a word.

But we never tried it. I was with her eight months and then when school was over, she went to the state of Washington to paint and to run her sister's bed-and-breakfast on the St. George River and she didn't come back. We exchanged letters for a while and then she wrote that she had met a man and I didn't write her anymore.

I kissed Wendy's neck. She shifted my left leg between her legs. I kissed all of her neck and then her collarbone, working my way to her breasts. I was in my underwear, but I was very aroused and rubbed myself against her leg happily. She breathed in gasps with genuine pleasure and when I put my mouth to her nipple, she whispered "*Papi*."

I sucked on both her nipples. The breasts didn't give very much, the implants were hard, but her skin was soft and smooth. And between her breasts there was the fruity, cheap smell of her perfume and to me it was an aphrodisiac. I positioned myself between both her legs and nursed at her breasts and rubbed myself against the sheet, fighting the impulse to come. She arched her hips up and rubbed the front of her panties against my belly and I felt what must have been her penis, it was soft, and she kept whispering "*Papi*," and I kept thinking, "Mommy."

I thought it was interesting that she was calling for the male parent and I was whimpering in my mind for the female. And then I thought I heard her say "Daddy." I wished I could say Mommy out loud, but I was too embarrassed, even though it wasn't really my mommy that I wanted when the word blazoned itself across my mind; for me it was simply a primal term for love.

Wendy continued to murmur *Papi* and I thought, while lying between her legs, that there were important differences between us. I had tried dressing up when I started puberty, as she had, but I more or less quit and she continued. She called for father, and I wanted mother. And based on Wendy, I made the assumption that all Queens called for their fathers. This made me think that since I called for my mother that perhaps I wasn't a repressed Queen, which was a genuine concern, and that maybe I was just a young gentleman.

I took a break from kissing her breasts and I asked sweetly, "Why do you say Daddy when I kiss you?" She had only said Daddy once, but I was translating all the *Papi*s.

"What? I don't say that," she said.

"I thought I heard you," I said.

"You are hearing things," she said, and she pulled away from me. She felt that I had accused her of something perverted. I had wrecked the mood. Maybe she hadn't said Daddy, and translating the *Papi*s, it turns out, was foolish. I didn't know it at the time but *Papi* is a common Spanish term of endearment. All my Freudian theorizing had been pointless.

I pulled her back to me, kissed her neck and then her breasts. She began to breathe heavily again with pleasure. I was making everything all right. Then I noticed in the glow from the television that on top of her right breast, near the armpit, there was a cut.

I hadn't seen it before. The cut was red, scabbed over. Because my eye was so close, it looked enormous. I pulled away, frightened. "What's that?" I asked and I pointed. I'm going to get AIDS, I thought, I've come in contact with an open wound.

"I'm having a problem with my implant. It happens," she said, and her tone was angry and annoyed. "I'm going to the doctor, he'll fix it."

Then she turned her back to me and lay on her side. I tried to think rationally. I hadn't kissed that far up on her breast, I had concentrated on the nipples. And it was only a little cut, really, maybe an inch, and it wasn't bleeding. I'm all right, I reasoned.

I felt bad that I had offended her twice in just a few minutes. She was watching the silent images on the television. I wondered if she would ask me to leave. I put my hand on her shoulder. She didn't pull away. I pressed myself against her back and I put my face in her dark hair. We began to rock a little. Through my underwear, I pressed against her rear. She pushed back to feel me. I was rubbing up and down. I reached around and squeezed her left breast. She was breathing in excited little gasps. Everything was all right between us. We rocked faster. I kissed the side of her face.

"Do you want to be my husband?" she whispered.

Her question was genuine; she wanted desperately to be loved, and in that moment she even wanted my love. And I felt overwhelmed by her need, by the hopelessness of it, but I was also flattered and the flattery excited me and I ejaculated in my underwear.

I held her tight and I shuddered, and then I lay there for a moment or two, in the blackness that comes after orgasm, but as soon as I was entirely conscious, I was panicked and I wanted to leave. Suddenly everything was sordid, the silent black-and-white TV, the sink sticking out of the wall, her wig hanging in the closet. I was in a narrow little apartment in Queens with a prostitute. I sat up and said, "I have to go."

I started to get dressed and she didn't seem to mind. She knew that men often had to flee after coming, that they didn't really make good husbands. She put on her robe, took a towel from her closet, didn't say a thing, and went down the hall to the bathroom.

130

As I was dressing, I had premonitions that my car would be stolen and that I would get a disease. Waves of self-loathing washed over me. I went out to the hallway and heard the shower. I didn't think it was right to leave without saying good-bye. I opened the bathroom door. She pulled back the shower curtain. Mascara was running from her eyes in black streaks; it made her look like a woman crying.

She was beautiful. Her Sophia Loren face, her full lips, her breasts glistening, her belly smooth and flat. And she held the shower curtain so that I couldn't see below her stomach. Like an idiot, I had to ask, wanting to be reassured, "Everything was safe, right?"

But she couldn't hear me through the water. "I want to clean up now," she said. "Come back to Sally's. We'll go out again."

I closed the bathroom door and ran down the stairs to the street. I was sure that my car would be stolen, that I would deserve to lose my father's car, but it was still there. Yet I had a problem: I had no idea how to get back to Manhattan.

I started to drive and the streets were empty of people; it was two o'clock in the morning. Twice I came upon solitary men, but they didn't speak English. And again I had this feeling that my great-aunt would lean out a window and see me and know that I had come to Queens, up to no good, while for years I never had the courage to drive there and visit her.

I wandered for about twenty minutes beneath the el, looking for a sign to Manhattan or someone who spoke English, all the while feeling guilty and ashamed of what I had done, when suddenly a lion leaped at my car. I swerved to the side of the road and slammed on my brakes. I screamed out loud, "OH MY GOD!" I had a million thoughts at once. I thought that a lion had escaped from the Bronx Zoo and had made its way to Queens. I was worried that it would be killed, run over by a car. But if I got out of my car to save it by calling the police, I'd be killed, mauled.

Then I looked in my rearview mirror to see if it was chasing me and I realized that it was a gigantic stuffed lion, like the kind you win at carnivals, and that someone had dropped it at me from the tracks of the el train above. It had hit the pavement and then bounced up at my car, paws aimed right at my driver-side window. I couldn't believe it. The most incredible thing in my life had just happened and I wouldn't be able to tell anyone, because how could I explain that I was deep in Queens late at night with a transsexual.

CHAPTER V

The Jewish Duke of Windsor

The lion proved to be a good omen because shortly after its attack I spotted a sign to Manhattan. But then I panicked between a confusing right and left and I made the wrong choice, and I ended up on the Brooklyn-Queens Expressway, where I was afforded the most fantastic view of the city skyline. Rarely had I seen it from the east, always I had approached Manhattan from the west, from New Jersey. It was almost like a different city from this side, you could see more of it, the whole long knife of the island, and in the middle of it all was the Empire State Building looking like it could kill me.

I imagined the point of the building puncturing my stomach and going right through me. I was still hating myself for being with Wendy, and my nerves were still jumpy after the lion. Surely I had done something wrong and I was going to be punished.

The expressway led me to the Williamsburg Bridge and from there I made it home. When I entered the apartment, silent like a criminal, I stared guiltily at Henry's sleeping feet. He was sticking to his experiment of keeping his head in the east. I tiptoed on the orange path and I felt that what little affection Henry had shown me, I didn't deserve.

I went to bed, and in the morning I woke up hungover and depressed. As I prepared to go to work, I found that there was some solace in playing more than usual the role of the young gentleman. I gave myself a close shave, strokes both up and down, which I didn't usually do, and I felt less depraved so smooth. I combed my hair with a vitamin oil that a barber had recommended, and I tied an especially good Windsor knot on my tie. I thought to myself, "I'm sort of a Jewish Duke of Windsor."

Then after I was all dressed, I thought of Wendy and I had to suddenly lie down and masturbate, opening up my sport coat and shirt. It wrecked the whole cleaning-up, young-gentleman-mood

I had started. I lay there spoiled on my bed and I thought, "I should just kill myself," which is the thought I often have after masturbating and when I can't take things anymore and I feel like an utter failure.

Usually after I think this, I concoct a suicide plan, but there's always some snag: I worry that I will only go into a coma with a drug overdose, or paralyze myself if I jump out a window, or if I do successfully kill myself, who will find the body? What a terrible thing to do to someone. So my suicide plans unravel, but the ten minutes or so I spend imagining them distracts me from my selfish agony, and soothes me somehow. But that morning, lying on my bed, my belly sticky with my problems, I didn't have time to think about suicide. I had to clean up and get to work.

Were There Animals?

On the job, I was haunted by irrational fears with each ring of the phone. I kept thinking that the police had somehow discovered that I had been with a prostitute and they had found me by first calling Henry and telling him what I had done.

I was also still plagued by the idea that my great-aunt had leaned out a window and recognized me. I hadn't been in touch with her very much since my mother had died, but I decided to call her. It would be a mitzvah, and maybe it would balance things out for me, a good deed erasing my bad deed.

"Hello," she said, her voice a little shallow and old. She was in her early eighties, though no one in our family ever knew her exact age. She had been a great beauty when she was young, a red-haired Jewish Holly Golightly. She was famous for all her boyfriends and she had married several times, but since her sixties she had been alone.

"It's Louis," I said, "your nephew." I half-expected her to say, "I SAW YOU IN QUEENS LAST NIGHT!"

"A stranger is calling!" she said, her voice coming to life.

"I'm sorry I haven't been in touch. I've moved to New York. I can come visit you now."

"You have a car?"

"Yes."

"I don't want you driving to Queens, it's too dangerous."

"I can do it," I said.

"You can take the subway . . . but that's dangerous. We'll have to have a telephone romance."

"I'd like to come see you. I will. How are you?"

"I'm all right for the shape I'm in. Are you eating?"

"Yes."

"What do you eat?"

I told my great-aunt what I ate, and then she asked why I had moved to New York and I filled her in on what had been going on with me.

I told her I'd call her when I could come visit and then we rang off. "Be careful," she said, and it made me feel good to talk to her.

I made it through the day, calling my ladies across America. I wasn't as gregarious as usual with them, because I was feeling secretly perverted, but I did the best I could. And I stayed in my cubicle as much as possible so as to avoid Mary; I didn't want to get set off again. In the late afternoon, I had a conference with George and he was pleased with my progress. Some of the museums and nature centers were beginning to order the bulk subscriptions that I was offering.

By the end of the day, I felt like I was almost back to normal, but when I left the office and was heading for the subway, I had a depressing experience. I was walking up Lexington and coming towards me was a homeless man without a shirt. It was cold out, but he did have a hairy chest, which I hoped provided him with some warmth. He was wearing dirty sweatpants and his face looked intelligent. He stopped momentarily to peer in a shop window with a dignified tilt of his head. And then as we passed each other, he said to me, "You're losing your hair."

He said this with utter authority and assurance, and he kept on moving briskly as if he had somewhere urgent to go. I stopped and looked in the store window to check my hair and it did look very thin. Even madmen were pointing it out.

*   *   *

That night it was Henry's turn to come home very late. I was lying in bed, not sleeping, and I was wondering where he was. He had his class that night and he usually made it home by eleven to watch *Are You Being Served?* but now it was well after one o'clock. I wondered if he'd had an accident, or if *he* was doing something sexual. I sensed that he was.

Around two o'clock, I heard the fumbling of keys outside the door, and the muttering of oaths. I became fully alert and awake.

"Are you sleeping?" he asked, as he entered the apartment.

"No," I said.

"You should be. But at least I can make noise."

"Where were you?"

"What?"

"Where were you?"

"I was out . . . with a friend. That's all I will say."

My suspicions were confirmed. He had been up to something. He turned the water on in the kitchen and washed his face and brushed his teeth.

"A lady friend?" I asked.

"What?" he asked, shutting off the water.

"You were with a lady friend?"

"I was with Bunbury," he said with great annoyance. "You won't get anything out of me. You were out late last night. Notice that I don't ask where you were?"

I figured that he was actually having sex with one of his ladies or he had gone to some gay porno movie. Was that where he took solace? Did Henry too need sex of some kind? To be touched?

Then in the shadows he passed my bed without looking at me and he went into the bathroom. As always, he flushed before he finished urinating. This drove me crazy, but I didn't say anything.

Finished in the bathroom, he walked past my bed again, and for a moment, in the silver light coming through my air-shaft window, I saw his handsome profile. He didn't turn to look at me; he wanted to afford me some privacy.

I listened to him groan and grunt as he undressed and lowered himself onto his small couch. Then he said, "It's all too absurd."

"What's too absurd?" I asked.

"Everything. There seems to be a curious maladjustment of things, as Thomas Hardy said. Perhaps because of original sin. That's my contribution, not Hardy's."

He didn't credit Hardy the previous time he brought up curious maladjustment, but I didn't point this out. I was more intrigued by the idea that maybe Henry was making some type of confession to me about his evening, with this mention of original sin. Then he asked, "Any final thoughts, comments, before I put my plugs in?"

"I almost had a strange sexual experience the night before," I said suddenly, bravely. I thought the climate might be right for me to confess somewhat to Henry. He probably had just had an escapade and therefore wouldn't judge me so severely. And I wanted to confess. All day I had been slowly rebuilding myself like a phoenix, and I wanted to unburden myself of my secret, to continue my recovery, but I wasn't so foolish as to confess the entire truth. Also, I hoped that if I opened up a little, maybe he would.

"I don't want to hear about it. Were there animals?"

"Yes," I said. I was shocked by his intuition.

"What kind?"

"A lion."

"That's dangerous!"

"It was a stuffed lion."

"You are stranger than Otto Bellman. But you can't get AIDS from a lion. I'm putting my plugs in. What happened with this lion?"

"To make a long story short," I said from my bed to his bed.

"No, make a short story interesting," he said, cutting me off.

"Well, this friend from work took me to this bar and I met a beautiful girl, but it turned out she was a transsexual. It's a bar where half the girls are transsexuals and my friend didn't tell me this, he was playing a joke on me, and he didn't let me know until I had offered this girl a ride home because she didn't have enough money for a cab. And then it would have been rude to back out."

"Transvestites?"

"No, transsexuals. They take female hormones and have surgeries. Transvestites only dress up."

"This story is too long. I don't like it."

"Well, I drove her home, I didn't want to be rude. And when we were in front of her building she suddenly embraced me and I did feel attracted, but that was all that happened. Then when I was driving back someone dropped a stuffed lion at my car from the tracks of the el train. I thought it was a real lion. And the lion bounced up right at my window. Can you believe somebody would do that?"

"This is all very suspicious. I thought you had more sense than this. You're completely naive. You're lucky they didn't drop a brick on you. And you shouldn't be driving strangers home, especially if you're uncertain of their sex. I might have to give you a curfew. Now the plugs are definitely going in. We are insane to still be awake. Don't ever tell me a bedtime story like that again."

This Is Only a Tape Recording

I stopped looking at the *New York Press* for a whole week and subsequently I was very well-behaved and imposed my own curfew by staying home again every night. And Henry, in his aristocratic way where problems are ignored, did not bring up the confession I had made.

Halloween came on a Friday and Henry was going to be with Vivian Cudlip. I had no plans. I came home early from work, around four o'clock, and Henry was in a frantic state. He had just received a phone call from Vivian's secretary telling him that things had changed and that the evening was now black-tie; they would be going to a dinner dance at eight o'clock at the Carlyle.

"This is terrible," he said.

"Why?" I asked.

"I don't have any studs. They were in my suitcase that was stolen in Poland this summer. My tax papers from the last eight years were in there also. Someone has my studs and all my financial problems."

"Why did you bring your tax papers to Poland?"

"To work on them during long train rides. The IRS is after me. I haven't paid taxes in years. I don't owe anything, it's all deductible, but if you don't produce the papers they don't believe you. It's all Poland's fault. I don't have good fortune with that country. I once cut my hand on a cheap container of Polish sardines."

Henry put his head in his armoire to search for another set of studs, in case there was a pair he had forgotten about. He was throwing dirty shirts on to the couch.

"I need studs!" he shouted with exasperation, as I stood helpless in the kitchen. "I can't wear my shirt without them. One can get away with it, of course, but I wouldn't enjoy myself. I will have to go out and find a set. I just hope that they won't be too expensive."

Henry put his raincoat on and while searching the pockets of his raincoat, he said with great resignation, "Now the keys are missing. They've gone the way of all flesh."

We started searching the apartment and I found his house keys wedged in the cushion of his throne-chair. He thanked me graciously, and having just performed this favor, I asked him for one, "Henry, do you think I could ever meet Vivian's granddaughter, like you said that time?"

I was thinking that some healthier diversions, other than the ones I had been coming up with, might be good for me. And it was the ultimate young gentleman's fantasy to fall in love with a wealthy girl and travel with her.

"I'll have to work on it," said Henry. "If I do set something up, you must never tell her how we live. It would be the end of my career. But I'm not sure you'll like her. She's very large breasted."

"I like breasts," I said.

"I like bread," said Henry, taking the moral and asexual upper hand. "I like the bread they serve at The Salt of the Earth. Yes. That café is a great addition to my life."

And then he walked to the door, and like a good squire I followed him and I said, "I hope you find some studs."

"Through troubles and into more troubles, that's my motto," he replied, and then he made his hero's exit, closing the door behind him with a theatrical flourish, and he looked a little wild as he left. His raincoat was open. His fly was open, as it often was since it was usually broken on most of his pants, and this was already the pair with the split seam. And his hair needed some of its mysterious dyeing. But despite all this, he still looked rugged and handsome.

I wasn't very hopeful that he would set me up with Vivian's granddaughter, but it was possible, and it was nice to fantasize about, especially after hearing that she was large breasted.

An hour and a half later, Henry returned. I was lying on my bed reading. "I found a perfect set of studs," Henry said as he came in. "I had to go to every thrift store on the Upper East Side, but then I found them."

"How much were they?" I asked, as I knew he had been concerned about the price.

"Twenty dollars."

"That's not too bad, I guess."

"What?!?" he shouted from his room, incredulous.

"Didn't you get them?" I asked.

"Of course not! Don't be so bourgeois. I came up here to get the car keys, which are missing, naturally. It never was easy, and it only gets harder. I am going to Spanish Harlem. I know a thrift shop where I can find studs for three dollars."

"Why did you bother going to the shops here?"

"To save gas, and once one store didn't have them—and they all used to have studs—I needed to prove that they still existed on the Upper East Side."

Henry found his car keys with surprising ease, and an hour later he returned from Spanish Harlem triumphant, having found a set of studs for only three dollars, just as he had said. But the whole thing had fatigued him.

"It's all too much, too much for me, something has to give," he said. "I will take a short nap. You can't go into society looking like you are deteriorating." He lay down and for fifteen minutes things were quiet. Then he called out, "I'm not sleeping. Macbeth has murdered sleep! Only the innocent can sleep."

"I'm sorry you can't sleep," I said from my room.

"I tried thinking of vices to help me sleep. I tried imagining random objects, such as a coffeepot. I tried thinking of pleasant people."

"Who would you think of for a pleasant person?" I said, hoping for a compliment.

"That was the problem."

Then he was in my room. He was only wearing his boxer shorts. His orange towel was draped over his shoulder and across his belly, and his belly was his weak point. It looked a little distended, though when he was dressed it was hardly noticeable. His body was mostly hairless except for a few strands in the middle of his chest, and some lines of hair on the shins. The rest of his leg hairs had been worn away by decades of wearing pants and socks. He looked at me lying on my bed with my book.

"It's cold in this apartment. Aren't you cold?" he asked.

"Not really," I said.

"Oh, that's right, I forgot, you have youth. Your blood still runs through your body warming you. My blood has stopped."

"It must still be moving," I said. "Your mind still works so well."

"Mind?" he asked. "What mind? That went years ago. This is just a tape recording." And with that he went into the bathroom and closed the door.

When he was all bathed and dressed in his black-tie outfit with his new shirt studs, he looked regal. He had also re-dyed his hair and had done a good job; there were none of those strange, mysterious crumbs.

The Queen Has Fifty Rooms

The next morning I went to The Salt of the Earth by myself. I had been restless and unable to stay in bed, and Henry was still asleep.

When I came back up to the apartment, Henry was sitting in his chair by the window and he was marking papers. He was wearing green pants and a green turtleneck. He smiled when he saw me and said, "I'm not celebrating St. Patrick's Day."

"You look like a leaf," I said good-naturedly.

"These are the only clean clothes I have," said Henry, and he laughed at himself. "But I should have gone as a leaf last night. Some people were in costume."

"How was last night?" I asked, and I was feeling good that Henry had smiled at me when I came into the apartment. Usually, he was too agitated with something to look at me that way.

"Well, there was quite an exciting moment in the limo when I told everybody about going to Spanish Harlem for my studs. There's nothing people with money like to hear about more than somebody getting a good bargain. But I'd better be careful—they'll start thinking I have money if I keep talking about bargains, and then they'll wonder why I never pick up a check."

"You'd better stop that right away then."

"Yes, right away."

I went and lay down; often after breakfast during the weekends I had this great urge to go back to sleep. Henry started heating a can of soup in the kitchen. He offered me some, but I said no thank you, and then he told me about his dinner dance with Vivian. As was often the case in our relationship, I was simply lying on my bed while Henry regaled me and moved about the kitchen and prepared his food:

"Someone said at the table that Fergie and Diana should be beheaded and have their heads put on spikes outside of Buckingham Palace. It was a judge who said this. But they shouldn't be tried, he explained, because it could be appealed. The Queen has some statute for decapitation without a trial. And then Andy will reform like Henry the Fourth and Charles will abdicate. I also think they should throw in the Duke of Edinburgh. He should be beheaded."

Henry was expressing his anger again about the Duke of Edinburgh, the Queen's husband, also known as Prince Philip. I think Henry envied him the way you envy someone who is at the peak of achievement of something you yourself aspire to. When Henry made the beheading remark, I said, "You really have it in for him, don't you?"

"He's nothing but a freeloader and he has a different girl in every vacation spot and he doesn't care if the Queen knows. And he has lots of gadgets, electric shavers, hair pluckers—he's never done an honest day's work. He's the stupidest man in England." He stopped talking a moment and then in a softer and forgiving tone, speaking of Prince Philip, he said, "Well, we all have our problems, as James Thurber said, and mine is being evil."

"Your problem is that you're evil?" I asked.

"No! That's what Thurber said about himself."

"What's your problem then?" I asked, and I opened a journal, which I had bought recently and had placed next to my bed. I had a pen ready as well.

"I don't know," said Henry. "I've never been interested in myself. Too boring. It's more stimulating to consider other people's problems . . . My only problem I can see is that I have no money. And the women who have money whom I could marry are all too depraved to sleep with, and if you are married that is expected, you know. But I don't like to sleep next to anyone, be it dog, woman, or whatever. If only I could have my own room, then I could get married . . . and that would solve a lot of problems with the IRS . . . I need a woman with a large house. That way you can hide from one another. The Queen has fifty rooms. That's probably just the right size."

Henry finished speaking and I didn't say anything. I was scribbling down notes. I had decided when I bought the journal that Henry made too many interesting remarks for me not to jot them down. I was writing quickly and he detected something in my silence, and he said, "What are you doing in there?"

"Writing down all the funny things you say," I whispered, half-confessing; I knew he couldn't hear me.

"What?"

"Just lying here, thinking of all the funny things you say." I put the journal under my bed.

"They're not funny," he said. "They're true."

CHAPTER VI

Four Gap-Toothed Dairy Maidens

On November 3, Clinton was elected president and Henry had a drunk-driving accident in Southampton. Henry said that Clinton's triumph had caused him to drink too much. He had driven off the road and hit a tree after a dinner party at Vivian Cudlip's estate. It was supposed to be a party celebrating George Bush's victory. Henry wasn't injured, but the car was damaged. He did manage to drive it back to New York, though he was uncertain of the Skylark's continuing reliability.

On November 7, a Saturday, it was my birthday. I mentioned this to Henry as we were walking back to the apartment after our coffees at The Salt of the Earth. "I'm twenty-six today," I said, trying to speak with a lighthearted tone. "It's my birthday." I had thought of not telling him—I had made it all the way through breakfast—but I wasn't very good at stoicism.

"I wish you hadn't told me," he said. "Now I feel obligated."

"I'm sorry," I said. "Maybe you could just take me out for a drink?" It was pathetic, but I did want a little attention from Henry.

"I'll get you a balloon," he said. "No . . . I'll give you an old necktie. You're growing up." When we got inside the apartment, he went over to his armoire and removed an ugly wide tie. It had a red background and was populated with large gray elephants. He handed it to me ceremoniously and said, "A young person can get away with it."

"Thank you," I said. I looked at the label on the back. Brooks Brothers. It was a high-quality tie, and I suddenly liked it a lot more.

"Just don't wear it if we should happen to go out with Marjorie, my ex-fiancée. She gave it to me for Christmas a few years ago."

"I won't," I said.

Then Henry went over to the dish cabinet and removed a red sport coat. "You can wear this with the tie," he said. "It never fit me right, too long in the arms." He handed me the jacket and it smelled of his sweat and cologne, but if I took it to the dry cleaner's it would be an excellent addition to my young gentleman wardrobe, and when I wore it I could imagine Henry wearing it and pretend a little that I was him. I tried on the jacket and it fit me well.

"Are you sure?" I asked and he nodded that he was. "Thank you very much," I said, and then I added, "You're lavishing me with gifts."

"No, I'm not," he said. "I'm throwing things away." Nonetheless, all this giving seemed to cheer Henry up, made him feel magnanimous, and he said, "Let's go to a musical tonight for your birthday and then I'll buy you an ice-cream cone."

"That would be great," I said, and I assumed we would sneak in somehow, so I didn't ask how we would afford it. And I was very happy that we were going to do something together; I had wanted to for more than a month since our trip to the opera.

"We'll leave at eight-thirty," Henry said. "Most of the shows have their intermissions around nine-fifteen. That's when you blend in with the smokers who are outside. Then you just walk in and try to find an empty seat. There's a moment of tension and anxiety until the lights go down, but I've never been caught." He said we'd choose our show depending on where we could find parking.

We spent a quiet afternoon together. I read and Henry graded papers. At one point, he called out to me and said, "I tried to teach my students something about life this week. I said to them, 'The only way you can be sure you are loved for yourself, and not for money or sex, is if you are unattractive and poor.' But then I explained that it's very hard to be loved if you are like that."

"I don't think that will help them," I said. "That makes love practically impossible."

"Well, they need to know what they're up against."

When it was time to leave we both were dressed in blue blazers, ties (I wore my new birthday one), and raincoats. I suggested that we take my Parisienne, but Henry wanted to use his Skylark, to test it after it had been resting on the street for a few days.

We were just heading out the door when the phone rang. Henry moved nimbly across the kitchen and living room to get it. I was impressed by his sudden burst of speed and agility.

"It might be an invitation to a free meal," he said to me over his shoulder. "And one free meal could lead to another!"

He answered the phone in his usual manner, "H. Harrison . . . oh, hello, Gershon." Henry widened his eyes to me. It was our mysterious, hulking downstairs neighbor; the silence between Henry and Gershon was over. "How are you? Is something leaking? To what do we owe the honor of this call? . . . You want to know how I am. Well, I went to Southampton and I skidded off the road. I went into a ravine, passed through some underbrush and hit a dead tree, which crumpled beneath the weight of my Buick. I missed a big healthy tree by a foot. I've been saved for the hanging. I will tell you of other disasters as they occur. I have to go now, Gershon. I will call you soon; I was just leaving."

Henry hung up and held his finger to his mouth, indicating that I shouldn't say anything. He whispered, "He might have pipes leading up here to listen to my every move."

Once we were outside, Henry said, "He broke down and called. Perfect timing. The car needs to be looked at. It has to make it to Palm Beach in a few weeks. The accident did something to the power steering and the oil is leaking. But Gershon can fix it . . . This *is* the longest he's gone without calling me. It's because of Bellman. I saw the two of them riding bicycles. Bellman needs the nearness of his own sex. The *menschen*. It's very German. That's why it was easy to get them together in the Luftwaffe. Together they *verk*."

We walked up to Second Avenue and Henry couldn't remember where he had parked the car. "I have the keys, for once," he said, "and now I've lost the car!"

We found the Skylark on Park Avenue and the only evidence of the accident was that the front bumper was hanging off at a rakish angle. Henry got in the car first, through the passenger door, and when he started driving he had to tug mightily at the steering wheel.

"If it was a Japanese car, I would be dead," said Henry, as we drove down Park. "For drunk driving you need an American car. I am prepared to make an endorsement along those lines. Yes."

When Henry made the left-hand turn down Fifth Avenue his lack of steering nearly caused him to hit a bus.

"It's all Clinton's fault!" he shouted. "He's destroyed my car. My freedom. I can't stand this country. It's all your fault. The truly great people of this country are going to withdraw into themselves. They could have asked for our help, but now it's too late. I'll have to move to Russia."

"I don't think my one vote swung the election."

"Yes it did."

"Well, we needed change."

"No! Youth know nothing. The more things change the worse they get."

I didn't respond and we drove in silence. It was my birthday and we both wanted to avoid a political argument. When I had told him a few days before that I had voted only for Democrats he had given me the cold shoulder for several hours.

We made it to the theater district—the steering seemed to loosen up as we went along—and we found parking right near the *Will Rogers Follies*. "Would you like to see that?" Henry asked sweetly, forgiving me on my birthday my vote for Clinton.

"Sure," I said.

"I've seen it three times. I like to go whenever they get a new Will Rogers, to see how they handle the role. I haven't seen this one yet—Mac Davis. It's a vulgar name, but maybe he can sing."

We hung around by the corner near the theater for about ten minutes and then the intermission crowd was let out. Henry became a little agitated and started whispering orders.

"Take off your raincoat and drape it on your arm; that makes it look like we've just come out." We both draped our coats. "Now let's mingle in." We walked from the corner and into the crowd. We stood about as if we were taking a breather.

After only two minutes, Henry said, for the benefit of any eavesdroppers, "Let's go back in. I need to use the rest room." When we entered the lobby, he whispered, "Get a program. It looks good to have one."

Near the velvet-curtained entrances to the theater were stacks of programs. I bent down quickly and grabbed two. No ushers seemed to notice. I passed one to Henry and said, "Let's roll them up. More realistic."

"Yes, good idea," said Henry, whispering out of the corner of his mouth. "Let's be bold and try for the orchestra."

We entered the theater and walked down the sloping carpet towards the stage and then stopped midway and leaned against the wall. We were eyeing two seats on the aisle. They had no coats on them and appeared to be free, but many people were still circulating in the lobby and going to the rest rooms.

"Let's hover here," said Henry, "and see if they're open. Try not to look too vulturish. If someone comes we'll go to the balcony."

People were standing about and talking; some were going back to their seats. One of the ushers seemed to glance at us.

"Oh, no, the *Polizei*," Henry whispered. "If she asks for our tickets I'll tell her that I dropped them in the urinal. She won't harass someone who she thinks is a senior citizen."

She walked away and we were both anxious that she might be returning with reinforcements, but she didn't come back. Then two older, white-haired ladies who were nicely dressed in wool skirts approached and sat in the two seats directly behind the ones we were interested in.

Henry looked at the women and said, "No one from Manhattan comes to Broadway anymore. Who can afford it? Only widows whose husbands had life insurance . . . Go ask them if those seats are taken. They are more likely to trust you than me."

The women said the seats were empty and Henry and I moved in. "Slump a little," he said. "We don't want to block their view."

The lights were lowered and the musical began. It was a bad show, quick moving and frivolous, and the women behind us were enjoying it very much. They were laughing at the most simple gags and exaggerated gestures. At one point Henry glanced at me skeptically when the women were both deeply guffawing and saying, "Oh, dear!" But he looked at me for just a moment. I knew that we both thought that the ladies were unsophisticated, but we didn't want to be judgmental as we felt guilty for somewhat obstructing their view, which had been unobstructed during the first act.

When the show was over and we were filing out, I did say to Henry with hidden, snobbish meaning, "The audience was really laughing."

"Yes. When you pay you have more at stake," said Henry.

"Without having much at stake," I said, "I enjoyed it. It was fun."

"It was worth the price of admission," said Henry, and we both snickered, and we were both happy. There's something very uplifting about sneaking into shows. And Broadway musicals are redundant and boring for two acts, but one act is just right—dazzling and amusing, even if it's a bad show.

We exited the theater on to Broadway and the air was cool. We were in the center of Times Square and Henry said, "Well, you can't say I didn't take you to a show on your birthday."

"No, I can't," I said. "Thank you very much. Did you like this Will Rogers?"

"He wasn't bad, but he has the look of a sex fiend . . . Instead of ice cream, let's go to the Sbarro for pizza."

The Sbarro was a block south of the theater, and we each got a slice, and Henry paid for both of us. The dining area was down a flight of stairs beneath the street level. There were many tables and the room was brightly lit. There were very few people there at the time of night, a little after eleven, but Henry sat us right near four very overweight young girls, all dressed in jeans and sweatshirts.

"I sat here," Henry said, "so that we could be next to these sylphlike, gap-toothed dairy maidens from Duluth High School. We might hear some interesting dialogue. I can use it in a play."

"Henry, please," I whispered. "Not so loud."

He ignored me and said, "They've never known a man, though they dress like men."

To get him off the subject of the girls, I said, "This pizza is very tasty."

"You have all these old-woman expressions—tasty—you have to get caught up to your generation. You're a square."

I ate my pizza in silence. Henry often put me down in little ways, and it always hurt. If only he really knew me, I thought, he would realize I wasn't a square. But what made me unsquare—my moments of sexual courage and craziness—was the very thing that would cause Henry to reject me. So I had to let him think that I was dull and boring.

We finished our pizza and headed out of the dining area. At the bottom of the stairs there was a counter with napkins, plastic utensils, and little packets of sugar, ketchup, and salt. Henry started grabbing sugar packets and clumps of napkins.

"Get some sugar," he said. "We can feed it to the cockroaches when they come back."

I grabbed about two dozen packets, and then as we climbed the stairs we knocked into each other because we were both concentrating on getting the sugar packets into our raincoat pockets, but raincoat pockets are very difficult to pry open, for some reason. The result of this bumping into each other was that we both dropped all our sugar packets down the stairs and Henry dropped his napkins as well.

"Some thief you are," said Henry, "spilling out the evidence like a trail . . . I don't think the cashiers can see us. You pick up the ones down there. You're young, you can bend. Leave the napkins. They are covered with disease."

Henry groaned as he was bending, and then he said, "OH, GOD, I'VE PUT MY HAND IN VOMIT!"

"What?!?"

"Oh, it's only the fake marble. It looked like vomit."

We managed to get out of there without further incident, though we were snickering in our usual manner as we exited the restaurant. Stealing the sugar was like sneaking into a show. I felt happy again and I forgave Henry for calling me a square. When we were in the car, he said, "Let's drive down Forty-second Street and see if there's any violence."

We only had four blocks to go and as we came to the stoplight at Forty-second and Seventh Avenue, we craned our necks to the right and the left, but there was no action. "It's quiet," Henry said. "The new Clinton depression is felt even here."

We drove up Eighth Avenue, right past Forty-third, just fifty yards away from Sally's. I impetuously said, "You know what? That transsexual bar I went to is right over there. I forgot that it was around here. Maybe we should go in. It's a real spectacle. You might get a kick out of it."

"No, I don't think so," said Henry. "I might see the president of my college, Dr. Rubinstein."

"You won't see your president," I said and I laughed.

"Oh, yes I will. You can't take risks like that when you don't have tenure."

I had proposed this to Henry wanting to show him that I wasn't a square, and I had at least expected him to scold me for such a suggestion, but instead he countered with the notion that Dr. Rubinstein would be there. He was inscrutable. But I was lucky that he didn't want to go in. I hadn't been back since the night of the lion, and if Miss Pepper or Wendy saw me and greeted me too effusively, Henry was sure to recognize the depth of my involvement and he would throw me out of the apartment just like he had Otto Bellman.

We drove home without any more mention of Sally's, and when we were getting ready for bed, he called out to me, "My life is in ruins!"

"Why?"

"My eye mask is missing. I can't sleep without it."

"But it's very dark in your room in the mornings."

"Not dark enough. Bellman may have broken in here and stolen it to torment me. It's the last straw."

"Will you be able to sleep at all?"

"I'll wrap a shirt around my head. It has worked in the past."

"Thank you for my birthday presents—the elephant tie, the red jacket, the Will Rogers, the pizza."

"We'll do it again next year . . . Now the plugs are in, the shirt is bound."

Fort Schuyler

The following morning Henry gave a scream around eleven-thirty.

"Are you all right?" I asked nervously from my bed.

"That means I'm up," he said.

"You alarmed me," I said.

"Don't be alarmed, this is a business relationship," he said, and then he screamed again as I heard him stand up. When he finished screaming, he said, "I would like to have a bed that ejects you. First it starts vibrating violently as a warning. You have a minute to get out and then it ejects you."

He finished his statement as he came striding into my room. An oxford shirt was wrapped around his head. The sleeves, still tied together, had covered the eyes, but were now lifted on to the brow. The rest of the shirt hung down from the back of his head like the little capes that French Foreign Legionnaires have on the back of their hats. He stopped at the foot of my bed and said, "You are picking up my bad habits. Sleeping late. But it's good for you. You might still be growing, and I need it because I'm disintegrating."

"Why do you think I'm so young all the time?"

"Everyone under thirty looks the same age to me. Somewhere around twelve."

Then he went into the bathroom and I listened to him urinate. Halfway through his urinating, as always, he flushed the toilet. The flushing stopped and he was still peeing a little. Why didn't he wait till he was finished peeing and then flush? I had conjectured that maybe he was playing a game to see if he could time the end of his urinating with the end of the flushing. This mystery had bothered me for weeks, and I was also bothered because often there was a bit of urine left in the water.

When he was all done he walked briskly through my room, but I stopped him. I felt that I had been living with Henry long enough in intimate quarters to take a risk, and I had already broached many sensitive topics like suggesting we go to Sally's the night before, and so I said, "Can I ask you a personal question?"

"I won't answer it, but you can ask."

"Why do you flush the toilet before you finish urinating?"

"I want to be done with it already. I'm too lazy to be bothered to wait."

"Some is still left in the bowl, you know."

"There is not."

"Sometimes there is," I said, holding my ground.

"Well, I like to save a little in case we run out," said Henry, and he walked out of my room. I laughed. It was a good way to start the day. We both got dressed and Henry put a record on. I watched him dance in the mirrors. He waltzed. He contorted. He spun and he shuffled. He sang along to the record: "The Army, the Navy, the Church, and the Stage . . ."

When he was done I went into the kitchen to brush my teeth and he was resting on his chair. I said, "You should make an exercise videotape for gentlemen, like Jane Fonda."

"No one could follow my steps. They're entirely original and intuitive, based on jungle rhythms."

While I was brushing my teeth over the kitchen sink, Henry called Gershon on the phone and asked him if he would take a look at his car. When he hung up, he said, "Gershon will examine the Buick! Bellman's influence might be waning. I think we'll go to the parking lot at Fort Schuyler. That's where I have Gershon do all my mechanical work."

"Where's Fort Schuyler?"

"The Bronx. It's quite beautiful actually. It's right on the water. The State University of New York has its Maritime Academy there. They have a very nice wooden practice yacht. It's the Annapolis of the Bronx!"

"Why do you go out there?"

"No one bothers you, and he can get under the car and have tools lying about. And I can be close to nature."

"How come Gershon does all this work for you?"

"I'm like a father to him—I don't approve of him at all, so he wants to please me. We've been in the building together for twenty years, and until Bellman came along I was his only friend.

Occasionally he brings a homeless person in to sleep on the floor, but they end up stealing from him."

"How does Gershon support himself?"

"He's a subway mechanic. Member of the union. He's one of the richest men on the Upper East Side. They can't fire him no matter how long his beard gets or how insane he becomes. I think he has syphilis from all the prostitutes. It goes to the brain, you know."

Then Henry went back into the bathroom and I knew that he was going to color his hair. But I still didn't know how. I had looked for dye on the shelves many times, but I never found any. And the shelves were loaded with things. They were like a totem pole of toiletries; each shelf probably represented the left-behind products of my predecessors. But there was no dye and Henry always went in empty-handed. How he colored his hair was a greater mystery than the urinating.

So sure enough five minutes after he went in the bathroom, Henry came out with dark brown, almost black hair, and he had gone in with brownish-gray. I made no comment about this transformation.

He asked me if I wanted to join them at Fort Schuyler. It sounded like an adventure and I always wanted to be with Henry so I said yes.

"Go downstairs and tell Gershon that I'm almost ready to leave," he said. "I'll never find his phone number. I have to look for the keys. Maybe I'll find my sleeping mask instead. Then I can go to sleep and pretend I don't have any car problems."

I went down and knocked at Gershon's door. On the other side, he said, "One minute . . . please."

There was silence and then the door opened slowly and shyly, until Gershon, with his great girth and height, filled the frame. He was wearing old gray sweatpants and a faded black sweatshirt.

"I'm Louis," I said. "Henry's roommate. I'm coming with you to Fort Schuyler. He says he's ready to go."

"Please . . . come in."

Gershon spoke in a whisper and his words came out slowly and with hesitation. It wasn't a stutter, just a very deliberate form of speech. I entered his apartment and I got my first good look at Gershon. Previously, the closest I had ever been was a length of hallway.

He stood about six foot three and he had the width of almost two men, though he was not obese. He was robust and thick. His hair was light brown and curled in rivulets down to his shoulders. He parted it on the side, sweeping it away from his forehead to reveal a brow that protruded and looked swollen as if he had banged his head long ago in frustration against some concrete wall. Recessed beneath his brow were his tiny, blue-gray eyes. The nose was blunt and appeared to have been flattened by the same banging that swelled the brows. The lips were pinkish-white and rather full and sensuous. His beard, like his hair, was naturally curly and hung about six inches beneath his chin.

"I have to put on my shoes," said Gershon, and he walked across the kitchen to his bedroom. The kitchen floor was covered with bicycle parts and newspapers, and two bicycles hung from the ceiling. I followed Gershon; I was rudely curious to see what his bedroom looked like. I stood in the doorway and he sat on his bed and tied on a large running sneaker.

His bed was made up of several mattresses piled on top of one another. Next to the bed was a lectern which supported a thick, opened volume of the *Oxford English Dictionary*. Resting on the page was a magnifying glass, and above the dictionary was a crane-like metal reading lamp, about four feet long. Gershon really was following Henry's advice to study a dictionary and to ride bicycles to help with his sex drive. But I did notice that all over the floor there were crumpled white tissues, and I knew immediately that Gershon, like myself, was a mad masturbator.

"Your room is the same size as mine," I said to Gershon, to somehow explain what I was doing poking my head into his private quarters.

"I can hear you . . . walking up there," he said matter-of-factly, without annoyance, and he put on his other sneaker.

I imagined the prostitutes lying on the mattresses with him. What did they think of Gershon? Did he crush them? Was he tender? I pictured him stroking them, admiring them, holding them. That's what I would do.

Gershon put on an orange down vest and grabbed a tool bag. We left his apartment and as we headed up the stairs, I said, "I hope Henry found his keys."

"He always loses them," said Gershon.

It felt good to be with someone else who knew about Henry's constant struggle with keys. It made me want to talk about Henry, to compare notes, to find out what Henry was like twenty years ago. It made me feel close to Gershon. With no one else did I have Henry in common.

Henry had found his keys and we went to his car. It was clear and sunny and fairly warm for November. Henry was wearing a light tan coat, which like all his clothing sported a variety of soaked-in stains. He was also wearing his stretch tan pants and his most destroyed loafers. It was an outfit for car repair, but his hair was combed back and he strode with his usual distracted arrogance. I was in my late-fall attire of brown corduroy pants and a green-and-brown plaid woodcutter's jacket, which I thought made me look very weekend sporty and young gentlemanish. Gershon was in his sweats and vest and carried his large black bag of tools. I thought of him as our bodyguard.

When we got to the Skylark, I sat in the backseat and found a pair of Henry's reading glasses. "I found a pair of your glasses," I said.

"Those eyeglasses have TB!" shouted Henry as he started the car. "Don't touch them! They fell off me into a quickly flowing stream, in the street, ridden with TB. I have to take them to a car wash to be scalded!"

I immediately dropped the glasses back to the newspaper-and-coffee-cup-covered floor, and I saw that on the floor there was a mascara applicator. This struck me as strange, as I realized that I had noticed a mascara applicator on Henry's coffee table. I wondered if Henry touched up his eyes. He had very nice dark eyes—they were perhaps his best feature—but I didn't say anything about the mascara.

Henry drove us to the Bronx with his slightly careening method, having to pull with exaggerated motions at the weakened steering wheel. I regretted somewhat my decision to come. I was afraid we'd have a car accident, and I needed to express my fear. I said, "There are no seat belts back here."

"Don't be a Milquetoast! If you are ejected Gershon will catch you."

"Unless . . . I go through the windshield first," said Gershon.

"You're both hopeless," said Henry. "No spirit."

Announcing my fear seemed to relax me, despite Henry's reprimand. I was able to sit back and admire Henry's knowledge and confidence in negotiating the crumbling and confusing roadways of the Bronx.

When we passed a McDonald's, Henry said, "The other day I saw the most incredible baby in the McDonald's. A wisp of a boy. He was with his mother who was in leather. She was not an S and M; she was perfectly charming. I was sitting behind them and the baby bent his neck completely backward to look at me. It was quite a phenomenon. I complimented the mother on having a gifted child. She smiled. If I could be surrounded by people like those two I would like New York. Instead there are all these ugly people."

I tried not to take offense at this remark, and Gershon didn't seem to care. Henry continued his speech. "Americans have lost their looks. People were better looking when I was young. It must be the war. If all the fit men get killed off you lose the good-looking genes. Sweden wasn't in the war and the people there have maintained their looks. I think Swedish women are the most beautiful. I said this in my class, and one student said, 'My girlfriend is from Haiti, what do you say to that?' What could I say? It's not racism. It's preference. But he wouldn't understand that."

"Haitian women can be very beautiful," said Gershon, in his whispery slow voice.

"That's not the point!" shouted Henry.

The Throgs Neck Bridge came into view. Henry wondered what a Throg was and asked Gershon to look it up in his dictionary when he got home. We passed underneath the bridge and drove through a working-class neighborhood.

"It used to be Irish poor here, now it's Italian. Look at all the cars," Henry said. "Where do all these people work? All over America you have houses and cars. Where are the jobs? That is the great mystery."

We approached the gate of Fort Schuyler and there was a little Checkpoint Charlie booth with a security guard. Henry slowed the car down and said to Gershon, "Tell him we're tourists from Russia and that we've come to see the fort. If they realize we've come to work on the car again they won't let us in. He'll believe that you're Russian Orthodox with that beard."

We pulled alongside the security shack and Gershon rolled down his window. In his quiet, hesitating voice, made worse by the pressure of the moment, he could hardly get the words out, "We're . . . from Russia."

The security guard couldn't hear him, and he seemed a little suspicious of Gershon's beard and the car's usual emission of smoky fumes. So Henry quickly shouted, "I am escorting two Russian tourists from St. Petersburg to the fort!"

Henry's authoritative tone of voice had a positive effect on the guard and he lifted the gate. The campus was shaped like an arrowhead, and on a single road, Henry pointed out, we could circle it. There were bisecting footpaths for walking across. We entered at the base of the arrowhead where the modern structures—dormitories and academic buildings—were located. At the point of the arrow, jutting out aggressively into Long Island Sound, was the massive, thick, and tall gray-stone pentagon: Fort Schuyler.

On the right-hand side of the road, as we approached the fort, there was a bay with a dock area. There were several small tankers and the large, old, wooden practice yacht that Henry had spoken of.

"There's the yacht!" said Henry, and he stopped the car.

"I'd like to buy a . . . yacht," said Gershon. "I could take a woman sailing . . . we could go to the Mediterranean and see the Blue Grotto."

This was a rather fantastic and beautiful notion and I admired Gershon for it, but Henry just ignored this musing about the Blue Grotto, and we continued down the road to the fort. We stopped alongside it, and at the top of the fifty-foot stone walls were turrets for cannons.

"It was built to protect New York against the British ships at the beginning of the nineteenth century," said Henry, wanting to educate me. "They were trying to teach us a lesson. They did manage to burn down Washington. Maybe they'll come back when Clinton is in office."

"It's perfectly situated to defend New York," I said, and I looked out across the gray waters. Even though it was November, there were many boats out, and New York seemed to me like a gigantic Venice, all of it broken up by rivers and sounds.

We drove around the point of the fort and to the other side, and high above the fort and the Long Island Sound, casting its shadow and acting like a partial roof, was the Throgs Neck Bridge. In its deep shadow was a parking lot and Henry stopped the car there.

"I need to find the registration in case I have to sell the car," said Henry. "I think it's in the trunk, but I may have lost it like everything else."

"I think . . . you're losing your mind," said Gershon, and in his own way he liked to give Henry a hard time. He was much braver than I in this regard.

"That's all right," said Henry, "losing my mind doesn't bother me. Everyone's afraid of oblivion. I think oblivion is good—who wants to remember? Also, I'm in the type of job where you don't need a mind. You just need your lecture notes from when you did have a mind."

We got out of the car and Henry opened the trunk and Gershon opened the hood, and there wasn't really anything for me to do, so I asked Henry, "Do you mind if I go for a walk?"

"No. I mind that you asked."

I walked out to the far edge of the fort where a few black men sat on rocks, fishing. I made eye contact with one of the men—he was older than the others, there was gray in his hair—and I said, "What kind of fish can you get when it's cold?" I knew that fishermen were always having to answer questions from non-fishermen, but I was hoping that he wouldn't mind.

"Black fish," he said.

I wondered if they were called that because they were black from pollution or if that was their scientific name. I didn't ask the fisherman, though, because I knew he probably ate the fish, and I didn't want to imply that it might be poisoned.

I sat on a rock and watched him and the others fish and I happily looked out across the gray, unconscious waters, which were quite vast, and I could make out the shore of Long Island, though it may have been the very end of Queens. My great-aunt and Wendy were out there somewhere. Then I thought about how the fort could have cannon-bombed any ship which had tried to pass on its aggressive way to Manhattan.

Thinking of war and water made me think of the Dead Sea. When I was seven years old my parents saved a lot of money and we went to Israel for two weeks for our summer vacation. My parents had friends in Tel Aviv—a married couple with two daughters a little older than me. These people, the Kanareks, were our tour guides. From that trip to Israel I have several memories, even though I was quite young, and one of the most vivid was of my experience in the Dead Sea. After a long car ride through the desert of eastern Israel (during which time my father's hat blew out the window and he couldn't retrieve it because it landed in a minefield, so he yelled at my mother) we arrived at the sea. On our shore was Israel, and on the distant, opposing shore, Jordan.

Across the water we could see the small red-brown hills of Jordan, and my father said, "That's where the enemy lives. If you swim out too far you can get shot."

My mother helped me get into my bathing suit, and as soon as I was ready and out of her hands, I went running for the water, as I loved to do when we went to the Jersey shore, our usual summer vacation spot. I saw that as I approached the water a soldier standing guard on the beach smiled at me. I felt proud. I knew that he must think I was cute—lots of people in Israel were finding me cute with my blond hair—and I especially liked having a soldier find me so. I had a great love for soldiers because of my G.I. Joe dolls, and so

I put on an extra burst of speed to impress him and I sailed into the water creating a great splash even with my little body.

For a moment I felt wonderful, especially after the long, hot car ride, but then I began to sting all over, especially in the eyes and anus, and the couples lolling quietly in the water near me all yelled at me in Hebrew. My parents and our Israeli friends were alongside the soldier and he was talking to the Kanareks and pointing at me and looking at me with anger. I was humiliated to have him look at me that way so soon after feeling beautiful in his eyes.

My mother came and took me out of the water and told me that the Dead Sea was filled with salt and that it stung people (which I knew) and that I wasn't allowed to splash or I would get in trouble with the soldier. She told me that I had to move very slowly in the water and that one could float without swimming because of the salt. She said I could go back in, but I felt too ashamed in front of the soldier, and so I sat on the rocky beach and looked at the hills where the enemies were, though you couldn't see anybody, and I watched the two Kanarek sisters float happily in the ancient water.

My other significant memory of that trip to Israel occurred when during one of our outings we took two cars and I was put in the car of our Israeli friends. I sat in the backseat with the two sisters, who had requested that I come with them, and I was flattered by this. They were very pretty girls with frizzy, golden brown hair, and they were probably ten and twelve, and I sat between the two of them.

They started tickling me quite a bit and I was shy, but I was loving it. They spoke English because they had lived in America for two years, during which time their parents met my parents, and the girls asked me if I knew how babies were made. I innocently nodded no and they told me that if I put my penis in their vaginas they would have a baby. I didn't know that I had such power. Then they began to grab for my penis during their tickling. They tried to open my fly, and I liked the exciting attention, but I also felt threatened and outnumbered. I knew that what was happening was bad and that we would get in trouble if they opened my fly, but their parents in the front seat were oblivious. There was no air-conditioning in the car, the windows were open, and so there was lots of noise from the road.

The girls urged me to take my penis out of my pants, since they couldn't, but I kept saying no. I told them I was afraid that they would get pregnant if they touched it. I had understood the concept that it had to at least touch their vagina—this must have corresponded with other rumors I had heard—but I was playing dumb with these two sisters, hoping that they would respect my fears. Also, I didn't want to take it out for them or let them get at it, because I thought their real goal was to make fun of it and maybe pinch it. But they were very persistent and it was a real struggle to keep my pants on.

While this little backseat sex lesson and tickling match was happening, my father, during a stoplight, pulled alongside the Kanareks' car. He was leaning out his window, smoking one of his horrible cigars, and he said something to the girls' mother and gave a sort of nasty laugh. Then the light changed and he pulled in front of us. Immediately, with a mean look on her face, the mother turned to her husband and mimicked my father's laughing and then said in Hebrew something about my father which was obviously derisive and cutting. I could tell that she was disgusted by him and I figured that she didn't think I would understand, but I did.

And it was the first time I had ever seen my father made fun of. I felt bad for him that he was being mocked by our hosts behind his back, especially when he had just thought he was sharing something funny, and so I pitied my father. He thought our hosts liked him, but I knew they didn't, and I couldn't tell him; I didn't want to hurt him.

But I was also ashamed of my father. His laugh and his cigar were gross to me as well, but since I was his son I was also ashamed of myself. I felt like I too had been made fun of, and I wished I could get out of their car. I didn't like them anymore. And the girls sensed a change in my mood. They knew that I had understood their mother, and they stopped tickling me.

But I was trapped. I didn't want to be in their car, but also I didn't want to be with my father. His behavior in Israel had been worse than it was back home. He was bad at traveling. He was moody, he yelled, he complained. And Mrs. Kanarek's mimicking of him, her repulsion, was confirmation for the first time from the outside world that my father was indeed a strange and abrasive man.

And so I wasn't the only one repelled by him, but mostly, even though I was young, I pitied him. It was a way to love him.

As I mused about all this, sitting on the rocks by the waters of Fort Schuyler, in the shadow of the Throgs Neck Bridge, the black man whom I had spoken to suddenly pulled a fish out of the water. To no one in particular, but to everyone, he said, "Got one." Right away he made preparations to clean the fish. Perhaps he wanted to head home having made his catch.

"That's a big fish," I said, complimenting him. It was shiny black with a gray belly the color of the water. I said, "Can I watch you clean it?"

"Sure," he said. "It won't take me long." He seemed glad to have an audience. I moved down a few rocks to be closer. The other fishermen pridefully ignored him.

He began by stripping off the skin with his long, serrated knife and I noticed that he didn't cut the fish's head off. He was cleaning the fish while it was still alive. He held it down with his free hand as it shook and fought him.

"Aren't you going to cut its head off?" I asked.

"It's going to die sooner or later. And they keep moving even after you cut off their head."

He tossed the skin and then the organs into the water like they were garbage, and he laid the white meat on the rocks. Even as it was being viscerated the black fish gave the occasional burst of movement to escape. Its eye stared straight up into the sky. When it was reduced to its spine and its head the man threw the fish into the water. I thought I saw it move, trying still to swim, to send messages to its muscles and organs which had been cut away. I wondered if it could possibly still be alive and then it disappeared beneath the surface of the gray sound.

"Thank you for letting me watch," I said, trying to be polite and not judge the man for his brutality; I was the one who had asked if I could look on. I started walking back to Henry and Gershon, and I felt weak thinking about the fish. I can never kill anything myself, not even a cockroach. When I go to step on one, I can't. I imagine that they—cockroaches, ants, whatever—have things that they are working on, that they have dreams, that they are loved.

I approached the car and Gershon was beneath it; only his thick legs and running sneakers were exposed. Henry, with the car's hood open, was looking at the black and mangled engine.

Henry said to Gershon, "Junior has returned from his walk," and then he said to me, "Gershon can't fix the car. He said it won't make it to Florida, and the amount of money to restore it is too great. I have to find a new car. If I can't go to Palm Beach, my life may be over!"

Breasts, Please

In the weeks preceding Thanksgiving Henry began to spend almost all of his free time looking for a car. He would read the automobile ads, talk to people in all the five boroughs, make appointments to see their cars, and then call back and cancel because he would realize that their voice had sounded ugly over the phone. He didn't want to meet someone who had an ugly voice. Some leads he followed up, but with no success. He was getting very nervous that he might not find a car that he could drive to Florida.

His budget was only five hundred dollars, which naturally made things more difficult. The Skylark was still running, though he was prepared to abandon it at the side of the road any day. It was better to have it die here in New York than somewhere on the road to Florida.

The weekend before Thanksgiving, he and Gershon went to New Jersey to look for cheap cars being sold out of people's driveways. They went to Warren County, the horse country of New Jersey, and stayed with one of Henry's lady friends. Henry brought Gershon along to inspect engines.

I was very lonely without Henry around and I weakened and returned to Sally's on Saturday night. I was half-hoping and half-afraid to see Wendy. I was scared that I would go off with her again, that I wouldn't be able to say no. But she didn't show up, and neither did Miss Pepper. There were many girls, though, whom I hadn't seen in my two previous visits, and it struck me that New York was filled with Queens. I thought how you didn't see them during the day, but that they came out every night to Sally's, beautiful and exuberant, ready to perform, just like the other actresses on the Broadway stages in the neighborhood.

I stayed for two hours, and then when I left I slipped into the peep show next door. I tried to make it look as if I had no intention of going in there: as I passed the peep show's door I suddenly let myself be sucked in sideways. I was like a vaudeville actor getting the hook. I did this because if any of the transsexuals I had met were on the street, I didn't want them to see me going in there. I wanted them to think of me as this young gentleman who happened to stop in at Sally's once in a while, but if they saw me going into the peep show they might consider me just another Times Square pervert.

The peep show had a citrusy disinfectant smell and was brightly lit. There were shelves of porno videos in brightly packaged boxes and there were booths for watching videos. Towards the back of the room, the cashier sat at an elevated desk, which enabled him to keep an eye on things, like a lifeguard. Next to him was a door to a much darker room. And over the door was a red neon sign that said Live. It was meant to be pronounced as an adjective rather than a verb, but one could take it both ways.

I approached the cashier and reached up very high and bought from him a two-dollar token for the Live entertainment.

I went into the dark room. It was lit only by a red bulb, and men hovered about in the crimson shadows in front of a series of doors that were attached in a semicircle. I opened a door and entered a booth—it was like a dark closet—and I put in my token. A panel in the wall raised up and a glassless window was revealed. Its similarity to the confessional must have been a source of great distress to lapsed Catholics.

I peered through my window and there were about half a dozen women, dressed only in bikini bottoms, standing on a semicircular stage. I could see the other men's windows; their pale, hangdog faces were in the shadows, just like my own dog-face. Some women were kneeling in front of windows. It was kind of like a crazy nursing station in the middle of Manhattan where upset males could come for relief.

A large middle-aged black woman with gigantic breasts came over to my window. "You looking for company?" she asked.

I thought that was a nice way to put it. It was respectful. I immediately liked her. I nodded yes to her question. She gave me a rundown on her prices. It was two dollars to touch her breasts, three for her rear, five for her most private area, and five again to kiss her breasts. I hesitated, I wasn't sure.

"You think about it," she said kindly, and she walked away from me. I looked at the dogs in the windows. I looked at the women. My panel came down.

I went back to the cashier at his lifeguard stand and he gave me another token. I went back to my booth and I put in the token and the panel raised. The black woman was still free. I motioned to her. She came over and I extended out my two dollars, which I had prepared, and I said, "Breasts, please."

She took the money and put it on the floor. She kneeled down, the stage was elevated, and she put her breasts in my window. I saw that some of the women had little carpeted prayer benches to kneel on. I felt sympathy for the Catholics. The place was filled with visual land mines.

I put my hands beneath the woman's breasts and I held them, like someone judging fruit in a market. They were brown and enormous and incredibly heavy. What a burden they must have been for her. I wondered what she looked like in a shirt. Would I be able to discern just how big they were?

I wished that I could smother my face between her breasts, but I did feel calmed just from holding them. After being in Sally's I was a little worked up, so it was therapeutic to touch someone. I thought of touching myself. I knew that most men masturbated in the stalls, that's why the place smelled of lemon-cleanser, but I was too embarrassed to add my mess to the black floor.

I brushed my thumbs across her dark and substantial nipples. In my most little-boy voice I said, "I don't have any more money, but can I kiss them?"

"You can kiss them, honey," she said very sweetly. So I gave each nipple a little kiss, but then I got scared thinking about TB and all the other men who may have kissed her breasts. I wasn't sure if the women washed between men, probably not since they would lose time on stage, and so I stopped kissing her nipples, and it was just as well because my panel started coming down and I withdrew my hands so they wouldn't be caught. She pulled her breasts away and she said, as the last sliver of light from the stage was cut off, "You can come back to me."

She must have known I had lied about not having more money, but she didn't mind. She had let me kiss her breasts for free. And I thought she was a generous person even if she had exposed me to TB.

Cut Off Your Hair Like Salome

Henry returned late Sunday night and I had purposely stayed up. I couldn't wait for him to be back. When he came in, I asked, "Did you find a car?"

"Of course not," he said. "My life is falling apart. It's all tragedy and it all centers around automobiles . . . I need to leave for Florida immediately after I finish teaching."

"When do you finish teaching?" I asked, having forgotten the exact date.

"Ten years ago," said Henry.

I laughed and then asked, "When do you finish this semester?"

"On December sixteenth. I want to be on the road by the seventeenth . . . it's looking very precarious. We did see one nice car, a Chrysler in excellent condition. But it was twelve hundred dollars. Gershon could afford it, but not I."

I couldn't help but feel happy that Henry hadn't found a car. It gave me hope that he wouldn't leave for Florida. I could make it for a weekend, I thought, but I didn't think I could survive in New York if he was gone longer. And then I asked, "How did your lady friend like Gershon?"

"Martha? She adored him. He was a great success in New Jersey. I told her that he was a Rothschild and she believed me. She loved his hair. She said, 'I'm going to come in when you're sleeping and cut off your hair like Salome.' She wants the hair for herself, she has terrible wigs . . . I could marry Martha. She's so dumb I'd find it restful. Though I don't think she has quite enough money to keep me in the style that would compensate for my loss of freedom. And she would probably want to have sex. To lose your freedom and have sex, that's too much. Freedom is everything."

You'll Get an Erection and Then What Will I Do?

Henry went to Connecticut for Thanksgiving to be with the Wallaces. They were his friends whose daughter, Virginia, had taken in Otto Bellman. I called my great-aunt and made plans to go to her apartment in Rego Park, Queens, for the holiday. Henry told me how to get there, and she called me three times in the morning before I left, always beginning with the question, "Are you still coming?"

She lived in a tiny rent-controlled apartment on the sixth floor of an old brick apartment building. I hadn't been there for several years, but the smells of the hallways, all the different cooking going on, brought me back to the many trips I had made to my great-aunt with my parents. For most of my childhood we would go visit her every two months or so.

My great-aunt greeted me at her door, which had a New York Mets banner taped to it (we both were baseball fans), and she was smiling so happily to see me. Her face was older, a little more sun-spotted since I had seen her last, but remarkably she had almost no wrinkles and she was in her mid-eighties. And her hair, cut in a bowl shape, had very little white. It was still strawberry blond and alive; it was practically the same color as my own, except her hair wasn't thinning. She looked cute and lovable and I hugged her to my chest. She was tiny, and I stroked her hair like she was a child. I figured she needed to be touched and held. I had stayed away for too long, afraid to drive to Queens. I had maybe done a bad thing with Wendy, but in an odd way it had brought me back to my great-aunt.

As I held her, she whispered the Yiddish she used to murmur into my ear when she hugged me to *her* chest when I was a little boy, "*Shana, tottela, ziessela.*" Beautiful little one full of life.

Then we separated and she was still squeezing my arm and looking at me. She didn't know what to do with herself, she was too full of love, so she shouted gleefully, "I HATE YOU!" Then she led me into the apartment and right away she had me sit down on the couch, and on the coffee table in front of me she had already prepared gefilte fish as an hors d'oeuvre. I knew we were on a schedule, that everything had to go as she had planned.

"Start before it all dries up," she said. She was nervous. I knew that to make her happy all I had to do was whatever she told me. I started eating the gefilte fish, but she stopped me, "Wait! Go wash up."

I came back, resumed eating, and then I asked, "Aren't you going to have any?"

"No. I don't want to fill up. I'm trying to reduce," she said, and then she asked accusingly, "Why don't you use the horseradish?"

"I didn't see it," I said, and I dutifully put the red horseradish on the gefilte fish. I ate and she watched me.

We had the main meal in her little kitchen. The whole apartment was tiny and filled with her antiques, and the walls were covered with her oil paintings of Paris streets and Maine harbors, and one of rabbis hovering over a torah. Her apartment was very neat and set up to impress guests who never came. For years my great-aunt had refused to have anything to do with fellow senior citizens. She didn't want to be old like them.

174

Instead of Thanksgiving turkey we had roasted chicken, and I tried to overeat to please her, but still she said disapprovingly, "You're not a very good eater." After the meal, I lay down on the couch so that she could clean up. It was just like the old visits and now I was in the role of my father, expected to sleep after the meal.

I took my shoes off and rested my head on a pillow. Like Henry with his couch, this was her bed.

Before I could close my eyes she came into the room, stood over me, and said, "I have something to give you. My friend Lillian entered a contest. She had to subscribe to magazines for it. She didn't even know what she was checking off. I told her not to do it . . . They sent her *Playboy*! What are they thinking? She can't even get out of bed. She's ninety-three years old . . . anyway she sent me the magazine; she's always having her niece mail me things. What am I supposed to do with it?"

She went to the other end of the couch where she had a little bin for magazines and newspapers and she lifted out the glossy *Playboy*.

"You want to look at it?" she asked teasingly, and she shook it in the air and did a mock sexy wiggle of her hips.

I hadn't looked at a *Playboy* in years. The pornography I bought on occasion was never that mainstream, but I was intrigued by the *Playboy*. "All right. Why not?" I said flatly, trying to hide my enthusiasm and act as if I was above such temptations.

She went to hand it to me, but then pulled it back. There was a naughty grin on her face and she said, "Wait. You'll get an erection and then what will I do?"

She had prepared a big meal, ordered me to take a nap, had a kitchen to clean, and this all gave her a great deal of self-satisfaction; somewhere in her mind she secretly acknowledged her age, so she was proud that she had the strength to take care of me on Thanksgiving. And needing to control everything, she thought that my erection would be something else she had to take care of.

"Let me see it," I said laughing, and I sat up and made a swipe at the *Playboy*. She pulled the magazine back. "I'll be all right," I said.

She handed it to me, still smirking, and went back to the kitchen. She had always been very sexual. That was part of her bad reputation in our family. In her day, she had been a beautiful, petite redhead with unusually large breasts, a sort of Jewish Mae West.

She had been a manicurist and for most of her career she worked at a men's social club, the Harmony, on East Sixty-eighth. As a result she met a lot of married men who wanted company. Supposedly she caused a few divorces, and even one accidental death: one of her customers, while cleaning his hunting rifle, had shot his wife. Six months later, he married my great-aunt. It was one of her three marriages.

And when she wasn't married she always had a gentleman friend, as she called them, who took care of her, even up until her late sixties. But then she had one of her breasts removed because of cancer, and her last rich gentleman stopped seeing her and didn't provide for her as he had promised. She had been his lover off and on for thirty years.

She lived off social security and the savings she had managed to gather. She didn't have any men leaving their slippers under her bed anymore, which had always been her euphemism for romance.

I looked at the *Playboy* and the girls were so pretty and washed-looking that I did get an erection. My great-aunt knew what she was talking about. Only because she had put the idea in my mind that it would need taking care of did I consider going into the bathroom and masturbating, but the meal had been too heavy, so I closed my eyes and took a satisfying nap.

After I slept, we sat at the kitchen table and played Hollywood gin, three games to two hundred. She chatted about different things and told me about an Italian man who had been courting her.

"I met him in the library a few weeks ago. He was following me around. I said, 'What do you want?' He said, 'You're a pretty lady.' Then I ignored him. I don't have much confidence because of this." She opened her shirt a little and pointed at her flesh-colored breast mold in her bra; she closed her shirt. "But I kept seeing him there every day. He wouldn't leave me alone. I said, 'Listen, I've had a mastectomy.' And he said, 'I still think you're pretty.' We went for lunch. He paid, but it wasn't much. His wife's an invalid, can't speak. He has diabetes and can't get an erection, he told me. What good is he? But I let him up here one night. My tussy was burning. It burns at night. I let him put witch hazel on it with a Q-Tip. Gave him a thrill. But I'm not going to let him up here anymore. I said I needed a new television and he didn't say anything."

My great-aunt used witch hazel for all ailments, and "tussy" was her odd word for her genitals, though it could have been for the whole area, I'm not sure. The word itself was most likely a combination of the Yiddish word *tuches* (ass) and the word pussy, and so it probably represented both at once, interchangeably or collectively. Ever since I was a little boy she had talked to me about sex and her tussy, and would tell me to eat potatoes to put lead in my *petzel*.

About the Italian man, I said, not wanting her to lose a potential friend, "Maybe he doesn't have a lot of money. A television is an expensive present."

"Well, then he shouldn't expect to have a nice, clean lady friend like me."

We kept on talking and playing cards and I found myself loving my great-aunt again. After my mother had died, I had lost almost all contact with my family. I didn't respond to invitations, and then they more or less stopped coming. I was sort of pretending that I didn't have a family, which wasn't too far from the truth—I had only a handful of relatives. So it was easy to just lose touch. All my grandparents were dead even before my parents, I had never really liked my few aunts and uncles and cousins, and, anyways, I was always the oddball. But I did feel guilty that I had selfishly neglected my great-aunt except for the occasional phone call.

I was nearing the winning score of two hundred in the first game and I needed just one more card for gin. I was waiting for her to throw down her card, but she was taking her time. I started to shake my leg. "Stop that," she said. "Sick people on the subway do that. It makes me nervous."

I won the first game and she won the second. We had always been evenly matched in gin, and the third game was close. I was trying to concentrate, but she started asking me about Henry. He had answered the phone when she had called in the morning and I explained to her that he was my roommate.

"How old is he?" she asked.

"I think he's in his late sixties."

"Has he ever been married?"

"No."

"Is he a *fagala*?"

She was quick, asking the essential question, the question that I myself was patiently waiting for the answer to. But I didn't want to upset her by telling her I wasn't sure of Henry's sexuality; in her mind that would mean homosexuality. So I said, "No, he was engaged for ten years and he has lots of lady friends."

"He must have money then."

"Well, not really. They pay for everything."

"They pay? He's a loverboy! Where does he get these women?"

"They're high-society ladies. He accompanies them to dinners, to plays, you know."

"He must be loaded. For a man to not pay for a woman, that means he has money."

"Not really. He lives very frugally. He sleeps on the couch and rents me the bedroom. And he does his laundry in the tub to save money."

"When you're that cheap you have money. He has you paying the whole rent, I'm sure, and he has his lady friends paying for dinner. They probably give him something extra too. He's a real operator. A user."

My great-aunt was a classic meddler; it was the other quality, combined with her sexiness, that had made her something of a black sheep in our family. She always had a way of pitting people against one another, creating distrust, and everything she said about Henry was true or could be true, but I didn't let her comments get under my skin. Even if I paid the whole rent, it was still very cheap.

"He's not a user," I said calmly.

"The Russians are users," she said. She sensed that I didn't want her bad-mouthing him so she made a convenient segue from Henry to the Russians who had moved in great numbers to Rego Park. "I have to fight them every day," she continued. "They call One Hundred Eighth Street Little Moscow . . . They rip open packages and stand in the aisles and eat. They don't move. I have to hit them with my cart. They're filthy. The women have bosoms out to here"—she made a motion with her hand out to the middle of the table—"and they wear fur coats, but they're on food stamps! Fur coats and food stamps. They use America. My parents didn't have it like that."

My great-aunt was one hundred percent Russian-Jewish, but she couldn't stand these new immigrants. I thought it was interesting how she and Henry were alike and yet also opposites. He loved Russians. She hated Russians. He came from a rich WASP background and was an escort to older rich women. She came from a poor Jewish background and had been an escort for older rich men. They both slept on couches. They both were old, but full of life from some lost age.

Her anger about the Russians helped her playing and she started really beating me the last few hands. I would check the deck to see what cards I could have gotten, and she would admonish me, "No postmortems. No postmortems."

She won the rubber match by a large margin and we were both a little tired, so it was time for me to leave. She packed up a shopping bag full of food and wrapped everything in foil and then little plastic bags and then large plastic bags and secured it all with rubber bands. It was going to be hell getting at the food.

"It won't go bad between here and Manhattan," I said, pleading. "You don't have to wrap so much." I felt that she was trying to get rid of the hundreds of plastic bags she had saved; she was of the Depression.

"Don't tell me about food," she said.

When she was done packing the food for the next century, she filled another shopping bag with several rolls of paper towels and a dozen rolls of toilet paper, which was very generous. I hugged her good-bye, thanked her for everything, and stroked her hair again. I picked up the two bags and she walked out with me to the elevator.

"You can give a little food to loverboy," she said. "But don't let him eat everything."

"He's a nice gentleman," I said.

When I was in the elevator, I held the door open and I thanked her again for our Thanksgiving, and she said, "Come out once a month, I'll cook. And when you're not here we'll have a telephone romance."

I let the elevator doors close and we smiled at each other in the diminishing doorway until we couldn't see each other.

You've Brought So Much Toilet Paper into My Life

That night when Henry returned from his Thanksgiving in Connecticut, I presented him with all the spoils of my trip to Rego Park. I offered to share the food and of course the paper goods. He was very impressed, especially with the dozen rolls of toilet paper. We were set for a long time. I told him that my great-aunt was interested in him.

"Of course she is. All women are," he said. And I had a private fantasy that maybe he would take her out one afternoon, show her a good time, but I didn't know how I could get him to do it since he expected the woman to pay, and she expected the man to pay. It was something I would have to think about. I asked Henry how his Thanksgiving was and he revealed that it had been upsetting.

"Bellman was there. The food was excellent, but he destroyed my appetite. They are engaged! The parents are shocked, but they don't seem to blame me, which is good. They didn't bring him to the club. It would have been too embarrassing. He's totally crude. No manners. Can't hold a fork and he dresses terribly."

"When are they getting married?"

"There's no date, so there's still hope. She's forty-five and he's twenty-five. He's doing it for the green card, I'm sure. He can't be trusted. I never should have let him in here. We can only hope that she'll come to her senses, but he's corrupting everyone I know. First Gershon, and now an entire American family in Connecticut. It may all be an act of revenge against me for kicking him out. He saw me as a father figure. He's very Oedipal, but at least there might be some truth to his attraction to her. Love of the mother. He once told me he admired her breasts. You share that with Bellman, but you are much more sane."

I didn't like Henry making any connection between myself and his antagonist Bellman. He was referring to our conversation about the large-breasted granddaughter of Vivian Cudlip, with whom he had made no effort, as far as I knew, to set me up, which was also painful: if Henry thought highly of me he would have done something. But I felt pleased that at least he found me sane.

That night before going to bed, I wrote a thank-you note to my great-aunt. It was the young gentleman thing to do and I knew she would appreciate some mail. I addressed the envelope, but had no stamps. I went into Henry's room with twenty-nine cents, obeying our rule of no obligations, and I said, "Can I buy a stamp from you?"

"I'll give you a stamp."

"No, that's all right," I said. "I have the change."

"I can give you a stamp," he said sweetly. "After all, you've brought so much toilet paper into my life."

CHAPTER VII

Fleas, Cars, and Florida

Between his automobile problems and the news of Bellman's engagement, things were going wrong for Henry. More than usual. And then they got worse. One night after Thanksgiving, I was home cooking some dinner and he burst into the apartment, his keys jangling in the lock. His face was red and flushed. He slammed the door shut, not so much in anger but as if to keep the world away. He rushed past me, his raincoat lifting up, trailing him like a cape. He went into the living room and sat on his bed. He held his face in his hands.

"Gertrude, oh Gertrude," he said, "my sorrows do not come as single spies, but in whole battalions!"

"What happened?" I asked. I was alarmed. He was being dramatic, but I had never seen him quite so defeated.

"I was trying to park on Park Avenue," he said. "But the steering is getting worse, and I overshot and struck the brass rail of a canopy. Luckily, I didn't bring the whole thing down. Of course the doorman was right there. He saw the condition of the car and came over and stared at me. Probably doesn't want it parked in front of the building. I don't blame him. And then to make things worse I had to slide out the passenger door. I had to admit to him that the other door didn't work. It was all too much." Then Henry lowered his voice, and in a confessional tone to me, his roommate, his houseguest, his would-be valet and squire, he said, "And on top of it all, I have fleas!"

"What?"

"Fleas."

"You have fleas? How do you know? Maybe it's itchy skin."

"No, it's fleas. I went to a dermatologist. He took a sample off my shin and studied it under a microscope. He's an expert. It was humiliating. I left him and went and struck the brass rail and abased myself further in front of the doorman."

185

"What did the dermatologist say you should do?"

"He feels that two flea bombs and my departure should put an end to the incident—the host must leave."

"Do you think I'll get them?"

"No. They need an experienced and charming host like me. You're too young, not enough experience. But they might stay on me until they've killed me and then go for you. They're mercenaries, vultures. We can only hope that the bombs will kill them first and then my removal to Florida will ensure their demise. It's more important than ever that I get there. I must find a car!"

I resented these fleas for giving Henry more impetus to escape to Florida. He had been thwarted in all attempts to find a car, and I had been growing in confidence that he would be spending the winter with me. "Where do you think you got the fleas?" I asked.

"I think Gershon picked them up from a horse in New Jersey. They probably went into his beard, saw that I had more to offer, and started freeloading on me."

Our apartment was like a wilderness that unfortunately we kept having to bomb. We had cockroaches, which were making a resurgence; we had several families of pigeons who lived on our windowsills and moaned all day long, and then with great fanfare they would fly away as if on an urgent migration; and now we had fleas.

That night I went to get a drink of water before going to sleep. Henry was sitting on his bed in his blue bathing suit and tuxedo shirt and he was consulting an old envelope with writing on it.

"What's that?" I asked.

"It's my list of things to do. What's 'trousers' doing on the list? Oh, yes, I have to have them repaired. Well, as long as one thing gets done each day. What did I do today? I went to the dermatologist. Still haven't done the income taxes. They're going to put me in jail in four months. They'll freeze my bank account. I've already started putting my money into traveler's checks so they can't get at it."

"Can't you find someone to do your income taxes for you?"

"I can't afford it. And all my receipts that someone would need to work with were in that suitcase stolen in Poland."

"I'm sorry about all this," I said.

"Well, it never was easy, and it only gets harder . . . If one day doesn't work, try another," said Henry bravely, stringing two of his personal proverbs together for extra courage.

He put the list down on the coffee table next to his bed and picked up a bottle of spray cologne. He sprayed his ankles and the smell was overwhelmingly sweet.

"Why are you doing that?" I asked.

"The fleas begin at the feet and move upward. I can only hope that the cologne will stop them, like a moat, and they will drown. I apologize for having brought them into our lives."

I noticed that there was a pair of boxer shorts stretched around his pillow. "Why do you have underwear on your pillow?" I asked.

"The fleas, of course. They are directing my every move. I am forced to wash everything constantly. I have no dry pillowcases."

I had noticed that Henry had been doing a lot of laundry in the bathtub, but I didn't know why. He had kept his suspicions secret. I guess he didn't want to falsely alarm me about the fleas until he had a professional opinion.

"What a life," Henry said, and he put in one of his earplugs. "Fleas, automobile problems, taxes. Can't make it to Florida. It's all too much, something has to give. And my eye mask is still missing. My life is becoming unbearable . . . It's a veil of tears." He bandaged his oxford shirt around his eyes, put in his other earplug, and seemed happier. He said to me, "I am off to the land of nod."

"Well, take solace in your dreams," I said. I didn't like to see him so beleaguered.

"Six dollars?" he asked.

"No. Solace. Take solace in your dreams," I said loudly, so he could hear me through his plugs. I was standing right near him.

"Dreams? I don't want dreams. I want oblivion. My dreams have no solace. I only have one dream. I'm always about to go on stage and I don't know my lines. And the curtain is always rising."

The Whole City Has Fleas

The next day I was at work and in the morning I had a brief but upsetting conversation with Mary. She was standing near my cubicle and she was wearing a thick, off-white cable sweater and a dark blue wool skirt and she said, "Oh, shit."

Hearing this utterance was exciting enough, and then I saw that she was stroking her calf. I knew what the problem was, but I asked, "What's the matter?"

"I just bought these panty hose and now they have a run."

"Oh, I'm sorry," I said, and she smiled at me for my empathy and then she left my cubicle area. I had purposely lured her into saying "panty hose," but I didn't realize how much it would bother me. It was just from hearing those first two syllables come out of her mouth: pant-ee. Panty.

For me it was a term of intimacy. And she didn't know it, of course, but I felt that by her saying panty she had acknowledged her sexuality to me: that underneath her blondness, her sweaters, her intelligence was a woman who was naked in the mornings, who rolled on panty hose over smooth perfect legs all the way up to her tussie.

It was too much to contemplate. I couldn't get the image out of my mind, the hose going up the legs, and this was accompanied in my thoughts by a whisper of the word panty.

I didn't know what to do with myself. I thought of going to the Barbizon Hotel. I went there at least once a day to use the bathroom. I didn't like to use the office toilet because I was very self-conscious. There was a can of deodorizing spray, but I felt that this was an admission of guilt and actually made the odors worse. The other people in the office used the spray and I didn't judge them, but I was afraid that they wouldn't show me the same tolerance. And besides odor I was also worried about noises. I thought that my officemates could hear me in there, even with the exhaust fan. There was also the problem of the false accusation. If I went in there and someone else had raised a stink and I didn't do anything objectionable, but as I came out and someone else had to go in—Mary, for example—I would be falsely accused. So I practically avoided the office toilet altogether. I wanted to be brave and not have toilet hangups, but they were too deeply ingrained. So I'd fallen into the habit of going to the Barbizon and using their toilet, which I enjoyed. It was like sneaking into a show with Henry.

And now after Mary and the whole panty hose incident, I was threatening myself with going to the Barbizon and masturbating in the stall if I didn't stop thinking about her. But it was only a threat. I didn't carry it out. What if the Barbizon security found me? I stayed at my desk and I reassured myself with my usual response to Mary: "I can just go to Sally's."

I had stopped in there a few times since that Saturday night when Henry was in New Jersey. I only went when I was sure that Henry wouldn't be home so that he wouldn't know I was out. Miss Pepper was sometimes there, but never Wendy. I didn't go off with any new girls, but I liked how they all put their arms around me and told me I was handsome. Then after Sally's I liked to go in the peep show, which I thought of as the breast store or the breast show, and touch the women in there. I began to associate the smell of the place, the lemon disinfectant, with pleasure. I had broken down, sunk to another level of shamelessness, and like the other men, I would masturbate in my stall as I touched the women. It was a whole routine—excite myself in Sally's and relieve myself in the breast store. Then when it was all done, I would leave Forty-third Street and I usually felt sick about my behavior for a few days, but never sick enough not to return.

By the middle of the day the word *panty* had finally left my mind, though it had lingered for hours like an annoying song. The rest of the afternoon, I had a headache and I could feel a depression following me like a shadow that wanted to overtake me and crush me.

When I headed home, I went to the very first car of the subway to try and cheer myself up. I loved to ride in the first car and look out the front window and watch the tracks. Sometimes I had to share the window with other people, though most subway riders didn't seem to know about the front window, how interesting it was. That night I shared it with a Hasidic man. We stood side by side, being very careful not to touch each other, and we stared out together and I said to him, "This is great, isn't it?"

But he didn't answer me. I imagined it was because to him I was a non-Jew, unholy, but he did smile at me, acknowledging that we were having a good time, while all the other subway riders were missing out.

My mood was lifted. Staring out the window was hypnotic: we raced ahead, careening on the narrow rails; the white headlights barely illuminated the dark tunnel in front of us; the rusted metal beams along the ceiling and walls were like ribs. I thought of the workers, the diggers, sixty years earlier, some of whom must have died when the earth would unexpectedly collapse.

The train hurtled along and filled the whole narrow passage, and then suddenly the platforms appeared in yellow light. They looked like faraway stages and the people waiting looked like an uneven chorus line. As the train would get closer a few people would always spot me in the front window, my forehead against the glass, and we would make eye contact, but they always looked at me with suspicion. What's he doing in the front window? they must have wondered, Is there something wrong with him?

But for once I didn't care what anybody thought; I was an intrepid explorer, an adventurer. Staring out that window is something that always brings me pleasure. I understand perfectly the boy who stole the A train and drove it from Brooklyn to Manhattan. In the city, the subway tunnels are an available otherworld, more easily reached than the ocean or the sky.

The Hasidic man got off at Eighty-sixth Street without even a nod of the head. I would have liked some acknowledgment, but I did have the window to myself for one stop.

I left the train at Ninety-sixth Street and I walked down the steep hill from Lexington to Second Avenue. Henry had told me that Manhattan was an Indian word that meant island of hills, though he liked to think that we lived at the base of an alp. It made our life seem more European. As I approached our building, I hoped that Henry would be home.

Near the garbage cans next to our door, where rats often rooted about, I saw what looked like the black metal frame of Henry's beloved couch. Something was going on. When I climbed the stairs to our floor I saw the mattress from the couch leaning against the wall. I knew that something extraordinary must have occurred.

I went into the apartment and Henry was standing in the living room admiring a white couch with light brown stains, which was against the wall where the old couch had been.

"What's going on?"

"I've thrown away the old couch. We are sorry to see it go, but its time has come. I haven't set the flea bombs yet, but that couch was obviously infested and I can't stand to spend another night on it."

"Where did you get this new couch?"

"I found it on the street."

"Do you think that's smart?" I asked. "We already have fleas."

"It was on Park Avenue, a very good address. I found it near the canopy I hit last night."

"Park Avenue could have fleas . . . How did you get it over here? Gershon?"

"No, he was out bicycling away his sex drive. I just found him now to work on it. He oiled it and tightened a few screws. To get it up here I recruited that little Irish bum from in front of the pizza place. I gave him five dollars. He collapsed in the hallway. I thought he died. His liver may have failed. He's probably too weak now to get drunk on the money he earned. But I can't concern myself with these things."

I couldn't believe that Henry and that bum, a little red-haired fellow who looked to be only in his thirties, had managed to carry that couch up four flights of stairs. I figured that Henry had gone into an irrational pique about the fleas and had taken it out on the old couch by throwing it away. And he had been so energized by his anger that he was able to carry up another couch. He was truly remarkable. I said, "I am very impressed that you carried it up here."

"Well, my dancing keeps me fit, though I may have ruptured something and will probably die in my sleep."

"Is it a pull-out couch?"

"Yes, and Gershon arranged it so that it opens very nicely. And it has a very good mattress."

Henry then began to cover the couch with white plastic garbage bags from the supermarket. "Is the plastic to protect you from the couch or the couch from you?" I asked.

"Both," he said. "I'll keep the plastic on for a few months. That should sterilize it. And I have a plastic sheet for the mattress. The dermatologist told me that the fleas can't survive on plastic. They can't survive on anything. Well, they could last on a curtain rod for a little while, but they need to be on a human."

When the couch was adequately covered with plastic bags Henry sat down on it with a look on his face as if he was wine-tasting. He came out of his reflections and said, "You know, when I picked up the couch with the bum, there were two dogs in a window looking at me. Their eyes were very sad. It must have been their couch. Then they started barking. I think they were trying to warn me that it has fleas! There's no winning for us poor. I have exchanged one flea-ridden couch for another. It could be an epidemic. The whole city has fleas!"

He Saw a Piece of Cheese and Made Havoc with It

The next morning I was at work and the receptionist buzzed me on the intercom. "A Dr. Harrison on line one," she said.

It was Henry. He only referred to himself as a doctor when he felt he needed to. He had told me that he had received a Docteur d'Université in dramaturgy from the University of Paris in the 1950s. Of his time in France he had said to me once, sentimentally, "When they had the communal piss trough in the Louvre, that's when Europe was still worth visiting. When they took that away the culture died."

I pushed the button for line one and said, "Henry?"

"Louis?"

"Yes, it's me. Are you all right? Is there a problem?" Henry had never called me at work during all the time I had been renting my room from him.

"I apologize for disturbing you, but I am going to set off a flea bomb and you must not return before six o'clock, otherwise you'll die."

"Thank you for the warning," I said.

"There's a chance I might set if off wrong and kill myself."

"Well, I hope not. You did all right with the roach bomb."

"In the event of my death contact my cousin in Charleston, South Carolina, Philip Harrison. He's a foot surgeon, but he's retired; he was always confusing which foot to operate on. He'll want me buried in potter's field, but tell him my pension fund from the college will pay for the funeral."

"Fine . . . but you're not going to die." I didn't like to think of Henry dying.

"And there's to be no ceremony of any kind. A single priest may follow the coffin . . . afterward they may have a short memorial mass in Latin. And the sermon has to be in Latin. Have it at seven p.m., that way no one has to get up early . . . I should put this in writing, but you'll remember."

He was enjoying this fantasy, so I said, "I'll see what I can do."

"What are you doing tonight?" he asked. "I have two lady friends who need escorting to an opening at the Historical Society."

"Well, I . . ."

"It might advance you socially. And there'll probably be food."

"I'd love to." I was finally getting my chance to be an escort, a rosen knight.

"We'll pick them up at seven-thirty."

"I'll see you at home then sometime after six."

"Yes, but not before. I don't want to call your great-aunt and tell her I murdered you by flea bomb."

As I headed for the subway that night after work, I saw the hairy-chested, homeless man again, who was still without a shirt. It was early December and cold, but he didn't seem to notice. He smiled at me as I approached. "Are you going to help me today?" he asked as if he remembered me, and he extended to me his open palm.

"I don't know," I said.

"Why not?" he asked, and he smiled at me. His eyes were playful, intelligent.

"The last time you saw me you told me that I was losing my hair."

"You are, so what? Are you going to help me?"

"Do you really think I'm losing it?"

"Bend your head down," he said. He was very authoritative and I followed his instructions. He got close to me and I felt compromised. He was very dirty, though he didn't smell bad. The whole thing was crazy, but going bald at a young age makes you desperate for counsel.

"You can see right through it," he said. "It's going. Get a rug."

I lifted my head and looked at his hair, at the odd dark strands forming a hedge at the top of his forehead. "Are those plugs?" I asked. I wanted to let him know that I wasn't the only bald one around here.

"Yeah, I used to be rich. I could get plugs. I could get anything."

"What happened?"

"Cocaine. Two hundred and fifty thousand dollars up my nose. I was a rich Arab Jew from the Eastern Parkway, like Crazy Eddie, and we both lost it. I had money. I had women. Lots of 'em. You should have seen me."

A fellow Jew. I had never met a Jewish bum before. I liked him. I liked talking frankly with him. But a pizza man, standing inside the door of his restaurant, smoking a cigarette, had been listening to our conversation, and he didn't like the homeless man to be in front of his establishment. Maybe he didn't like Jews. He interjected himself into our discussion and said meanly, "So what. Look at you now."

The homeless man acted like he didn't notice or care, but he must have because his face darkened and he suddenly walked away from me without saying anything. I caught up to him and gave him a dollar. He just grabbed it, didn't thank me, and kept on moving.

When I arrived at home there was a slight bitter odor from the flea bomb, but not too strong, not as bad as the roach bomb. And more striking than the smell was the fact that the living room had been rearranged again. The old couch was back! We now had two couches. Henry had pushed a lot of clutter around to make room. Some new patches of cleaner-looking orange carpet were visible.

Henry was sitting on his throne-chair and before I could even say hello, he said to me, "Who wrote: 'Here lies one whose name was writ in water'?" He liked to test me on famous quotes and usually I had no idea who the author was. My only correct answer had been Oscar Wilde. I made a guess. I said, weakly, "Whitman?"

"No, I don't think Whitman cared about immortality," Henry said. "He just wanted to be left alone to scratch his belly."

"Well, who wrote it?" I asked.

Henry yelled at me, "Keats, of course! . . . What was said on W. C. Fields' tombstone?"

"Your mind is really on death today," I said. "It doesn't look like the flea bomb killed you."

"Don't avoid the question."

I was exasperated. "I have no idea," I said.

Henry yelled at me condescendingly, "Keats and W. C. Fields! You've missed the main cultural movements of our time! His tombstone said, 'I'd rather be in Philadelphia.'"

I was sufficiently demoralized, but also a little angry, so I put a question to Henry to get him on the defensive. "Why did you bring the old couch back?"

"I missed it," he said, somewhat embarrassed, and then he added, so as not to seem overly sentimental, "And that new one is too much of a bother to open every night. It can be our guest bed. Or if we get an indentured servant from Russia, they can sleep there. How much do you think it would cost? The wage in Moscow must be one dollar a day. That would be seven dollars a week. We could split it. Only three-fifty each. Not bad." He raised his eyebrows at me, hoping to entice me with the economy of it.

"They would escape," I said. "They'd go work at The Salt of the Earth and wash dishes."

"No, they'd be illegal. They would have to stay with us. That would be our control. And if we got a woman she could stay in your bed." He was trying to further seduce me into the idea, and also apologize for the difficult Keats and W. C. Fields test.

"Maybe we could get a wet nurse then," I said, half wanting to playfully annoy Henry and half giving over to fantasy.

"You're depraved. An American sex maniac," he said, and he was silent for a moment, pondering the notion of a wet nurse. Then he said, "I should think that Russian milk would be very potent."

"Yes, because of Chernobyl," I said, and we both laughed.

I wanted to be rested for Henry's ladies, so I went to lie down, and Henry came into my room on his way to the shower. His orange towel was draped over his shoulder and he was in a pair of faded yellow boxer shorts.

He paused at the end of my bed, looked at me gravely, and said, "This evening is very important to me. One of the ladies you will meet is Lois Huber. I've stayed in her guest bedroom down in Palm Beach for the last four years. She's the one I went to Europe with this summer, but we had a falling out when I insulted her and I haven't seen her since we came back."

"I'll try to make a good impression," I said.

"Well, we both have to do more than that. I don't have a car that can make it to Florida, but I haven't given up hope that I will find one, and so it's crucial that I get my room back in Palm Beach. I don't really need her down there. I have my tent. I can sleep on the beach. But there would be no way to reach me for invitations. A phone is necessary. I'm out with Lois, but I have to get back in."

"How are you going to do this?" I asked as I moved into a sitting position on my bed.

"I have two plans. The first one involves you. Your youth might have a powerful effect on her. It could help to lower her guard.

She's oversexed. You have nothing else to offer, but that's all right as long as you have youth."

"I don't know about this," I said. "I don't know if I'm up for it."

"You don't have to sleep with her. You just have to smile and be pleasant."

"I didn't think that I'd have to sleep with her, I just don't know if I'll find the right things to say."

"You don't have to say anything. You just have to be young. It will distract her. She invited me, I think, as a test. She said she would only accept constructive criticism. So if I am very good to her she might take me back. Or it could be a trick to tease me into thinking I have a chance at my old room and then reject me as revenge for my insults."

"How *did* you insult her when you were in Europe?"

"I told her that she has no taste in clothes, that she's vulgar in her response to things, that she has no sense of social strata, that her ass is too big, that she's saddle-back, and that she's probably a moral imbecile . . . I think that's constructive criticism. She should take that as a foundation and build up. She can go for classes at an etiquette school."

"You really should apologize. That's an incredible string of insults," I said.

"I can't. It's all true. But I won't criticize her further. That will be a form of apology and I will present you. You are being used. But that's how it works. In return you'll get free hors d'oeuvres and drinks, and maybe dinner."

I was afraid that I would let Henry down, but I said to him bravely, "I will do my best for you."

"Our biggest problem is the other woman, Meredith Lagerfeld. She used to be a good friend. She knows I'm out with Lois and she's trying to replace me. She wants my room in Palm Beach. She's been angling to get invited down there for years. She's putting all her charms to work, promising Lois that she'll introduce her to men. The only thing she can get is old fruits. She's the worse type of social climber. She could never make it in Palm Beach. She'd be on the D list."

"What list are you on?"

"I move from list to list. A to Z. I go wherever there is a free meal, as long as the people are interesting . . . I guess I'm on the A list, but I wouldn't say I'm a mad success. You never know. One year you're in, the next year you're out . . . And what we must make sure is that Lagerfeld is permanently out. While you are softening up Lois, I will keep Lagerfeld occupied. Then we'll switch women. Lois thinks Lagerfeld can get her men, but I can offer her something Lagerfeld can't: a part in one of my plays!"

"Which play?" I asked.

"The George Eliot play, *The Dead Hand*. I found the title page when I threw the couch out last night and it gave me the idea."

"Where's the rest of the play?"

"It must be in one of the valises in the kitchen. I'll find it."

"Do you think *Henry and Mary Are Always Late* is in a suitcase?"

"No, it was on the floor in the spring during the Bellman era. He's probably having it produced in Yugoslavia and getting rich off the proceeds. Some day we'll find it, or he'll confess to stealing it. But *The Dead Hand* is perfect for Lois. I'll set up a reading in Palm Beach and let Lois be George Eliot. She's always wanted to be an actress and she's taken a great interest in my work over the years, and my offering of this role is my best chance to win back my room!"

Henry took a shower and then I quickly washed up and began to dress. I put on my gray pants, blue blazer, white shirt, and a good tie, and Henry was putting on the same outfit in his room. He called out and said, "Our strengths are your youth and my play. The combination of the two could do it."

"I don't know how youthful I look," I said. "You know I'm balding."

"No you're not," Henry said. "You're obsessed with your hair." He came into my room, half-dressed in pants and T-shirt, and he said, "Let me look at it. Bend your head down." It was incredible. Two inspections by different kinds of madmen in one day. I had combed my hair back so that it didn't readily appear that I was thinning. It was my tricky combing and my blondness that fooled most people. But by bending my head down I exposed to Henry, as I had a little while earlier to the homeless Jew, the weakness in the middle of my scalp.

"Yes, I see," said Henry. "It's very odd. You're not losing it at the front or the back, but in the middle . . . I think you have mange."

I snapped my head back. I said, "I don't have mange! Just forget about it." I was upset and Henry knew it. He tried to patch things up. "Well, your face is young," he said. "As human beings go you're not bad looking. From the profile you look like George Washington." This mollified me completely. It was the first compliment regarding my looks that Henry had ever given me.

He went back to his room to continue dressing. I was finished and sat in the kitchen to watch him. He took out the ironing board, placed it across the stove, and ironed a pair of thin gray socks. I asked him why and he said, "To dry them. They are wet from the shower. The flea bomb may not have killed all the little vampires and they are particularly fond of my ankles. So I must continue to sterilize my socks."

When the socks were done, he said, "Now which dirty shirt will fit? That is the next question." Finally, he was dressed, having chosen a shirt whose stain was hidden by his tie. Then he had me smell both his blue blazers.

"You are the royal smeller," he said. "Lois has complained in the past about the odor of my clothes. She doesn't realize that filth is the privilege of the aristocracy, but I need to please her tonight."

Henry was really trying to butter me up since he saw me as instrumental to his success that evening. First, I looked like George Washington, and now my sense of smell was being appreciated, rather than mocked.

I chose one of Henry's blazers as smelling less full of life's experience than the other. He gratefully put it on, but as a precaution dabbed some cologne around the lapels. We were ready to leave, but then with great despair the issue of the keys, as always, reared its ugly head. "The keys. The keys are gone," Henry said. "That's it. They've disappeared. Last seen heading for Butte, Montana."

The keys were found next to the phone and we left. As we headed down the stairs, Henry gave a groan. "What's the matter?" I asked. We stopped at the second-floor landing.

"These pants are cutting off circulation. The sperm will be killed."

"What did you say?" I asked, amazed.

"The sperm will be choked."

"I thought you were retired from procreation," I said.

"No. I am at the height of my powers."

I was shocked. Henry was always preaching chastity. So I couldn't believe this sudden mention of sperm. I think he was in a good mood because we were going out. He felt alive, but still, I pressed him on the issue. I said, "You told me that you were retired from sex when I interviewed for the room."

"Retired? No. The word was retarded." Henry laughed at himself and I laughed too, and then we descended the remaining stairs and left the building. I loved it whenever Henry spoke about sex. I couldn't get enough of it. Each time it came up, I felt that I was closer to knowing the truth about him. As we headed for Henry's car, I was incredibly happy that we were together. I didn't envy the world for anything.

We took the Skylark, though I had offered to drive the Parisienne, but he never wanted to go in my car. He didn't say it, but I knew that he didn't trust my driving ability.

I was alarmed to be in Henry's Buick, but my desire to be with him was greater than my fear. As we careened down Fifth Avenue, he said, "The steering could go at any moment, killing everyone near us. I have to try and rectify this with my conscience. I will warn you and you can jump out. I plan to drive into a wall, sacrificing myself. It's the least I can do."

I kept my hand on the door handle, but the car seemed to be all right. On our way to the museum, we crossed through Central Park with the dark, lonesome trees above us on both sides, and Henry said, "I must tell you that Lagerfeld is quite enormous. She can barely walk, she has a cane. That's why she has stayed friends with me all these years, because of my cars. I can give her rides. But even without me she goes everywhere. A free concert in the Bronx, a play in Brooklyn, if it's free she's there. Especially if there's food. And if you need an invitation to something she can still get in. With her Brünnhilde locks flowing and her cane she'll go up and say, 'I haven't had time to respond to my invitation.' That's how she's managed to get us into many things. We've been sneaking into parties and plays and operas for years. Sometimes she claims to be a journalist with the *Yorkville Ladies' Home Journal*; that also works very well."

The way Henry spoke of her I knew that he must still admire her, despite her attempt to steal his room in Palm Beach. He continued talking about her. "Her heart was broken when she was sylph-like. She probably was very beautiful then. Her face isn't bad and her hair is good . . . Well, we all have something, even Lagerfeld. Of course some people have nothing, but they have the consolation of knowing that they can't get any uglier as they get older."

We parked the car on Central Park West and went into the Historical Society building, which was near the massive granite American History Museum. As we rode the elevator to the appropriate floor, Henry said to me, "Don't expect the A crowd."

The opening was in a long, elegant room with a high ceiling and a beautiful wooden floor. We paused at the room's entrance and read a card on the door which explained that this was an opening for a recently donated collection of nineteenth-century portraits of individuals and families of the Hudson River Valley. After reading the card we saw that at the far end of the room there was a long table arrayed with fruits, crackers, cheeses, and meats.

"Oh good, there's food," Henry said, and then asked, "Who said, 'He saw a piece of cheese and made havoc with it'?"

"I have no idea," I said dejectedly, missing out once again on an opportunity to show Henry that I was bright.

"Hazlitt about Wordsworth," he said, and then we advanced hungrily to the table, making our way through the small crowd. There were about thirty people and no one was looking at the paintings hung on the wall. They were all clustered in small groups, sipping wine from clear plastic cups.

I was scanning quickly for anyone beautiful, but it was very much an older, grayish collection of people. Henry whispered to me, "There's Lagerfeld. She's at the food now. Blocking the whole thing. We'll be lucky if there's anything left."

When we approached the table Lagerfeld's back was to us—she was leaning over a tray—and Henry said politely, "Meredith, you look lovely tonight." As she slowly turned, with a piece of cheese in hand, to see who it was, Henry was able to slip past her girth just enough so that he could get at the cheese himself; while he did this he continued complimenting her. "That's a lovely cape you're wearing," he said.

"Oh, it's you, Henry," she said. "I'm happy to see you."

"Allow me to introduce Louis Ives," Henry said. "My house-guest, and a native of the great state of New Jersey." I was glad that Henry often expressed his admiration for New Jersey. He thought that the people there were honest and that the automobiles they sold were inexpensive.

Lagerfeld demurely offered to me her large but soft hand, and I held it gently. She smiled at me with great gaps in her teeth, and she said, "So nice to meet you."

She was quite large, about five foot nine, but because she was a woman she seemed even taller. She was also quite wide and she was wearing a black cape and beneath the cape a diaphanous black top, which was darkened over her breasts, but then became more sheer as it went down, and I could see, as if through a veil, the flesh of her belly. She wore a long red skirt and she leaned on her cane. The skin of her face was white and pure. Her hair was a lustrous strawberry blond and flowed to her shoulders. Her eyes were magnified strangely by her glasses and they seemed to shift about, scanning the crowd for someone on the A list, or at least the B list.

She said to Henry, "The George Gillies are here. She's involved with Lincoln Center and is having a big party next Thursday. We should try to talk to her." Henry was greedily preparing himself another cheese-and-cracker sandwich—one was already crumbling in his mouth—and he said, "Yes, we must get invited. But where is Lois? I don't see her."

Lagerfeld pointed to the far corner, past the crowd milling around the drinks table, to a solitary lady looking at the pictures.

"Louis and I will say hello to her," Henry said, "and then I will circulate back around to you and we can pursue the Gillies. I will tell them I know Vivian Cudlip."

We left Meredith and stopped at the wine table. There was an attractive young girl pouring the wine and Henry said to her, "Are you Russian?" He said it in a flirtatious way and the girl blushed and said, "I'm American."

"I will always think of you as Russian," Henry said and he smiled at her. I tried to smile at her too, but she didn't seem to notice me. She was still blushing from Henry's remark. He was looking very handsome and he was acting like a gentleman-rake. We took two glasses of wine from her and stepped away from the table. Henry said, "The people here are very dreary. That Russian bartendress is the only attractive woman. And the men are the walking dead."

We each took a quick sip of our wine and then Henry said, "Now on to Lois and our real mission." We walked towards her— she was still looking at the pictures—and Henry said to me, "Oh, God, look at that dress. Where does she find them? I told her that she has to get dresses that fool the eye. Everything she wears draws attention to her most glaring defects." Her dress was a tightly wrapped leopard-print affair, which did highlight her somewhat swollen rear, which in turn made her back indeed curve like a saddle.

She was gazing at a portrait of a family and even before saying hello to her, Henry said, "There's a dwarf in that picture!"

Lois looked at him and said, "Only you would think that child is a dwarf. It's not a dwarf, it's a small boy."

"It's a dwarf, obviously a dwarf. Or a child who is a dwarf, but will never grow."

"It's a lovely child," said Lois. "You always try to make things ugly."

"I have an eye for the grotesque!" said Henry, and I could see he was almost ready to insult her, they had so quickly launched into an argument, but then he reined himself in. He must have thought to himself: FLORIDA! He peered closely at the painting and said, "Upon further inspection, I must agree with you. It is not a dwarf. It is a child with a large head, but not an unattractive head. Speaking of children, let me introduce my young houseguest, Louis Ives. He has moved to New York to find himself, and at the moment he is involved with magazine publishing. Louis, this is Lois. Your names are meant to be spoken together. They roll off the tongue."

We shook hands and Lois gave me a very pretty smile. Henry suddenly said that he was famished and needed more cheese, and so he quickly took his leave from us, but before doing so he fixed me with his eyes to remind me of the importance of my task.

Lois and I walked to the next picture. I was very aware that she had lots of money and I was hoping that she would like me.

"These are very good paintings, I think," I remarked.

"I don't like them," she said, "but I think it's a shame if nobody looks at them."

"Yes," I said, "I see what you mean."

I hadn't done very well with my opening comment and so as we walked to the next picture, I said, "I like your dress very much. It's interesting."

My tone was sweet and sincere and Lois smiled. She thanked me for complimenting her dress. She was a very short woman and her face was pretty. Her nose was tiny and nicely shaped, though slightly square at the tip. I suspected a nose job, and a face-lift, because it seemed as if she should have some wrinkles, but didn't. Her lips were painted a gaudy red and she wore a frosted blond wig, which was tipped rather low on her forehead. I figured that she was in her mid-seventies. Being with her made me long for my grandmothers, both of whom had died many years before. But at least I still had my great-aunt.

And while Lois and I stood in front of a painting, and I thought of my grandmothers, I felt a sudden compulsion to hold her hand. I looked at her fingers. They were bony and the nails were a gaudy red, but her tininess made her seem sweet and fragile.

"What exactly do you do with magazines?" she asked, oblivious to my tender feelings.

"I work on the marketing side of things for an environmental journal called *Terra*. I'm just getting started. But I think I'd prefer to eventually be an editor or a writer someday," I said, playing the dutiful, ambitious grandson.

"Henry's a very good writer, you know. Have you read his plays?"

"I haven't," I said, "but I sense that they must be very smart."

"I've read them. He's a good playwright, but he can be a very rude man, you know."

I could see that she was wanting to open up to me already. "Well, he can be a bit cranky sometimes," I said.

"He insulted me terribly this summer. Meredith suggested that I should give him a second chance tonight, but I don't need friends who criticize me the way he did."

"I'm surprised," I said. "He speaks very highly of you." I wished at that moment that Henry could have heard how expertly I was helping him.

"Well, we were good friends once. Platonic." She looked at me to make sure that this point was perfectly clear and then continued talking. "He was a very good companion while my husband was dying. He passed away last spring. Then Henry and I went to Europe in the summer and he turned on me." She said this bitterly and angrily.

"I'm sorry to hear about your husband," I said, hoping to take her mind off her anger with Henry.

"It's all right. I would have divorced him five years ago, but he took ill so I never had the papers served. But then right before his last collapse he was very mean to me and so when he was on his deathbed I told him that he could go the last mile without me."

She was a tough old lady, and I think she was telling me all this knowing full well that I would report it back to Henry. I felt a little scared of her and I had lost all desire to hold her hand and play the dutiful grandson. I didn't think Henry had much chance of getting his room back in Florida. We looked at some more paintings together and then we were joined by Lagerfeld and Henry.

"This is a terrible crowd," said Henry. "I think they're a group of shut-ins who all decided through kismet to come out tonight."

"There's another opening at the Whitney at nine o'clock," said Lagerfeld. "We'll have a much more interesting crowd there. I only have three invitations, but you can talk your way in, Henry. Tell them you're a friend of Vivian Cudlip's. She's on the board. You should be able to get in that way."

"This crowd is dead," said Henry. "But the crowd at the Whitney will be depraved."

"Stop complaining," Lois said.

Since we had time before the Whitney opening they decided that we should have dinner at Lois's. They were all, including Lois, very cheap, and eating in was the cheapest option. Lois was to make a salad and Henry and I were to pick up a ready-made roasted chicken. We left the museum and Henry and I walked the two ladies to Lois's old white Mercedes. He held the driver's door open for Lois and I aided Lagerfeld. She held on to my arm and I steadied her as she lowered herself into the car. There was a brief moment of imbalance and she stared up at me pitifully with her magnified eyes. I felt bad that her heart had been broken when she was sylphlike.

Once the ladies were off, Henry and I returned to his car and we recrossed the park. I gave him a full report of everything Lois had said, how she had opened up very quickly, telling me about abandoning her husband for the last mile, and Henry shook his head. "It's looking very bad," he said. "She's equating me with her dead husband as yet another man who's wronged her. She doesn't realize how much she needs me down in Palm Beach. Without me she won't get any invitations, she has no idea how it works . . . And it's very interesting that it was Lagerfeld behind tonight's invitation. She only does something for you if she thinks she can get something out of you. That's what makes her a good friend, she's not just a taker, she does give a little . . . Well, we must press on. Your youth has failed, but I do appreciate your efforts. It gives me a better idea of what I'm up against. And we still have my play. All is not lost."

I was glad to be of some help and I was enjoying our adventure. We went to a chicken place on Lexington Avenue and it was very busy and so we waited on line. Henry asked one of the chicken servers if there was a bathroom he could use. When he was informed that there was no toilet for the public, he told me he couldn't wait, that the cheap wine from the opening was giving him bladder pain and that he was going to step outside for a moment. He left me on line, rushed out the door, and then returned rather quickly, which I found strange. Then it was our turn to order a chicken and Henry paid for it and very grandly refused, with a wave of his hand, my offer of money. "You are a paid informant," he said. "This chicken is your fee."

He handed me the bag with the chicken and we stepped outside. I looked to see if there was a bar next door that Henry must have slipped into to use the bathroom, but there were no bars or restaurants near at hand. We began to walk towards the car and I said, "Where did you find a bathroom? I don't see any bars around here."

"I went in the street."

"I can't believe it. Where? In a doorway?"

"No, right there, by the bumper of that car."

The car was right in front of the chicken place! And this was a well-lit, well-to-do part of Lexington Avenue, and it was only around eight-thirty in the evening.

"How can you pee on the street?" I asked. "Somebody could have seen you. You could have been arrested!"

"You have to be more aristocratic," Henry said. "Aristocrats know that they can piss on the streets."

"But weren't you worried about being seen? How did you do it?"

"Well, you have to be discreet. You walk out into traffic as if you're going to cross. But you think better of it and so you start stepping backward. Meanwhile secretly your pants are undone and you put your hands in the pockets of your raincoat and hold the coat out in front of you in a wide arc to act as a shield. And so as you walk backward, preferably between two parked cars, you piss and no one knows what you're doing. And the walking backward keeps you from pissing on your own legs and from walking back over your own piss."

While Henry told me all this, he gave a quick demonstration of how to hold open one's raincoat (I was also wearing my raincoat) and how to walk discreetly backward. Then we went to the car and drove over to Lois's building.

During the elevator ride up to Lois's floor the chicken fumes were very strong and then Henry suddenly said with urgency, "Don't say anything about the fleas. Because then if she gets them she'll know they're from us and I'll never get my room back . . . I'll try not to sit on her couches. The dining room chairs are made of wood, that should be all right . . . She has a dog! I'll try to give them to the dog. That will save us. He'll want to be petted. He likes me very much."

Lois's apartment was large and high in her building, with a fine southward view that let me see the million lights of Manhattan. I felt like a rich person looking out the window. The apartment's decor was flowery and pillowy and much of the furniture was surfaced in mirror. It aspired to be feminine and pretty, and yet like Lois, in her leopard-print dress, there was a hard, cheap edge to it.

Her dog, named Lovie, was tiny and had silky long brown hair, and was the type of breed that continually trembles. He raced all around yelping when Henry and I arrived. And he was wearing a plastic cowl around his neck and head, which made him look like a Victorian woman. After greeting the ladies, Henry said of the dog, "He's wearing a royal bib!" And he scooped up the dog and stroked him affectionately, hoping to transfer the fleas as quickly as possible, while Lovie squirmed.

Then Henry, after releasing the dog from his flea-ridden hands, followed Lois to the kitchen to assist her in setting the dining room table. Lovie resumed his racing and yelping, and Lois yelled at him, "Lovie, go to bed!" It was a command she would repeat throughout the evening.

Lagerfeld and I sank into the soft pink couch in the living room.

"Why does Lovie wear that plastic shield?" I asked Lagerfeld.

"He's too high-strung. It keeps him from chewing on himself. He bites his paws until they bleed and then he drips blood all over the carpeting."

"Oh," I said, and I looked out the window to the elegant building across the way and peered into people's homes. I wondered if I would see other dinner parties. "What a great view we have up here," I said to Lagerfeld. "We can see everything."

"Oh, yes," said Lagerfeld, not responding directly to my comment, "I grew up in this neighborhood."

I wanted to say, "What was it like back then?" And though my intention was innocent, I knew it would be rude. She appeared to be only in her late fifties, a good deal younger than Henry or Lois, but still it wouldn't have been right, so all I said was, "Really?"

"It was wonderful," she said. "We were the most popular family. All the children wanted my parents for their parents. We were always doing the funnest things, taking everyone to plays or concerts or going to Coney Island on a weekend afternoon. If on a Saturday night we didn't have anything planned then my father would take us down to the night court. It was great entertainment. We never had a dull moment. I thought all families were like that."

She smiled the whole time, but I thought she was sad, sad that she wasn't part of the most popular family anymore. When we were called to the dinner table, I helped her get out of the couch and she steadied herself with her cane. At the table, Henry with great effect graciously poured the wine into our glasses. "For you, my dear," he said to Lois. But then he noticed a spray can by Lois's glass. "What's this?" he asked. "Roach spray?"

"Don't be disgusting," she said. "It's spray-on butter. It's not messy. I don't like messy butter dishes."

"Well, you never know, it might also kill roaches," said Henry. Lois looked at him with anger. The fleas had put bugs on his mind; he was sabotaging his efforts to get on Lois's good side. I stepped in to save him. I praised Lois for her salad, and then Lagerfeld praised the roasted chicken. We were both peacemakers, and everyone started eating. I avoided the spray-on butter, ate my roll plain, and nibbled at the chicken, which was greasy.

But things were a little too quiet and Lagerfeld sensed this and started talking about her problems finding a good doctor for her knee. Henry said, "I hear the royal family has terrible doctors, but they live despite them. It gives the rest of us courage." This led to a discussion of the family's scandals, and Henry very passionately said, "They should execute Charles and Diana, put an iron mask on Edward—he's a homosexual, you know—and lock him in Château Villon in Switzerland. The Queen can last another ten years and then one of Charles's children can take the throne. There'll be a boy king!"

Lagerfeld said, "I met one of Diana's cousins. Very good looking. And he defended her, saying that she had tried very hard to make the marriage work, but that Charles ignored her and wouldn't sleep in the same bed with her."

"English men are very cold," said Lois. "My second husband was raised in England and he was the least affectionate man I've ever met." And then she yelled at poor, panicked Lovie, who wouldn't shut up, "Go to bed!"

"All the English upper class are homosexual," said Henry. "It's the public school, you know. They never get over it."

I had heard that one before, but Henry was not bashful in my presence to restate his favorite theories, and the ladies giggled and nodded their heads in agreement. And I wondered what they thought of Henry. Was his sexuality apparent to them? Or were they confused like me?

We had ice cream for dessert and then all of us were anxious to get to the Whitney. We took two cars again, since Lois's Mercedes was a bit small for four, and Henry's backseat was dirty and cluttered with old coffee cups, TB-infected reading glasses, and other such things unfit for ladies to sit on.

When we were in Henry's car, he said, "I'll have to get Lois alone in the Whitney. I almost started talking about the play when we were setting the table, but I didn't think the timing was right. My conscience wasn't clear. I was thinking about the fleas I had passed on to Lovie."

It began to rain and Henry started the car. The Whitney was south and west of us, only about fifteen blocks away. We were laboring up the hill of Eighty-ninth Street and we were almost to Third Avenue when suddenly the car stalled out.

"Oh, *scheisse!*" Henry shouted. He often cursed in German to lend greater profundity to his aggravations. He tried to start the car back up, but it wouldn't turn over.

"Are we out of gas?" I asked.

"Of course we are!"

Like a schoolteacher, I said, "You shouldn't have let it run down so far."

"I always keep it on empty. In case I have to abandon the car I don't lose any money on gas."

Henry ordered me to get out and push the car backward, on an angle to the left, to an open parking spot he had sighted. It was a one-way street and it wasn't hard pushing the car down the hill, but getting it to cut to the left was difficult since the steering wheel, without any power, had died completely.

I pushed valiantly against the hood and I was getting soaked in the rain. Through the windshield Henry looked tragic, twisting and turning his neck, trying with all his might to budge the wheel. I began to laugh, I was a little drunk from the wine at dinner, and it felt incredibly funny to be getting wet and pushing a car with no gas.

As I vainly struggled like a backward Sisyphus, two young men around my age approached the Skylark. They were both very tall and sturdy. They wore long, gray winter coats, but had no hats or scarves or umbrellas. Their faces were unremarkable, but well fed.

"You need help?" one of them asked.

"Yes," I said and then they took over. One of them began to push with me and the other had Henry roll down his window and through the opening he reached across Henry and grabbed hold of the steering wheel. Henry and I had been unable to get the thing to budge and in about a minute they had the car parked.

"Thank you," I said, and they began to walk away without saying a word. Henry slid across the front seat and got out the passenger door and said to their retreating backs, "Thank you, I am deeply indebted to both of you," but they didn't even turn to acknowledge him. They were strange and solemn. We stood in the rain staring at them walk away, side by side. "They are silent heroes," said Henry, and then he noticed a sign next to the car and exclaimed, "Oh, God, it's a diplomat's spot! No wonder it was open." But then suddenly he liked the idea, it pleased him. It felt suitable to Henry's sense of station and romance that a diplomat would understand a fellow-gentleman's predicament.

"I will have to write a thank you note and put it in the door and explain what happened and that we will be at the Whitney, but returning shortly." I think Henry and I both fantasized that somehow when we returned to the car that there'd be an invitation from the diplomat to come have a drink in his lovely brownstone. But Henry couldn't find a decent piece of paper for the thank you note and ended up scrawling "Out of Gas" on an old, oily paper plate and leaving it on the dashboard.

We took a taxi to the Whitney in the rain. It's a fantastic modern museum, and as we approached it in the taxi, the Whitney looked like a gigantic brick about to topple on to Madison Avenue. When we saw the museum, Henry said, "It's filled with pornography. Every exhibition is the same: sex organs and toilet seats. America is dying. The culture is dying. What nobody realizes is that all sex, homo and hetero, is boring. It will take them years to figure that out."

"But why is everyone so crazy about sex?" I asked.

"People have too much to eat. They don't have the survival problem which would keep them sane. We need to cut the rations."

We shared the cost of the taxi and walked across the bridge that connects the sidewalk to the museum. Underneath the bridge is a concrete moat and the large windows of the basement floor. Through those windows I could see a teeming party.

At the museum's door, we showed the one invitation that Lagerfeld gave us and Henry explained to the door person that he lost his and it was easy to get in. We checked our wet raincoats and Henry said, "I have to get Lois alone and offer her the George Eliot role. See if you can't distract Lagerfeld somehow. Don't knock her over or do anything violent, just get her away from us."

We went down a flight of stairs to the party and the place was packed with at least two hundred dazzling people. There was a jazz band in the far corner and the combination of the music and the multitude of conversations made for a deafening cacophony.

"We'll never find them!" Henry shouted to me and just then I sighted Lagerfeld's hair at the bar. "I see Lagerfeld's head!" I shouted to Henry. I was proud that I was the one who spotted her. I felt like an Indian scout. The whole evening, because of our secret mission, had a military feeling, and I wanted Henry to think that I was a good junior officer.

We made our way to the bar, and our two lady friends, Lois in her leopard dress, Lagerfeld leaning on her cane, looked very striking amidst the stylish young people—the women with their beautiful hair, the men with their interesting eyeglasses.

"I apologize for leaving the two of you unattended," Henry said. "But my car ran out of gas and it looked as if we would be trapped in the middle of the road until the police came along and fined me for numerous violations. But then out of nowhere two Penn Staters came to our aid. They must be in ROTC—they had us parked in no time at all." And then Henry added with dignity, "I am in a diplomat's space."

The ladies laughed at the perils-of-Pauline nature of Henry's story and then Lagerfeld conspiratorially told the three of us that we could get free drinks in the VIP room, rather than pay for drinks here at the main bar.

She led the way through the crowd to the elevators. There were two large elevators and then to the left a smaller elevator. In the small elevator stood a black man in the uniform of a museum guard. Lagerfeld said, "Please take us to the boardroom." I saw the man hesitate—I think you needed a special Whitney Museum pin—but Lagerfeld was an intimidating figure, as Henry said, with her flow-ing strawberry locks, cane, and gigantic eyes, and she confidently limped past the man into the elevator and we followed her.

The guard took us to the top floor and the door opened on to a large, private boardroom with a long black table. A single paint-ing hung on one wall, a large, red Rothko reproduction. A bar had been set up at the end of the room, away from the table, and a few elegant people were mingling about. There was a tangible atmosphere of elitism, and there was one plump woman in a very low-cut dress showing a daring amount of cleavage. I was immediately drawn to her, and Henry saw her and said, "This must be where they have the orgies."

The four of us sidled up to the bar and ordered drinks. The woman in the low-cut dress hailed Lagerfeld and approached. She and Lagerfeld knew each other and we were all introduced. Her name was Gloria Milton. "Any relation to the poet?" Henry asked.

"Actually, yes. He's several times my great-uncle. Seven times actually," said Gloria, proud of her famous pedigree, especially in an artistic setting like the Whitney.

"Have you read *Paradise Lost*?" asked Henry.

Gloria Milton squinted at Henry and didn't answer. How embarrassing not to have read her own forebear.

"I must sit down," said Lois to all of us. "Please excuse me."

Lois took a seat at the board table and Henry and I joined her. Lagerfeld and Ms. Milton stayed at the bar and continued talking.

"That dress is outrageous, even for the Whitney. I'm sure she's a fraud," said Henry.

"I'm exhausted," Lois said. "I hope I'm not coming down with anything."

"It's the weather," Henry said. "You'll be fine as soon as you get to Florida . . . When are you planning to head down?" Henry asked his question politely and casually, but I knew that the time had come for him to make his proposal to Lois.

I was prepared to take action against Lagerfeld should she suddenly sit down with us. I thought to myself, I could spill my drink on her cape, I could accidentally kick her cane. So I prudently kept my eye on her, and Ms. Milton's bosom, which she had powdered to conceal some freckles; and I discreetly listened in on Henry's conversation, all the while pretending to stare at the Rothko.

"I'll be flying down in ten days, but I have lots of errands," said Lois.

"I imagine there's much to do . . . yes," Henry said. And then in his most intimate and humble tones he continued, "You know, Lois, I am going to try and put on the Eliot play down in Palm Beach this winter. Vivian Cudlip can help me get one of the ballrooms at the Colony. It will be perfect for a reading and I was thinking of you for George Eliot, with me playing the lover, of course. You've read the play. I think you would be wonderful."

"Oh, are you going to Palm Beach this winter?" she asked, knowing full well that Henry went every winter.

"It is my intention. And I hope, of course, to be in constant contact with you."

"Well, I'd like to play George Eliot. But I will be very busy this winter. My daughter is coming down, and my son. And I do have a new gentleman friend, whom I met in Southampton this fall, and he'll be in West Palm. It's going to be hectic . . . and if you were thinking of staying in the guest room I really can't have you this season. Meredith is coming down. I think the sun will be very good for her bad knee."

"Lagerfeld!" Henry expostulated. His worse fears had proven true, she had usurped his room. Lois shot him a dirty glance when Henry exclaimed Meredith's surname. Lagerfeld herself looked over, but Gloria Milton was talking rapidly and was demanding attention. Henry quickly regained his composure and said to Lois, "Yes. That'll be very good for Meredith's knee, the sun cures everything. And you needn't worry about me this season, I've made other arrangements. You've been very generous to put up with me the last few winters . . ."

"It's nothing, Henry. I'm glad you found something, and you know I probably can make some time for rehearsals and a performance."

"Yes, of course, we'll be in constant touch. You'll be a great George Eliot."

I was sure that Henry had no intention now of putting on the play, and soon after this terrible defeat we left the boardroom. We were all tired. Before going to the coat check Lois used the ladies' room. The three of us waited for her and Lagerfeld said to Henry,

"I was wondering if you're free tomorrow. I found an inexpensive sports doctor for my knee out in Brooklyn. It would be wonderful if you could give me a ride and then after my appointment there's a free violin concert we could go to at the library. I think they'll have wine."

Henry was short with her. "I have to teach tomorrow. I can't help you."

After we all got our coats we headed for Lois's Mercedes. Henry and I managed to squeeze into the backseat. It had stopped raining and we drove to First Avenue, where the gas stations are, but none of the stations would lend us a gas can to transport the fuel back to Henry's car. You had to buy a can, but my three companions were too cheap to pitch in for one. Then Henry spotted a plastic soda bottle on the street. He had an attendant fill that with gas, and then we drove off to replenish the Skylark. Henry, sitting next to me in the backseat, held the gasoline-filled soda bottle between his legs. "I hope I don't blow us all up," he said.

Lois drove us back to Henry's car and there was enough gas in the soda bottle to get the car started. We bid adieu to the two ladies and just as they drove off, I stared at Lois, who seemed too old and too tired to be driving. She was sitting up high on a special cushion and her wig was practically touching the ceiling of the car. She looked pathetic and yet there was something brave about the way she grabbed the wheel and stared straight ahead. Before they disappeared around the corner, I caught a last glimpse of Lagerfeld's hair.

We began to drive home and I said to Henry, "I'm sorry it didn't work out."

"Nothing works out anymore," Henry said. "It never used to be this way. Bills got paid, I had cars that could make it to Florida, I had rooms in Florida. It's only in the last ten years that I've had these problems. Where can I go? Russia. There's always Russia. But there's no social life in Russia."

"We had a lot of social life tonight," I said.

"Yes, and just when we're about to fall asleep the full horror of what we experienced will jolt us awake. It's all madness. The whole evening was engineered by Lagerfeld to get me to drive her to a cheap knee doctor in Brooklyn tomorrow. Of course she doesn't want to ask Lois. She doesn't want to do anything to jeopardize the room now that she's got her hands on it. It's all very depressing."

"Do you think you can be friends anymore with Lagerfeld or Lois?"

"Friends? We never were friends. We've used each other. And I'm sure we'll use each other again. When they need me they'll call. But *I* don't really need *them*. I only need a little pleasure once in a while—good food, good orchestra, and good wine, there's nothing wrong with wanting those three things . . . That roasted chicken tonight was good. I will have to concentrate my thoughts on that."

We pulled up in front of our building and Henry told me to get out. I said, "I'll come with you to park the car."

"No, it could take forever. No sense in both of us being out here."

"Really, I'd like to come. It's not good to be alone on the street." I knew that he often parked in Spanish Harlem.

Henry was suddenly angry—the frustrations of the whole evening had ignited his temper—and he shouted at me, "Do you think I'm an old man? Get out!"

He didn't realize that I didn't want to separate from him, that I felt I would miss him even for those few minutes I'd wait until he came home.

"But it's probably safer if there are two of us walking together," I said, almost pleading, not wanting him to be angry with me.

"I don't need you!" he yelled. "Now get out!"

CHAPTER VIII

Straightish

We hardly acknowledged one another for a whole week after Henry had screamed at me. Only the most necessary communications were exchanged. There had been a viciousness to his "I don't need you" and I felt too ashamed to be around him very much. He didn't need me, but I was in some kind of love with him.

I avoided the apartment as much as possible. I went to Sally's and stayed there late. When I came home Henry would be asleep or watching television and I'd go straight to bed. It felt odd now that I was living with and renting a tiny room from someone I hardly knew and yet whose opinion of me meant everything.

At Sally's I often bought drinks for Miss Pepper. She never asked me anymore if I wanted a date. We had a platonic friendship. One night I asked her if she knew Wendy.

"What does she look like?"

"Kind of like Sophia Loren. Really high cheekbones and a hook nose."

"A Puerto Rican girl?"

"Yes."

"She has long curly brown hair, a nice body?"

"Yes."

"I know her."

"What's happened to her? I haven't seen her around."

"She was arrested. She's going to be upstate for a while."

"What did she do?"

"She and another tranny tried to steal a date's car. Those girls were crazy."

I couldn't believe it. Wendy had liked my car. I wondered if she had wanted to steal the Parisienne. But I didn't think she did; she had genuinely seemed to like me. She had enjoyed playing my girlfriend. We had held hands while we drove to Queens. I felt bad for her. She had probably tried to steal the car to have money to put towards the surgery. I wondered if she could take her hormones in jail. If she couldn't, would she lose her looks? That would devastate her.

"How long will she be in for?" I asked Miss Pepper.

"Probably six months. Unless you hurt somebody they don't keep you in very long. Costs too much."

"Have you ever been in jail?"

"Child, I have a sheet this long for pross." Miss Pepper spread her hands wide like a fisherman talking about the one that got away.

"Pross is prostitution?"

"Don't be a dick, child." She was annoyed that I was slow, but then she continued. "Going to jail is part of the lifestyle. The cops have a quota. Every night they have to bring in a certain number of regular whores, drag Queens, and fags. Sometimes they count Queens as fags. I was arrested last week just walking down the street here in front of Sally's. They had a sweep."

"Do they put you in with the men or with the women?"

"Do I look like a man?"

"No, I'm sorry . . ."

"They put us with the whores, otherwise we'd be raped all night."

After Miss Pepper told me about Wendy, I concocted this fantasy in my mind that I would visit her in jail. I would bring her things, take care of her. We'd fall in love. It was a romantic fantasy because I'd be in love with someone in jail, which is always romantic and noble, and it would be doubly noble because I'd be going against all of society by loving her. But how could they laugh at me when they saw she looked like Sophia Loren?

But I was only brave in my mind. I didn't find out what jail she was in. I knew that I couldn't really live out such a thing. I was afraid that if I wrote her a letter that she wouldn't remember me.

In the world of Sally's, Miss Pepper was kind of like my Henry: she liked to talk at me and have me listen like a pupil. One night she explained to me where I fit in socially at the bar.

"Child," she said, "there are three kinds of men who come to Sally's: closet Queens, bisexuals, and tranny-chasers. Most men in here are closet Queens. Our bread and butter. We need them. They want to dress like us, be like us, but they can't, they're too scared. And they only want to give blow jobs. That's all they like to do. They're easy to deal with. A lot of married men are closet Queens.

"Then you have bisexuals. They come in once in a while because they want to experiment. They want to do everything. They get their money's worth. But they usually figure out that they want a woman when they want a woman, and a man when it's time for a man.

"Then there's the tranny-chaser. That's what I think you are. If a Queen settles down with somebody it's usually a tranny-chaser. We'd like a straight man, but everybody wants a straight man—gays, women, Queens. There's too much competition. And when a straight man finds out a Queen is a Queen, they always run away. Every girl in here will tell you about a straight man who fell in love with her and then left as soon as he found out that the girl had a dick. Sometimes they try it once, they're curious, then they run away.

"So the next best thing is a tranny-chaser. I was in the bathroom tonight and a girl was sniffing coke and getting all excited and she said, 'I hope there are some tranny-chasers out there.' Tranny-chasers appreciate our beauty. That's why she was hoping some were out here."

"What's a tranny-chaser like? What am I like?"

Miss Pepper looked at me square. Her face was beautiful and dark, her eyes were large and perfect. They were eyes that liked me.

"First of all you're cute. Most girls would die for your blond eyelashes. And you dress nice, like a gentleman. And you have a good personality. You treat Queens with respect. You're a typical tranny-chaser. You're not really straight, but you're not really gay. You're straightish."

My Analyst, Gershon Gruen

The night Miss Pepper told me all this, the silence between Henry and myself came to an end. When I got home, he was waiting up for me. He was sitting on his throne-chair and for once reading a book rather than watching television. It was a book for his class, and he looked up and said, cheerfully, as if there had been no problems between us, "How are you?"

I was surprised. "All right," I said quietly, in a reserved, sullen way.

"I was thinking," he said. "I have a proposal that would save you money. Let me pay for your car insurance and I'll take the car down to Florida for two months. And then when I come back, we can share the car until I find a new one. I'll pay most of the insurance, but since we would be sharing it, you should pay a little. So you'll save money, and this would be a great help for me. I need to get to Florida."

I couldn't believe it. We barely talk for a week and then he proposes this car deal. He just wanted to use me. He was a user. My great-aunt was right. But also a part of me wanted to do it—to help him, to have his approval. But if I let Henry have my car, I was sure he would destroy it. He neglected all things, and my precious car, my Parisienne, would be wrecked. And it had been my father's last car, my inheritance.

"I don't think it helps me very much," I said. "You would probably destroy my car." I was being nasty because I was hurt that he had broken our silence not for apology, but to try to get something out of me.

"No, I wouldn't. I know how to take care of a car."

"Why should I help you? Why haven't you introduced me to Vivian Cudlip's granddaughter?" I suddenly asked, implying that my lending him of my car, even if he paid for the insurance, was an equal favor to an introduction to a young heiress, which wasn't true, but it felt true.

"It wouldn't be right," said Henry, and he wouldn't look at me.

"You think I might embarrass you?"

"Possibly, and it could affect my standing."

"So you're just worried that something about me might make you lose out on one free meal."

"It could be more than one meal. It could be many," said Henry.

For a brief moment the haughtiness was gone from Henry's face. He was a little embarrassed by this admission, because in a sense he was saying that he valued a free meal more than he valued me. But this didn't mean that I was extremely low on his list of what was important, because free meals were perhaps the highest.

So I forgave him everything. He was being honest and I guess that's what won me over. And it was funny. I loved the craziness of it. My anger dissolved. He had spent so many years pursuing the free meal that he couldn't allow anything to endanger his relationship to his best source, Vivian Cudlip.

And I didn't blame him for being embarrassed about me. I had told him a scandalous half-truth about going to Queens with a transsexual and having a lion dropped at me; and he knew I was Jewish and that the granddaughter wouldn't really be interested in me (she was from an old Philadelphia WASP family), so why should he introduce me? He had only mentioned that I could meet her early on before he knew I was Jewish. And regarding the car, I knew the economy of Henry's life: you tried to get things from people. That's the way it was.

But I didn't want to let him use the Parisienne. If he destroyed it, the last evidence of my father would be gone. I wasn't sure Henry would forgive me this—I was perhaps his best chance to get to Florida—but I calmly told him, "I'm sorry, but I can't lend you my car. It has special value for me. My father left it to me. I can't take the risk of anything happening to it."

"I understand," said Henry, and then, with great civility, we took turns brushing our teeth in the kitchen sink before going to bed.

I thought that things would be very cold between us, but Henry was wonderful. He didn't bear me any ill will, despite how much he wanted and needed to get to Palm Beach. Rather, our talk seemed to clear things up. It was cathartic for both of us. He was pressing on to the next event, and we started carrying on as before—watching *Are You Being Served?* and talking from our beds. As always, I went to sleep laughing from the things he said, and I was sort of happy. I stopped going to Sally's and the peep show. I was doing my best to just be the young gentleman, to go to work each day in my jacket and tie, to be clean-shaven, to read my books, to be pure.

Henry finished teaching on the sixteenth, and he began to spend all day every day looking for cars. And he often convinced Gershon to take off from work to help him. But they had no success, and I was encouraged that Henry would just give up on going to Florida.

A few days before Christmas, I came home from work and Henry wasn't around. I made a little dinner for myself and then lay down on the orange carpet and watched the Knicks play for a while, and it wasn't a close game. They were losing and I couldn't bear it, so then I watched a violent movie. Henry came in around nine o'clock, saw me lying there, and said, "What did the Bible say? Lie down with fleas, raise up with bites?"

I got off the carpet and sat on the white couch. Some of the plastic had slipped off, but there were still a few protected areas. Henry saw the violent movie and said, "Americans and their guns. They can't outwit anyone so they shoot them."

I shut the television off and Henry began to prepare some food in the kitchen. "Did you find a car?" I asked.

"No. Gershon and I gave up for the day. I'm not a very good Puritan, I always want to goof off. I couldn't take another day of used cars and frustration. So we went to the Met, and then to the movies. The Met was interesting. Some art students noticed Gershon. They wanted to draw him as Bacchus."

"What did you see at the Met?"

"We saw the Greek exhibit, but we make too much of them. They were purely photographic of young men and athletes. And all the statues have permanent waves. I'm sure their hair wasn't like that . . . Then the Romans copied the Greeks and made a vulgar display of wealth and power. The greatest period in the history of art was French Impressionism and Tchaikovsky . . . Gershwin is the apex of popular music . . . And Ibsen is the greatest artist of all time. Yes," said Henry, and he was picking up speed, lecturing me on the history of art, while he filled a pot with water, lit a burner, and doused a dinner plate with hot then cold water. "Molière is funny the way Abbott and Costello are. Racine is absurd. Shakespeare is overrated. The English keep promoting him because they don't have

226

to pay royalties. Only a few of his plays are any good, the rest were commercial to get the audience in. *King Lear*, as Noël Coward said, 'is too long.' The good ones are: *Romeo and Juliet . . . As You Like It . . . Othello . . . Hamlet . . . The Merchant of Venice.*" Then Henry laughed, acknowledging that was a lot of plays, but recouped by saying, "Well, *Coriolanus*, *The Winter's Tale* are all shit . . . That's it. That covers everything." Henry laughed at his compression of Western culture. "Any questions?"

"What about American literature?"

"Doesn't exist. Hemingway was a spastic jerk. Faulkner is unreadable. Fitzgerald had talent but drank too much Coca-Cola. Yes. There's been no one in the English language after Dickens. Read the Bible and read Ibsen . . . Do you want some chicken? I'm going to roast one in the toaster oven."

"No, thank you," I said. I never used the toaster oven, but Henry often did.

"Don't worry, all the roach and flea eggs are killed by the heat, or so we hope."

"I already ate," I said. "But thank you . . . How did Gershon like the museum?"

"He felt elevated, improved. There was an embarrassing moment, though, which is the risk of going out in public with him. We were in the café, I bought him milk and cookies, and I saw Harold Harold, who is very big with the Public Theater. I didn't want him to see me, I was dressed like this—in poet's rags." Henry had on his usual costume of tattered sport coat, stained tan stretch pants, stained shirt, and wrecked shoes. "But he came over to our table."

"That's his real name? Harold Harold?"

"Yes. He's an urning. He came right over to the table and I had to introduce the two of them. I said, 'This is my analyst, Gershon Gruen.' I think Harold Harold believed me. He shook Gershon's hand very respectfully. But it wasn't good to be seen in poet's rags. He'll think my career is over and that I'm in analysis because of it."

I Felt Something Under My Rear

On December 23, on the eve of Christmas Eve, Henry's Skylark finally died. He made it home around nine o'clock and told me of his misadventure.

"I was in Queens following automobile leads. But all the poor have cars which are far too expensive. That's the problem with this country—the poor have too much money. Then the Buick began to fail. Kept passing out and starting again. I limped my way to the Queensborough parking lot. I thought the car was out of gas. I went to a station and filled up that soda bottle. I managed to put some gas in the car, but I spilled most of it on the parking lot, made a puddle. I was worried that a student would set it on fire with a cigarette butt. I convinced the security guard that *I* should set it on fire. The guard said, 'That's not a little puddle.' I told him it was little. But it *was* deep. Made a big thing of black smoke. I tried to start the car to get out of there, but it wouldn't turn over. I skulked away. I've had so many run-ins with security. I can just hear it, they'll say, 'Dr. Harrison is at it again. He left another big black mark on the parking lot.'"

The next day, Christmas Eve, Henry and Gershon went out to Queens to look at the car. They returned in the early afternoon. The car was now officially dead due to various causes, and I felt selfishly reassured about my decision not to lend him the Parisienne. To lend the car to Henry would be to kill it.

Henry was resigned about his situation—no car, unable to get to Florida—but he was not devastated. He had to pack. He was spending Christmas Eve and Christmas Day at Vivian Cudlip's Philadelphia house. She was sending a limousine to pick him up to have him in Pennsylvania by dinner. While he packed, he and I talked about my helping him to find a car. We would start when he returned from Vivian's, as I had several days off from work. I felt good about this—it would give me some time with him, and make up for my not lending him the Parisienne, though I knew that with Henry's budget we were unlikely to find anything and so I wouldn't really be helping him to leave.

I was sitting on the white couch during our talk, while he searched for clean tuxedo shirts, and I felt something under my rear. I ignored it at first, and then I reached under myself. It was a beige mascara applicator. I held it out to Henry. "What's this?" I asked, and then good-naturedly joked with him, "Have you had a woman up here?"

"I will not say," replied Henry with gravity.

"Why not?"

"One doesn't speak of such things."

"Well, then I might think you had been using it yourself."

"Yes," said Henry quickly, and happily, "I've been cross-dressing."

"You readily admit to cross-dressing, but not to entertaining a woman?"

"Yes."

He finished packing and he looked at me. I was still holding the mascara applicator. His face took on a humble expression. The eyebrows relaxed, the cheeks sunk a little. He didn't want me to come up with my own ideas about the mascara, or to believe his cover story about cross-dressing.

"I use the mascara for my hair. I start at the root and brush it back. It changes the whole color. It's a trick I learned in the theater."

The mystery of Henry's hair was finally revealed! I tried not to smile too widely, but I was overjoyed. I was slowly figuring him out, piece by piece. I knew why he prematurely flushed the toilet, I knew about his hair . . . if I was patient, I'd get to the bottom of everything.

And I admired the use of the mascara. It was ingenious. He could hide the applicator in his pocket and emerge from the bathroom transformed, mystifying me. No dyes, no potions for snoops like me to find. And then I remembered the mascara applicator I had seen in the car. There had been clues.

"I should tell you," I said, "that sometimes there are tiny smudges on your forehead . . . like Ash Wednesday." I had always been too embarrassed to say something, but since the truth was out,

I thought it was appropriate to give him this constructive criticism. I was hopeful that the religious reference would soften the blow.

"Yes, I know. There are always problems. We have too many problems. But it's best not to think about them. It's better to give each other gifts than to think about problems."

Henry reached into his armoire and removed a clear plastic bag with about a dozen used Christmas balls.

"I forgot to give these to you earlier. I picked them up at a garage sale when Gershon and I were in New Jersey. Now you can have your own collection."

Henry went into the kitchen and put the Christmas balls in a soup bowl and carried them into my room and put them on the window ledge. We stood a moment and admired them. There was now a bowl of Christmas balls, like a bowl of jewels, in Henry's room and my room. I liked being the same as him. And the Christmas balls seemed to be Henry's way of acknowledging that I had achieved some kind of permanency, that I wasn't going anywhere.

"Thank you," I said, "but I feel terrible, I didn't get you a present." I had been afraid that Henry would reject anything I bought, and that he would be annoyed that I had wasted money.

"That's all right, I didn't really get you a present," he said reassuringly. "I thought I would use the Christmas balls myself. I couldn't resist them. But my bowl is overflowing. So don't feel bad, *and* they only cost twenty-five cents . . . I did spend more money on Vivian. I picked up a fake silk Chanel scarf on Canal Street for ten dollars."

"That's very nice of you," I said.

"It's the least I can do for all she gives me. And of course to ensure that she keeps on giving," Henry chuckled to himself. He was half-sincere, he wasn't really *that* mercenary. "But even if she stopped treating me I'd still give her something. I like her. But that's the burden of the rich—never knowing if you're loved for yourself or for your money."

"Well, that's something we don't have to worry about," I said.

"Yes. But *you* are loved . . . Your great-aunt loves you." He was struggling to think of other people who loved me, and then he said, "And I . . . I am a friend."

Are You Having BMs?

Henry went to Philadelphia for Christmas and I went to Rego Park. My great-aunt and I followed the same routine that we used for Thanksgiving. Gefilte fish hors d'oeuvres. Roasted chicken dinner. *Playboy*. Nap. Hollywood gin.

Over cards she told me that she was going on a Slim-Fast diet. I didn't know if this was a good thing for someone her age. I tried to counsel her against it.

"You don't need to lose weight," I said. "You look wonderful."

"Look at this belly," she said, and she lifted up her cotton housedress to show me her stomach; it was rather swollen and jutted out strangely from her small body. "I should go to the doctor," she continued. "I'll tell him I'm pregnant. He'll look up my tussy and a moth will come out."

We both laughed at that image; I saw in my mind my great-aunt lying on an examining table with her legs open and a white moth flying around her doctor's head. Then my great-aunt said, "I need mothballs up there. Nobody uses it anymore."

She really was too bawdy and I wanted to get back to the issue of her diet. I didn't want her to make herself sick with the Slim-Fast.

"Instead of those powder drinks," I said, "you should eat lots of fruits and vegetables, and drink water."

"I boil a jar of water every day," she said.

I wondered if boiling made the New York water worse, somehow purified the lead. "You can buy springwater," I said.

"Don't be ridiculous. I'm not going to spend money on water."

"Well, you really shouldn't do the Slim-Fast. You're just bloated. Are you having BMs?" (We always called them BMs in my family.)

"I go every day. It's a religion with me. I don't leave the house until I go. I smoke a cigarette; that usually gets me started."

I wondered if there was a scientific basis for that, or if it was psychological. It made some sense in that the nicotine might get her blood pumping and send blood to her intestines and genuinely help her.

She won all three games of gin and then packed up two bags of food for me to take home. She told me that loverboy, Henry, could have some. She also gave me a toaster since she was now off bread. I tried to refuse the toaster, but she insisted. I also had no luck advising her against Slim-Fast.

We said good-bye at the elevator. "Thank you for everything," I said. "I love you."

"I love you more," she said.

The Essential Man

Henry spent an extra day in Philadelphia and came back late at night on the twenty-sixth and I was half asleep, but we spoke briefly and made plans to drive to Long Island in the morning. Henry remembered seeing a car for sale in a driveway in Southampton when he was down there for Vivian's Election Day party. In fact, he had noticed the car just a few hours before he struck the tree with the Skylark, and Henry wondered if this was a sign. A sign that this was the car that would take him to Florida.

I woke up early on the twenty-seventh and I showered and dressed. I was excited to be going on a day trip with Henry. I sat on the edge of my bed, and like a child waiting for the special adult in their life, I waited for Henry to wake up.

I did get a little bored, so I read a few Somerset Maugham short stories to put me in the mood for a trip, and I wrote in my journal.

Around eleven, I heard Henry groan, and a few moments later, he came staggering into my room and his shirt was tied around his forehead in place of the still-missing eye mask. He saw me sitting on the bed fully dressed and he gasped and raised his arms in horror. He didn't stop or say anything, just continued into the bathroom and urinated, flushing prematurely, saving some as usual.

He came out, a little less shocked to be awake.

"Do you want some coffee?" I asked. "I could go out and get it."

"I can't make decisions yet, it's too early."

I waited patiently for him to get dressed. He groaned melodramatically every few moments, knowing that I was listening. When he stopped groaning and he was dressed, I went into the kitchen to show him the toaster and the different foods that my great-aunt had sent me home with.

"This toaster is clean," I said. "It gives us a fresh start without having to worry about roaches or fleas."

"Your great-aunt and I have the perfect relationship for a man and woman," said Henry. "She sends me presents and we never see one another."

"Maybe you could see her some time? Take her out for lunch," I said, hopefully.

"No. That would destroy everything. We're in perfect harmony. She idolizes me from a distance. It's best to keep it that way. I don't want to disappoint her."

I didn't press him any further about my great-aunt and we went down to The Salt of the Earth to give us courage for our expedition to Southampton. We sat at our regular tables right next to each other, and I asked Henry, "How was Christmas at Vivian's?"

"She had a dinner for one hundred people in the ballroom Christmas Day," said Henry. "All the knights were gathered. Barbarash, the one who's trying to have me removed. Spencer Mooney, an unprincipled old fruit who spreads vicious gossip. Aresh Farman, a weepy, exiled Persian. Neville Henry, an impoverished yachtsman who likes jelly beans and has gout. He's the only one I like. He at least has some soul. He needs the free meals. The other two have some income. But of all the freeloaders, I have the most integrity."

"Are you sure?"

"You should see the others."

"Can a freeloader have integrity?"

"Of course! I bring Vivian happiness in exchange for food. I bring her all my talents. Bit professor. Bit playwright. Bit walker. Bit psychopath. Bit intellectual. Bit fascist. Bit communist. Bit royalist. Bit gigolo. Bit escort. Yes."

"Bit extra man?"

"No," said Henry, forgetting that he had told me once that he was an extra man. "I am more than extra. I am essential!"

We finished our coffee and then walked a few blocks to where I had left the Parisienne. It was a cold and sunless day. There was a heavy ceiling of gray clouds.

We got in my car and Henry moaned with pleasure and smiled widely. He liked the cushioned velour seats. Finally, he was in the Parisienne, and I was proud of my beautiful car.

When we came to a stoplight at First Avenue, an attractive woman in her forties, wrapped in a rich fur, crossed in front of us.

"*A quel destin inconnu se dirige-t-elle?*" asked Henry.

"What does that mean?" I asked.

"'To what unknown destiny is she directing herself?'" answered Henry. "I always say that when I see a beautiful woman. What will happen to her? Where is she going? Where has she come from?"

We took the FDR Drive heading north. To our right was the East River, which would soon merge with the Harlem River. The water was a dark gray and the waves were high and choppy. It was like driving beside the ocean. I put on the radio to give us some music. It was tuned to a Spanish station and some salsa music blared out.

"Can we change this to something the cow didn't die from?" asked Henry with immediate annoyance.

I put on a classical station and he visibly relaxed.

"Is this FM and AM?" he asked.

"Yes," I said.

"*Quelle luxe* . . . what a radio. You Americans with your radios and cars. Sounds as if the piano player is sitting on the dashboard. I'm not used to a car with its own orchestra and two working doors . . . And no fumes!"

I liked having Henry praise my car. I took it personally. And he didn't make any criticisms about my driving, which was only right, since I was an excellent driver.

He decided that we should quickly pass through the Italian neighborhood by Fort Schuyler and search the driveways for cars for sale before heading to Southampton.

The whole trip was starting to seem a little crazy to me. It was past noon, we were making a detour, and it was going to take two hours just to get to the Hamptons. The sun was going to set by four-thirty, and so we would have maybe an hour or two of light to find a car that Henry had seen two months before—and he confessed to me that he wasn't sure of the car's exact location.

I felt like Sancho Panza trailing after Don Quixote as he sallied forth on an absurd knight errantry. Quixote sought immortality, Henry sought a car, and both were convinced of impractical methods to achieve their aims. Sancho complained a lot about following his knight, but even if our trip was crazy, I was happy to be Henry's squire.

As we approached Fort Schuyler, Henry observed the numerous empty, gutted Bronx buildings and said, "Look at that! What you've got to do is put the homeless in there and give them a paintbrush. But that only works in communist countries. The only thing that works . . . Why do I concern myself with these things?"

"Because it's distracting and you don't have to think about your own problems?"

"Psychological problems or automobile problems?"

"Psychological."

"Yes, I've never cared for introspection. I have an idea what lurks inside me and it's best to ignore it. I recommend that you do the same. What we really need to do is get out of America. Look at these buildings. This country is dying. The culture is dying . . . Just have to let it die. Russia is all I can think of. I want to go back to Riga. You can get a bottle of champagne for three dollars and a room for two dollars."

"You must have really liked it there," I said.

"The people have soul. Their eyes are beautiful," said Henry.

He had mentioned Riga before. It was his Xanadu. It possessed qualities that were most important to him. Low prices, champagne, and beauty.

We drove around the Fort Schuyler–Italian neighborhood and the houses were packed closely together, and each driveway was crammed with two or three automobiles. And yet there were none for sale. I thought fondly of our trip to the fort with Gershon.

"There are no cars," said Henry. "You could always find a car . . . I'll have to learn Russian." He was alluding to his eventual and necessary move out of the U.S. "I'll put an ad in *The Village Voice*: 'Wanted: Russian language lessons from native Russian in exchange for wives and husbands.'"

"Where will you get these wives and husbands?"

"Well, there's Gershon and you, and all the women on Vivian's staff are single. That should do it."

"I'm flattered that you would offer me," I said.

"Don't be, they're marrying you for the citizenship. But even if she doesn't love you, she'll be a very good friend. That's the way Russians are."

We headed out of the Bronx and we passed a go-go bar and Henry said, "Go-go bars do their best business on Mother's Day. They all want to look at udders. Once I stopped at a place in Trenton and one of the strippers was a transvestite, an urning. The stripper took off her brassiere and it was a man. And the truck drivers just sat there, no change, mouths open, they could care less. And the announcer, who was also a transvestite, it turns out, shouted, 'We're just fellas like you!' But it made no difference to the truckers."

Henry was always bringing up cross-dressing, transvestites, and urnings! I knew what an urning was from Krafft-Ebing. It was a man who felt himself to be a woman trapped inside a man's body. So it wasn't just me who was concerned with these issues.

"How did you feel seeing the transvestites?" I asked. I had him trapped in my car and I wanted him to open up once and for all, to let me know what it was that lurked inside him.

"How did I feel? I felt nothing. I observe."

"You weren't stimulated? Aroused?"

"It takes more than a transvestite to stimulate a great intellect . . . One of the truck drivers said, 'I could go for that.' I still don't think he was aware it was a man."

He so easily dismissed the notion of being excited by transvestites that I was terribly disappointed. He wasn't like me at all and I felt rather small-minded, the opposite of a great intellect, since I was so fascinated with Sally's. I dropped the conversation, and following Henry's directions I got on the Long Island Expressway.

We had turned the radio off to help us concentrate while in the Italian neighborhood, and so we drove along in silence, except for Henry's murmuring of a song to himself. It sounded French. Then suddenly there was a spinning hubcap in the road and I swerved to avoid it.

"*Scheisse!*" I shouted with indignation.

"You don't say it with the same feeling. You're too young. You don't have problems," said Henry with some propriety, aware that I was using his favorite malediction.

"I do have problems," I said.

"You don't sleep enough. You don't eat the right things. And you don't think the right thoughts. That's why you have problems."

"What thoughts should I have?"

"I follow the Church of Rome. They tell me what to think. But it's the same thing a rabbi would tell you: Know God and love God in this world and be happy with him in the next . . . but it's not easy. Who said, 'There are a thousand men who have found Paris, to only one who has found God'?"

"Baudelaire?"

"I would have given it to you in the French!" said Henry, annoyed with me as always for not knowing the source of his quotes. "The Princetonian said it. Fitzgerald. At least he tried. He went to a Jesuit high school. But he got lost. Prohibition made alcohol too appealing. He was too weak. He was one of the thousand . . . There are two ingredients to truth: good food and good wine. If the wine is good then you fall asleep and you don't need sex. You are in a state of euphoria."

"What about Fitzgerald then?" I asked.

"That was liquor, not wine."

"Sometimes wine makes you want to have sex," I said. Henry was of course seeing sex as the obstacle to truth and God.

"No. A truly good wine is so ecstatic that nothing compares.

But so few people can afford a sixty-five to seventy-dollar bottle of wine . . . How does one explain the rich?"

"You mean they don't find truth and yet they have good food and wine?"

"Yes. The rich have lots of sexual problems. They are constantly divorcing. Vivian's daughter has been divorced nine times. But some do find God and some don't. And the poor—poverty is no guarantee of virtue. The Russians, interestingly enough, look down on divorce. They think it bourgeois . . . Pioneers. That was a good life. A good way. Building houses to burn off the sex drive, and they lived so far apart they had no one to sin with except their wives. When they did get together, they square-danced." Henry paused a moment in his contemplation of what peoples—the rich, the poor, the Russians, the pioneers—might find God, and then said, "What are we doing? This is dangerous. I didn't expect to give a sermon. We'll both get carsick."

Henry began to sing to himself again and we drove along quietly. We passed an attractive woman in a silver Mercedes.

"Her hair should be flying in the wind at these speeds," said Henry.

"That woman?"

"Yes. She's sitting inside. Nothing's happening to her . . . What's that ring you're wearing?"

Henry had never noticed my Rutgers ring before, with its engraving from the Honors program. "My college ring," I said.

"Can you put it in wax and seal letters with it?"

"I don't think so."

"Is it gold?"

"Yes."

"It's a hedge against inflation. You can always pawn it and get the last drink."

Henry started singing the French song again. "What are you singing?" I asked.

"What?"

"What are you singing?"

"It's from a French operetta. *Pas Sur La Bouche.* It's about a man who doesn't like to be kissed on the mouth. That's the whole plot and theme. The great song is," and Henry began to sing, "'*Un baiser, un baiser, pas sur la bouche, pas sur la bouche.*'" Henry laughed to himself, then translated for me. "'A kiss. A kiss. Not on the mouth. Not on the mouth' . . . I agree. I think kissing on the lips is disgusting. There's all that saliva, bad teeth, bad breath . . . What's the other problem? . . . Germs! I almost forgot. People shouldn't kiss. It's uncivilized. Rubbing noses is fine. Or they should suck nipples when they meet."

"What? Women too? I can't believe *you* would suggest such a thing," I said.

"It's much more sanitary, you know, and a better sensation. The mouth is for eating . . . Do you want to pull over soon? I need something to eat. I have to keep thin. I want to play some tennis in Palm Beach, so I can't have anything I like. What's slimming? A leg of chicken."

"Fruits and vegetables," I said. "They're filled with water. They'll clean you out."

"You can't clean the fruit, that's the problem. And they don't sell fruit at 7-Elevens . . . I could drink. That's the thing to do. Have a drink. Yah," said Henry slipping into his German accent, "a bottle of brandy. We'll give them your ring. Stop in Half Hollow Hills, it's coming up in a little while. They have a good 7-Eleven."

We pulled off about ten minutes later, and Henry got crackers with phony orange cheese and I bought a small bag of popcorn. We ate while parked, and Henry devoured his crackers ravenously, extravagantly. He was performing for me, and making lots of crumbs. "I'm weak. I'm weak. These are fattening, but the pleasure is too great," said Henry. "And I need calories and strength to find a car."

While we ate, we watched a man at the Exxon station right next to us put some gasoline in his pickup truck. He was bending over to get the nozzle in, and he was very fat and his jeans were low on his hips. His down jacket was high on his back and we could see the chafed red slice of his ass.

"Look at that!" Henry said, laughing, happy because of the crackers and the spectacle of the man's ass.

"Oh, God," I said. "It looks disgusting."

"Don't be an old woman. It's not disgusting," said Henry, defending the man. "We're not seeing the ass*hole* . . . Do you know in Florida they've made it illegal to expose the ass crack? I wonder why in Florida. The redneck mechanics and construction workers are claiming it's discrimination. I agree with them. I am only politically correct when it comes to defending rednecks."

We left the 7-Eleven after that and Henry started singing a new song, Gershwin's "Lorelei." I recognized it from a record that Henry had danced to recently, and as he sang, I heard the lyric "I can only dream of love."

I said to him, "Have you ever been in love?" I wanted to get the conversation back on to sex, sucking nipples, and urnings.

"Love? What an absurd question," he said angrily. "Do you know what love is? If you can tell me, I will answer."

I was silent. I had offended him. We drove on. He started singing again, and he didn't seem that angry anymore. And then without solicitation from me, he said, "Constance Seehusen, Lettie Linfield, Virginia Gunn, these were the great romances that lasted years. Now Marjorie Mallard, who's threatening to write me out of her will again if I go to Florida. But she's rewritten it so many times that you can't trust her."

Henry was suddenly talking to me about love after all, and so I asked, "What were you like when you were my age? Is that when your romances began?"

"When I was twelve the other children were outside playing baseball. I stayed inside and drank my mother's perfume and read the biography of Noël Coward. It shaped my whole life."

"At twelve?"

"I was an unusual child."

"Why did you drink her perfume?"

"For the alcohol."

"Didn't it taste horrible and make you sick?"

"No. It was very good. I'd still drink it. I thought of drinking your cologne the other night. It's much nicer than all the colognes I have."

"I'll have to hide it," I said, laughing, but then I asserted, "I'm twenty-six, not twelve. What were you like when you were twenty-six?"

"Oh yes, that's right, we celebrated your birthday, and you have a driver's license. You're driving right now, and not so fast. We don't want the *Polizei* to pull us over," said Henry, and then he continued, answering my question. "I was traveling through Europe when I was in my twenties. I wanted only to roam, to loiter. I looked for beauty. That's all I wanted, to keep moving, but also to be virtuous and as uninvolved as possible. Initially, it was my soul I was developing. I'm still developing my soul, but I do like an invitation once in a while, with some free food and dancing."

"How did you afford your traveling?"

"I had a small inheritance. All my relatives were dead by the time I was twenty-five. There was no pressure on me to do anything. No one cared, and I certainly didn't care."

"Both your parents died around the same time?"

"No. My father died when I was two. I was raised by women. My grandmother, my aunt, and my mother. Mostly by my aunt."

"Why not your mother?" I asked. Henry had never revealed so much to me before. I felt excited, privileged.

"She was afraid of me. My aunt understood me. Gave me the Noël Coward biography. She taught literature at Johns Hopkins, one of the first women professors. She was ahead of her time. She was fascinating. She was always taking ships to Europe and having affairs. She told me of a Spanish man on a train whose hair came out in beautiful curls because it was very hot. That's what I remember from conversations with my aunt. She was quite beautiful, but never married. Her great love died in World War I. She died of TB. All the interesting people back then died of TB."

"Is that why you went to Europe, because she did?"

"Yes."

"How long were you there for?"

"Ten years. Spent every cent."

"Was this after the war?"

"Maybe," said Henry elusively, not wanting me to be able to estimate his age.

"What happened after your money ran out? Is that when you started teaching?"

"Yes. It was terrible. Had no money. Had to work. Grade papers. I didn't know about the papers. That's what makes teaching so demoralizing: the papers. So as soon as I got my salary I immediately spent it on pleasure. I was always borrowing money."

"You still managed to go to Europe?"

"Yes, I had to go to Europe. Life would have been intolerable if I didn't go."

"When did you tour around with your plays? The seventies?" I was trying in my mind to put together Henry's life chronologically from the bits and pieces of what he had told me.

"That sounds right . . . This is very suspicious, all these questions. Are you working for Winchell? Or are you planning to write a biography of an unknown playwright whose greatest work was stolen? . . . I will have to give you as misleading an image as possible," said Henry, and then he paused a moment, contemplating me as his biographer. I think he liked the idea, the attention. He said, "You can write about me if you want, but you will never capture my soul."

"I'm just curious about you," I said.

"Don't be. I'm not curious about you," said Henry.

I was a little wounded, but I tried to ignore that remark. "When did you start going to Florida?" I asked.

"I always went. Florida in the winter, Europe in the summer. I used to go to Key West before it was built up. Tennessee Williams was there. He liked to be near the sailors. And I went to Coral Gables. Palm Beach I've only been doing for about . . . 'seventy-five? 'seventy-six? . . . that's almost twenty years . . . We're coming to Lake Ronkonkoma," said Henry, suddenly, reading the sign at the side of the highway, and then he repeated the word, emphasizing each syllable, "Ron-konk-oma."

"Is that an Indian word?" I asked.

"Yes. It's a glacial lake. It's very, very deep. You go down and come up in Darien, Connecticut, or someplace."

"It goes across the sound?"

"Under the sound and then pops up again."

Then Henry resumed his singing of "Lorelei." He had told me a lot about himself, so I didn't pester him with any more questions the rest of the way.

We arrived in Southampton a little after three and had about an hour and a half of meager sunlight. We couldn't find the street where Henry had seen the car, but we did come across a Chrysler New Yorker being sold by a gas station. It was a burgundy color and in excellent shape. "It has very good lines," Henry said. "All the other cars look like cough drops."

But the price of the New Yorker was over two thousand dollars, there wasn't much hope there. As we drove away Henry said, "That was too lovely for the likes of me. But even a cat may look at a Queen."

"Where's that from?"

"I'm not sure. Some fairy tale about a cat who fights for her right to watch the Queen go by in a procession. But it might be a mouse. Even a mouse can look at a Queen."

We drove alongside mansions, which I couldn't see very well because they were surrounded by gigantic hedges or brick walls. Henry showed me Vivian Cudlip's estate, but mostly I saw its locked gate.

We drove down one road to see the ocean, and always in winter I find it surprising that the waves are still crashing in their solitude, as if they should only exist in summer when people can swim in them. We stepped out of the car to smell the ocean air, but it was too cold to smell anything, the wind was freezing, and so we continued our quest.

Darkness came and we drove around for more than an hour searching for the street with the car for sale. And it wasn't easy, because there were no streetlights in Southampton.

Henry was very frustrated and then he remembered that he had seen the car in Easthampton, not Southampton. He had gone for a long drive before the drunken Election Day dinner at Vivian's estate. The dinner which had resulted in the accident.

So we drove up to Easthampton, and I was sure that we wouldn't find the street or the car, but Henry recognized the street immediately, and sure enough there was the grail of our journey in the driveway of a modest, wood-shingled house. All the tires were flat, one of the door panels was rusted, but the car had a certain charm. It was an old Oldsmobile Cutlass. Henry knocked at the door of the house, though the place had a dead look to it. No one came to the door.

"Let's take a look at the engine," Henry said. There was a lamp on the edge of the driveway, probably on a timer, and it gave us some light, but I was a little uncomfortable with poking around the car. It seemed to be a part-year-round and part-summer neighborhood—there were lights in some windows—and if someone should see us or if a policeman should drive by, it might look funny if we were spotted opening the hood. But I didn't say anything. I didn't want Henry to tell me that I was a Milquetoast.

We tried pressing down on the hood so that we could get at the little lever, but it wouldn't budge. Henry took his frustration out on me. "What good are you? You're not mechanically inclined. I should have brought Gershon!"

"Gershon doesn't have a car to get you out here," I said, standing up for myself. It was freezing cold out, and even I couldn't take any additional abuse.

"That's true," said Henry, being somewhat conciliatory. "You do have some good qualities."

Henry tried to get in the car to find the hood release, and inside the car there were several old suitcases, and we both wondered as to the meaning of this. All the buttons on the doors were down, but one of the back doors actually opened. The lock was faulty. Henry got in the car, but he couldn't find the hood release. He had me look, but I couldn't find the damn thing either. It was a mystery, and we were trying to rush, as even Henry was tense that the police were about to show up.

We closed the car and made one last effort to pop the hood again, but with no success. Henry grabbed hold of the hood ornament, which looked like a squarish tuning fork, and found that it bent backward.

"This might be a secret hood-handle," said Henry, and he began to push it farther back. I knew better; I had the same kind of bendable hood ornament on my Parisienne. They are designed to bend with the wind or with a car wash's scrub brushes. Before I could say "Don't!" Henry bent the thing all the way back and it snapped off.

"*SCHEISSE!*" he shouted. "Let's get out of here! The *Polizei!*"

We scrambled into the Parisienne, and Henry still had the incriminating ornament in his hand. "Memorize the phone number in the 'For Sale' sign," he said. "Now that I have this ornament I will have to buy the rest of the car to go with it."

I memorized the number and then backed up a little wildly. "Don't draw attention," ordered Henry, and we made our getaway. Vandals. We stopped at a Greek diner to calm our nerves and have dinner. We were both famished, having not eaten since the 7-Eleven in Half Hollow Hills.

We consulted the Talmudesque laminated menus and ordered our food, but we were both depressed—the day had been particularly fruitless. We had driven two hours to Southampton and Easthampton to see one Chrysler New Yorker that was beyond Henry's budget, and one Oldsmobile Cutlass with four flat tires, whose hood ornament we had stolen.

Henry was especially demoralized, but his breast of roasted chicken seemed to revive him. After we ate he was going to try the phone number which I had jotted down on a piece of paper. He wasn't going to confess his crime. He was still interested in the car, and if he bought the car he could glue on the tuning fork himself.

"They won't suspect me," he said. "Who would be crazy enough to break off a hood piece and then call to inquire about buying the car that goes with it?"

"But you're sort of like a criminal returning to the scene of a crime," I said.

"Don't depress me with your detective-novel logic," he said. And then a policeman came into the diner. Henry whispered, "I'll tell them you didn't know a thing . . . Perhaps I could plead insanity. Driven mad by a culture centered around automobiles." The policeman ordered a cup of coffee to go and left.

Henry made the phone call and got an answering machine, which gave a Manhattan number where the occupants could be reached. He wasn't prepared for that, so he had to make a second call. He borrowed a pen from the waitress, which he dropped at the crucial moment, and missed the number. "*SCHEISSE!*" he exclaimed again, and several people looked at him.

He was ready to give up, but I offered to make the third call. "This car has already cost me fifty cents!" Henry complained.

I paid for the third call and was able to successfully record the Manhattan number that the voice on the machine had left. I wanted to help Henry so that he would appreciate me, but on the other hand, I didn't want to help him so well that he would be able to leave New York. But getting the number for Henry felt safe. I didn't really think that Cutlass was going to be his salvation.

CHAPTER IX

Whatever Happened to Danny Kaye?

We returned to New York and the next day, Henry called the owners of the Cutlass. They were a married couple, the Fleischmans, obviously Jewish. Henry dropped some names of people he knew in Easthampton and Southampton and this impressed the Fleischmans. He arranged to meet with them on the afternoon of the thirtieth to discuss buying the car. Henry thought that in person he could negotiate a better price than over the phone.

Henry had a good feeling about the Cutlass and so he stopped all other car hunting. He spent most of his time with Marjorie, his ex-fiancée, since he was abandoning her New Year's Eve to be with Vivian Cudlip.

I slept a lot and went to a few movies. It was relaxing to be off from work, and I read two Graham Greene novels and they weren't about gentlemen, but they were very English, so they made for good reading.

I was tempted a few times to return to Sally's, but I wanted to discipline myself and stay out of trouble. I knew that if I spent much more time there, I was sure to do something I might regret.

For his date with the Fleischmans, Henry dressed up in his gray slacks and blue blazer outfit and went to their apartment on Fifth Avenue and Seventy-second Street. He was very hopeful that this would be the end of the great car search, but he returned from the negotiations defeated and disheartened.

"I'm making progress towards nothing," he lamented as he sat in his throne-chair. "The season in Palm Beach is advancing without me."

"The Fleischmans don't want to sell the car?" I asked, secretly pleased.

"It needs too much work. The ignition is dead, the battery is dead, the radiator is rusted. The hood ornament is stolen. But the husband would sell it. Gershon could get it running probably, but the wife wants to keep it as a spare closet. That's why they have all that luggage in there. He intimated, when she left the room for a moment, that she can't throw or give anything away because of the Holocaust. They are survivors."

"They were in the camps?"

"No, they got out before that, they fled Germany, but they were quite wealthy and lost everything. He owned a leather factory. The Nazis destroyed it."

"How did they get rich over here?"

"Another leather factory, but they have no friends, she said. They want me to advance them socially. I told them all I know: cultivate only those people that can help you, trample over all others, and get involved with charities—that's where you meet the right people."

"That's beautiful advice," I said.

"That's the way it works. Women in New York are always yelling, 'He called me every day. I introduced him to everyone. Now he never calls.' So what. You are friends with people until they introduce you to more attractive people, then you drop everyone who brought you along to begin with. That's the nature of society."

"Don't you feel funny, then, being a member of society?"

"I am not a member. That's where I get my free meals. Nowhere else do I get free meals."

The next day was New Year's Eve and it snowed. Henry was to be with Vivian that evening and since he had something to look forward to, and the snow kept us from resuming the car search, Henry did his best not to think about his automobile woes. We stayed in all afternoon and watched a series of Danny Kaye films on the Classic movie channel: *The Secret Life of Walter Mitty*, *Court Jester*, and *The Inspector General.* Henry warmed up some apple juice on the stove and added rum, and we sat on the two couches and got drunk.

I said to Henry, "Do you think we drink too much?"

"Men face reality, women don't. That's why men need to drink," he said.

That sounded like a good maxim, so I enjoyed my drink and the movies. And it turned out that we both loved Danny Kaye. This made me feel happy. I kept an accounting of all our similarities like money in a bank.

After the second Danny Kaye movie, Henry said, "What ever happened to Danny Kaye? It's strange. He just disappeared and it was before AIDS."

"You mean Danny Kaye was gay?" I asked.

"Of course!" said Henry with annoyance. "He and Olivier were lovers."

"Olivier too?"

"Why don't you know these things?" asked Henry, exasperated with my innocence.

"I'm not an expert like you on the sexuality of twentieth-century figures," I said, fighting back.

"You don't have to be an expert. Olivier was British, and the British are all homosexual because of public school. They never really get over it."

"I know. You've said that before."

"Well, some things need to be reinforced."

"I can't imagine Danny Kaye and Laurence Olivier," I said.

"Oh, yes," said Henry, with assurance. "Opposites."

I tried picturing them in bed. "Who played the woman?" I asked, phrasing my question in nineteenth-century terms that I thought would appeal to Henry.

"Danny Kaye, I imagine. He could do a lot of accents. That way Olivier could have a different woman every night . . . But they were both very versatile."

After the movies, Henry wanted to take a nap to be ready for the night's festivities. And I was tired from the rum and apple juice, so I also lay down.

When I woke up, Henry was in his tuxedo pants and shirt and when he saw that I was no longer sleeping, he put on his Ethel Merman record of Cole Porter songs. It was his favorite album, and she was singing "Anything Goes."

"Dance with me," he shouted over the music.

This was a first, and though I felt shy, I joined him on the orange carpet. Our dance floor. We didn't hold hands and we didn't look at each other, at least Henry didn't look at me. We moved privately, but in close proximity. Henry thrust his arms into the air, twisted his neck, and shuffled sideways, criss-crossing his legs like Fred Astaire. Then he spun. He skipped. He elevated his eyebrows to the beat of the music to exercise his forehead. He sang along with Ethel Merman in breathless whispers. My feet shuffled a little. I swayed at the hips, jumped once or twice, and felt very happy.

"Loosen up!" he commanded me. "It's almost 1993."

I shuffled more energetically. We didn't have much room, only about seven feet of carpet, so we moved with our backs to one another like flamenco dancers. I was dazzled. The next song came on. Outside the window it was a black winter night. Snow in the moonlight, in the city lights, glowed like white paint on the roof of the building across the way. Our orangish apartment radiated warmth. The mirrors and Christmas balls sparkled. Cole Porter was a genius. Ethel Merman sang to us and we sang along: "'You're romance. You're the steppes of Russia. You're the pants of a Roxy usher. I'm a lazy lout who's just about to stop, but baby, if I'm the bottom, you're the top!'"

Then right at the end of the song and the record, Henry screamed and collapsed to his knees like he had been shot. He's had a heart attack, I thought, he's going to die. His head fell to the carpet like a Muslim praying.

"My sciatica!" he bellowed. "Wine!"

I dropped to my knees beside him. "Are you all right?"

"Wine!"

I dashed into the kitchen. I filled Henry's wine goblet with the cheap red wine that was always around. I rushed back to him. He was still in the prayer position. I cleared a spot on the coffee table for the wine goblet.

"Can I lift you on to your bed?"

"No." His eyes were closed in pain.

"What should I do?"

"Give me my wine."

He was on his elbows and knees, but he was able to raise his head a little. He lifted up his right hand and I gave him the wine goblet. He tilted his head and spilled half the wine on the carpet, like spilling gasoline at the Queensborough parking lot, and he swallowed the rest. He handed the goblet back to me and said, "More."

I refilled it; he spilled and drank. Then he lowered himself completely, groaning in genuine agony, until he was lying prone on the floor in a fetal position. I took his pillow and rested it under his head. I lifted the needle off the spinning, soundless Cole Porter.

"Henry," I said, "should I call an ambulance?"

He was silent. His eyes were closed. His face was clenched in agony. I was kneeling right beside him. I waited for him to tell me what to do. Was he dying on me? His lips were stained from the wine. Did he need mouth-to-mouth? I would have done it. He opened his eyes and said, "You looked like Danny Kaye when you were dancing."

There was no irony to his voice. It was the most affectionate and praiseworthy thing he had ever said to me. Even better than comparing me to George Washington. He closed his eyes. "I have to sleep," he said. "My spine is dissolving. Call Doubles and leave a message for Vivian Cudlip. Say that Dr. Harrison has taken ill and is unable to attend, with the most profound regrets."

I took Henry's blanket off his bed and lay it over him. I took off his shoes. He didn't say anything to stop me from behaving so intimately. I called Doubles and spoke to the maître d': "Can you take a very important message for Mrs. Vivian Cudlip?" I wanted Henry to hear how I was taking expert care of him.

"Oh, yes," the man said with genuine deference.

"Please tell her that Dr. Harrison—Dr. Henry Harrison—is ill and is unable to attend, with the most profound regrets. Those words please."

When I hung up Henry thanked me and said, "If you could, refill the wineglass and leave it next to me in case I need it . . . This sciatica comes every few years, like a locust. I may be in bed, or on the floor, for the next few days."

I shut off the lights in his room and said, "I'm staying in, so if you need me, I'm here."

I lay in bed reading. It was New Year's Eve 1992. A few hours after his attack, around ten o'clock, he called out to me.

"Louis?"

"Yes? Are you all right?"

"I'm still alive."

"Do you want me to help you on to your bed?"

"No. But I found some aspirin and codeine on the coffee table and knocked them to the floor. I swallowed several and drank the rest of the wine. This might be important if the coroner needs to know cause of death. After he examines the body, I'd like to be buried in a tree like an Indian. But they won't let you do it. You have to own the property and even then they won't let you do it. Try to come up with something."

"What about the mass in Latin?" I asked.

"No. I've changed my mind. I want a Native American burial."

"Gershon and I will take you to a tree in New Jersey. We'll find some woods."

"I'd like a tree in Monte Carlo. That would be nice. Or Ireland. Lagerfeld would take the body to Ireland if her expenses were paid, though she'd probably have it dropped in the sea."

"What about all your possessions?" I asked. I was hoping he'd say that he'd leave me something. It would be another sign of affection, like the Danny Kaye remark.

"Everything goes to Catholic charities. I'd like to leave the car to Gershon for all the work he's done. He could sell the parts. And the royalties from my plays, which will skyrocket after I die, will also go to Catholic charities. Can you write all this down?"

"Yes," I said, playing along with him, a little disappointed to not be left anything.

"None of this would have happened if I was in Florida. My back needs sun. They used to have solariums in Coney Island in the winter, but that's all gone . . . And during the summer you could go to Atlantic City if you were tired of Coney Island. You know they used to have the moral police in Atlantic City. Women would patrol the beach in blue skirts and fine you if you were caught embracing. New Jersey has always been very virtuous. They have the moral police in Saudi Arabia, you know. That's a good idea." Henry's voice was a little slurred; the codeine and wine were having an effect. "I'm all for moral police. My ideal country would be communist with a king and an archbishop to instill moral order. England is that way, but the Queen has no power and the Church of England can't make up its mind on anything. Iran is a good setup. If I was the bishop, I wouldn't go into people's apartments, I would make allowances for private orgies . . ." He trailed off and he was silent.

"Henry?" I said, and there was no answer. I got out of bed. How many codeine had he taken? Could he have overdosed? It was unlike him to just stop talking. Was his last word going to be "orgies"?

I ran into his room and his breathing was audible. He was asleep and he looked comfortable on the floor. I adjusted his blanket around his shoulders. Then I decided that I had better sleep on his couch. If his breathing stopped, I would be there to revive him. I just hoped that I would wake up instinctively, like a mother hearing her child cry.

I got my blanket and pillow and sheet, which I put over his sheet. The fleas were probably gone, but Henry wasn't the cleanest man and I wanted the reassuring smells of my own bedding. His little couch was narrow but comfortable. I had a sense of how Henry felt each night. I liked it. My feet dangled off the end. My head was in the east. I could see the refrigerator in the west. We still hadn't defrosted it.

We both made it through the night, his breathing didn't stop, and I woke up before he did, which was good. This way he wouldn't know that I had been on his couch. He wouldn't have liked my playing nurse that way.

That morning, January 1, he was in a good deal of pain. He stayed in his tuxedo pants and shirt, but he did manage to get off the floor and sit in his chair by the phone.

"Is there anything I can do for you? Should I take you to a doctor?" I asked.

"No. Doctors can't do anything for sciatica. I need endless pleasure and no responsibilities, so there's no hope. Any time I have to do something, like move, my back gets worse . . . Take me to a horse show. That would get my mind off my back. Dorothy Glade, the soap opera actress, invited me out to New Jersey once, to the horse country. And she also invited these two fairies. The type of homosexual they don't make anymore. Real urnings. They had dyed blond hair and they were sitting on a red fire truck watching the Essex Hunt and Steeplechase, looking perfectly bored while everyone else was in a frenzy. I'll always remember them on that red fire truck. That's the kind of thing that would distract me. That's the kind of thing that happens in New Jersey."

I was happy. When Henry complimented New Jersey, he was complimenting me. And then I asked, "Why were those men on the fire truck so poignant?"

"Because they didn't care at all about what was going on. It was a great example of utter indifference."

I went to The Salt of the Earth to get us coffee and rolls and newspapers, and when I came back to Henry with our breakfast, he was just finishing a phone conversation with Vivian Cudlip. After they rang off, he said, "Vivian asked me how I was. I said, 'My spine is deteriorating.' She said, 'That's so true. I know what you mean.' I don't think she hears half of what I say. But it's not good to tell her about problems. It bores her. She only likes people who are pressing on, like her. Usually, I am pressing on. But now I'm on the verge of a total breakdown. Sciatica. Taxes. Cars. Fleas, possibly. It's an absurd existence."

I didn't know what to say to comfort him. We drank our coffee and read our papers. In spite of Henry's condition, it was a moment of pleasant domesticity that lasted for about fifteen minutes until it was interrupted by the phone. Henry answered.

"Oh, hello, Gershon . . . Yes. Happy New Year. What's happening with me? Still no car and my spine is going."

A few moments later Henry hung up and said, "Gershon is coming up. He has devices to fix my back. He's worked on me before. When he can't fix my cars, he fixes my back. He's a dilettante. Now he's into boats. He wants to join the New York Yacht Club. I told him he first has to shave that beard. He has enough money to join, but not the right look."

Gershon knocked at the door and I let him in. I hadn't seen him for a few weeks. Under his arm he had a shoe box and a book. He looked at me and he had a shy person's tentative, sweet smile. We shook hands. "Thanks for coming up to help out," I said with spirit. I had adopted Henry's attitude of superiority towards Gershon, even though he had more money than the both of us.

"I like to help," he said.

"You're getting more Bacchus-like every day," said Henry. He tried to raise out of his chair to greet Gershon, but instead he emitted a King Learish groan of pain and could not move. Gershon strode purposefully into Henry's room and put his things on the white couch.

"Let me lift you up . . . and lie you on the floor," said Gershon, in his usual halting, near-stuttering way.

"What?"

"I have my book on . . . acupressure . . . I've read what spots I need to put pressure on."

"I can't be touched! Only by royal-family-approved physicians!"

"Don't be difficult," said Gershon in a whisper, but with uncharacteristic force. "I fixed you two years ago."

"You did not. You made it worse."

"You could walk again."

And then Gershon grabbed Henry by the hips with his enormous meaty hands and lifted Henry up into a standing position.

Henry's face turned scarlet with anger. "Bellman sent you up here to kill me."

"Let me crack your back like I did two years ago . . . then I'll lie you down and do the acupressure." I hadn't expected Gershon to be so commanding. His devotion to Henry was apparent. He knew that the only way to help him was to defy him.

"Tell Bellman he can keep *Henry and Mary Are Always Late*," said Henry. "And you can have the car. It's already in the will. Louis wrote it last night when I thought I was going to overdose on codeine and wine."

Gershon ignored Henry's bribes and put his arms around Henry and hugged him to his enormous stout chest in an effort to crack his back. Henry strained his face to the left, trying to avoid Gershon's beard.

"Gershon, please, be careful," I said.

Gershon then kneeled down, still holding Henry to him. He was a powerful man, capable of lifting car engines and volumes of the *OED*. He somehow maneuvered Henry on to the floor. Henry, inert and stunned, lay with his face turned towards me, his right cheek on the orange carpet. Then his eyes widened.

"Under the bed . . . I see my eye mask!"

I retrieved the eye mask, and squatting next to Henry, I put it in his hand. He rubbed the silky black eye-patches fondly between his fingers. Gershon was turning the pages of his book. He found what he was looking for: a large diagram of the human body with black dots in various locations.

"I'm going . . . to put pressure . . . above both butt-ocks."

"What? Don't use your hands! Germs. There's a broomstick behind my armoire. Use that."

I retrieved the broomstick for Gershon. He put the acupressure book next to Henry; it was open to the diagram as a guide. Then he stood above Henry, straddling him, and squinted his eyes at the book. He needed glasses. Then he dug the broom handle into the left side of Henry's lower back. He reminded me of a gondolier. Henry screamed, but the angle of his head and the carpet muffled his cry.

I have to admit that it was strangely pleasurable to watch Henry be tortured. Gershon held the pole into Henry's back until the cries subsided, then he dug it in afresh to more cries, until he finally released it. He kneeled beside the book to find the next spot.

Henry was resigned. He said, "I give up. As Napoleon said, 'When rape is inevitable, sit back and enjoy it.'"

Gershon lodged the pole into two more spots. There was something primitive to the whole cure. It was like I was watching Henry be bled or exorcised of demons. He would scream and then moan with pleasure.

Then Gershon stopped using the broomstick, and he took from the shoe box a gleaming silver contraption. It was shaped like a barber's clippers, but with a large silver knob at the end. It had an electrical cord and Gershon plugged it in. The device also came with a black Velcro wrist-strap and Gershon secured it to himself like a carpenter with a sander. He turned it on and the silver knob spun rapidly and brilliantly and made a whirring noise. Henry twisted his neck and saw the sparkling instrument, and Gershon kneeled down. Henry, rejuvenated by the acupressure with the broom handle, was able to roll onto his back like Gregor Samsa. He put his hands up defensively and said, "I have suffered enough. That thing is only for depraved women!"

"It's for massage," said Gershon.

"No!"

Gershon's shoulders relaxed. I could tell that he wanted to use the device—he was a man of tools—but he also seemed a little worn out from battling with Henry, and he relented on this part of the treatment.

"With this wrist strap . . . you can treat yourself . . . just reach around. I'll leave it here, and the book."

"Thank you, Gershon. You are a great friend. Now if you would both be so kind as to help me on to my bed." We lifted him up— Gershon did most of the work—and then Henry, comfortably secure on his couch, said, "I need to sleep. I want to try out my eye mask. I've missed it terribly."

The Men Are Still in Charge Down There

The next day, the second of January, I returned to work at *Terra*. I called my ladies and they told me about their holidays. But things were a little slow, a lot of my contacts were still on vacation, so I called my great-aunt to check on her, and she told me that a repairman had come to fix the refrigerator.

"He was bald, forties, big belly, blue eyes, and he was the sweet-est guy," she reported. "He had to use the bathroom and he put the seat back down. A gentleman. He was a pleasure to have in the apartment. I always have luck with repairmen."

I checked on Henry in the morning and he was feeling all right, and then I called again late in the afternoon, but there was no answer. I was a little concerned. I rushed back to our apartment as soon as work was over and I found Henry just beginning to pack one of his large suitcases.

"What's happening?" I asked. "How are you feeling?"

"Much better. A little stiff, but the burning has stopped. Gershon cured me with that broomstick."

"But why are you packing?"

"I'm leaving for Florida immediately. I'm taking a bus. There's one at nine o'clock tonight. There's a six-hour layover in Jacksonville. I could take a direct bus tomorrow, but I can't stand New York for another day. My health depends on it. I need pleasure."

"I'm sorry there's no pleasure here for you," I said.

"I did have some pleasure today. The Jewish Guild for the Blind is taking my car. They even agreed to tow it off the Queensborough campus. I can write it off as a charitable gift, if I ever do my taxes."

"Why does the Jewish Guild want your car?"

"They sell old cars for scrap and then use the money to print books in Braille."

I was proud that a Jewish organization had helped Henry. Like the qualities that he attributed to New Jersey, I hoped that Henry would see the actions of the Jewish Guild as a reflection of my own character.

But I didn't want him to leave, and so I said, hoping to put fear in him, "Do you think your sciatica can handle a bus ride? You might have another attack and be in some terrible bus station."

"Just knowing that I will be in the sun should give me courage if the pain returns. And I have plenty of codeine; I went out and refilled an old prescription."

"What about a car?"

"I'll find one down there. I'll rent a bicycle until I do. I like bicycles."

I retreated to my room to let Henry pack without distraction. I was shocked by the suddenness of his decision. I lay on my bed and I felt sort of trembly and scared about him leaving.

While he packed, the television was on with the news. Clinton's inauguration was to take place soon, and there was a lot of uproar about the new president's stance on gays and the military. A reporter for the news show was on the street asking people, "Do you think homosexuals belong in the armed forces?"

Henry said from his room, "This country is losing its hypocrisy. We need to hold on to it."

"You think we need hypocrisy?" I asked.

"Yes. It keeps people from getting at each other's throats. Clinton doesn't understand this. He's going to destroy the Navy. They were happy homos the way they were. We were so much more sophisticated years ago. If you were gay you joined the Navy and you were perfectly happy. And if you couldn't get in the Navy, you tried to go to jail. Clinton wants everything out in the open. It won't work. It's nobody's business what you do for sex . . . Maybe hypocrisy is not the right word . . . Discretion. Yes. Discretion in sex and in mail fraud."

I lay on my bed. I agreed with him that it was nobody's business, but I wanted to be the exception in Henry's case: I wanted to know what he did for sex. But I hid my immature curiosity. "Why discretion in mail fraud?" I asked.

"You have to be careful. The post office has its own police, you know." Then he was silent a moment before calling out, "Have you seen my social register?"

"No, I haven't," I said.

"I need it to call a lady friend in Palm Beach. I don't have her number in my address book. It's hard to lose a social register. This is very odd. Gershon probably took it, sending out late Christmas cards."

I came out of my room to help him look for the book. It was thick and black and on its front cover, in orange printing, was its year, 1988. Henry had an old one. The social register is reprinted every two years, and over one thousand of America's leading families are listed. Addresses, phone numbers, universities attended, club memberships, and other pertinent information are all printed for everyone to read. I had looked at it a few times and I had taken pleasure in seeing that a number of Iveses, though of no relation to me, were registered.

We found the book underneath Henry's green trousers. Henry contemplated taking the pants with him to Palm Beach.

"That's the problem with having such an extensive wardrobe," he said. "Difficult choices have to be made. These might look very good at night, but in direct sunlight all the stains will be visible. Things have to be clean down there. You can see everything."

Henry threw the pants on to the white couch. He looked up his lady friend in the register and found her number. He was going to ask her if she would put him up for the season.

"She's not seen much anymore," he said. "She might jump at the opportunity to have me. Young blood."

He picked up the phone and sat in his throne-chair and adopted a posture of confidence and popularity.

"Betty, this is Henry. Henry Harrison . . . Yes, the playwright . . . I'm still in New York, but I'll be in Palm Beach in two days. I'm taking a bus, I've been having all sorts of automobile problems . . . I'm sorry to hear that. All our trials come in different forms . . . I would love to see you . . . Yes. It would be wonderful to stay with you . . ."

They rang off and Henry admitted that she was wise enough to know why he had called, but she didn't mind. He needed a room and she needed company.

"Things are going your way," I said.

"Yes. My eye mask. The Jewish Guild. And now I have a place to stay. She's in a wheelchair—emphysema from smoking—but they have ramps at the Everglades Club, where she's a member. I'll have most evenings free. It should be fine. The main thing is the sun."

Henry kept on packing and I couldn't stand to watch, so I went out to eat. He declined my offer to bring him back something. His excitement had killed his appetite. When I returned he asked me if I would drive him to the Port Authority at eight-thirty.

"Of course," I said. "I expected to."

"I'll give you five dollars," he said.

"Don't be ridiculous," I said.

"I want no obligations!"

I didn't want to argue with him on his last night, so I relented and he gave me the five dollars immediately. Then he said, "I want to show you something. I found my old album in the armoire. It has a picture of my aunt. I thought you might want to see her."

We sat on his bed and Henry flipped through the fragile-looking pages of his thick album to find the picture he was looking for. He was holding the book away from me so that I couldn't see anything, but I peeked around his shoulder and saw briefly what looked like an old-fashioned black-and-white college yearbook photo.

"Is that you, Henry?"

"No."

He found the pages he wanted and opened the album for me to see. Two facing pages were devoted to his aunt. One whole page was a large black-and-white portrait photo. She was wearing a high Victorian lace collar. Her hair looked thick and beautiful, like Henry's. She was distinguished looking and lovely. There was a forthright cast to her eyes. She was not a demure woman.

"She has your eyes and cheekbones," I said to Henry.

"I have hers."

On the opposite page there were two old newspaper clippings of Baltimore society columns. In both columns there was a photograph of Henry's aunt. One of the photos was a copy of the portrait on the other page, and the other picture showed Henry's aunt wearing a white dress and standing with a group of people at a wedding. The headline of the column with her portrait was "Grace Rutherford Leaves for France Today."

"Back then society columns were really society columns. Now it's all Hollywood scandal," said Henry, as he looked at his aunt. Then he closed the album and put it back in the armoire.

"So there we are," said Henry. "Where are we?"

"She was very beautiful," I said.

Henry was silent; his excitement about leaving drained out of him. I think he was engaging in a rare moment of sentimentality, having looked at his aunt's picture. He was missing her. But then he began to pack a few more things, dirty shirts mostly, until he said with renewed vigor, "The great moment has come—the closing of the suitcase!" He sat on it, but couldn't get it to buckle. "I need a valet . . . Sit down with me," he said.

I sat on the large suitcase with him—we were back-to-back—and we both tried to hop up and down a little, but we couldn't get the buckles to click into place. Then I gathered all my strength, pressed down as hard as I could, and was able to snap the thing shut. This impressed Henry very much. "They could use you in the Army," he said. "They always need good packers."

Even though it was a silly compliment, I always felt good when Henry praised me. We put on our winter coats and I carried the suitcase down to the vestibule. I had Henry wait there while I went to get the car.

As we drove to the Port Authority, Henry mused about his trip. "I have a bottle of vermouth to go with the codeine. I'll probably end up sharing it with all the others on the bus—paroled convicts and black domestics. There is no one else like me in America. I live like the very poor and the very rich . . . You know, Jacksonville is very interesting for its redneck culture. I'll have to go to a bar during my layover and do some research. The women have no teeth in Jacksonville. Not because they lost them, but because the men knocked them out. The men are still in charge down there. They don't know what they are doing, but at least they're still in charge."

We arrived at the Port Authority and the traffic was thick on Eighth Avenue. It was close to nine—there was nowhere to park—so I double-parked next to the taxi line. I wanted to leave the car and carry Henry's suitcase into the station, but he wouldn't let me.

"You'll get a ticket," he said.

"I don't care," I said. "I'm worried about your back."

"Worry about the eighty-five-dollar ticket. Not my back. I have thirty codeine pills. One for every hour. Just get the suitcase out of the car and I can roll it inside on its wheels."

I lifted the bag out of the trunk, and we stood by the taxis. The traffic flowed past us on the other side of the Parisienne. Henry practiced lifting his suitcase.

"I'll have to get help in Jacksonville. I'll have to be like Blanche Dubois," said Henry, and then he slipped into a sultry Southern-woman's accent and said, "I can't lift my suitcase. Are there any pickaninnies who can lift this for me? I always had pickaninnies carry my bags into the Tarantula Arms."

As he finished his Blanche Dubois speech, he pushed and kicked the suitcase between the two taxis next to us and managed to lift the bag over the curb and onto the sidewalk. He resumed his kicking and pushing. I ran to the curb, leaving my Parisienne, and I said, "Good-bye, Henry."

He turned to look at me and said, "Get back to your car. The *Polizei*. Don't be a fool."

I retreated back to my Parisienne and I watched Henry make it to the glass doors of the Port Authority. He spoke to a thin, dark, black boy who was standing there, most likely a hustler. The boy picked up the bag with effort and carried it inside. Henry didn't look back to see if I was still there. After he went through the doors I couldn't see him. He didn't even shake my hand good-bye.

I got into my car. I thought of going to Sally's, which was only one block away, and getting drunk. It would taint my good-bye with him, which was what I wanted. That way I wouldn't deserve to miss him or to have him think about me on the bus. But I didn't go to Sally's. I drove right past Forty-third Street, surprising myself. I raced all the way home, somehow insanely hoping that Henry would be there even though I had just left him.

When I entered the apartment I was struck by its ugliness. The clutter and dirt and smell were unhealthy and nauseating. How could I live here? Henry's leaving had sucked out all the grandeur and glow that my eyes had been filtered with like a scrim. He had made the apartment seem like a star's haphazard dressing room.

I went straight for his armoire. Before I opened it up, I saw on the floor a ticket. His packing had disrupted everything. It was a speeding ticket from New Jersey, dated around the time that he and Gershon had gone looking for cars. The policeman had written down Henry's license number, address, and date of birth. It was March 23, 1920. Henry was going to be seventy-three years old. He was more amazing than ever. I put the ticket on his coffee table, so that he could find it when he came home. I lay it upside down so that he wouldn't think that I had seen his age.

I opened the armoire and underneath several tangled shirts I found the album. I sat on the white couch and started looking at the pictures. There were about a dozen black-and-white photos that seemed to cover Henry's college years and his twenties.

The most striking picture showed Henry sitting on a bicycle. He was maybe twenty-five years old and he had no shirt on and he was wearing shorts. He was on a dirt road at the top of a cliff, and down below you could see the Mediterranean and what looked like Monte Carlo. His body was lithe and beautiful. His stomach was flat; his arms were perfectly shaped. His face was handsome and clear. He wasn't smiling. He had a young man's expression of melancholy and romance, as if he'd always be beautiful.

Then there were three or four color photos that represented, I think, Henry in his thirties. They all appeared to be taken the same day. First there was Henry in front of a French château. He was wearing a blue blazer and raincoat and nothing was stained. The next two pictures showed Henry at a cocktail party with a group of attractive-looking, fashionable people. He was still handsome, but there was the beginning of the cast to his face of amused yet weary detachment, which was now permanently etched.

For a whole life, Henry had saved very few pictures. The album was mostly empty. In the back, unattached to a page, there was an actress's old black-and-white head-shot. She was very beautiful and her name was Constance Seehusen, one of the women Henry had mentioned as one of his loves. I wondered if it had really been a romance, or if he had auditioned her for one of his plays and had held on to her picture because she was beautiful and it was a lie, a fantasy that they had ever been together. But a lie that he himself had come to believe. Like once when I was thirteen, I had carved a girl's initials into a tree to pretend that I had a girlfriend, and then years later when I saw the initials, I smiled happily because I momentarily believed my own falsehood. I had changed the history of my life, but then I remembered. Did Henry do the same thing with this woman's picture, but not remember the truth? I didn't know what to think about Henry and love.

I went back to the picture of him on the bicycle. He was so flawless. Then I looked at his narrow bed across from me with his ragged, dirty clothes piled on top, his empty bottles underneath. I tried to look into that beautiful young man's eyes. We were very close in age. I wanted to warn him, and I started to cry a little. I was crying because that boy had no idea what he would become, that fifty years later he'd be sleeping on a mean little couch in a filthy room.

I was crying for what had happened to that young man, and I was crying because the old man he became had left me behind.

CHAPTER X

She Wanted Me

I was starting to think that all women were transsexuals. I couldn't tell the difference. It was frustrating. I was on the subway heading to Sally's—I didn't feel like driving—and I saw this young Hispanic girl sitting on her boyfriend's lap. She was pretty and she liked it on his lap. So I immediately thought that she must be a transsexual, but I couldn't believe that she was behaving so openly on the subway. As a Jew I was raised to keep a low profile, not to attract attention and ridicule, and I had observed the same thing in transsexuals. Outside of Sally's they weren't demonstrative, they blended in.

This girl looked like the Hispanic girls at Sally's: jeans, work-boots, down coat, overly painted red mouth—but maybe she was a real girl. The problem was I hadn't seen a real girl on a man's lap in a long time. I thought that only transsexuals acted sexy with men. So I studied the young couple. It was the boy that convinced me that she was a real girl. He was too relaxed and natural. He was a real boy and she was a real girl. I figured that maybe in the Hispanic community the old roles were still in place. I envied those two. They kissed. I wanted to be both of them. I wanted to be strong enough to hold someone, or lovely enough to be held.

I used the dark subway window as a mirror. I was twenty-six years old and going bald. I couldn't stand the way I looked. My face was tormented, and my young gentleman costume of corduroy pants, tweed sport coat, and overcoat was a sham of respectability.

Because of the happy, vital couple I went into Sally's feeling sorry for myself. With Henry gone I was at the bar several nights a week and most of the time the place put me in a good mood. The girls were beautiful and their beauty made me feel alive. But that night I felt like I wouldn't be able to shake my self-pity. I sat at the large oval bar and ordered a rum and coke. I looked for Miss Pepper, but she wasn't there. The place was smoky and crowded.

There were dozens of girls, half as many men. The girls looked sexy, the men looked ashamed.

A tall blonde approached me. She was in a tight red dress, which showed off her nice breasts and good legs. I'd seen her around, but this was the first time we had ever talked.

"How are you tonight?" she asked.

"Fine," I said. "A little depressed." I tried to open up sometimes with the girls. I kind of hoped that one of them could help me.

But the blonde snapped at me. She was tough, maybe in a bad mood. She said, "I don't want to hear your problems."

"OK," I said. But my face must have showed a little hurt and she still wanted a chance at my money, so she said, "All right, why are you depressed?"

"Because I'm crazy."

"Why are you crazy?"

"Because I'm here."

"You're not crazy," she said. "God made you this way. You like Queens. So what? Would God make a mistake? I'm beautiful—did he make a mistake with me?"

"No."

"See, God doesn't make mistakes . . . So, do you want to go on a date? I know you'd like to see my big cock."

A lot of the Queens, like this blonde, had some type of religious philosophy. They needed it to survive. The whole world was against them. But the blonde was only trying to convert me to get at my money. I didn't mind that, but she was too rough for me. I liked it when the girls acted feminine and didn't mention their penises. For me it is better if I forget about the penis and then act surprised and a little excited if I should see it later. I said to the blonde, "I don't think so. Not tonight."

"Your loss," she said, and she did give me a sweet smile, keeping open her chances at getting me some other time. And then she grabbed my crotch and took a quick measurement. All the Queens did this, and then she walked away.

I felt better. I was back into the swing of my Sally's life. I finished my drink and ordered another and then I spotted a young

Hispanic girl who was voluptuous. She was wearing a shirt buttoned very low to show off her beautiful, soft-looking breasts. They looked very real to me. She looked real to me. Her skin was flawless and olive and she had dark eyes. Her brown hair was naturally curly and went to her shoulders. Because of my own balding I often worried about the girls going bald. They looked good in wigs, but they really looked much sexier when it was their own hair. I wondered sometimes if the female hormones stopped them from balding. I wondered if a small dosage might help my hair.

The Hispanic girl was just as pretty as the one I had seen on the subway and eventually as she cruised the bar she sat next to me. We started talking business. I had some suspicion that she might be a regular prostitute. I was getting annoyed and frightened. I couldn't perceive the world properly anymore. Real girls were transsexuals, transsexuals were real girls.

She said the date would cost one hundred and fifty dollars, plus the hotel room. I tried to get her lower, but she said she had standards. She was tough and sullen and arrogant.

I said to her, "You're the prettiest girl in here." I always told the girls that they were very pretty, even the ugly ones. They wanted to know that they looked on the outside how they felt on the inside. My compliment softened her up a little. She gave me a smile for a second, and that's when I knew that she was a transsexual. She appreciated and needed the compliment. Then she was tough again. She said, "I know I am. So do you want a date or not?" She didn't play the game at all. I needed the illusion of sweetness and so I told her I couldn't afford her prices.

She moved on and I kept watching her because I was quite attracted to her. She started talking to this old fellow near me who was wearing a tuxedo. It was the first time I had ever seen anyone in black tie at Sally's. He was thin and tiny and had this little shock of white hair. He was lit up with drink. He had a radiant smile. He wasn't embarrassed to be there, like most of us were. I wondered if he was a headwaiter somewhere or a crazy rich man. He got the Hispanic girl to sit on his lap and I heard him say with enthusiasm, "I want to see it."

They went to the farthest, darkest corner of the bar, which was beyond the dance floor. There were some tables and chairs there in the shadows and he sat down and she stood before him. I followed them part of the way. I stood by the two carpeted stairs that led to the dance floor. The old man and the girl were about fifty feet away from me. Two girls were dancing by themselves on the dance floor so I could pretend to be watching them. I saw the old man give the girl some money and then she dropped her jeans a little. She dug her hand in her panties and it looked like she was struggling to get it out. She must have really tucked it up there or maybe tied it to something. But then she released it and he put out his greedy, old-man hands. I couldn't see her penis because my angle was mostly from behind and I was trying to be discreet.

He had a big smile on his face and he only held her penis and maybe gave it a kiss or two for about a minute. That must have been all the time they had contracted for. She backed away from him and with effort retucked herself. She left him sitting there. He still looked happy, fearless. She walked back across the dance floor. I shrunk back against the wall and as she passed me I could see that her face was less arrogant, less tough. She seemed momentarily unsure of herself and I felt surprised. Something about being with the old man had been distasteful to her. Maybe it was less easy to whore herself than she let on, or maybe his single-minded interest in "seeing it" had punctured for a little while her own illusions about being a beautiful girl.

I continued to lean against the wall and I watched everybody. I stood there maybe ten minutes observing the endless cruising, and then an Asian girl came and leaned against the wall near me. I hadn't seen her before, and she struck me as a wallflower, shy and daunted by the competition for men. She had a very pretty face, her cheekbones were pronounced and high, and her nose was delicate. She had shiny black hair to her shoulders. Her arms were thin and white. She was wearing a jean miniskirt, and like most of the Asian girls there seemed to be no hint of her original sex.

I started talking to her. Her name was Sylvia, and she was careful with her English, but she spoke well.

"Where are you from?" I asked.

"Manhattan."

"I mean before Manhattan."

"Korea."

"How long have you been in the States?"

"Five years."

"What do you do besides come here?"

"I go to F.I.T."

Many of the Asian girls I had spoken to were studying fashion. They came to Sally's to pay for school. Then Sylvia asked me a question. "Do you want a date with me?"

"How much?"

"Seventy-five dollars." Nobody said seventy-five dollars. She was new to Sally's. I became very excited, and I agreed to go with her. Getting a bargain made me feel like I wasn't doing something wrong. I could almost convince myself that she wanted to be with me.

We went to the money machine up by Seventh Avenue. Then I got a taxi and in the backseat we held hands. She didn't seem to mind. It was only a nine-block ride. We went to her apartment on Thirty-fourth Street, right across from Madison Square Garden. I thought about the Knicks. They were playing well the last few games.

We went up four flights of dirty wooden stairs and when we got inside she checked the bathroom to make sure nobody was in there. She said she shared the apartment with another girl. It was just a good-sized room with no kitchen. There was a big bed right in the middle, a bureau, and a nice armoire with a mirror. I paid her the money up front and she hid it in the top drawer of the bureau.

"Is that where you keep your underwear?" I asked.

"No," she said and laughed. I wanted to look at her underwear, at her panties and bras, but I didn't ask, I wanted to seem a little normal. I sat on the corner of her bed and she began to undress before me. She seemed much more relaxed and confident here in her apartment than she had been in Sally's. Her eyes were almost playful now. The clothes came off and her body was luminescently white and hairless. We hadn't turned on the lights; it wasn't neces-sary—the glow from well-lit Thirty-fourth Street infused the room with a silvery light. Only her panties were left on. She was lovely and demure. She had no breasts to speak of, but there was a swell-ing, like that of a young girl, around both nipples.

"How long have you been on the hormones?" I asked.

"A few months," she said.

It was like she was just starting puberty and I stared at her breasts, and I thought of Cindy, a twelve-year-old girl whom I had become attracted to during my first year of teaching at Pretty Brook. Her desk had been in the first row and she had yellow-white hair bleached by the sun. I'd find myself looking at her when the class had to be silent and do their work and her beautiful head was bowed. She had traces of gold on her arms and little lines of it beneath her knees, which I could see under her desk when she wore skirts during those first weeks of school. And when she lifted her head her lips were the wet pink of the inside of a shell and her eyes were blue. But it was the hint of hair beneath the knee, this intrusion of animalness, that drew me to her.

Because it was a private school we often went on weekend hikes with the children. In early September we took a bus to the Worthington State Forest by the Delaware Water Gap. We were going to hike up a small mountain and see the Appalachian Trail. It was a very hot, brilliant day and before beginning the climb the children were running around a field at the base of the mountain. Cindy was about twenty yards from me and I watched her run from some boys who were chasing her. She ran quickly, but her legs were too long and thin. She was half-grown, colt-ish. She screamed and then she disappeared behind some cabins with the boys after her and I felt aroused thinking of her young blondness. I imagined her nude and pure. To kiss her gently. I felt guilty for my thoughts, but it was safe enough to only think. And then someone jumped on my back. I was shocked. I said, "Who's on me?"

It was Cindy. She wrapped her legs around my stomach. The boys who were pursuing her surrounded us. She laughed and said,

"Protect me, Mr. Ives!" The boys looked like dogs, hot and want-ing. Their noses, too big from puberty, were like snouts. My only advantage over them was my size and authority. I wanted to chase after her too. I told the boys to leave her alone. That enough was enough. They dispersed and I touched one of her thighs, which was by my ribs, to steady her. I allowed myself to have a moment of illicit joy in that touch and then I said, "You can get down, Cindy." I tried to make every part of me awake as she slid off my back so that I could feel everything. She said, "Thank you, Mr. Ives," and then she was off running after the boys, hoping they'd chase her some more. I stood completely still, not wanting to lose the memory of her weight against me.

During the hike we split up into groups of ten and Cindy was in my group. I had five boys and five girls and as we walked through the woods it was very hot and one of the boys asked me if he could take off his shirt. I told him he could and Cindy said, "I wish I could take off my shirt. It's not fair that girls can't take off their shirts."

I thought to myself, Is this possible? Am I being tested? I said, "Well, it's good for girls to have some mystery."

"I don't have any mystery," she said. I stopped walking and so did she. The other children kept going; they hadn't paid attention to what she had said. Her face was turned down and sad. Because of my own embarrassing late start at puberty at the age of fifteen and a half, I knew she was talking about her little breasts, only the nipples seemed enlarged, which I found beautiful, but most of the other girls in the class were more developed and she was obviously comparing herself.

"Don't worry," I said, "in time you'll have lots of mystery."

She turned her eyes up at me and said, "Mr. Ives, you're the best!" And she gave me my second hug of the day. I cherished the contact, and then she ran after the other children. I was proud that I had helped her. And I was happy when her family moved a few months later and she was no longer in my class.

Sylvia liked how I was staring at her breasts and she affection-ately put her hand in my hair and said, "Take your clothes off."

There was a chair by the window and I neatly put my clothes on it and hid my wallet in my shoes. I kept my underwear on and got into bed with her. I lay there, nervous, but she smelled good. I liked cheap perfume. She said, "What do you want to do?"

"Nothing unsafe," I said. "It would be nice just to hold you."

So side by side we held each other. I went to kiss her on the cheek and she moved her face quickly. She thought I was aiming for her mouth, but I wasn't. I was glad she was like that. It was the old-fashioned rationale: if she's like that with me, then she's probably like that with the others, so most likely she's relatively disease-free.

Then she turned and lay with her back against me. I held her arm. I smelled her hair. I was happy. She said, "Why do you go to Sally's?"

"Because I'm lonely."

"Don't you have a wife?"

A lot of the men who went to Sally's were married. "I don't have a wife," I said. "Do you have a boyfriend?"

"No. It's not so easy to get a boyfriend."

"But you're very beautiful. There must be lots of guys who want to be with you." I thought of saying, I could be your boyfriend.

"No, it's not easy being a girl like me," she said. "The gay men want men, and the straight men, when they find out, don't want me."

That left only one kind of man for her, but she didn't seem to consider that an option. So I felt a little dead lying there and I regretted losing my seventy-five dollars. But then she reached back and took hold of my penis and rubbed it against her panties, against her rear. I wrapped my arms around her and I kissed the back of her neck. We both were excited and then she lay on top of me. I was erect in my underwear and she raised up to a sitting position, straddling me. She looked truly beautiful in that light. I reached up and I held her little breasts in my hands. I touched her swollen nipples. She took off her panties and I saw the small offering of her penis.

She took her penis in her hand, it was very slight, not threatening, and then she took one of my hands and had me hold it. It didn't fill out or anything. I massaged it between my thumb and fingers and I didn't know if it was so small because she had a small one or if the hormones had weakened it.

Then she got off me and pulled my underwear down. She took a condom out of her purse. She put it on me and began to suck. I watched her. I felt I was going to come too soon and I wanted to make my money last so I asked if we could rub against each other some more. She agreed and she lay on her belly. Her panties were off and I lay on her back and rubbed against her. She said, "Don't go in me."

"I won't," I said.

So we kept rubbing and the wet condom was sliding between her buttocks and she got genuinely excited. She started moaning and then raised her ass in the air, pushing me into a kneeling position. The white globes of her cheeks were beautiful. Her silky black hair lay across her shoulders. I knew she wanted me to put it in, and I was excited that she wanted to give me this after she had warned me not to, but the excitement was too much for me. It was daunting to have her ass in the air, that I had really made her aroused, and I shriveled in my condom and it slid off a little. I sort of flailed against her crack and with half a hard-on, I had a strange, yet pleasurable orgasm.

I lay beside her. She took the condom off me and carried it to the bathroom. She came back from the bathroom with a hot washcloth, which I hoped was clean, and she gently soaked me. She dried me with the sheet and then I got dressed and looked out the window to Madison Square Garden. I thought about the Knicks, whom I loved. I thought about how powerful they were. I unfairly compared myself to them, thinking that they would laugh at me if they saw me making love to transsexuals. I tied my shoes. Sylvia put on a robe, and at the door I said, "Maybe I'll see you again at Sally's."

"Maybe," she said, and she gave me a little kiss good-bye on the cheek. She really was very gentle.

But as soon as I was down the stairs I began to review in my mind if there had been any dangerous moments. I began to terrorize myself with the thought that my penis had been a little exposed when the condom slid off. I could get something from her rear area. And then as I walked to the subway in the cold I went over in my mind the possible moments of danger with Wendy, the open wound on her breast. I'm doomed, I thought.

When I got home I took off all my clothes and I hid my sport coat and overcoat in the bottom of the closet. Everything else I put in the laundry bag. I always felt like my clothes had betrayed me when I had an episode, and I couldn't wear them again until they were washed or several days had passed. Once all the clothes were taken care of I took a long, hot shower. I washed my penis several times. After the shower I put on a clean T-shirt and clean underwear and I felt new. I got into bed and in the darkness I thought about Sylvia. She wanted me.

People Are Dying, New Ones Are Coming Up

I stopped going to Forty-third Street. I was scared. I had liked it too much with Sylvia. I had liked it too much with Wendy. What had I stumbled upon in Sally's? I wanted to be part of the regular world. I wanted to be able to go out with normal girls. I didn't want to have to pay to hold someone's hand. I didn't want to end up like the other men at Sally's. I had only intended to be a tourist there, to observe an unusual place, but I felt myself being drawn back there helplessly again and again.

I started plotting furiously to work up the courage to ask Mary out. It would be awkward in the office, but it had to be done. She was going to save me.

I thought of things we could do together. I could take her to the second act of a Broadway show; she'd be impressed by my ingenuity, by my knowledge of how to do fun things in New York cheaply. We could even try to sneak into the opera. I'd explain to her the need for the reentry ticket.

I was pretty sure that she didn't have a boyfriend. I had overheard her speaking to the receptionist a month earlier about a breakup. And I had the utmost respect for Mary and assumed that she hadn't yet fallen into a new romance.

So I tried to approach her a few times when she was near the coffeepot in the office's little kitchen. I'd take a step in her direction and then I'd make a sudden retreat back to my cubicle. I was so attracted to Mary that I was repelled. My attraction doubled back on itself. I was like a magnet trying to touch another magnet.

But I was determined to overcome this. I was going to ask her out, though I knew that if I did speak to her that I would have no personality, that only the most banal things would come out of my mouth. So I scripted out an opening remark, something that a handsome young gentleman out of a Fitzgerald story might say.

I made my decisive move one day in early February. I timed my departure from the office to coincide with hers. When we got on to Sixty-second Street, I abandoned the script and said, "It's very cold."

"Freezing," she said.

At the corner of Lexington, I had to walk uptown for the subway and she was going downtown.

"Have a nice night," she said, and she smiled. She was always friendly with me. This encouraged me and I gave her the line that I had rehearsed.

"Would you like to get a drink at the Barbizon?" I asked. It was a moment of courage, bravery.

"What?" I could see that she was genuinely shocked that I was trying to communicate with her beyond the most perfunctory pleasantries.

"We could get a glass of sherry at the bar in the Barbizon. That's a good drink for six o'clock," I said cheerily. And in my mind I was trying to pretend that I was someone who had friends at the Yale Club, friends I could meet for dinner after having a drink with the girl I worshipped. If I gave off the air of the Yale Club, I would seem confident and appealing.

"I have to go downtown, I'm taking a photography class at the New School," she said.

"Maybe another night," I said.

"I take a lot of classes, and usually after work I'm really tired," she said and she smiled at me, trying not to hurt me. She suddenly seemed incredibly large. She was towering over me. The whole street was tilting up, I was at the bottom of a slope, she was at the top. I called up to her, pretending that I was still the same size, "Of course . . . have a good class."

We both waved good-bye and I turned. I was sliding down the hill, Lexington Avenue was going to fall on my head. I went into my deli for shelter. Roberto, the cashier, was still working. I bought an old muffin. I started to regain my height. I was at about eye level with the counter.

"The Knicks are playing great," he said. "They're not scared of anybody."

I looked at his dark hair. I wish I had your hair, I thought. I felt so ugly. "The Knicks are playing great," I said, and then I lied to Roberto. I needed to build myself up, but it was a good lie because in it there was an element of truth. I said, "I went to the Garden a few days ago." And he looked at me with awe, and I let myself be looked at that way.

That night I was watching *Are You Being Served?* and the phone startled me. Sometimes when the phone rang, I had this crazy, delirious hope that it was Mary. It was the same kind of misplaced hope that I had for the mail; somehow each day I expected some wonderful letter to be in my box, a love letter, an invitation to a glamorous dinner party, but nothing of the sort ever arrived. And Mary never called, but at least this one evening I knew for sure that she wouldn't be calling, that there was no need to engage in fantasy.

I picked up the phone. "Hello," I said.

"Louis?"

"Henry!" I shouted. He had been gone a month and this was the first I had heard from him. And I hadn't been able to reach him because his departure had come about so suddenly that I didn't ask for the phone number of his lady friend in Palm Beach. And I only knew her first name, Betty. I had searched the social register for Elizabeths in Palm Beach, but there were too many. I was sure that he had forgotten about me altogether. "I'm so glad to hear from you," I said. "I was concerned."

"Don't worry. You would have heard from me if I died."

"From the beyond?"

"No, nothing so dramatic. A collect call, maybe."

"I'm watching *Are You Being Served?*," I said. I wanted Henry to see that I was maintaining our habits.

"How is Mrs. Slocombe?"

"Her hair is orange tonight, and she's trying to seduce Mr. Humphries."

"I would like to meet Mrs. Slocombe, the actress, that is. She may be the greatest comedienne alive."

"How is it down there? The social life?"

"People are dying. New ones are coming up, not as interesting . . . Have you defrosted the refrigerator?"

"No . . ."

"Try to do that. I think there's a steak in there. We can have it when I come back. You can freeze meat for a long time . . . How are the fleas?"

"I haven't seen any."

"The incident may be over. I have been soaking in the ocean."

"How is your sciatica?"

"The sun has cured it, the warmth, and free meals. What's your weather like?"

"Very cold, but the apartment is overheated, I think."

"Of course it is. The whole culture is overheated."

"Are you getting lots of invitations?"

"Yes, far more than I deserve, considering I never entertain. I'm averaging four dinners a week, and three cocktail parties. I'm having a very good season. And there's enough food at the cocktail parties to almost count them as a dinner."

"Are you getting along with your lady friend?"

"Oh, yes, she's good company. She's in the wheelchair, we can move around pretty quick. We have lunch at the Everglades Club. But after that she's too tired to do much else, so it's restful. There was some fuss one day. One of the waitresses at the Everglades is new and told someone, 'Enjoy!' Caused a great uproar. Staff is not supposed to do that."

"Was the woman fired?"

"Severely warned."

"Have you seen Lois or Lagerfeld?"

"Of course not. They can't get invitations to anything."

"Is Vivian Cudlip there?"

"She has a whole floor at the Colony Club, and now *she's* in a wheelchair. Just happened a few days ago, but it's not permanent. She has an infection in her hip replacement. I pushed her around the dance floor at Au Bar; the wheel crushed the foot of an Arab race-car driver, but he was very good about it. It was mentioned in the paper the next day, not about the Arab's foot, but that I was pushing Vivian, and I immediately received several invitations from other chair-bound women."

"Have you found a car?"

"No, I've been borrowing Betty's, and riding a bicycle for exercise."

I wanted to tell him that he looked beautiful on his bicycle when he was a young man, but that would be admitting that I had looked at his album, which was like reading someone's diary.

Instead I asked Henry for his phone number and we discussed some bills from the electric and cable-television companies, both of which were overdue, though I had already paid my share to Henry. He told me to send ten dollars to each and that would keep them from shutting things off. Having conducted our business, he asked me how I was.

"I had a drink tonight with a young woman at the Barbizon Hotel," I said. I was full of lies that day.

"Did you wear a condom?"

"We only had a drink," I said, and I was offended for Mary. "She's a very nice girl."

"The last time you had a drink with a girl, it was a transvestite who didn't have carfare."

"Well, she's a real girl, and very pretty."

"This is long distance . . . Do you have anything else to declare?"

"It's quiet around here without you . . ."

"You're supposed to say what Wilde said when asked that question by American immigration."

"I don't know what he said." I was resigned. With Henry, I was eternally the student who would never please his tutor.

"I thought you at least knew your Wilde. He came off the boat and they said to him, 'Do you have anything to declare?' He said, 'Only my genius.' His first words in America. So there we are. Where are we? I'll see you in a month, the first week of March. Don't smoke in bed."

"You know I don't smoke," I said. But Henry had already hung up.

Otto Bellman Collects His Mail

The next evening, soon after I returned home from work, the phone rang again. Mary? My heart was hoping again for a miracle. I had hid myself from her all day. Maybe she had changed her mind. Maybe she did want to go for a drink one night.

"Hello," I said.

"Are you Louis?"

"Yes."

"I am Otto Bellman. I lived there with Henry. I am downstairs with Gershon. Henry is away, yes?"

"Yes."

"Is there any mail for me?"

"There is," I said.

"I would like to come up and collect it now."

"All right," I said. "Come right up."

Henry had been putting Otto's mail in the front bin of the refrigerator, next to an old bag of defeated brown carrots. Putting the mail anywhere else in the apartment would have caused it to be lost and sucked away forever. Henry hadn't called his friend Virginia to tell Bellman about the mail, not wanting to speak to him, but Henry had too much conscience to throw it away altogether.

I felt my heart palpitating as I removed the stack of envelopes,

285

which had attached themselves to the bag of carrots. I was finally going to meet the infamous Bellman. He was Henry's Professor Moriarty, a shadow on his life, blamed for everything: for missing eye masks and plays, for stealing friends, for evil seductions, and for a general undermining of morale.

Bellman knocked at the door and I let him in. I had a sudden urge to strike him (Louis: faithful squire, defender of Henry!). We shook hands, and somehow only my fingers managed to go into his palm; it was one of those embarrassing handshakes, and he crushed my digits. Swiss yodeler.

"Good to meet you. Henry's new tenant," he said. "You have my mail?"

I handed him the envelopes. He took them and walked into the living room and sat in Henry's throne-chair in the corner. I thought it was disrespectful, and it was unusual to see anyone else sitting there.

I sat on the white couch and studied him while he fingered his correspondence. He had sandy blond hair and a pleasant face with an upturned nose and dark brown eyebrows. Because he was bent over looking at his mail, I could see the outline of a meager hump, the size of half a cantaloupe, protruding from just behind his right shoulder. He wasn't really a hunchback, as Henry had said, but there was some kind of lump there. Henry had also said that his profile looked like Brigitte Bardot's, and I did see a resemblance in the dark eyebrows.

Bellman looked up from his letters, having quickly opened and read one of them, and said, "I don't forget this place. It is the most dirty home I ever lived in."

"Well, the rent is cheap, as you know," I said defensively.

"What do you think of Henry?" asked Bellman, and there was an ironic smile on his face and a glint in his eyes. He was inviting me to conspire and gossip with him. I should have been asking him about missing plays being produced in Yugoslavia.

"I am very fond of him," I said.

This response bored Bellman. "He is very original, don't you think?" he asked, without pausing for me to answer. "Sleeping in mask very original. Dancing very original. He goes to parties with his colleague Lagerfeld, and they are not invited. She is also original. Henry and I, we went to the opera five or six times. And always we sneak in. And you know he doesn't take just any tickets. He only wants the best. This is very original."

"I know," I said, dying a little. "We went to the opera. Saw Pavarotti." Henry had taken Bellman six times in six months of living together. And we had only gone once during my four months. I was jealous and slighted.

"Do you think Henry is homosexual? I was never sure," said Bellman.

I was surprised by the boldness of this question. I found it tempting. I suddenly wanted to confide in Bellman. To see what he thought about Henry's sexuality, to conspire and gossip after all. It would be a relief to talk about it with somebody. I almost plunged into it, but I caught myself. I didn't want to talk behind Henry's back. I decided to take the moral upper hand with Bellman.

"I believe in discretion when it comes to sex. Discretion in sex and mail fraud."

"What is mail fraud?"

"When you steal mail, or do things illegally through the post."

"I thought Henry might steal my mail."

"He would never do that," I said.

"Why was my mail cold?"

"He was keeping it safe in the refrigerator."

"See, very original."

Bellman's English was good, but he was fixated on the word original. I didn't know how to ask him to leave, so I continued our interview. "I understand you're getting married," I said.

"Yes. I'm marrying Virginia in May. Henry doesn't approve, I know. He thinks I owe him twenty-seven dollars for a phone bill. I don't, but I told him I'd give him the money. But he won't take it. I still want him to be my best man. He introduced us and he was the first person I met in this country."

"Have you asked Henry?"

"No. I will ask him when he comes back from his holiday."

This was going to kill Henry. If he said no, he might offend Virginia and her parents. He would be in a terrible bind. "Why don't you ask Gershon?" I said. "Isn't he a good friend?"

"No, Henry is better as a best man. Virginia doesn't want Gershon to come to the wedding because of his appearance. But I am going to fight for him. I like the way he looks. He is natural. I have to wear a tie for the wedding, but I don't want to. We're getting married in a club in Connecticut."

"Well, you have to dress a certain way in society, especially for weddings," I said.

"I don't care about society. But I know in America they care. You're like Henry. He once measured my legs with a ruler. And then he went out and bought a pair of gray flannel pants at the used store. He wanted to take me to a party but only if I wore the pants. I said, 'Henry, I go with you, but I won't wear these pants.' He didn't take me to the party."

The phone rang. It was Gershon calling for Bellman. I handed Otto the phone. They spoke a moment and then rang off. "I go now, Gershon is making dinner," he said. "I am glad to meet you. Gershon said you were a nice person."

"Thank you," I said. Gershon didn't invite me for dinner, but I did feel good that he thought I was a nice person.

I shook hands good-bye with Otto at the door. I managed to give him a good squeeze, making up for our initial greeting, and while our hands were momentarily joined, I said, half-jokingly, "You didn't take the play, did you?"

He ended our handshake and his green eyes darkened. "He convinced you of my guilt," he said. "Don't listen to him. He's diminishing. He read me the play one night when I was trying to sleep. It woke me up, it was very good. I said, 'Henry, take that to the theaters, you can make a lot of money.' And then he lost the play and blamed me. I think he may have thrown it away with the newspapers. Always he's talking about the play and the phone bill."

I didn't say anything and he pursed his lips at me in consternation; I think he had been hoping that we might become friends. He left me and walked down the hall. I closed the door. I half-believed him about *Henry and Mary Are Always Late*, but like Henry I found myself preferring to think that Bellman had stolen it. This way there was still hope that the play might be recovered.

I poured myself a glass of red wine and Bellman gave me an idea: I sat in Henry's throne-chair, which I had never done. I liked it. I drank three glasses of wine. I got a little drunk. I tried to set my face like Henry's face. Distracted. Arrogant. I crossed my legs the way he crossed his legs. I sipped my wine like a king. I admired my bowl of jewels. I pretended that someone like me was in my room and I called out to this person, "There seems to be a curious maladjustment of things, perhaps because of original sin . . . So there we are. Where are we?"

Then I put on the Ethel Merman record of Cole Porter songs. I danced enthusiastically. I cut across the orange carpet. I pointed my toe and dragged it. I leaped. I threw myself to the floor and popped back up. I twirled. I danced like Astaire, like Henry. I spun around and dizzied myself. I stopped.

I looked at myself in the mirror and my face was flushed and I thought I was handsome.

Brassiere Revisited

The dance did something to me and I had three good weeks. I stayed away from Sally's, I visited my great-aunt, I worked hard, and I read the whole second book of Don Quixote. But then I had more bra trouble.

Mary didn't mean to, of course, but she set me off. I had avoided her or been humiliated in her presence ever since the Barbizon-and-sherry line, but I had been pressing on and surviving. Then one day, I went to photocopy a letter to one of my ladies at a nature center in New Mexico, and it was about an hour after our lunch break. Mary was sitting on the edge of her desk holding out a brassiere for inspection to the other young woman in the office, Paula, whom I also found attractive, but not in the painful, blow-to-the-stomach way that Mary appealed to me. There was a shopping bag at Mary's feet that said The Limited, a woman's clothing shop on Madison and Sixty-fourth Street, just a few blocks from our office. She must have gone there during lunch. And she was holding out to Paula this flimsy, delightful black bra and Paula was feeling the material.

"It's beautiful," Paula said, just as I approached, and the two women looked at me and smiled at me in a caught, yet dominating way. I was a small squire intruding on a princess and her handmaiden while they talk about sex. The vulgar handmaiden then abuses the squire, since they are of the same class.

"What do you think, Louis?" Paula asked, joking. She was a sturdy bosomy brunette, who liked a good hamburger for lunch. Her princess and my princess, Mary, was wearing black stockings, a white silk blouse, and a black wool skirt. She was smiling at me—she had beautiful teeth—but she was also a little embarrassed. She knew it wasn't fair for me to see a bra she would wear after she had rejected my offer to join me for a glass of sherry at the Barbizon Hotel.

"I have one just like it," I said, answering Paula. It was a moment of wit, bordering on honest longing, and the girls laughed appreciably at the emasculated squire.

I turned to the copy machine to discharge my duties there, and I felt a burst of wild sexual passion. I could have leaped the few feet from me to them, gathered both of them in my arms, and taken them at the same time. Not in a way that they would have hated me, but in a way that would have been an homage to all things masculine and feminine. Unable, of course, to do such a thing, I held it all in and hit the copulate button with force, Xeroxing my letter.

Correspondence in my paw, I retreated like a monster of desire to my cubicle. I thought of Mary's gentle, small breasts being held in that black brassiere. I saw my hand moving towards them; I saw the perfection of her collarbone, her neck, her hair, the smell of her hair . . .

This incident with her brassiere was worse than the incident with the run in her panty hose. Just the word brassiere, or its shortened form, bra, was enough to stimulate me, and to say to myself "Mary's bra" was deadly. I had once looked up the word brassiere in the dictionary, and I had been aroused: "A woman's undergarment worn to support the breasts." I even looked it up in another dictionary just to be excited by the different wording.

So after seeing Mary's bra, I really threatened myself that I was finally going to go to the bathroom in the Barbizon and masturbate, but I didn't. Instead, I stayed at my desk and waited the rest of the afternoon for her to leave the office at four o'clock, as she did most days, to get a cappuccino or a frozen yogurt. And true to form, though at ten minutes after four, ten minutes when I thought I would be saved and deprived at the same time, she left *Terra* to get one of her creamy pleasures.

I took a letter over to the copy machine, glanced down in the shopping bag, looked behind me, and I thought of my childhood rabbi. He had once said that a good man was a man who never had to look behind him. I chased my rabbi out of my mind and I saw that I was unobserved and I stooped over and plunged my hand into the bag through the tissue paper just to touch the bra.

There were some packages of panty hose in the way, but I found the bra and I touched it. It was sort of scratchy, too scratchy for Mary's skin, I thought. Then I started squeezing the bra into a ball. I was unable to let go, like Lennie in *Of Mice and Men* crushing a mouse, crushing a woman, and I was in the grip of something myself, I wanted that bra, and so I took it and shoved it into my sport coat pocket. I rushed back to my desk. The bulge in my pocket was noticeable, but no one saw it, no Heads of Lower Primary like Mrs. Marsh at Pretty Brook were suddenly appearing to catch me.

At my desk I put my hand in my pocket and felt Mary's bra. Even though it was a little coarse, it was also delicate and sexy. It was rimmed with black lace. Touching it was like touching Mary.

Why had she bought such a sexy bra? I didn't like to think of her wearing it for a man, pandering to him. I wanted to think that she was too perfect for all men and didn't need any of us, that she was happy to be alone.

I put on my lined raincoat and my wool cap, and I went to George, who was in charge of me. Things were relatively lenient at *Terra*, I was a good worker, and so already dressed to leave, I approached my well-haired WASPy superior, who was conscientiously hunched over the copy of an article about the plight of the North American wolf. I told him that I wasn't feeling well, that I wanted to head home early. He distractedly nodded his head and gave his assent.

I said to myself, "Go to the copy machine and throw that thing back in the bag, don't do this," and even though I had just been given permission to leave, I headed for Mary's desk, but Paula was there copying something. I took this as a sign that I was meant to steal the brassiere, but I yelled at myself, "Just wait, she's almost done," but then Mary returned, her afternoon cappuccino in her hand. There was no way to return it now.

I walked past Mary, leaving the office, and I was certain that she would be able to look with x-ray eyes through my two layers of coats and see her just-purchased brassiere. I rushed to the subway.

I waited for the Number 6 train at Sixty-eighth Street and my thinking was panicked. I was sure to be accused. Paula was definitely a larger breast size, so Mary wouldn't think that she would take it, and had anyone else seen the bra besides me? Probably not. And I had asked Mary for that drink. She would think I had stolen the bra as an odd lashing out. But that wasn't the case. I would have stolen it had I never asked her out.

I could think of only one chance for getting away with it: Mary wouldn't realize the bra was missing until she was home, and she would think that it was stolen out of her bag on the subway.

When I got to the apartment, I rubbed the brassiere all over my face, felt the thin, almost sheer lining of the cups, and then flung myself to the bed hugging the bra to my chest. Mary had probably tried it on in the fitting room and I smelled it for any trace of her, but there was no odor. I thought that maybe there would be at least be a new bra odor like a new car odor, but it smelled of nothing, of nothingness.

This lack of smell was disappointing, but I had the bra, so I had to soak it for all the crazy pleasure I could get out of it. I wanted to put it on, but since I was insane enough to steal it I decided that

I should do a complete transformation. From my pile of newspapers to be recycled, I found a *New York Press*. I saw Ms. Hart's Recession Spankologist ad and I smiled thinking about her, a fellow nut, but I skipped her number and I called the cross-dressing service in Bay Ridge, Brooklyn.

I spoke to the woman I had spoken to months before and she said that she had an opening at seven o'clock that evening, in two hours.

"I have my own bra I'd like to wear," I said. "Is that all right?"

"Lots of my clients bring their own clothes. Do you have anything else? Panties, a dress?"

"No."

"What size shoe are you?"

"Eleven."

"What size women's shoe?"

"I don't know."

"Really? You should know these things . . . You have big feet. Eleven. I have two pairs that will probably fit you."

She gave me directions to Bay Ridge and told me that her name was Sandra and I told her that I was David. The price was still eighty-five dollars, and she said at the end of our conversation, "You know there's no sex, right? Other places will give you a release. But not here. You have to wait till you get back home for that. I offer only cross-dressing. No release."

"I understand," I said.

Deep in Bay Ridge

As I drove to Bay Ridge, I alternated between zany happiness and self-persecution. My happiness was a kamikaze happiness. I had gone absolutely too far and, as Napoleon said, I might as well enjoy it. But in the moments when I couldn't give over to it, I felt like I was moving towards insanity and wouldn't be able to come back. I had enormous problems, compulsions I couldn't control, and was going to Bay Ridge to be dressed as a woman and it could only make me more isolated from the world, shroud me in more secrecy and humiliation. And yet I wanted to do it. I wouldn't have turned my car around for anything. And I couldn't turn my car around. I was compelled to go through with it.

I took the FDR Drive to the Brooklyn Bridge to the Brooklyn-Queens Expressway to the Gowanus Expressway to Eighty-sixth Street in Bay Ridge. I had come a long way since my initial days in New York. I could drive anywhere. I was less of a Milquetoast.

Bay Ridge was its own little city. People didn't have to leave it. There was every type of store imaginable. It was part of the city of New York, but it had taken me an hour to get there from the Upper East Side of Manhattan.

Sandra was on 101st Street, off Fourth Avenue. The streets were clean looking and lined with houses or brick apartment buildings, and above all the rooftops I could see—because it was so gigantic—the arched, lit peaks of the Verrazano Narrows Bridge. It dominated the evening horizon like a mountain.

I parked at the end of Fourth Avenue, which seemed to be the end of Brooklyn. There was a highway in front of me—the sign said the Belt Parkway—and then there was the Atlantic Ocean.

It was cold near the water, there were icy winds, and I hurried down 101st Street on the left-hand side checking the numbers, looking for Sandra's building. I saw that at the end of the street there was a Checkpoint Charlie and a sign that said Fort Hamilton. There was a soldier in the booth. It was an active military base. And on the other side of the street from me there was a little grassy park with an enormous bronzed cannon pointing at the ocean. It must have been part of the old, original base.

The defense of New York became clear to me. Fort Schuyler protected the north, and Fort Hamilton protected the south. In my travels around the boroughs I was becoming a military expert.

Even though it was cold and dark, I decided to walk into the park and to really see what the view was like from the end of Brooklyn, to take advantage of having traveled all this way. I walked past the enormous cannon and at the far edge of the grass I was on a sort of cliff. Down below was the highway and then the ocean glittering with moonlight. To my right, the bridge towered over the water, connecting Brooklyn to Staten Island. It was a wild celebration of a bridge; it looked to be at least a mile long and seemed as if it would never be destroyed.

It was all very beautiful and Staten Island across the water was like a giant black shadow. It looked primeval and untouched. And further south there was another long shadow with some lights twitching, the Jersey shore. And to the east was just ocean and a black horizon defined by moonlight and starlight, and I thought of old-fashioned steamer crossings to France.

I was freezing, but I was mesmerized by the view. My back was to the world and I stood above the coast of Brooklyn. Then the coldest, cruelest wind yet came off the water, and I put my hands into my pockets for warmth and I felt Mary's bra. I was snapped out of my tourism. I had almost forgotten why I was visiting Bay Ridge: I wanted to wear a stolen bra and feel beautiful. What a strange, petty desire it felt like in the face of all this nature and the end of land and army bases and cannons and bridges.

But I still wanted to do it. I looked at my watch and it was a few minutes past seven. I walked back quickly across the park and found Sandra's building. It was a brick walk-up and she buzzed me in and I climbed five flights of stairs. My legs were in shape, but my thigh muscles started feeling squeamish with nervousness. I wished that I had eaten a banana for energy before leaving. I knocked on her door, very aware of the other doors on her hallway, her neighbors. Did they know why men came here? They probably thought she was a prostitute. Would the truth be better?

The door opened partially; it was still chained. Two green eyes looked at me. They were circled with black eyeliner. It was like looking at a raccoon. There was also a freckled nose.

"David?"

"Yes," I said. It was always strange to respond to my phony name, but it helped to remove me somewhat from the situation. Made me more of an actor, less responsible. Sandra's eyes scanned me, and satisfied with my neat, gentlemanly appearance, she undid the latch and let me in.

I was immediately struck by the nauseating smell of cat urine. It covered my face like a putrid cloth.

"I hope you don't mind cats," she said.

"No, I don't mind."

We were in a kitchen and she walked me into her living room. It was an ugly, coarse room with battered furniture. It wasn't a good room for cross-dressing. Several cats were lying like harem members on a worn, frayed couch. "How many do you have?" I asked. I wondered if it was dangerous for her to breathe in so much cat urine all the time.

"Eight," she said. "I can't say no when I see a stray."

"That's very kind of you," I said.

"It's easy," she said. "I'm a cat person."

We smiled shyly at each other. She was a professional and I was out of control and there to be cross-dressed, but we were both bashful, which we were covering over with cat banter as if we were ordinary people.

She led me across the living room to two glass doors with lace curtains. Ah, the feminine boudoir, I thought hopefully.

She opened the glass doors and the dressing room wasn't at all feminine. It was a bare room with a long mirrored wall, a wall with a large bookshelf, and a wall with heavy-metal rock posters. She closed the glass doors and shooed a cat away.

"I don't let them in here," she said. And the smell was less putrid in the dressing room, but I was breathing through my mouth anyways.

"You can hang up your coat there," she said and she pointed to a coat tree in the corner. Next to it was a large glass case with a pale green lizard inside. It was about two feet long and had a branch to crawl on. I hung up my coat and looked at the lizard's home. There were untouched bowls of sliced apples and raw hamburger meat. The lizard was remarkably still, pretending to be camouflaged in the desert in case I was hunting him. I asked Sandra, "What kind of lizard is that?"

"An iguana."

"Is it supposed to eat fruit and meat?" I asked. It was very rude of me to presume that she might not know what she was doing, but I didn't think that a desert creature had that kind of diet.

But she wasn't offended by my question. "Oh, yeah, that's what they love to eat. I have another one in the bedroom. I'd like one more, but it's too cold this time of year. They die if they leave the pet store . . . Sit down—I want to study your features."

There was a simple wooden chair in the middle of the room. I sat down and she appraised me for a second like a portrait artist, and then she said, "I always forget, let's get the money out of the way." I took out my wallet and paid her. Then she studied me and I studied her. She was short, about five foot two. She was wearing black army boots, an orange miniskirt, and a black turtleneck. Her clothing was matted with cat hair. But underneath the clothing and cat hair, she had an attractive, compact figure. Small breasts, strong legs. She appeared to be in her mid-thirties; her skin was sun-worn and freckled. Her hair was dyed blond and the roots were dark. I thought she was cute.

"Is this your first time getting dressed?"

"I tried it when I was a teenager, but I looked ugly," I said.

"You won't look ugly today. You're thin, which makes it easy. Some of my clients are very big, and it's difficult for them to get a realistic look, but they all are happy with the way they turn out. So don't worry, you're going to look good."

She circled me, holding the money in her hand, and she studied my features from all angles.

In front of me was the mirror and in its reflection I looked at the bookcase. On the top shelf were about twenty Styrofoam woman-shaped heads with wigs of all colors. They looked like twenty decapitations.

She put the money between two books on the case and said, "Let's choose a wig. You probably want to be a blonde. Everybody does. But looking at your skin, I think a redhead would be good for you."

"Blonde would be good," I said. Mary was a blonde. I could become Mary and go out with myself.

"I think redhead would be better," she said.

"I like the idea of blonde," I said. I wanted to assert my rights as a paying client.

"All right," she said with very little enthusiasm, and she pointed to two of the blonde wigs for me to choose from. I chose a curly Dyan Cannon wig and I grabbed the Styrofoam head, since Sandra was too short to reach it.

I noticed that along the shelves, in front of all the books, which were all science fiction, there were dozens and dozens of *Star Wars* figurines. Sandra had all the enthusiasms of a suburban teenaged boy: heavy-metal bands, lizards, science fiction, and *Star Wars*. And all these pimply-boy hobbies didn't give me confidence that she would be very good at feminizing and cross-dressing me.

I handed her the Dyan Cannon wig and I sat back down. She put it on my head and it did look terrible. The false blonde hair made me look completely washed out.

"I really think red," she said. Maybe she did know her business.

We put on a red wig and she combed it out. It was better. She explained to me that the wig was the first step and from the wig she could figure out clothing and makeup. She told me to undress and I stripped down to my underwear.

She rifled through the drawers of a cheap cardboard dresser, looking for panties for me. She gave me two choices, a black bikini or a pair that was wide-bottomed. I took the bikini pair. I turned my back to Sandra, but I did glance over my shoulder and I was sure that I saw her peek at me.

The panties felt like they had been washed a hundred times, and I was a little let down. Both she and Miss Hart had worn-out panties and I wanted first-class stuff, but the bikini gave me an erection anyways. Sandra acted like she didn't notice it. She was probably inured to men getting erections from panties.

"You said you were bringing a bra. Do you have it?" she asked.

I got Mary's bra out of my coat and Sandra said, "I don't think that's going to fit."

"It has to," I said. I put my arms through the straps and Sandra got behind me, but it wouldn't fasten. It was a thirty-four and

Sandra told me that I was a thirty-eight. I had jeopardized my job for a bra two sizes too small! My folly, my stupidity, was incredible. I felt myself get hot under my wig. I was a fool. My only comfort was that I was getting what I deserved.

"You should know your size before you go out and buy things," said Sandra. "This is an expensive bra."

My guilt towards Mary was compounded. I wondered how much it cost. I had no sense of the price of bras. I would have liked to ask Sandra what she meant by expensive, but then I would have to admit that I had stolen it.

"If you like," said Sandra, "I can take you shopping sometime. It's a service I offer my clients. You can go dressed up. Then after shopping we can go to a movie or a bar. Then you really get the full experience of being a woman. It's fun."

I was thinking that this would be my only cross-dressing experience. I would see the woman inside myself once and for all, and then I'd put her back in forever and I wouldn't have any more problems. So I resented Sandra's implying that I was only going to fall deeper into cross-dressing, but how could I protest? I had come this far, hadn't I?

She put Mary's bra on top of the dresser and dug around in the drawers for another one. She chose a large black one to go with my black panties. I sat back down and she put it on me. It felt good. I always like bras. Then she inserted two rubber, tear-shaped breast molds into the cups. They were flesh-colored and very heavy and were the same kind of prosthetic mold that my great-aunt used for her missing breast. I then thought of her alone in Queens and I was shot through with guilt. She would be sickened if she knew how I had spent eighty-five dollars.

After the breast molds, Sandra gave me a pair of black tights. She showed me how to put them on—I had to roll each leg up a little and then push through with my toes and unfurl the material slowly. The leg parts were like condoms. Then I pulled the whole thing up over my bikini panties and she asked me if I wanted a corset.

"No, I don't think so," I said.

299

"I only asked because a lot of clients like them. They want to feel that restraint. But you don't need a corset, you have a nice figure."

Undergarments taken care of, she opened the closet and pointed at a variety of ugly dresses, and every one I chose she disagreed with. She recommended a black, cat-hair-covered miniskirt and an orange top with a cowl neck to cover my chest hair, which protruded from the little indentation at the bottom of my neck. When I was finally dressed I realized that she had fashioned me, unconsciously or consciously, after her own image, but upside down. She was wearing an orangish miniskirt and a black top. We both were in Halloween colors.

She had one pair of shoes that fit me and she had me walk around the room to get the feel. She thought I would like it. I teetered awkwardly and I felt gangly instead of sexy.

"How are they?" Sandra asked.

"They're tight around the toes."

"That's the way it is for all women," said Sandra snappily, and I sat back down. She didn't like my complaining; she was picking up on the fact that I wasn't having a good time. I felt guilty.

"If you don't get into it," she said, "then it's hard for me to get into it. And that's when it's fun for me, when I'm making somebody feel good."

"I am feeling good," I lied. "You're doing an excellent job."

"I'm going to start the makeup now. You can't really judge how you look until the makeup is on. It's the most important part."

She thought I was unhappy because I wasn't looking good yet, but that wasn't the reason. I was unhappy because my behavior was insane and being cross-dressed was tedious.

From the closet, she lugged over an enormous fishing-tackle box and opened it up. It was multitiered inside and was filled with cosmetics instead of fishing lures. In the middle of the tackle box was a Ken doll dressed as a woman. He was in a brunette wig and he was wearing a yellow skirt and a white blouse with falsies. He had stolen some of Barbie's clothing. For some reason, I was offended by this. Ken looked ridiculous.

She removed my wig and had me take off the cowl-neck blouse. I sat there in miniskirt, stockings, high heels, and my black bra with its two rubber weights. The bra and panties felt good, but that was about it.

Sandra put her fingers in a jar of flesh-colored makeup and started smearing my face and neck. I was concerned that the jar had been previously opened. I thought it was unsanitary, that I could get pimples or a rash or a fungus from the other men's skin.

I knew I shouldn't say anything, I wanted to be a good client, but I couldn't control myself. "Is it all right to use that makeup for everybody?" I asked, certain that it wasn't.

"It's only my fingers touching you," she said, and I could tell she was annoyed. She was used to strange but simple men who didn't have my kind of neuroses. In fact, she was a strange but simple woman herself.

I wanted desperately to tell her that her logic about the makeup was faulty: her fingers touched her clients, picked up germs, and then went back into the jar with the germs. But I didn't ask Sandra to open a fresh jar of makeup; I let her put the germs right on my face. I am the kind of person who doesn't like to share a fork and have someone taste my dessert, but I always let it happen because I don't want to seem prudish.

While the makeup was being applied the phone rang. She picked it up and was addressed by someone, and then she gave her location and fee and asked the party to call back in two hours. She returned to me and then the phone rang again. I wondered if this was going to start happening throughout the session.

She picked up the phone, listened to the other party for a moment, and then her little body seemed to rise in the air with anger, and her face was red and she yelled into the receiver, "I'M WITH A CLIENT. DON'T FUCKING CALL ME, YOU ASSHOLE!"

She slammed the phone down and returned to me and resumed smearing on the thick makeup. I was shaken up. I figured that some strange client of hers was stalking her and calling all the time and perhaps the person was outside the building and would attack me in a jealous rage with a knife when I left. I would have to crawl bleeding for help to the soldier in the Checkpoint Charlie.

I was about to ask Sandra if she often received such phone calls, but before I could ask, she said, "I'm sorry you had to hear that. But my parents are retired in Long Island and call me all the time. They want to talk. They're bored. That was my father."

"Your father?" I asked.

"Yeah, he called just before you came here. They don't leave me alone."

"Do your parents know what you do?"

"Of course. I'm not ashamed of it."

She continued to smear on the flesh-toned makeup—she was really working it in and putting on several layers—and then the phone rang again. We both girded ourselves. She stomped over to it. "Hello," she said professionally in case it was a client, but then she bellowed with venom, "I JUST TOLD DAD NOT TO CALL. WILL YOU GUYS LET ME DO MY JOB. DON'T CALL ME AGAIN TONIGHT. I'M FUCKING PISSED OFF AT BOTH OF YOU!"

She slammed the phone down. I couldn't believe it. I felt like I had a remarkable life. Amazing things happened to me. The woman who's cross-dressing me has trouble with her parents and curses at them in the most foul language. But at least they were understanding parents, I thought; they didn't mind what she did.

She was simmering and I was politely silent. She massaged more makeup into my face. Then she began to work on my nose, contouring it just as Miss Pepper had once suggested, and the concentration that her craft required calmed Sandra down.

I asked her how she came into this business, and she told me that she was a professional makeup artist and that she worked in television and for theaters. And she started cross-dressing men when an actor confided in her and asked her to help him. He then introduced her to some of his friends and she built up a business. She did it part-time.

"You like doing this?" I asked.

"Do you mean does it turn me on?"

She was perceptive. "Yes," I said.

"I told you, I like to make somebody feel good, but it doesn't do anything for me sexually. This is what I was trained to do. I like to see the finished product."

"Do you ever have trouble with your clients?" Even though it had been her father calling, I was still thinking about vengeful madmen.

"In the beginning, I had some weirdos, but you learn to weed them out."

Then she began working on the eyes. I've never liked anything near my eyes and I had a lot of difficulty while she put on my eyeliner and mascara and painted my eyelids.

"Hold still," she kept instructing. And it was while she was doing my eyes, even though it was scary, that I became genuinely aroused. My hard-on from the panties had long since disappeared, but now it came back: her thigh was pressing against my thigh, and she was looking so intently into my eyes that it felt like the look of a lover. Then she got between my legs to really get at my eyes and her face was close to mine and I could taste her breath. It was sugary. I wanted to kiss her. And it seemed like the thing to do. Somebody only looked into your eyes, the way she was looking into my eyes, if they liked you.

I was about to do it, I was working up the courage to just lean forward and kiss her, surprise her, make her happy, but she finished my mascara and she backed away. I wanted her close to me again, I wanted to feel her leg against my leg, but I was afraid to ask. She had said no sex over the phone.

The application of all the makeup took about forty minutes and the final touch was a well-applied dose of red lipstick, which she had me do myself with her instructions. Then she carefully helped me with my orange blouse and then she put my wig back on, with a little brushing to get it right. I had avoided looking at myself as much as possible, but she had me stand up and appraise her work in the mirror.

I squinted and I almost looked like a tall, sexy, red-headed woman. My legs were long and had a nice shape in the tights.

From the side, my breasts looked large, which excited me a little. And the makeup on my face gave me a much healthier look than my own late-February pallor. And my scarlet lips and my vampish raccoon eyes were seductive. She had made my eyes like her eyes.

But when I looked at myself closely and didn't squint, I looked like a man who wanted to wear women's clothing despite how terrible he appeared. My shoulders were too big, my hips too narrow, my rear too small and flat, my face too waxy, my breast molds too lumpy. I looked like the amateurs who came to Sally's and sat quietly at the bar by themselves and received no attention from the men. At first you noticed these cross-dressers and then they became invisible.

"How do you feel?" asked Sandra, smiling. She was proud of her work; she was a craftsman.

I didn't want to disappoint her, but I felt like a fool. My shoes hurt. I tried to walk and feel sexy. To get something out of it. I said to her, "You did a great job."

I looked at myself again. The cowl neck really was unflattering. It was a hideous orange trough around my neck; it looked like those plastic bibs they put on dogs to keep them from biting themselves. It looked like Lovie's bib. And the cat hair on my miniskirt enhanced my ugliness: I was dressed as a woman in dirty clothes.

I was not in any way transformed. I was not a pretty girl for one second, let alone my old requirement of ten minutes. So my dream of at least twenty-two years, which had started with that Porky Pig cartoon, had finally come to an end. And just as Porky had slammed into the ground after floating in the air as a girl, I had crashed in Bay Ridge. He had at least felt beautiful during his descent, but I would never know beauty that way.

But there were other benefits, I realized. Standing there in front of that mirror in a wig and heels and lipstick, I felt like a man. Perhaps more so than ever before in my life. I knew that there was no woman inside me wanting to get out. I wanted the women outside of me. I wanted one of them to love me. I wanted Sandra to look into my eyes again.

I wondered if I should try to kiss her. Maybe she was attracted to me. She had peeked at me, I was sure, when I took off my underwear. And she was a small woman, she would be delightful to hold. But I was afraid that if I tried anything she would immediately reject me. She had been so firm on the phone about the release happening at home.

Her service was all build-up. Once you were fully dressed, then you started getting undressed. There was nothing else to do, but she offered to take photos of me for ten dollars and I declined, and then she said she would do it for the price of the film, five dollars. Drawn in by a bargain, I went along, figuring that I might as well have the whole experience and it would give me more time with her; maybe I *could* make a move.

Before our little photo shoot, she showed me an album of her clients and the various poses they were in, so that I would understand how to position myself. There were over two hundred men. Many of the photos showed the same men in different outfits—they were regulars. And the men pictured were all different races and ages and body types—slim men who almost looked like women and great big men who had the bodies of laborers—yet they all had the same odd dream and they came to Sandra in Bay Ridge and put up with the cat smell and hairs so that she could help them realize this dream.

Sandra, to me, was a wacky nurse for wacky men. All the women I met in the sex field (Miss Hart, the Live women) were like nurses to me. Peep shows were emergency rooms. Sex listings in the back of free newspapers were the names of nurse practitioners that your insurance company would let you see. I went to these women for help and I paid them and they did the best they could.

Sandra directed me like a fashion photographer and took shots of me sitting with my legs crossed; lying down on my belly with my feet kicked in the air; lying sideways on the floor, my hand seductively on my hip; standing up looking over my shoulder like a woman acknowledging a handsome pursuer; everything but a direct shot, which she said often didn't come out well. Then she gave me the film in its little black tube. She told me that her clients used the pictures for cross-dressing newsletters. She suggested that I get a subscription. I didn't know if I would ever develop the film.

I undressed and she led me to the bathroom where I washed off the makeup. It was hard work. She helped and worked on my eyelashes. My face took on a rosy shine as if I was wearing rouge. She said this would last for a few hours and that I shouldn't try to rub it off, that I'd only make it worse. She also warned me that I might find little pebbles of mascara in my tear ducts, but not to worry, just rinse them out.

I got dressed in my young gentleman costume, and it was like putting on shoes after ice-skating. I was myself again. She walked me to her door and she said, "You didn't like it very much, did you?"

"I think I would have liked it more a few years ago," I said. "To be honest, I felt more interested in you than I did in being dressed up."

I said this forthrightly, not thinking that I had any chance with her, but I wanted her to know that I liked her.

"Thank you. That's sweet of you," she said, and I wanted to tell her that the best part of the whole night had been the pressure of her leg against mine, and the way she had looked into my eyes, but I didn't have the courage to say it.

"If you ever do want to try it again, call me," she said. "Going out dressed up would give you the best experience. Like I said, we could go shopping, to a movie. A lot of my clients do that."

"All right," I said, and she was convinced that I was destined to be a cross-dresser for the rest of my life. I knew that I would never do it again, but I didn't think she would believe me.

I offered her my hand, though Henry had told me never to offer my hand to a woman, that I was to wait for her to do so, and only then could we shake. But I wanted to touch Sandra good-bye. We held hands and she looked at me. Her hand was small and she let it stay in my palm. What did she think of me?

We said good-bye and she closed the door. I walked down the dimly lit staircase, and I wondered if I could have embraced her. I suddenly realized that she *had* sort of liked me, that she had smiled in a genuinely flattered way when I said I was more interested in

306

her, and her hand had stayed in mine a few seconds longer than just a shake good-bye. But I had been too much of a gentleman to suggest anything. If I went back up and knocked at her door, she would think I was just another desperate pervert.

When I got to the car, I realized I had left Mary's bra in the apartment. I thought of it as an excuse to return, but then I was afraid that I would be wrong about how Sandra felt about me—I was doubting myself again—and so I left the brassiere there as a donation for some slighter man who could fit into a thirty-four.

All the Queens Were Dead

I didn't want to go home and think about the trouble I was in. How could I possibly return to work in the morning? Mary would tell George that I had stolen her bra. I was sure to be fired.

So I drove from Bay Ridge to Sally's. I was hoping that Miss Pepper would be there. She was the one person I could talk to about what I had done.

I was happy when I saw her at the bar. It was around ten o'clock and I took the stool next to hers, and she was showing another Queen a little pocket photo album. I didn't intrude. I ordered a drink and looked around. I was more impressed than ever with the girls. I had been so ugly dressed as a woman that it made me truly appreciate how beautiful they were, how much work it took. Only men could have the single-mindedness of purpose to turn themselves into women.

When Miss Pepper was done talking to her friend, she said hello to me and asked me to buy her a drink. She had her usual rum and coke and I didn't want to launch into my story right away. I asked if I could look at her album. She opened it up for me and it was my second album of the night, a strange coincidence.

The pictures were all of beautiful, glamorous Queens that Miss Pepper had known. Many of them were her friends from Los Angeles from when she had lived there in the mid-eighties. And as she pointed to each one, she'd say, "That Queen is dead. And that Queen is dead." Almost all of them were dead.

The last picture was of Miss Pepper with her mother and her sister. They were all dark-skinned and luminous and smiling. Her mother was old, but still a handsome woman, and her sister was good looking, but Miss Pepper was more beautiful.

"Your mother's really smiling in that picture," I said.

"She loves it when we're all together."

"I don't mean to be rude," I said, "but she's very accepting of you?"

"She loves me the way I am. She has no use for men. My father left us a long time ago; she likes just having a house of women. When I get sick I'm going home to North Carolina to be with her. She said she'd take care of me."

I didn't say anything. No one ever spoke about AIDS in Sally's. They only alluded to it when they said that they were safe when they made their propositions. I didn't know if Miss Pepper had HIV or if she just assumed that she would get it.

"But I've lived this long," she said, "so I might as well keep on having a good time." She took a drink of her rum and coke.

"Thank you for showing me your pictures," I said. There was no need to tell her what I had done that night.

"You're welcome, child," she said. "I've liked you since the first time I saw you. It's those blond eyelashes." She stood up and took her drink and said, "I'm gonna see if I can make some money." She walked away from me and circled the bar looking for a man.

I drank two beers and Sylvia showed up with a date, a business-man in a creased suit. They came through the doors that led from the Carter. He was already drunk and he was buying more drinks. He was playing the big shot. He was bald and he was keeping her close to him. She and I briefly made eye contact and she seemed to smile at me. But she was working. And I had no claims to her.

The businessman was ugly. He kissed Sylvia. Her face was still sweet and innocent, but I felt like I could see it darken. She was tolerating the intolerable. She was becoming a prostitute. I was no better than the businessman.

I left the bar. I thought of Miss Pepper's pictures. Her friends had all been so beautiful. I wished that I had somebody I could talk to about everything. I got in my car and I headed home.

I was on my way up Third Avenue and I hit a series of green lights; it was something I usually liked, a freedom to fly through the city, but it was merely hypnotic this time, and I just let the Parisienne carry me. I imagined lying in bed with Sylvia again. I saw my hands on her hips, her beautiful rear, the line of her white back, her black hair as fine and as shiny as the grooves of a record.

And then I realized I was going through a red light. The series of greens had come to an end. Right in front of me was an enormous white garbage truck. I swerved and headed for the sidewalk. An older black woman stared right into my eyes. She was wearing a belted overcoat, carrying a purse. I was going to kill her. It was only a second, but she looked at me with fear and anger. What are you doing? her eyes screamed. I'm sorry, I'm sorry, I pleaded with my eyes.

But then the woman and I realized that I was going to hit the light pole instead of her, and I was thankful. It was a silver, sturdy pole, and I thought, "My poor little life." I didn't have a whole flashback or anything, just those four words.

And then I slammed into the base of the pole as cruelly as a hammer hitting a tooth. The black woman and I met eyes again for just one second—she was curious now and was afraid for me—and then I was asleep.

I woke up and got out of the car. I leaned against the door.

"Are you all right?" asked the woman. Some other people had gathered, staring.

"I'm all right," I said.

The police arrived. A big weight-lifting fellow came out of the blue-and-white car with its beautiful flashing red lights.

"I'm sorry, Officer," I said, and I started crying. I was so scared. I was in trouble. "I'm really sorry," I said. "I didn't mean to."

"What happened here?"

"There were all these green lights and I was daydreaming and I didn't see the red."

"Have you been drinking?"

"I had one beer," I said. I was crying and I was lying, but only by one beer.

He gave me a sobriety test. I stopped crying. I had to walk in a straight line, touch my nose. I was a good boy, a good student. I passed the test.

"Are you all right?" he asked. His breath was steamy. I was suddenly very cold.

"I'm OK," I said. "I had my seat belt on."

I walked with him to the front of the car. The other officer was talking to the old woman. I heard her say, "He went right through the red light. I thought he was going to hit me."

The big policeman and I looked at the front of my car. Both wheels were flat and the hood was popped open. The grill had fallen off. Green fluid was bleeding from the engine. Steam coming off the engine, hitting the cold air, was causing a fog. The whole car was tilting forward like a bull on its knees.

The policeman knelt down and looked under the car. "You snapped the front axle," he said. He stood up. "It's a pretty old car," he said. He was trying to console me. The car was totaled.

"My father is going to kill me," I said. "It's his car." I thought my father was still alive. I must have been in some kind of shock, or hit my head on the windshield. I started to sob and I held my face in my hands, embarrassed. The policeman was kind. "Just calm down, buddy," he said. "You're going to be all right."

I liked the way he was handling me. I thought that he had seen many things and he didn't hate me for going through a red light. And then I remembered, with something almost like joy, that my father was dead. I wasn't going to get into trouble; he wasn't going to kill me.

I didn't tell the policeman. I was still crying and they were true tears, but I also thought that my hysteria was helping me. He pitied me. He didn't give me any tickets, but there would be a fine for damage to the pole and a charge for towing.

The truck came and took away the car. I watched it disappear up the street, dragged off like something dead. I felt a terrible guilt, a sense of destruction. I had committed a crime. I walked home in the cold.

Then I started feeling devastated that my father wasn't alive; for a few seconds he had been. My fear of him had been so real.

What a strange trick I had played on myself. I wished desperately that he was at our old house and I could call him. I wanted my dad. I wanted him to be alive, even to yell at me, to kill me for wrecking his car.

CHAPTER XI

I Was Like Don Quixote and Sancho Panza

I woke up very ill the morning after the accident. I couldn't stop coughing. It was probably bronchitis. The shock and the walk home in the cold had done it to me.

I didn't call in to work. I didn't have the courage. I waited for them to call me and fire me.

I figured that George might want more than just Mary's word, and he would contact Pretty Brook to see if I had exhibited strange behavior in the past. Mrs. Marsh would get on the phone and say, "I found him in the teacher's room wearing a colleague's bra over his sport coat."

George called me around eleven.

"Louis, are you all right?"

I couldn't read anything into his voice. "I'm sick," I said. I figured that covered all the bases.

"You sound terrible," he said. "But you should call in when you can't make it."

"I'm sorry. I fell back to sleep. I think I have bronchitis."

"Do you have a doctor?"

I didn't and he gave me the name of his doctor. George was a guileless person. Mary hadn't said anything to him. He was calling me out of a genuine concern.

"I also had a car accident," I said.

"When?"

"Last night."

"What happened?"

"I almost hit a garbage truck and went into a light pole."

"You're OK?"

"Yes, just banged up, and I woke up with this cough, bronchitis."

He told me to stay home for as long as I needed, and not to come back until I felt one hundred percent. He was kind.

I stayed home for a week. I coughed constantly, and my body was very sore. I hadn't realized it right after the accident, but I was bruised all over. I must have hit the steering wheel with my shoulder, the seat belt did something to my ribs, and my Club, which I had on the floor of the car, must have slammed into my right ankle because I had a thick blue-green welt there. I was like Don Quixote and Sancho Panza after one of their many pummelings.

I contacted the Jewish Guild for the Blind and they accepted the car as a donation so that they could sell it for scrap. But before they could claim the Parisienne, it was necessary for me to get myself out of bed and take a taxi to the holding yard on the West Side to remove the license plates and my few personal belongings.

I limped among the dead cars, and thought how once they had all been new and people had been happy to own them and go on trips. I found my poor car and I unscrewed the license plates, removed the paperwork from the glove compartment, and from the trunk I took my nice cotton summer hat, purchased in Princeton at the English Shoppe for young gentleman strolling.

I petted the smashed-up hood and I said to my car, "I'm sorry, I'm sorry." Then I sat in the driver's seat one last time and I cried a little. I held on to the steering wheel. I closed my eyes and I thought of my parents sitting in the car. My father at the wheel, my mother next to him, me in the backseat. I could see it all very clearly.

That's All I Have to Say About America

I left behind, between the two front seats, the little canister of film that Sandra had taken of me. When I realized this back at Ninety-third Street, I had a moment of great anxiety imagining a sighted person from the Jewish Guild developing the film. They would see me in all my mock seductive poses. They had my name and number. They might refuse the car, since it had belonged to a pervert.

I did consider going back over to the West Side to get the film, but I became rational and figured that no one would find it. And

I thought it fitting that my ugliness should be crushed in some compactor like an enemy of the Mafia.

The accident was on a Wednesday, and by the following Thursday I was ready to return to work. All week I had expected George to call back and fire me, but he didn't.

The night before I was going to return to *Terra*, I woke up around two, coughing; I wasn't entirely well yet. I got out of bed, put on my robe, and began to boil some water in the teakettle. I had found that hovering over the kettle and breathing in the steam was the only thing that made the coughing stop.

I was steaming myself for a few minutes, thinking that it was also good for my skin—my great-aunt steamed herself—when I heard a familiar jangling of keys outside the door. Henry could never find the right key. He was home! Part of me wanted to scream in delight, and another part wanted to go hide in the bathroom like a child overly excited.

I had known he would be coming back soon: it was the beginning of March and he was due to start teaching the spring semester at Queensborough, but I had thought he would at least call and warn me of his arrival. I shut off the gas burner and bravely opened the door for him.

"Go back to bed. I wasn't supposed to wake you," he said, snapping at me. He was tan and more handsome than ever. He had the look of adventure about him. His large suitcase was at his feet. I considered for a moment that I should hug him, but thought better of it. I was only in my robe and underwear.

"It's all right, you didn't wake me," I said. "I was up. Let me take your suitcase."

"Since you're up," he said, and then he strode past me, through the kitchen, and into his room and I followed behind, carrying the bloated luggage.

He put on two lamps and stood in the center of the orange carpet with an amazed expression on his face.

"This is one of the most charming places I've ever been. Much nicer than anything I saw in Palm Beach," he said.

"Really?" I asked.

"Oh, yes. There's an overall ambience here. And all these possessions. I didn't know I had so many things. It's like a surprise inheritance. With Christmas balls yet!" He looked at his gleaming bowl. I sat down on the white couch. The apartment seemed brighter. I felt a sort of quiet, ecstatic happiness that I had only read about in nineteenth-century novels. Rapture.

"I have a new car," he said. "It's quite beautiful. A 1976 yellow Cadillac. It has an instrument panel. Was owned by an aeronautical engineer who put in extra dials along the dashboard to remind him of a cockpit. So I have cabin pressure, altitude, tire temperature, everything. It's very exciting."

"I can't wait to see it. You finally found a car."

"I won't have it for long. I am financially ruined. As soon as I registered the car, the computer discovered hundreds of dollars of unpaid parking tickets. And not just for my last car, but the one before that, a Regal. I should get up at the crack of dawn and move the car out of state, but I'll let the marshal have it. It only gets eight miles to the gallon anyways, and I'm feeling suicidal. Now the next problem. Where is the cocoa butter?"

Henry took off his raincoat, opened his suitcase, groaned, and managed to sit down on the carpet like someone by a campfire. He began to rummage in his suitcase, going through the tangle of his dirty shirts and pants.

"What do you mean, the marshal?" I asked.

"I received a letter from the Manhattan marshal saying that the car would be taken off the streets unless I paid eight hundred dollars immediately. And of course I don't have that kind of money."

"Where did you get the letter?"

"An old Palm Beach walker lets me use his address so I can get Florida insurance. But the marshal knows that I spend a lot of time in New York because that's where all the tickets come from. He's probably having it towed at this very moment."

Henry was back with new disasters, troubles, and catastrophes. I thought of telling him about my car problem, but I was afraid that he would reprimand me and say something disparaging. There was also the news of Bellman's wedding, that it was being planned for

May and that Henry was the first choice for best man, but I didn't want to tell him this and spoil his return. I started coughing again.

"What's the matter with you? TB?" asked Henry.

"I'm getting over bronchitis."

"Well, you look much better now that you're dying. You look like Hamlet." I had grown a reddish blond beard, having been too ill and depressed to have shaved for the last week.

"Thank you," I said.

"I bought a gift for you. An organic piece of soap made by Fabergé. I got it at Eckerd's. They were having a sale. If I can find the cocoa butter, I'll find the soap."

Henry unearthed a toilet bag and unzipped it. "What's in here?" He began to remove the contents. "Two neckties. A bottle of vermouth. Shampoo. Sleeping mask: essential. No cocoa butter. No organic soap." He began to rummage further and then asked me, "Did you know that Mary Martin, Jean Arthur, and Janet Gaynor were lesbians?"

"Where did you hear this?" I asked, not really able to put faces to the names of these old actresses.

"I read it."

"Where?"

"It doesn't matter. If it was in print, it is true . . . I have found the cocoa butter, but not the Fabergé soap."

He squeezed the butter into his hand and smeared it over his tanned features. "I've been wanting to do this for forty-eight hours," he said. "But I was too lazy. I made the mistake of opening the suitcase the first night on the road. Then I was barely able to close it. I didn't want to go through that again."

"How long did it take you to get up here?"

"Three days, the usual."

"Did you camp out?"

"No. The motels are getting cheaper with the Clinton depression. It's quite wonderful, actually, the only good thing he's done. But I almost had to use the tent because I ran out of gas. It was quite an adventure. You might like this story. It's about human nature . . . I was in the bayou of Georgia, on some back road—I don't like the highways, too ugly—and I went for miles following a sign that said gas, food, whatever, but of course in this depression everything is closed.

"I finally ran out of gas right at the foot of an Episcopal compound where they teach old people, who probably have one more year to live, about ecology. A man was right there when I pulled over; I almost hit him. He was out walking, communing. He was one of the Episcopal staff and I told him I was out of gas and right away he wanted to know if I would give him money if he helped me. I told him I would and so he led me to the compound down a dirt driveway, almost a mile long.

"While we walked he started talking about child abuse. Everything in this culture is abuse, abuse, abuse, even in the woods of Georgia. You would think that they, at least, would be unaffected by these things. I told him that sometimes not to abuse a child was to abuse them, that the Japanese idea of hitting them in the head if they made an error in grammar was good."

Henry paused a moment, and he removed his blazer and shirt and began to rub cocoa butter on his arms energetically; he had been driving all day but he was electrified. He continued with his story, "The man said, 'No! No! You must never touch a child.' And I told him that some children need to be hit, as Noël Coward said about women, as regularly as gongs. I told him that parents should bring back the hickory stick. He was horrified. He said the sadists in the world were all abused. I told him that if you're going to be a sadist it's in the blood, whether your parents hit you or not.

"Then he started going on about Jesus, that Jesus was only a man, not a part of the Trinity, but that he liked Jesus because Jesus taught that you should love everyone, and I said that I thought this was very naive. And he said, 'Are you calling me ignorant? I think you're ignorant.' Meanwhile we were finally at the compound and another one of these loving Christian souls, a woman, approached. He asked if we could borrow her car to drive me for gas, but she said no. She was actually more rational; she sensed something and thought I might murder him, which I might have. But he didn't care, he wanted the money I was going to give him. He tried to siphon gas out of her car with a plastic tube, using his mouth, and he almost fainted from the fumes.

"Then a Chinese came along and he took us for gas, he wouldn't accept money, and the other one insisted on coming along, still hoping to get a commission, but I had no intention of paying him. Then we started talking about child abuse again, he wanted to know the Chinese's opinion. I told the Chinese about the Japanese and grammar, and he was much more receptive since they're fellow Mongolians, and so I finally got gas and left that compound, glad to have escaped . . . that's all I have to say about America."

"That's some story," I said.

"Yes, a bedtime story. Now we must sleep." Henry got up and went to the bathroom. I crawled into bed, coughing lightly, and listened to Henry urinate and flush prematurely. It was like music: he was back. I pulled my blankets happily to my chin. He came out of the bathroom, looked at me, and said, "Wake me when you get up. That's close to the crack of dawn. I'm feeling less suicidal. I'll take the car to New Jersey. The marshals won't look for it there."

"I wake up pretty early," I said.

"I'll sleep in New Jersey," he said, and he walked out of my room. Then he came back in and said, "I met the owner of a 963-carat emerald in Palm Beach, and this person needs to sell it. If you help me find someone to buy it, I will split the commission. It could save me from the marshals."

"Who owns the emerald?"

"A Russian countess. She does very well in Palm Beach because she has a title, but she needs the money . . . Think about it," Henry said, like one businessman to another, and then he left my room.

I listened to him groan as he descended into his bed, and then he called out, "I don't feel like I live here. I feel like I'm visiting you. Thank you for having me."

"I'm glad to have you," I said.

321

JONATHAN AMES

The Life of a Fugitive

I woke Henry at seven and I was very surprised but he didn't put up much of a protest, despite only sleeping a few hours. When I came out of the shower he was putting on music for dancing.

"Thank God, I've come back to New York so I can exercise," he said to me when I came into the kitchen.

"Didn't you exercise in Florida?" I asked.

"I had no time. Something was always going on. It's very competitive. Trump tried to break in again. He threw a big party at Mar-a-Lago the night of the Red Cross Ball. Said he was going to have beautiful models. They were nothing but prostitutes, and then at the end of the party they did the inevitable—jumped into the pool. So he's finished for another year. Too vulgar."

"You couldn't go for a walk in the afternoon?"

"I didn't want to be in the sun. I'd only do my exercises after five o'clock. I was invited to play tennis, but no one wanted to play after five."

"How did you get so tan?"

"I was in the ocean a few times to kill the fleas, but that was it. I wore white gloves to protect my hands from the sun, but then I lost the right one. Had to keep my hand in my pocket, which isn't very attractive."

Henry began to dance and I was coughing again so I put on the water to steam myself before going to work. While the water boiled, I retreated to my room to give Henry some privacy. When I heard the kettle's whistle, I came out. Henry was dancing to an Ethel Merman record.

I put my face in the steam and I draped a towel over my head to get the full effect.

"What is that? A croup kettle?" Henry asked.

"Yes."

"You are like someone out of a Jane Austen novel, and yet you've never read Jane Austen . . . Do you have to do that now? I can't be seen while I dance."

"I've read Jane Austen," I said. "And I've seen you dance before. We've even danced together."

"But we're strangers again."

"I can't see you through the steam anyways."

"All right. Since you are dying. This isn't bad, actually, it's like living with Keats."

So Henry danced and I steamed. I peeked out from beneath my towel and watched him. And being around him again, I realized how difficult and lonely it is to make it through life by yourself; I realized how hard the last two months had been for me, and now how everything felt easy with Henry back in the apartment.

After exercising Henry rested in his throne-chair. I finished steaming and sat down on the white couch.

"I think that music really made me feel better," I said.

"Oh, yes," said Henry, "Ethel Merman can cure you of anything."

"Where in New Jersey are you going to go?"

"Martha's."

"That's where you got the fleas."

"It's either the fleas or the marshals."

"So you're going to leave the car there and take a bus back?"

"No, I'll stay there with the car and come back Monday when I have to teach. Then I'll race back to Martha's. To safety. I can't even live in my own city. I'm leading the life of a fugitive!"

"Do you really have to go to New Jersey? What's the chance that they would actually find the car here? The city is so gigantic," I said, trying to convince Henry to stay; I didn't want to lose him again after just getting him back.

"They can tell from the tickets the vicinity in which I commit most of my crimes . . . I do have one person I can call for help—my friend in the Mafia. He might have some advice . . . This country is sick, driving me to criminals. Well, he's not Mafia, he owns a hot dog stand near the college. But he acts like he's in the Mafia, and he knows his way around the law. He's always getting fines for his hot dog stand and he never pays them."

Henry tried calling the hot dog man, but even though it was early he wasn't in. So Henry packed a small bag for going to New

Jersey and there was nothing I could do to stop him. At least it was New Jersey and not Florida.

"Before you go," I said, "there are two things I need to tell you."

"You're getting married? Good. That's what you need. Is she white?"

"I'm not getting married. But Bellman is."

"What?"

"Bellman is marrying Virginia in May in Greenwich. It's definite. He came here for his mail and told me."

"It's all my fault. I sent him there for one night, he stayed for six months, and now he's marrying her. I never should have had him as a tenant. I put the wrong ad in the paper. It was the drama teacher ad. It attracts all the psychotics."

"You listed yourself as a writer in the ad I responded to."

"Yes, the writer ad gets a much better type of person, but there are more actors than writers, and if I need someone right away, I use drama teacher."

I felt a little conned that Henry's initial bait for me had been so thought out, but I was also proud that I had responded to the writer ad, since in Henry's mind this attracted a better quality of person.

"Bellman also told me that he wants you to be the best man," I said.

"He's out of his mind. I won't do it. He's entirely Oedipal. He wants to kill me. I'll have to come up with a good excuse to decline. I'll try to think of something on the way to New Jersey."

Henry picked up his bag and headed for the door.

"I wanted to tell you one more thing," I said. "You're not alone with car problems. I had an accident."

"How bad?"

"Totaled."

"That's good. You don't have to spend money on repairs. Were you drunk?"

"No. Maybe a little."

"Was it your fault? You might have a lawsuit."

"It was entirely my fault. I drove through a red light and almost hit a garbage truck, and then I almost hit a woman on the sidewalk, but instead I hit a light pole."

"You've been living here too long. It is the curse of the House of Harrison—terrible luck with automobiles. Did you call the Jewish Guild for the Blind? They were very good about my car."

"Yes, I called them."

"Well, you're learning the essential things—donate the cars you destroy to the Jewish Guild. So don't worry about it. It's the best thing that could have happened to you. A car in the city is an extravagance. I need it, of course, for my freedom, but you don't need freedom as much as I do."

He was magnanimous and understanding. He even took partial blame for my accident by attributing it to my contact with his house. I had told him about it expecting to be yelled at, the way my father would have yelled at me. In some ways, I had wanted him to, so that I could be punished for what I had done. But he didn't humiliate me. He left to go hide in New Jersey.

I Was Like Lady Macbeth

I stopped at the deli, said hello to Roberto, and then went to *Terra*. I slinked in and went straight to my cubicle. No Mary. I sat at my desk and looked over my accumulated messages from all my contacts from around the country. My ladies had missed me.

I called George from my phone, rather than walk thirty feet to his office, and he wasn't in, so I left a message on his voice mail. I started to return calls: business was going well, more museums were going to buy bulk subscriptions of *Terra* and offer it as a gift to their members. I was increasing our circulation significantly. But while I spoke to my telephone lady friends, I kept waiting to be summoned into George's office and finally have the question of the missing bra put to me. I figured that he hadn't called me at home because he wanted to confront me in person.

Then it happened: George stopped by my cubicle and asked me to come to his office. As I walked down the brief hallway behind him, I could smell myself. It was fear and it was a burnt odor, like a street vendor's pretzels. I clamped my elbows to my ribs to keep the smell from escaping.

We sat down and George asked, "How are you feeling? We were all concerned."

"I think I'm ninety percent, still a little cough," I said.

"How did the accident happen exactly?" He stroked the outside of his bony, thin nose. He arched his eyebrow in patrician concern. He was only in his mid-thirties, he had a full head of hair, but he had the mannerisms of an older man.

"To be honest," I said, "I was foolishly daydreaming and I went right through a red light. It was all my fault."

"I'm the same way," George said. "I use driving as a time to meditate. I'm lucky I'm still alive . . . Listen, we all signed this get-well card for you and then it got buried on my desk. I thought I had put it in the mail." George handed me a baby-boy blue envelope. I wondered if I could use the unmarked stamp. I held the envelope without opening its seal.

"Thank you very much," I said.

"I want to talk to you about something," he said, and he paused a moment and looked down.

I composed my whole speech in my mind in a fraction of a second: I have a sexual problem. I just wanted to look at Mary's bra, but I couldn't let go of it. I will reimburse her, plus interest, and I'll go for counseling.

George continued, smiling. He said, "I'd like to give you some copyediting to do and have you read manuscripts that come in unsolicited. We've been sort of overwhelmed lately and I think that you'll do a good job. It'll be more interesting for you than just phone sales." He smiled at me. He was feeling like a beneficent superior addressing a promising subordinate. He didn't know that he was letting a pervert off the hook, and I graciously thanked him for the opportunity to do some editing.

I walked back to my desk and I thought that Mary had obviously not said anything. And even if she did suspect me, she had most likely convinced herself that it was paranoia to think that her quiet, nicely dressed coworker could be mad enough to steal a brassiere.

So sitting back at my desk, I began to feel some confidence that I was going to get away with my odd crime of passion. But I did feel guilty about the money Mary had lost on the bra. I called her woman's shop from my cubicle.

"The Limited," answered a young woman's voice.

"I was wondering," I whispered. "I'm shopping for my girl-friend's birthday, and I have a certain budget, and I was curious about the price range of your more expensive brassieres."

I got a little excited talking to a woman about lingerie over the phone, but I reprimanded myself. How much more trouble did I want to get into?

She told me that the most expensive bras cost forty-five dollars. I thought of sending Mary an anonymous money order for that amount, but then she would conclude that the bra had been stolen by someone she knew, and I was sure to be the primary suspect.

I thought of buying the same bra and staying late one night and throwing it under her desk. But I didn't know the cup size. I could call Sandra and ask her the size or just ask her to mail the bra to me, but I was afraid to call her; she would think I'd want another cross-dressing appointment. And I was afraid I'd set up one just so I could see her, and I'd have to be uglified again. And if she did mail it to me, almost two weeks would have elapsed and then the bra would suddenly appear under Mary's desk. Fingers would again point in my direction.

I realized that I should have called Sandra while I was recuperating, had her mail it then, but I couldn't really think straight that whole week, and I had been expecting to be fired anyways. So there was nothing I could do. I resolved to simply not steal any more of Mary's clothing; it was the best I could do as an amends.

Then I opened the blue envelope that George gave me and I cut away the stamp; I didn't want to be wasteful. The card had a picture of a young boy all bandaged and dirty wearing a soccer outfit. Inside was the inscription: "Feel Better. The team needs you."

It was a get-well card for a small boy on a soccer team. I didn't know what to make of it. Did they all perceive me as an athlete? As immature? Was it meant to be humorous? Were they so perplexed by my personality that no other card seemed suitable?

I then began reading their banal inscriptions and blanched and felt a tremendous wave of cold fear when I read Mary's: "Come bra soon." It was a hidden, secret, damning accusation. I thought of running out of the office.

And then I realized the word wasn't bra but "back"; her handwriting was sloppy. I was like Lady Macbeth seeing blood where there was no blood.

That's Very Good Cheese He's Eating

Henry eluded the marshals for more than a week, though he said that Martha didn't liked housing a fugitive since he wasn't really visiting.

He was able to stop hiding out in New Jersey when Queensborough advanced him two paychecks. He paid off the marshals, had his name erased from the list of most-wanted scofflaws, and his Cadillac was now safe on the streets. But no sooner had the marshals been paid off than the IRS increased their efforts to get Henry to pay his back taxes for the last eight years. He was a scofflaw and a tax dodger. He really did abide by his motto of "Through troubles and into more troubles."

The IRS sent him numerous letters, and they also telephoned once a week, so Henry no longer answered the phone. I took all the calls and I was instructed to say that Dr. Harrison was abroad.

"I am hounded by tax collectors. By publicans!" he bellowed one night, looking at all the IRS envelopes.

I wanted to get his mind off his problems, so I asked him, "What are you teaching this semester?"

"The same as always: 'Composition and Expression.' But I'm thinking of proposing a change. A course about ideals instead of the essay. They'd have to read Genesis, Exodus, and Matthew; *Das*

Kapital and *Mein Kampf*. But they'll never let me do it. Not a city university. There'll be a great hue and cry. They'll say he's a Nazi and a communist. They won't look at the literary value of the course. But they shouldn't protest. The students have to see what was what. Of course I would try to show that the Bible is good and the others bad. But they'll never let me teach it. My life will have no meaning. It will be spent with taxes and judgments . . . Who was that critic? Wilson? Of course you wouldn't know. He was destroyed by tax problems. Just as I will be."

Henry tried to make some extra money when there was an enormous blizzard in late March. He recruited Gershon and they were going to drive around the city and offer to dig people out for twenty dollars. But after they dug out the Cadillac, they slid into a snowbank a block later, couldn't get out, and the venture came to an end.

Then spring arrived and Henry called out to me from his bed, "Do we push the clocks forward or back?"

"Spring ahead, fall behind," I said.

"Where did you learn something so wise?"

"New Jersey."

"Of course, all good things come from New Jersey."

And as the spring really started to set in, the IRS stopped calling and writing. It was like both the shadow of the government and the winter had been lifted from our apartment. Henry was in much better spirits and this elevated my mood as well. If Henry was despairing, I despaired. If he was happily enjoying *Are You Being Served?*, then I was happy.

In my life apart from Henry, I wasn't getting into any more trouble. Henry's return and my car accident seemed to have neutered me. I wasn't interested anymore in sex. Mary had no power over me and I never went to Sally's.

I did have some concern about this utter lack of interest and feeling—I wondered if the seat belt during the accident had bruised a nerve—but mostly I found it peaceful.

Henry wasn't going out as much—most of his lady friends were still in Palm Beach—and I hardly went anywhere, though I did go to Queens to be with my great-aunt for Passover. She sent me home with matzo and Henry liked to eat it with cheese.

There was no word from Otto Bellman about the wedding, and when Henry asked Gershon if he knew anything, Gershon claimed ignorance. And Henry didn't call Virginia or her parents; he was hoping that the problem would just go away, that the wedding had been called off.

One Saturday afternoon, he did see Bellman and Gershon on our street. And he ran into our building to avoid them, but really to avoid Otto. He came into the apartment out of breath and told me of his narrow escape.

"Gershon was on his bicycle," said Henry. "His body hung over the seat, his flesh is like lava. And Bellman was jogging alongside him. He looked like a hunchback schoolmaster. He should have had a flock of boys behind him. He waved at me and I ignored him. It's a good thing I was rude to him. It has to be apparent that I'm not cut out to be his best man."

The warm spring weather brought a guest to our apartment. One night, Henry and I were watching *Are You Being Served?* and midway through the show a brown mouse appeared from beneath the white couch, where I was sitting, and ran across the orange carpet and went underneath Henry's bed, where he was sitting. We both looked at the mouse and I was silent for a moment and then I said, "Oh, God," and Henry said, "Oh, no, it's under my bed. It's going to defecate into my shoes. I can't believe this life. We'll have to buy traps."

"Can't we just let it live off our crumbs?"

"No!"

"What about one of those traps where it's just caught and we let it go outside?"

"No! He'll just come back. He knows there's lots of dirt and places to hide and old food up here."

Henry bought traps and over the next week the mouse somehow kept on eating the cheese without releasing the guillotine. "What a houseguest!" Henry said. "Not even a thank you note. I don't pay my taxes, but I always write thank you notes. That's very good cheese he's eating."

So he kept trying to kill the mouse, especially now that he perceived him as rude. But then in a fit of hunger Henry ate the rest of the cheese himself.

The mouse ran around and made noises, but we didn't do anything about it. The empty traps just lay about and I was afraid to remove them because I was sure I would lose a fingertip.

Then Henry realized that he liked feeding the mouse. He saw him as a fellow traveler in search of a free meal. So he went out and bought more cheese to put in the traps for the mouse to eat, and if the mouse happened to die then it was destiny. Each day we checked the traps to see if he had finally been caught, but he was a magnificent thief, and I was grateful that he kept eluding death, and so was Henry.

Lagerfeld Is Back In

Towards the end of April, Henry's social life picked up again. Two ladies were out of the hospital; Vivian Cudlip and a few others had returned from Palm Beach; and Marjorie Mallard, his ex-fiancée, was calling again—she had forgiven him for going to Florida and claimed to have written him back into her will. Also, Lagerfeld was calling. "Lagerfeld is back in," he told me, and he explained that she'd had a fight with Lois over a dinner check. Therefore she was out with Lois and in with Henry.

The first weekend of May, Lagerfeld invited Henry to an opening at the National Arts Club. He asked me to join them. I was very happy. Henry and I hadn't done anything together in some time.

On his way to the shower that Saturday evening, in preparation for our going out, Henry made his usual stop at the end of my bed, while wrapped in a green towel, to address me as I lay reading. "I wonder what Lagerfeld will have on," he said. "The last time I saw her she was wearing her Barbara Bush pearls and was looking slim. She said, 'I'm getting there.' Where she's going, I don't know. She was wearing a button that said, 'Do It.' Do what, do you think?"

"Sex?" I asked.

"No. She's not interested in sex. She might tell a bawdy joke if she's trying to get a homosexual critic to give her a free ticket, but that's the extent of her sex life," he said, and then he went into the shower.

When he came out there was a reflective look on his face. He had put the mascara on his hair, the green towel was now wet and clung to him, and it was a moment so often repeated for us—me lying on the bed reading (*The New York Times Book Review* this time) and Henry coming out of the bathroom ready to press on to the next event—that it gave him a moment of pause.

"This is like a play," he said solemnly. "We're just two people bobbing up and down, up and down . . . One plot could be the battle of the haves versus the have-nots. Except I don't battle with the haves, just with my own have-notness. I don't take any of the necessary steps to change."

He walked away from my bed looking unusually resigned and went into the kitchen. As he did we both heard the mouse rustling about.

"We must catch that mouse," he said from just beyond my doorway. "That can be one of the motifs. In *The Three Sisters* they're always trying to get to Moscow, but never go. We're always trying to catch that mouse, but never do . . . I talk about Russia, but never go. We don't do anything. The same thing with defrosting the refrigerator . . ."

"Or finding *Henry and Mary Are Always Late*," I said.

"Well, that's hopeless," said Henry, but then my suggestion sparked an idea; we were *collaborating*. He continued, "That could be the climax, when it's found."

"Maybe when the refrigerator is defrosted it will come flowing out of an ice block. That would be a good end for the play—another play being discovered."

I couldn't see him, I was still lying down, but he was now in his room by his armoire (I knew every sound in the apartment), and he laughed at my proposal for the ending of the play about us, and this made me feel good. It was rare that I could make Henry laugh. And it was especially pleasing to hear his laughter this time because he seemed genuinely sad about his have-notness and our state of simply bobbing up and down.

But he was energized by our discussion of the play. He started rifling through his armoire and called out, "Now the eternal problem—a clean shirt. But it's only Lagerfeld, it doesn't have to be too clean."

I kept on reading the *Book Review*, though I needed to get in the shower myself, but in the *Review* there were printed excerpts from Edmund Wilson's journals that he had kept near the end of his life, and they were very interesting.

Despite Henry having said to me a few weeks earlier that I didn't know who Wilson was, I did know him, and I wanted to point out my sophistication to Henry by reading to him a brief passage from the journals, which I had just come across. It mentioned Chekhov, and Henry only moments before had brought up *The Three Sisters*. It was too good a coincidence to pass up. I called out, "I want to read something to you."

"Why aren't you getting ready?"

"I'll hop in the shower in a moment."

"What do you mean hop? Where do you get these words? That sounds ridiculous."

I ignored this and said, "It's a passage from Edmund Wilson's journal written in 1961. It's very good. He wrote, 'As a character in one of Chekhov's plays says he's a man of the '80s, so I find that I am a man of the '20s. I still expect something exciting: drinks, animated conversation, gaiety: an uninhibited exchange of ideas. Scott Fitzgerald's idea that somewhere things were "glimmering." I am managing to discipline myself now so that I shan't be silly in this way.'"

I finished reading and I said, "I like the Fitzgerald glimmering part."

"Glimmering," Henry mused. "I like what Kerouac said better. He was looking for IT."

"You've read Kerouac?" I asked. I had read Kerouac in college, but hadn't been swayed from my devotion to English writers writing about English gentlemen, though I had seen the American romance in *On the Road.*

"Oh, yes," said Henry. "Kerouac and I are of the same generation. He was a great experimenter. Typed everything on a single roll of toilet paper. He was like Rimbaud. He had a great friend, Cassady . . . Lagerfeld and I are like Kerouac and Cassady. We like to drive at high speeds looking for It! It! It!"

Lagerfeld was really back in if he was talking about her like that, and so I hopped into the shower since we were to pick her up shortly.

Showered and blue-blazered, we left the apartment and as we headed down the stairs, the back of Henry's blazer momentarily lifted and I saw that he was wearing his pants with the split seam and his bare white rear was visible.

"Henry, your pants are split! And you're not wearing any underwear."

"Yes. Underwear is fattening. This is a much slimmer look."

"But if your jacket lifts up, I can see your rear."

We stopped at Gershon's hallway. Henry buttoned his blazer and this kept the jacket from lifting up. This was enough for Henry, as he didn't want to climb up the one flight and change his pants.

"As long as there are no urine stains on the pants, they're all right," he said. "And if the ass is exposed, they won't know what they're seeing anyways. It's going to be a bunch of old ladies. They'll think it's a new design."

"Well, if it does becomes visible, I'll give you a signal," I said.

"It's a good thing I'm not in Florida. I'd be arrested. You're not allowed to show the ass-crack anymore. That's why they call them Southern crackers. But now they're trying to get all the crackers and rednecks out of the South. It's discrimination."

"I know, you told me," I said.

"Why do you memorize everything I say, but can't identify a single line of poetry?"

I didn't say anything. I was a dog. Henry kicked me and kicked me, but still I trailed after him, and when he gave me a little snack, a little compliment, my love for him was unbounded, all wounds were forgiven.

We headed out of the building and got into Henry's car. I had seen it parked on the street, but this was my first trip in the Cadillac. It was a canary yellow Eldorado and it was even bigger than my Parisienne. None of the dials on the dashboard worked and there were newspapers and coffee cups strewn on the floor, so the car already had the feel of Henry's Skylark.

"This must be difficult to park," I said. "It's so big."

"That's not the problem. It only gets four miles to the gallon. It's destroying me financially."

We drove through the Upper West Side on our way to collect Lagerfeld, and at Ninety-sixth and West End Avenue Henry pointed out a building and said, "I had a friend who used to live there. When he moved into the apartment there were whips left by the last owner and thank you notes from John Gielgud complimenting the food."

"That's strange," I said.

"Yes."

Lagerfeld's building was on 100th Street, between West End and Broadway, and she was waiting for us in the lobby. She limped out to the car—her knee was swollen, she said—and I held open the door for her and she sat in the front seat.

She had her cane with her and she was wearing her signature thick glasses and a large black dress with a white collar. She may have reduced a little, but she still was very large, probably two hundred pounds or more. I rode in the back and stared at their fine heads of hair: Henry's mascaraed movie-star swept-back helmet and Lagerfeld's strawberry-blond Brünnhilde locks. I thought of them as some kind of latter-day Kerouac and Cassady in search of free meals and drinks and gaiety.

We caromed down Broadway in Henry's Eldorado, its wide yellow hood leading the way. Lagerfeld mentioned a fund-raising party she had attended for St. John the Divine and this started Henry complaining about the new priest at his church.

"He's English," said Henry. "He looks tormented. At the end of his last sermon, he said, 'Why don't you leave with a smile? The

Baptists smile. And what can the Baptists offer that we can't? So smile.' I thought it was very bad taste. The Church used to accept you if you felt guilty and sinned. Now they're trying to whitewash everything. The whole point is the agony and the ecstasy, none of this sunshine smiling shit. We're not saved just because we go to church. We have to work on our souls."

Lagerfeld didn't like Henry preaching at her, so she gave him a dig. "When's Otto Bellman marrying Virginia?"

She obviously knew that this was a sore point for Henry. "I haven't heard anything," he said. "She might be on to him. He should be kicked out of the country."

"I have a new German roommate," said Lagerfeld. "She's a graduate student at Columbia. She's very nice."

"Most German-speaking people are," said Henry. "Except when they start wars, or move into my spare bedroom."

From the backseat, like a child, I interjected myself into the adults' conversation. I recounted my meeting with Bellman when he came for the mail. I did an impression of him. In my best German-Swiss accent, I said, "Henry is very original. And Lagerfeld is original. She is his colleague. The two of them sneak into parties where they are not invited. Very original."

This caused Henry to snicker and Lagerfeld to laugh heartily.

"He's very good," said Lagerfeld. "He sounds just like that wily Swiss."

"Henry sneaks into the opera and he doesn't want just any seats, he wants the most expensive," I continued in my best Bellman. I enjoyed entertaining the adults.

"You have some ear," said Lagerfeld, still laughing.

"Yes, he's very good at mimicry *and* memorizing what people say," said Henry. This time he meant it as praise and I lapped it up. We were a laughing, happy family, like Lagerfeld's family long ago.

We parked near the National Arts Club, which was on Gramercy Park South. The club was in an elegant old brick building and our opening was on the ground floor, in a two-room gallery. It was a show of ink drawings. The subjects were landscapes and also obscure city streets that looked Italian. They had an etched quality and were moody.

We armed ourselves with drinks, but there was no cheese, which annoyed Henry, and then Lagerfeld limped around searching for contacts and future invitations. In twenty minutes, Henry and I each had three white wines, and we looked at the drawings together, which pleased me, and he was keeping his blazer buttoned so his rear was not on display. It was an older crowd, as he predicted; even the artist was an old man in his seventies who had long fleshy ears.

Standing next to me, as I finished my third glass, was a woman who looked a little bit younger than most present. She was maybe in her late fifties, and she was wearing a droopy, flapperlike hat with small, sewn flowers pinned around its brim. Her hair, a mixture of brown and gray, was in a thickly twined braid and it came out of the back of her hat like a tail. She seemed to be looking at me. And then she spoke to me.

"I like your nose," she said. "It's the best nose I've seen since Paris ten years ago."

"Thank you," I said. She was trying to say something witty, but she had sad green eyes. But despite her eyes, I was sexually flattered.

"I like your hat," said Henry to the woman. He had overheard her remark and he was butting in.

"Why?" she asked.

"I like its shape," said Henry. "It takes great courage to wear hats. People should wear hats again."

"It's all I have left."

"Your hat?" asked Henry.

"No. Courage."

"Why? Have you lost everything else?"

"Yes."

"But why?"

"I'm being facetious."

"Oh."

"I'm an actress," the woman said. "I was acting."

"Oh," said Henry, dismissively.

"Are you a writer?" she asked him. "You look like a writer."

"No. I'm a thinker."

"My name is Louis Ives," I said, not wanting to be left out. "This is Henry—"

"Don't ever give my name," he snapped at me. "I might be recognized and accused of something."

"Are you pulling my leg?" the woman asked Henry.

"I would never pull your leg," he said with pride, and there was a strong element of double entendre to his remark. The woman was a little eccentric and sad, but also bright, and she caught Henry's meaning. She reddened somewhat and walked away from us.

I felt bad for the woman. She had been nice to me, she liked my nose, but Henry had driven her away.

"Very rude of her to try to pick you up like that," he said, and he left me and went to the wine table.

I went to look for the woman in the flapper hat. I wanted to apologize for Henry's behavior and have her compliment my nose again. But she wasn't in the second room of the gallery and so I went to look for her in the lobby.

I was a little drunk and I quickly manufactured a fantasy about the two of us falling in love. Her eyes were pretty and she was slim. In the dark it would be nice to hold her and make her feel young. I imagined her resting her head on my chest. I would stroke her thick hair. And how decadent it would be to have her delight in me. She would probably hold my penis and smile with memories.

She could mother me until I had confidence, perhaps after five years, to pursue women my own age. In the meantime, we could travel together. I hoped that she had money to travel. I thought it would be nice to see Italy, because of the drawings.

But she wasn't in the lobby. She had fled. Henry's remark had been too rude. Her eyes had already been sad before we spoke to her.

I knew she had left the club, but I went up a carpeted flight of stairs off the lobby to look a little bit more for her, just in case, and on the second floor, in a large, elegant wood-paneled drawing room, there was another party going on. There were lots of people and a big buffet table. I didn't see the lady with the hat.

I went back to the gallery and asked for another glass of wine. I found Lagerfeld alone and stood alongside her.

"Having a good time?" she asked.

"All right," I said, and then I added, "I feel sort of bad. Henry was rude to this woman I was speaking to." I was talking behind Henry's back; I was suffering from *in vino veritas*.

"He's terrible to all women," she said.

"Why?"

"His heart was broken years ago when he was young and handsome and still had money. He's never gotten over it and takes it out on all women. You have to know how to handle him and then he's a lot of fun."

"How was his heart broken?"

"He was in love with a Catholic girl. But her family wouldn't let her marry him. She ended up marrying a rich banker. He's pretended to be a Catholic ever since, but he started out Presbyterian. Now he likes the Church because it lets him be a religious snob."

"I didn't know any of this."

"He likes to be secretive. No one can figure him out. He's too crazy. Even I can't really understand him."

"Otto Bellman thinks he's homosexual."

"That's what everyone says. He was in the theater, after all, and actors need to be homosexual or bisexual so they can say their lines with feeling. But Henry is the opposite. He has no feelings."

He approached us then and we both gave him false smiles. I felt guilty having gossiped so willingly. Henry said he was ready to leave and Lagerfeld agreed.

"I'm hungry," said Henry, as we walked out of the gallery.

"I noticed a party on the second floor," I said. This was my chance to redeem myself for my sin. I had slandered Henry, but now I could feed him. "There was a big table of food. Maybe we could sneak in."

This excited my two companions, and Lagerfeld struggled up the stairs, but the thought of another party gave her strength. We were able to go right to the buffet table unobstructed and mingle in with the crowd. They were gathered for an antique auction for Brown University.

The food was excellent, pâtés and meats and shrimps and cheeses. And it was especially delicious because it was free, and the three of us ate a great deal and drank more wine.

We didn't move far from the buffet table and Henry opened his blazer so that he could breathe more comfortably and I saw a flash of white out of the corner of my eye. The back flap of his blazer had opened and his ass was right next to a wheel of Camembert cheese.

Before I could say anything, Lagerfeld spotted it. She smiled, and then our eyes met and she grinned knowingly at me. She looked like she wanted to smack Henry's ass with her cane. I whispered to Henry, "It's showing."

"What's showing?"

"Your rear."

"This is tiresome. I don't want to button my jacket. People should feel privileged . . . but I am close to the food. I can understand objections," he said, and he buttoned his blazer.

We left a little while later and drove Lagerfeld home. We double-parked in front of her building. It was once grand, but now it looked neglected. Before she got out of the car, she said to me, "You did very well to find that party." And then she said to Henry, "He's learned a lot from you."

"All the wrong things," said Henry.

I got out of the car and offered myself to Lagerfeld. She put her arm through mine and I walked her to the double-glass doors of her building. The doorman at the far end of the impersonal, dirty, fluorescently lit lobby buzzed her in. I watched her walk across the lobby with her cane and she waved hello to her doorman. I could see that she was wanting to play the role of the society woman who has returned home for the night. But the doorman hardly looked up from his newspaper, and Lagerfeld disappeared into the elevator.

A Tie Is Dipped

Henry and I went home and drank more wine and watched television. At eleven o'clock *Are You Being Served?* came on. The episode revolved around a London rail strike. All the store's employees couldn't go home and so they were spending the night in either the camping or the furniture department.

Mrs. Slocombe, in the furniture section, made a nice little bedroom for herself and was trying to seduce Mr. Humphries, a thin blond with terrible British teeth and a pursed mouth. Just as Mrs. Slocombe's pussy was the source of much canned laughter, Mr. Humphries' effeminate personality was also the fodder for many jokes. But he was trying not to be rude in denying Mrs. Slocombe's advances. He cared for her and didn't want to hurt her feelings.

"She's the only one who can't see that he's an urning," said Henry.

"Yes," I said.

"They're all great actors, but now they're hopelessly typecast. Mr. Humphries will always be Mr. Humphries."

Rather than reject Mrs. Slocombe and crush her spirit, Mr. Humphries closed his eyes and started to kiss her wildly, but he was saved by the appearance of the dour Captain Peacock, who was confused by finding the two of them in bed. Captain Peacock had thought he was sure about Mr. Humphries.

I was fairly intoxicated from a whole night of wine drinking, and midway through the show I lay down on the orange carpet. I took a pillow from the white couch to prop up my head so I could see the TV. My shirt lifted up and my belly was slightly exposed. When the show was over, Henry stood behind me and began to undress by his armoire, and then his necktie began to descend in front of my face. It was red with blue paisleys. I thought he wanted to give it to me and was dangling it for my inspection. But the tie kept going, moved south, and poked its tip into my navel, which was surrounded by a small tuft of dark blond hair.

"What are you trying to do there?" Henry asked, referring to my exposed navel, and there was an edge of flirtatious accusation to his voice.

The tip remained in my navel. We were umbilically attached, and I felt a profound embarrassment. We had never touched one another in all our months of living together. We had been very careful never to even brush shoulders, and our apartment was small and cluttered. What now inspired this tie to dangle in my belly button? Was he jealous of the woman who had complimented my nose? Did her attraction to me make me more desirable? Or had his esteem for me grown because of the way I was like a third partner with him and Lagerfeld and had found us all a free meal?

I looked up at him along the length of the tie and there was an odd, conflicted smile on his face that I had never seen before. He was trying to be seductive, playful, but at the same time he didn't want to be.

I pretended that I didn't fully comprehend his question and I said distractedly, "Not doing anything," and I pushed my shirt down, knocking the tip of the tie out of me. He reeled it in and I stood up and went to my room.

We lay in our beds and I thought about how it took Claudia Chauchat and Hans Castorp years before they ever kissed in *The Magic Mountain.* Henry and I lived at the base of a small hill on the Upper East Side, so it had only taken us a few months, though it wasn't exactly a kiss, a necktie in a navel, but it had the effect of one.

But still I was unsure. Nothing was ever clear. Had he tried to touch me? Had Henry finally revealed himself to me? If he did, I didn't want to see it. I didn't want him to need anything, anyone. I didn't want him to be weak like me.

CHAPTER XII

It's Your Fellow Old People Who Tear You Down

After the night of the necktie, I realized that I didn't want Henry to be desperate the way I was desperate, but I did want, more than anything else, for him to like me. Had his tie in my navel meant that he liked me?

If it did, I found myself hoping that he would try to touch me again. I didn't want to have sex with him; I just wanted his approval. One night I lay down on the carpet and I reexposed my belly button, but nothing happened. I felt foolish and didn't try any more stunts like that.

So our relations stayed the same. We both pressed on. We both kept bobbing up and down. I lived for his approval and was never sure that I had it.

On the Wednesday of the third week of May, I was at work and my great-aunt called me in the morning. She was going for a hearing test at the Ear, Nose, and Throat Hospital, which was right near my office, and she wanted to know if I would have lunch with her. I readily agreed and we made plans to meet in the lobby of my building at noon.

At eleven-thirty Henry called me. He had locked himself out of the apartment and wanted to come to *Terra* to get my keys. He was calling from The Salt of the Earth. I told him to meet me in the lobby in half an hour. I didn't tell him about my great-aunt; this was a chance for them to meet and I wanted to invite him to lunch with us, but if he knew in advance he would try to back out, since my great-aunt couldn't offer him anything.

Henry was the first to arrive. We were alone in the narrow lobby except for the doorman. I gave Henry the keys, except for the mail key, and we arranged for him to leave my set in the mailbox so I could get back in. Then I said, "My great-aunt is going to be here any minute. She came into Manhattan for a doctor's appointment. We're going out for lunch. It would be great if you could come with us."

"I'm in no shape for lunch. I have a tooth that is killing me."

"Well, can you just stay here a moment to meet her?"

"You're trying to destroy a perfect relationship. We never see each other and she sends presents."

"She'd like to meet you," I said, and then to stall him, I asked, "What happened that you locked yourself out?"

"My friend Howard, the one who follows gurus, called me up out of the blue. Still trying to recruit me. I let him in the apartment, which was a mistake. He told me I looked old. I told him you never tell an actor that. I was so angry after he left that I went to the park without my keys, sat on a bench, and a young woman reading *Life* magazine tried to engage me and I snarled at her."

Henry was wearing his loafers with the backs crushed down, his stretch tan slacks and a blue windbreaker, and I said to him, "I think you look very young. You have good color from the park and you look like a yachtsman in your windbreaker."

Henry was mollified somewhat by my compliment. He said, "My anger must have caused the blood to start pumping again, rejuvenating me . . . That girl in the park smiled at me, I must not have looked too old." Then he thought a moment more about my compliment, weighing its validity, and added, "Young people always think old people look young. It's your fellow old people who tear you down."

Then my great-aunt arrived. The doorman opened the door for her and she smiled at me widely, so happy to see me. She looked tiny and frail outside of her apartment. She was wearing a plaid skirt and a light-wool blazer. Her red hair was in a bowl cut.

"Aunt Sadye," I said, "this is Henry Harrison, my roommate." I hoped that Henry wouldn't mind being called that. But I wanted to be sure that she knew who he was. She always just called him loverboy.

She was surprised, but she puffed herself up—her small, five-foot body—and she tried to arrange her face into a sophisticated countenance suitable for an introduction: she pursed her lips.

I could see that she wanted him to find her attractive and for him to be aware that she was a woman of class. She demurely offered her small, sun-spotted hand. Henry took it, behaving nicely, and she said, smiling sweetly, "It's a pleasure to meet you."

"Yes, I am happy to meet you too," he said. "Thank you for all the food, the matzo, the toaster . . . But I must run. I was locked out, I'm on the verge of a breakdown, and now a tooth is draining."

I was annoyed that Henry was being so abrupt and I saw my great-aunt wilt a little, but she held on to his hand so that he wouldn't run away, and she asked, "Are you looking after my nephew?"

"No. Absolutely not. It's every man for himself. I can barely manage my own life. But really I must go. It was good to meet you," he said, and she released his hand. He gave a tiny bow and said to me, "Thank you for the keys. I'll try not to lose them between here and Ninety-third Street." Then the doorman opened the door and Henry was gone.

My great-aunt took a breath and she slumped down. She let go of her meeting-a-man posture, which she didn't get to use too much anymore. I saw she was disappointed that he hadn't been more attentive, and I was heartbroken for her. She didn't need any more defeats. And my own vanity was wounded—this was my great-aunt, he should have liked her, been more respectful.

But she was strong, she was already fighting back. She said dismissively, "I could have spotted him a mile away. He doesn't look clean, but he's not bad for his age."

We had lunch across the street in the Greek diner. A despondent old man sat at the counter holding his head in the palm of his hand. My great-aunt dug around in her purse looking for her lipstick and said, "You need a Geiger counter to find anything in this bag."

She found the lipstick, freshened up, and then she told me a story about working in a salon in Saratoga Springs in the 1930s during a racing season, and the advances that a wealthy lesbian had made on her in the Grand Union Hotel.

"I went up to her room at midnight, I was drunk, but she said she wanted a manicure. All of a sudden my clothes were off. I don't know how it happened." Her split-pea soup arrived. She took a sip and it was cold to her, and she called to the waiter, a tall stately Greek with a chin already charred with the day's new beard. "It's cold," she said to him. He took her bowl away without a word, sympathetic; he understood old ladies who needed to have their soup reheated even if it was hot. She smiled with pride, having received good service, having been shown respect, and continued her Saratoga story. "And then she's kissing me you know where. Right on the tussy. It sobered me up like a cup of coffee and I got out of there. But I forgot my shoes. Had to walk barefoot. I was psychologically affected. I sat in the bathtub for hours, but I felt dirty for weeks. Can you imagine?"

"Did it feel good?"

"What?"

"Being with a woman?"

"For a second," she said, and she smiled at me mischievously. "That's why I was psychologically affected."

Daphne Wants to Drink Cough Medicine and Smoke Cigarettes

When I arrived home from work the apartment was pitch-black. Usually Henry's stained curtains were open, letting in the end-of-the-day sun, but they were closed.

I put on the kitchen light and then walked across Henry's dark room to open the curtains and realized that Henry, in the shadows, was lying curled up on his bed. He was supposed to be teaching at Queensborough. I was a little shocked and momentarily frightened. "I'm sorry," I said. I could see that his eyes were open. "I didn't realize you were home. Aren't you supposed to be at school?"

"Don't want to go," said Henry in a whispery, girlish tone.

"What voice is that?" I asked.

"I'm speaking through a medium, a child's voice."

I sat down in the darkness on the white couch. I liked that Henry was talking through a medium. I asked, "What is this child's name?"

"Daphne," whispered a little girl.

"Is there something wrong, Daphne, that you don't want to go to school?"

"I have a toothache."

I thought the toothache had been an excuse to avoid lunch with my great-aunt. I asked Daphne, "Is there anything I can do? Anything you'd like?"

"Cough medicine."

Daphne was naughty. I tried to think of another question for the child. There was something exciting about Henry playing a little girl. I spoke to her in a soothing adult voice. "What does Daphne like to do?"

"Smoke cigarettes," she lisped coquettishly from her shadowy bed.

"How does smoking cigarettes make Daphne feel?"

"Good."

"Does Daphne feel guilty when she smokes?"

"Yes."

"What happens when Daphne gets caught?"

"Daddy—"

The phone rang, ending our game, and I wanted to know what Daddy did to Daphne. I picked up the receiver. It was Vivian Cudlip's secretary. She said, "Mrs. Cudlip would like to speak to Dr. Harrison."

I gave the phone to Henry and I sat back down on the white couch. Henry was silent a moment, then said in his normal voice, which sounded strange after Daphne's, "Vivian, stay in bed. Cancel everything . . . Don't strain yourself talking on the phone. You have a leaking heart. Even addressing cards is exhausting . . . All right, we'll confirm tomorrow."

He hung up the phone. "Oh, God."

"What's the matter now?"

"She wants me to take her to *Will Rogers* tomorrow night. And tomorrow I'm going to the dentist for this tooth."

"You don't mind seeing *Will Rogers* again?"

"I don't go for the play. I go for the dinner afterward. But they have a new Will Rogers. That's always interesting. The one we saw looked like a sex fiend."

Sex reminded me of Daphne, so I said in my soothing voice again, "What does Daphne's daddy do when she smokes cigarettes?"

"She's gone. I can't bring her back."

Disappointed, I returned to our adult conversation and said, "What's wrong with Vivian?"

"Her anemia. But she doesn't care. I tried to get her to stay in bed so that I don't have to take her tomorrow night. They may pull this tooth."

"Vivian will understand if you have a bad tooth."

"She won't understand. She has a hole in her heart, but that doesn't stop her from pressing on. You cancel once and it could all be over. She's been in the mood for banishing lately."

"I thought you said it's good not to be too available."

"It's good to appear that way, not to be that way."

The phone rang again and Henry picked up.

"Yes, I tried calling," he said into the receiver, and then to me in a whisper, "It's the IRS," and then he continued talking into the phone. "I got nothing but busy signals and tapes. Tapes calling tapes . . . And you need a push-button phone, but that's too expensive, I have rotary . . . I need the form that says I'll pay something every month. I lost it . . . When I get money, I'll pay someone to do my taxes so that I don't have to pay my taxes . . . Yes, send it here . . . Yes, lost that too. Hand deliver? Which office? . . . I can't go above Ninety-sixth Street, too dangerous, fever line . . . Church Street . . . Yes, good-bye."

Henry hung up the phone and said to me, "They say 'Have a nice evening' after they destroy your life with taxes. They're after me again. This country is sick, attacking the poor with taxes to pay the greater poor to have babies or to abort the babies. It's all Clinton's fault . . . I need a crooked accountant. I'm always driven to criminals . . . Though there is some hope—the IRS agent said if I keep it up they may label me uncollectible."

"What happens then?"

"Probably a citation. A medal of honor . . . This tooth is killing me. There's no recourse but oblivion. Drink with me."

It was a work night, but I wasn't going to refuse Henry. We

started to share a bottle of wine. He said, "What a life. Whose fault is it? Mine or the world's?"

"I know that I'm the cause of all my problems. Most people are."

"But the world made me and made my problems. It never used to be this way. I didn't have problems . . . I don't blame man. He is so imperfect and his systems so imperfect that there's nothing you can do . . . Where can I go? In Riga they don't have these problems . . . It's not like I have money. That's what usually causes problems. Though all the problems I have stem from money. Well, it's good to have only one problem. It's better than a spiritual crisis, though of course the money problem is a result of a spiritual, psychic problem: I've never liked to work."

"You worked on your plays. If we found *Henry and Mary* you could sell it."

"Samuel French was interested once. But you have to put a cover on it."

"You can buy a cover."

"No! There must be a cover around here. I only spend money on pleasure and judgments from the police."

We finished our bottle and Henry sent me out for a second. I walked down Second Avenue, ebullient, feeling like a boulevardier. I bought two bottles. I loved to drink with Henry, to be drunk and happy with him, to receive his full attention.

When I came back up to the apartment he was dancing. He shouted over the music, "I'm dancing so I won't get a dowager's hump, or an Otto Bellman hump. You know, he could probably be straightened out if we placed him under a steamroller or put him in bed with Lagerfeld."

Then he finished dancing and we opened the second bottle. We listened to an Eddie Cantor record. Henry was singing along. I tried my best to keep up with the lyrics and sing along too.

When the record was finished, Henry suggested that we sing patriotic songs and spirituals. The singing and the wine kept his mind off his tooth and his taxes. We belted out bits and pieces of "Dixie," "Star-Spangled Banner," "John Henry," "America the Beautiful," "Green Mountain Boys," and "Ol' Man River."

Then midway through the third bottle, Henry stopped singing and turned melancholic. He said, "My friend drank himself to death. He wanted to write a play but couldn't, and he didn't want to run the family business. He was a homosexual, but I don't think that bothered him. I'm going to call his mother."

I didn't know whom he was talking about. I asked, "When did this friend die?"

"Nineteen fifty-eight, I think," he said, and picked up the phone. Before dialing, he said, "If you want to commit suicide, get drunk and call everybody you know all over the world and then when you're done, think of the bill and kill yourself."

He dialed the number. "Did I wake you? . . . It's Henry . . . Henry Harrison . . . I woke you, but now you're up . . . How are you? . . . Me? I'm living on a dangerous edge, but I'm used to it, so it's not so bad . . ."

I went to the bathroom and when I came back Henry was off the phone.

"I don't think she knew who I was," he said. "But she is old. Older than Vivian. At least ninety-five."

"When did you speak to her last?"

"Twenty years ago."

"It's amazing she's still at the same number."

"Oh, people stay at the same number for years. When you get a good one, you hold on to it . . . But I can't even commit suicide. No one who likes me is still alive for me to call and run up a big bill."

"You could call me," I said.

"You don't like me," Henry said.

"Yes, I do. I like you a lot."

"You only fool yourself into believing you like me. Otherwise it would be unbearable to live here."

"I do like you."

Henry drank from his glass and didn't look at me. "I don't need like," Henry said. "I need love."

"You need love?"

"Yes. I'm having financial problems, it affects my thinking."

"What if you didn't have financial problems?"

"Then I wouldn't need love . . . The greatest sign of love is when someone gives you money because then they are truly helping you. Few people realize this."

"Do you need anything from *me*?"

"I need to talk to you. You're the only sane person I know."

I gave him something no one else did. I was an *only* for him. I was proud. "Thank you for thinking I'm sane," I said.

"You're welcome."

I had never felt closer to Henry. I wished that I had money to give him to show him my love. We sipped our wine in silence. I had an idea.

"Why don't you ask Vivian Cudlip for a loan?" I said. "Or maybe she would even give you the money if she knew your tax problems."

"No, that isn't done. You never ask for money. I could ask her to marry me. I sleep late, she visits doctors in the afternoon, the day would almost be over and I'd be provided for . . . but everyone is always proposing to her. I can't lower myself that way."

"Couldn't you just be honest with her and ask for a loan? That's not ignoble."

"Any man who is honest with a woman is a fool."

"What about a man who is honest with a man?"

"Any man who is honest with a man is a fool."

"But you still think I'm the only sane person you know, right?"

"Yes, you're sane. A little old-fashioned, but sane."

Thank You, Dear Boy

The following afternoon, Henry called me at work. He sounded like he was in bad shape. He had been to the NYU dental clinic.

"What did they do?" I asked.

"Pulled a tooth. Only gave me local anesthesia. My whole face is swollen. But it's a great opportunity for you. I want you to take Vivian to *Will Rogers* tonight. Then afterward she'll probably take you to the Russian Tea Room."

My heart raced. I was getting a chance to escort all by myself. "Does Vivian mind that I'm a stranger?" I asked.

"She doesn't know yet. We'll wait until the last possible moment. You pick her up at seven, we'll call her at six, six-thirty. That way she can't call any of the other knights."

I was to come home immediately after work and at that time Henry would give me full instructions and make sure that I was properly dressed.

When I got out of *Terra*, it was a beautiful spring evening and I walked quickly to the subway, excited to be off on my mission.

On the stairs up to our apartment, I ran into Gershon. His hair was nicely combed, his beard had some shape to it, and he was wearing khaki pants and an oxford shirt. I had never seen him dressed so nicely. He was usually in sweatpants.

"Hello, Gershon," I said.

"Hi, Louis," he said, and the corners of his mouth lifted gently into a smile.

"Where are you going?"

"To a lecture at the Freud Society."

"Are you a member?"

"No. They have lectures open to the public . . . one of Henry's friends thought I was an analyst . . . I thought I should investigate."

I nodded and took a step up the stairs to pass him and then I said, "Henry's in a bad way. He had a tooth pulled."

"People are like cars," he said. "The older they get the more maintenance they need."

"Yes," I said, and I headed up to Henry, and Gershon continued on to his Freud lecture.

Henry had just finished speaking to Vivian when I came into the apartment. He lied to her. He told her that he had a lecture to give at the college, which he hadn't properly recorded in his calendar. She wasn't angry; she didn't mind if someone had to work, and she was also intrigued by the notion of meeting a young person, me.

I took a shower and shaved—for the second time that day— and got dressed. I wore my best white English cotton shirt, a blue silk tie, gray wool pants, and blazer. I combed my hair neatly with vitamin oil and I brushed my teeth. Henry said, "Perfectly presentable."

My instructions were to watch her like a hawk at all times, never discuss our living conditions, and don't let on that I had seen the second act of *Will Rogers*; she'd want to feel that she was treating me. At the door, I said to Henry, "Thank you for this opportunity. I'm very excited."

"Yes, the first time is like that," he said.

I took a taxi to her house which was on Forty-eighth Street between Third and Second avenues. Henry told me that all the houses on Forty-eighth and Forty-ninth shared, in their backyards, a block-long private garden called Turtle Bay. Some of the people who shared the garden with Vivian were Katharine Hepburn and Stephen Sondheim. It was one of the most exclusive neighborhoods in New York City.

I was about to ring her bell and then I thought how flowers would be a very nice opening gesture. Henry had told me early on that rosen knights were knights who brought roses. I was a few minutes early and so I ran down the street to Second Avenue. At the corner of Forty-ninth there was a deli, but all the roses were expensive. I was a cheap knight. But I did buy several lovely purple irises for four dollars, and I ran back and rang Mrs. Cudlip's bell.

I was greeted by a uniformed maid, and Mrs. Cudlip was waiting for me in the entrance hallway, sitting on a chair like a small child. She was looking at her feet, her hands were in her lap. She was wearing a strawberry blond wig, a red dress, stockings, and white pumps.

The maid helped her stand up and Mrs. Cudlip was still looking straight at her feet. I saw that she had a horrible swollen hump at the base of her neck. It was a grotesquerie of calcification. It forced her to permanently stare at the tops of her shoes. She was bent over like a shrimp. She was about four and a half feet high. The maid took her hand and led her to me. She took tiny little steps and I couldn't see her face. Her wig advanced toward me.

She tilted her head slightly and peeked up at me. I saw a pointy chin. Henry had told me that she had lost most of her chin to cancer. "You're Louis? Henry's young friend?" she asked.

"Yes," I said. "It's very nice to meet you. I've heard so much about you." I was nervous, but under control.

"If it came from Henry, don't believe a word. He's full of stories," she said, and because she was looking straight down, I could hardly hear her and her speech was a little raspy because of her bad chin. But for a woman in her nineties, she seemed very sharp.

"I have some flowers for you," I said, and I held them between us at what I thought was her eye level. She reached out a gnarled, bejewelled hand and took the flowers and smelled them.

"That's very thoughtful of you," she said, and she handed the flowers to the maid. "The car's waiting outside. Let's go."

She took hold of my arm and I led her slowly down the front stairs and into a black limousine. It was like leading a blind person since she couldn't look straight ahead.

During the car ride we talked about the weather: it was beautiful. And why she loved musicals: they made her feel good.

The driver parked in front of the theater and I escorted her into the show, and I was continually frightened that she would get knocked over and break something. But we made it to our seats and I really was like a human walker.

We were right next to the orchestra and I pretended artfully that this was my first time at *Will Rogers*.

"It's a very nice set," I said.

She craned her neck, but I didn't know how much she could see. I didn't know if her field of vision extended above the lip of the stage. But then the music began and I could see her smiling under her wig. Midway through that first act, I put my arm on the armrest and she lay her hand on top of mine. It was a bony, gnarled hand with enormous emeralds and diamonds on each finger, but its placement over mine was a tender and sweet gesture.

During intermission, I was worried that she would want to go to the bathroom, but she didn't ask.

"How do you like the show?" she inquired. "I think it's a scream."

"It's wonderful. Thank you for taking me."

"Don't thank me yet, it's not over."

When the curtain did fall, I managed to get her back to the limo, and the driver hopped out and opened the door for us. I liked being in the limo. I felt very rich. He took us to the Russian Tea Room and on the way over, I thanked Mrs. Cudlip for taking me to see *Will Rogers*, and then I added, "I'm so glad that Henry asked me if I could take his place. He felt terrible about forgetting about the lecture."

"Henry's a great friend," she said. "But he'd like to be more than friends. He asked me to marry him last week."

"Really?" I said. "I didn't know."

"What he said was, 'It's time I got married.' But I pretended not to hear him. I'm not marrying anyone. I love too many men . . . My friend Aresh is meeting us for dinner. He was a diplomat from Iran years ago. Exiled now. He's a nice gentleman. I like to have dinner with men. They're much more interesting than women."

At the Russian Tea Room, the dark-haired maître d' greeted us: "Mrs. Cudlip, always a pleasure. We have your table ready." He led the way and the restaurant was crowded and nicely appointed with samovars and lamps and pink tablecloths.

The staff stopped moving and respectfully watched our slow progression. Mrs. Cudlip was shuffling forward bravely and happily, squeezing my arm, her strawberry blond wig at the fore like the prow of a ship. Many of the diners at the other tables looked up: she was a person of power, which was obvious by all the deference shown to her, but people were also staring because she was so disfigured.

Aresh was waiting in the booth. He was a short bald man with a fine gray fringe around his egg-shaped head. His eyes were heavy-lidded and beautiful. He was impeccably dressed in a black suit and his fingers were small and manicured.

"Vivian," he said, and he leaped up and took her arm from me and guided her into the banquet, and the maître d', with the help of a waiter, pulled out the table.

"I want a drink," she said. "Champagne."

"Right away, Mrs. Cudlip," said the maître d', and he gave an aggressive nod of his head to the waiter, who hurried off.

"Anything you need, Mrs. Cudlip, just ask," he said, and he gave a little bow and left our table.

Soon we were drinking and Aresh was effusive in his compliments of Mrs. Cudlip. "It's so good to be with you. You're the most beautiful . . . the most sophisticated . . . the most cultured . . . the most prominent . . . the most popular woman in New York."

It was really too much; he seemed to think that he sounded sincere. But I don't think Mrs. Cudlip was really listening, because she was drinking her champagne with a straw and it was making a lot of noise. Because of her mouth cancer she had to use a straw.

We started off with Beluga caviar at eighty-five dollars an ounce, and I watched how Aresh prepared it on the toast with the crushed bits of egg and onion. He made little pieces for Mrs. Cudlip as well. But he seemed bothered by something, and then he announced that he was displeased with the wait staff. He said, "They're not serving right this evening."

He was trying to exhibit his sophistication and worldliness, but Mrs. Cudlip said, "It's perfectly fine. I love the Russian Tea Room. What do you think, Louis?"

"This caviar is wonderful," I said, diplomatically, avoiding the issue of the wait staff. So I was my usual boring self, but I was sincere—the caviar *was* delicious, like little silky pellets of salt.

After the caviar, we ordered our dinners, and switched from champagne to white wine. I had cold borscht, beef à la stroganoff, and then Mrs. Cudlip wanted more caviar, so we had caviar blinis. But it was difficult for her to eat; she had only a few crooked teeth that I could see on her bottom lip, and when she spilled things on the front of her red dress, Aresh would wipe her off with the restaurant's pink napkins.

Halfway through the meal, the maître d' arrived with a tiny envelope for Mrs. Cudlip.

Inside was a phone message, Mrs. Cudlip said, from Barry Barbarash. I knew that name as one of the men in Mrs. Cudlip's court who was a rival of Henry's. She read the phone message aloud to us: "I know you're out with boyfriends. Go home at once."

This enraged Aresh. He thought it was incredibly rude. He conjectured that either Barbarash had informants in the Russian Tea Room or he had called her house and had pried information out of her servants.

"You shouldn't fall for that Barbarash," said Aresh. "He is charming and has wonderful long legs, but he spies on you in Palm Beach, you know. He has binoculars and watches you undress in your room at the Colony."

"Stop it right now," she scolded him. "He's a very good friend."

Aresh brooded and when it was time for dessert, Mrs. Cudlip asked him what he wanted. "Only Barry Barbarash's head on a plate," he said.

"You're very jealous," she said.

"How can I be jealous? He's so handsome. So charismatic. Such long legs. I can't even compare, so how can I be jealous?"

"What do you think, Louis?" she asked.

"Well, wanting his head on a plate with flaming cognac sounds jealous to me," I said. I added the detail of the cognac because I was a little drunk. Aresh looked at me with hatred, but Mrs. Cudlip appreciated my frankness and said, "I like you," and this made me feel very good.

And then a party of six people arrived at the restaurant, three couples all in their early forties. Mrs. Cudlip knew them and waved them over and insisted that they join us. More chairs were brought to our booth, more bottles of champagne, and more caviar. Aresh was slighted by all this—slighted that she should want anyone else's company. He had not considered me to be a true rival, but I had watched him over the course of the meal slowly crumble and lose all confidence. When the couples started drinking their champagne and enjoying the caviar, he said that he wasn't feeling well. So he stood up and said good-bye to Vivian, intending to injure her with his sudden departure, but she hardly seemed to notice. His eyes were full of humiliation, and he stepped away from the table.

I felt bad about my cognac remark and so I walked him outside. I needed some fresh air myself after so much food and drink.

"Can you make it home all right?" I asked him as we stood on the sidewalk of Fifty-seventh Street.

"She doesn't know how she hurts me," he said. "I've lost my country. My career. My identity. Everything. She could help me so easily, but she doesn't even think of it. I'm through with her."

He walked away from me without saying good-bye, a little man destroyed in a perfect suit.

I returned to Mrs. Cudlip and our party was loud and boisterous, and with Aresh gone I was the one who took the pink napkins and cleaned the caviar off her chest. I enjoyed tending to her like a nurse. I felt charitable and important at the same time.

She drank and ate a great deal, but not once did she ask me to take her to the bathroom. I suspected that she wore a diaper.

We closed the restaurant and everyone thanked her for her generosity, but she was too drunk to sign the check. She had her own account at the Tea Room, and the maître d' discreetly asked me to sign her name; his manner led me to believe that many escorts before me had done this. It came to over twelve hundred dollars. I was worried that I was about to do something wrong, and so I asked the maître d', "Does this include the gratuity?"

It did and so I penned out her name with a great flourish. Then I practically carried Mrs. Cudlip out of the restaurant. I had my arm around her knobby, stooped body, but I didn't mind, I wasn't repulsed. I liked Mrs. Cudlip.

The maître d' held open the door for me, and on the sidewalk of Fifty-seventh Street, Mrs. Cudlip was swaying happily and I was very worried that I would drop her. I waved at the limo driver, who was parked several yards away, but he appeared to be asleep in the front seat. I thought how it was just me against all of New York. I'd have to fight for Mrs. Cudlip. Anyone could come along and try to knock us over and steal the rings off her fingers. She was incredibly vulnerable and I carried her quickly to the limo, and holding on to her I tapped at the window. The driver woke up and was very apologetic and helped me get her into the car.

In the backseat, she held my hand and rested her head against my shoulder and then she fell asleep. How easily I could slip a ring off her finger, I thought.

The maid answered the front door and the driver and I carried her up a flight of stairs to her bedroom. Her house was in shadows, but I could see that the living room was elegant, with fine furniture, a chandelier, and a grand piano. At the top of the staircase we went to the left and the maid whispered, "To the right."

Mrs. Cudlip woke up as we turned her—her feet were barely touching the ground—but she did a little dance step to coincide with our change of direction. She had great spirit.

We took her to her bedroom and placed her on her bed, and lowering her down brought me to my knees. I was able to look into her tiny eyes for the first time that night. She reached her arms around me and clasped me to her red dress, stained with food and champagne, and she said, "Thank you, dear boy."

Life Rushes By

The limo driver gave me a lift home. He said, "I don't think she has any blood left. It's all alcohol."

Henry woke up when I came in. He had purposely left the plugs out so that I would wake him and tell him what happened. And after I brushed my teeth, I lay in bed and gave him a full report, though I didn't mention that I had heard of his marriage proposal.

I told him all about Aresh and how sad and pathetic he looked walking down Fifty-seventh Street, and Henry said, "He desperately wants to marry her or just get some money. He cries every time they're together, but she puts up with it. He may have been tortured when the Shah was kicked out."

I told him how Vivian had clasped me to her at the end of the night.

"You weren't supposed to do so well," he said. "I sent you to keep my rivals at bay, not become one."

"She's very sweet," I said. "It's not hard to be nice to her. I feel bad. She's this tiny crippled woman and everybody wants her money and stares at her rings."

"Don't feel bad for her. She's not sweet. She's a monster. She treats her staff like something out of Peter the Great. Well, she's a sweet monster . . . Tell me about the food."

I gave him a rundown on all the caviar and borscht and champagne, and he said, "Stop it. I shouldn't have asked. I'm starving to death because of this tooth."

"How is it doing?" I asked.

"The swelling's gone down quite a lot, but I probably picked up AIDS from the dental instruments. But what can I expect for twenty-five dollars? Used to be when you went to a clinic, you waited with the Irish poor. Now it's all drug addicts and homeless. I don't know what the answer is. The conservatives pay attention to no one. And the liberals pay too much attention to the majority—the poor. We need a visionary leader. We need great people in government, like myself. But they've made it impossible. So this greatness is untapped."

"I'd vote for you," I said.

"I should hope so. Because of me you ate caviar all night. But I don't think I can give all the voters caviar . . . And they don't want caviar. They want hamburgers. So there we are. Where are we? I'm putting the plugs in."

In the morning, as I was getting dressed for work, I was hungover, but the previous night had been worth it. Then the phone rang. It was Mrs. Cudlip's secretary. Both Henry and I were invited to lunch at Mortimer's that afternoon. Henry was asleep and I took a risk and accepted for both of us. I didn't think he would miss two free meals in a row. After I hung up, I nudged him awake and gave him the news. He felt his face and the swelling was down. I would see him at the restaurant at one o'clock.

At *Terra*, George gave me permission to take an hour and a half lunch. Mary saw me as I was leaving and she said, "Nice jacket."

I was wearing my seersucker jacket from my Princeton strolling days, and I looked bashfully at her perfect white knees and said, "Thank you," and then I hurried out of the office. I still was like Raskolnikov around her, but her compliment was quite a gift. I felt very handsome.

I walked to Mortimer's—it was just thirteen blocks up Lexington—and when I got to the restaurant there was no Vivian, but Henry was at the bar and so was Aresh. I shook hands with the exiled diplomat, but he glanced at me sheepishly. He was back for another meal.

Henry and I shook hands for the fun of it, but then he looked at me closely and said, "It's all wrong. Blond people can't wear seersucker. You look all washed out. Your face has disappeared. You need something stronger."

This remark canceled out Mary's compliment. I looked at Henry to try to find something with which to undermine his confidence for once. He was wearing his bright green sport coat. "Your jacket's *too* strong," I said.

"Yes," he said, laughing at himself; I couldn't hurt him. "I look like a Puerto Rican funeral director from the South Bronx."

I ordered a club soda and looked around the restaurant. Mortimer's was plain, bordering on ugly, but this was obviously part of its allure for its patrons, the wealthy of the Upper East Side. They could pretend that they were having a casual lunch, though Henry had told me that this ugly little place was famous for its exclusivity. You had to know the owner to get a table, which was obviously its most attractive feature.

Then Vivian arrived, escorted by a tall, thin man with jet black hair, yellow skin, and a wild look in his eye. All the Upper East Side ladies hushed up, and the maître d' and Henry and Aresh and I all rushed to Mrs. Cudlip and buzzed around her until we were taken to our table and seated.

I was placed next to Mrs. Cudlip and over the course of the meal, the gentleman with the dark hair, an antique dealer from Philadelphia named Philip, and I took turns wiping at her dress with a napkin.

The conversation was inane, led mostly by Philip and Henry, and somehow *Bonnie and Clyde* was being discussed. Philip was drinking heavily—this was the cause of his wild eyes and yellow skin—and he said that Bonnie was actually a dwarf and that the movie had beautified her.

"Some dwarfs are beautiful," said Henry.

And then the conversation got on to dwarfs, and Philip said that Alexander Pope was a dwarf, and Aresh, who had mostly been quiet, cited Toulouse-Lautrec, and I said, "Lautrec wasn't a dwarf; it was a bone disease that shortened him."

"Really?" asked Philip.

"Oh, yes. He hated himself because of it. And it came out in his paintings; his subjects were all grotesque. He was fascinated by the grotesque," I said. I had read about Lautrec and I felt very knowledgeable, but Henry was lifting his eyebrows at me angrily. I immediately recognized that I shouldn't be talking about the grotesque with Vivian right next to me, but I had ceased to really think of her that way.

"This is very interesting what you are saying about Lautrec," said Philip.

But before I could put my foot into it any deeper, Henry said, "It's all par for the course."

"What's par for the course?" asked Philip.

"That's what I say whenever there's a lull in the conversation, or I say this line from *The Red Shoes*, 'Life rushes by, time rushes by, but the red shoes go on dancing forever.'"

"There was no lull," said Philip.

"I'm wearing red shoes," said Vivian.

"Of course you are," said Henry, and the conversation moved off dwarfs. Philip started talking about space exploration and how astronauts suffer radiation in their testicles and can't have children, and Henry said that Henry James burned his testicles, and Vivian found it all very amusing, and Aresh pouted, and I kept my mouth shut the rest of the meal.

When we were done, I thanked Vivian for lunch and she told me that I'd have to come to Philadelphia some time and meet her granddaughter. I was very pleased. I really was making it as a young gentleman.

We all said good-bye on the sidewalk, Philip and Vivian went off in her limo, Aresh got in a cab, and as soon as Henry and I were alone, he said, "I can't believe what an idiot you are."

"Why?"

"So rude to talk about a fascination with the grotesque."

"I don't think she was offended."

"You have no tact, no sensitivity. You were trying to show off."

Then something quite embarrassing happened. All the months of criticism had finally gotten to me, and I became hysterical. "Why are you always putting me down?" I screamed right in public, right in front of Mortimer's. "Why do you always have to make me feel stupid?"

And then I started crying, and I couldn't face Henry and I ran away from him.

I went to two movies that night and came home late. Henry was in bed and I tiptoed to my room.

"Listen," he called out. "I'm sorry I criticized you. But you shouldn't be so sensitive. But I apologize. So let's just sweep it under the carpet. There's plenty of dirt under there and loose change and probably an old eye mask, but there's room for other things."

"It's under," I said, and I began to undress. I was very relieved that Henry wasn't angry at me for having yelled at him and then for having cried.

You Look Practically Middle Class

The following week, Otto Bellman, with Virginia on the line as backup, called and asked Henry to be his best man. I was in the kitchen, making dinner, when it happened.

The wedding was that coming weekend. They had waited until the last minute so that he couldn't say no. But Henry made certain stipulations. He wanted them to use the King James version of the

Bible, which wasn't their first choice. Virginia wanted to use the Revised American, but she conceded on this issue of holy text. And the bridegroom, Henry insisted, was to be properly dressed, and Otto harrumphed when he heard this, but Virginia reassured Henry that they would buy a suit.

"I have to do it," Henry told me. "I couldn't say no with her on the phone. But they did give in on the Bible, that's what's most important. They were afraid I wouldn't come otherwise." Then Henry slipped into a W. C. Fields accent and boasted, "They're afraid I'll cut them off without a penny." Then he thought about this, about his actual financial worth, and he said, "I'd like to leave someone my debts. I'd like to leave Bellman my debts. I'll give his name to the IRS as a wedding present."

"Why do you think it was so important to him that you be best man?"

"Do you know the opera *Das Rheingold*?"

"No," I said, but Henry didn't castigate me.

"It's the story of Alberich, who has a dwarf whom he keeps locked up. Then one day the dwarf gets out and when he comes back he says to Alberich, 'You didn't tell me there were women!' And Alberich was upset; he wanted the dwarf all to himself. Bellman is like Alberich and I am the dwarf—he wants me all to himself. He was very jealous when he lived here, didn't like me going out, always had to tag along. I enthralled him . . . You know, wizards have the power to enthrall. I seem to have that power. I've prided myself on it. Of course it does no good. There is no money in being a wizard, but there are other benefits . . . Now I will lie down and think how hopeless and difficult life is and gain some strength to make some spaghetti."

All week long there were calls about the wedding, and I asked Henry if I could go, but it was to be a very small affair. Only family and a few friends of the bride and groom were invited. Even Henry wasn't supposed to bring anyone, but he threatened not to come and so they were letting him bring Lagerfeld.

"Lagerfeld doesn't know she wasn't invited," Henry told me. "She'd be very offended. She knows Virginia. I don't want her to be hurt."

"You're good to Lagerfeld," I said. "She really is your closest friend."

"Yes, she's the one who tries to exploit me the most."

Gershon was invited and since Henry was allowed to bring a lady friend, Gershon was bringing a woman he had met at the Freud Society. Henry figured that it was an analyst who wanted to study Gershon, but I believed that he had really met someone.

Gershon needed clothing for the wedding and so Henry took him shopping at the thrift stores. Gershon also agreed to go to a barber for a haircut and a shave, but he wouldn't let Henry come with him. So the new Gershon had yet to be seen.

Saturday was the big day. The ceremony was scheduled for four o'clock, followed by a dinner at the parents' club in Greenwich. Then they were all going to spend Saturday night in a bed-and-breakfast, paid for by Virginia's parents. On Sunday they were going to have a post-wedding brunch and then return to the city. I was very jealous to be left out of all the festivities.

Around noon on Saturday, Gershon came up to the apartment. I let him in, and Henry and I saw him at the same moment. Sometimes when a man has a fresh, clean shave and his skin takes it well, he radiates light and well-being. This was the case with Gershon.

"My God!" Henry said. "You look practically middle class."

Gershon was in uniform: black lace-up shoes, gray trousers, a white shirt, red tie, and a blue blazer. In a blazer he looked barrel-chested in a handsome way, and without his beard it was revealed that he had a beautiful smile and a manly wide jaw. His hair was closely cropped, and it was only the forehead and brow that remained Gershonesque—they still protruded and cast a shadow over his kind, blue-gray eyes. He was a formidable figure.

"You look great," I said, and I shook his hand as a gesture of congratulations.

"Thank you," he said.

"Yes," said Henry. "Now you can join the New York Yacht Club. You have the right look."

Then Henry searched for his keys and found them in his pants pocket, and so he and Gershon took off for Connecticut, for Otto Bellman's wedding.

A Girl as I Must Have First Imagined Girls

Left behind in New York, I went to Sally's for the first time since the accident. I got there late, after eleven; I had been fighting the urge to go, but then gave in to it.

I ordered a drink and despite myself I was happy to be back. I loved the mingled smell of cigarettes and perfume. I loved looking at the Queens. I marveled at their beauty.

It was crowded but Miss Pepper wasn't there. I figured that she had landed a date and would probably be back. Dates didn't last very long; rarely did they go the full hour that was promised. Sylvia wasn't around either. And Wendy, I assumed, was still in prison.

I asked the beautiful bartender if Miss Pepper had already been in that night.

"No," she said.

"You think she'll show up?"

"She moved, baby."

"Where'd she go?"

"I'm not giving out personal information."

"Please, I'm her friend," I said. "You've seen me drinking with her many times. Did she go back to Los Angeles?"

On principle the bartender had been tough with me, but she could see that my motives weren't strange or harmful. "She's down in North Carolina," she said.

"She went to her mother?"

"Yeah, that's what she said. We had a going-away party for her."

I was quiet. If Miss Pepper had gone home, then she had gone home to die. "Do you have her address?" I asked.

She laughed at me. "I don't write letters, baby."

I took my drink and went to one of the tables by the dance floor. I felt all weak in the shoulders and in the legs.

A young Queen came up to me. She had shiny black hair to her shoulders and there was a curl in the middle of her forehead like the letter *j*. She was of medium height, maybe five foot eight with her white platform high heels. She was wearing an off-yellow summer dress with a flower print. Her legs were smooth and delicious looking. And her mouth was a beautiful red thing.

"What are you doing tonight?" she asked, and she had a slight Spanish accent. She stood in front of me and I didn't get out of my chair.

"I'd like to go out with you," I said.

"Are you a cop?"

"No."

"Are you sure?"

"Yes. How old are you?"

"Twenty-one."

"How old are you really?"

"You're not a cop?"

"I'm not a cop."

"Sixteen."

"What's your name?"

"Maria."

"Let's go."

"It's one-fifty."

"All right."

She smiled at me and she moved her hips in a nice lazy circle. She brushed the front of her sweet summer dress against my leg. She lowered the straps of her dress, revealing two little budding breasts with swollen brown nipples. She lowered them to my mouth. I was shy, but I licked them. They tasted of perfume. Other men watched. She knew they were watching.

She pulled her dress back up. "OK," she said. "Now we go."

We went to the cash machine on Seventh Avenue. She held my hand. She was happy. It was a spring night. She was a pretty girl.

I took out the money; I didn't really care how much it cost, I felt half dead. But then I got a little cheap. I didn't want to pay for a hotel room. "Let's go to my apartment," I said, and she agreed.

We took a taxi. We held hands in the backseat. I admired her profile, the *j*-shaped lock of hair on her forehead. Then she turned to me and smiled and said, "What's your name?"

"Louis."

The driver looked at us in the mirror. I'm sure he thought that Maria was a real girl, but the redness of her lips, the short dress, and all her perfume let him know that she was a prostitute. But I didn't care. I liked holding her hand.

He dropped us off on Second Avenue and I bought us four wine coolers. Then we went up to the apartment and no one spotted us on the stairwell; it was after midnight. I didn't turn on the lights. I didn't want her to get a good look at the apartment. I just put the light on in the bathroom to give us a little glow in my room and she said, "This place wouldn't be bad if it wasn't so dirty."

"I just rent a room here from an old man," I said. "If it was my place it would be cleaner."

"Where is he?"

"He's away."

"Do you sleep with him?"

"No," I said, laughing.

"Where does he sleep?"

"There's a couch in the other room."

She looked at me skeptically. I knew she thought that if I lived with an old man that I must be exchanging sex for rent. She asked me for the money and she put it in her little purse.

We sat together on the edge of my bed and we clinked our wine coolers together. I didn't want us to drink out of glasses; Henry and I each had our one glass that we kept clean and that was it. I put my hand on her knee. I kissed her neck. She put her wine cooler on the floor and fell back on to my pillow and smiled up at me. I lay beside her. She was a beautiful teenage girl. She was only sixteen, she had probably barely started puberty as a boy, but was already on female hormones. She was androgynous, a changeling. I put my arm around her and hid my face in her neck. I smelled her perfume.

She seemed to like me. She wasn't trying to rush away, leave.

"Why are you down?" she asked. "You're too quiet."

370

"Do you know Miss Pepper?"

"Kind of old, real dark, but pretty?"

"Yes," I said. "Do you know what's happened to her?"

"No, I haven't seen her around lately."

"I heard that she went home. I think she has AIDS. That's why I'm down."

"Oh, yeah, a lot of the old Queens are sick. It won't happen to me. I love myself too much to get AIDS."

Then she kissed me and I didn't care where her mouth had been. She looked so young and clean. And who else did I have to kiss anyways? Who was I trying to preserve my health for? I touched her breasts through the light cotton of her dress.

"You like my titties?" she asked.

"Yes," I said. "You are adorable." She smiled a genuine smile. She pulled down the straps and I kissed her small, swollen nipples.

Then she rose up and removed her heels. She stood in front of me and I sat on the edge of the bed and I smothered my face against her belly, against her soft dress. She put her hands in my hair. Then she stepped out of her red panties and lifted her dress just the slightest, and her uncircumcised penis dangled in front of me. I looked up at her clear, gentle face, her full red lips. The straps of her dress clung to the sides of her arms, her dark-tipped breasts were revealed to me, and now too her dangling soft penis, not ugly. What odd beauty she had. It was a girl as I must have first imagined girls.

"Kiss it," she said.

I took it gently in my hand and kissed the side of it and she laughed and threw herself on to the bed. I had done something incredible, perverted, kissing it was like kissing electricity.

"Take your clothes off," she said. I did and then I took a big drink of wine, and then I lowered myself to her, and naked we lay on my bed. We kissed and rubbed against each other. She was perfect and beautiful. I could have kissed her a thousand times. I felt like I was in love with her.

She took hold of my penis and stroked it and then led my hand to hers. It wasn't really hard because of the hormones, and then I felt something at the base of her penis. In the dim light of my room I could see a scab. It was right near her pubic area.

"What happened?" I asked. I was repulsed, scared.

"A date bit me two weeks ago," she said. Her voice was angry. She looked at it with concern. "I went to a doctor. He said it would be all right."

"Why did he bite you?"

"I don't know. He was smoking crack. He was crazy. It was bloody."

"What did you tell the doctor?"

"That I woke up that way."

"The doctor believed you?"

"Yes." Then she started to pick at the scab.

"Don't pick it," I said, like a mother. She was injured. She seemed young and vulnerable. Things were somber between us. There was no more kissing. A date had bitten her. I was a date.

She was thirsty and wanted some water. She took my glass from the side of my bed and went to the kitchen. I listened to the water come from the faucet and through it I heard Henry's keys jangling outside the door. Henry's home, I thought, and I felt my usual, immediate happiness. But it was momentary. I was twenty-six years old, and I don't think I could have had a heart attack, but my heart did seize. And there was a moment of sheer terror just like the moment before I hit the light pole on Third Avenue.

I ran into the kitchen to drag her out of there, to hide her in my armoire. I was counting on Henry not to find the right key. I grabbed her arm forcefully but didn't say anything, I didn't want him to hear. She looked at me angrily—we had just been talking about the date who bit her. The slight jingle of the keys outside the door had meant nothing to her. I heard everything. She pulled away from me. The door opened. I jumped back. I covered myself with my hands. Henry saw her, not me, and screamed. It was high-pitched and unusual. A sound I wouldn't expect from him, but he was terrified. He had a small overnight bag and he threw it at her defensively, reflexively. He thought she was some kind of intruder. The bag missed.

"Fuck you," Maria said. She was undaunted, tough. He stood in the light of the doorway; his momentary blindness from fear was passing. He realized that she was nude, less threatening. He stepped all the way in and saw me. His eyes ran over my naked body, my foolish hands protecting my penis.

"Henry . . . I'm sorry," I managed to get out in a hoarse whisper.

He looked at her, saw her breasts and penis, and she walked into my room.

"Get out of here," he said, he could barely speak, and clumsily he slammed the door shut. I ran into my room. She was already dressing. I put on my clothes. I felt weak and yet there was that cold feeling that everything was perfect. That I was meant to destroy everything.

"You're fucking sick!" Henry shouted from his room. I had never heard him use the word *fuck* before. Then he threw something, and there was the breaking of glass.

"You'd better get out of here. Move out of here!" he shouted with venom, but there was also a weakening in his voice, a disgust, a trembling.

"He's an asshole," she said. I wanted to hit her. But I also knew she didn't understand. We got to the front door. I dared for a moment to look into his room, the light was on. His back was to me. He had thrown a wine bottle against his armoire and there were pieces of green glass on the orange carpet.

Maria wanted to get away from me and I didn't blame her, but I couldn't be alone, so I offered to buy her something to eat. She accepted my offer—she must have been hungry.

We walked to the Greek diner on Eighty-sixth and Second. All the waiters stared at her. She looked like a girl to me, and probably to them, but there was something, and they picked up on it. And she was a young Queen, but she already had the courage not to care about people gawking at her. We sat in a booth in the back. A few other people were in booths. It was around one o'clock in the morning.

"You shouldn't have brought me there," she said pragmatically and easily.

"He wasn't supposed to come home," I said.

"He must be in love with you to get that angry. He's jealous." She said this with confidence, as she glanced at the menu. This was the kind of thing she said to her girlfriends.

"No. I'm not supposed to bring people there."

"But if he didn't want you for himself, why would he care?"

It was too complicated to explain to her. I didn't tell her about the first rule of the apartment: No fornication. But I also heard what she said. But if he did love me, then I had destroyed it. He thought I was sick. And yet also I felt a certain terrible satisfaction that he had seen her. She had looked beautiful in the light from the hall.

She ordered fried chicken fingers and ate them with great pleasure. I liked watching her eat. For once I was the old person. I wanted to tell her she shouldn't eat such greasy food late at night. But she's young, I thought, she can handle it and not lose her beauty. I was having tea. I thought that if I ate anything I would throw up.

She was silent while she ate, but I needed her to talk. I said to her, "What are you thinking about?"

"About my show. I'm in a ball tomorrow night. I'm wondering if I'll look good." We had just been thrown out of my apartment by a hysterical man, and she was thinking about her show. It made me like Maria even more. She didn't feel shame or tainted by what had happened.

Then she said with confidence, "But I'll look good. I dress to impress because I'm an impressive person. They'll see that I have character."

After the chicken fingers, she ordered a large salad, and smeared the iceberg lettuce with thick Russian dressing. "I could just eat the dressing," she said.

I wondered what would become of her. I was glad that she was eating lettuce, vegetables. I said, "You're very beautiful. Do you think you'll always be a woman?"

"Probably."

"What about when you get older?"

"I'll retire from the scene, save my money and get the surgery. Then I hope I have a husband. And we'll have a home, but not in New York or Puerto Rico. Somewhere nice . . . like Wyoming or Ohio. I want to be somewhere beautiful."

She had a piece of cake, and then smoked a cigarette she borrowed from a waiter, who smiled at her. He liked her. I fantasized about making a lot of money and having her be my girlfriend. I would pay for her surgery. I would help make her a woman. Buy her love.

I asked her if she was still in high school. And she told me that she went to a special high school in the Village where it was OK to be a Queen. But she didn't go too often because she lived in the Bronx with her aunt. Her parents were still in Puerto Rico.

Then we left the diner and I felt proud that I could treat a young person to a meal. I liked Maria and when we were outside, I asked her for her number, but she said she couldn't have dates calling because of her aunt. She told me we would see each other at Sally's.

I wanted her to take a cab back to the Bronx, but she wouldn't, she wanted to take the train. She insisted that she would be safe in the subway.

"I know how to take care of myself," she said.

"Why won't you take a taxi?"

"I don't like to spend my money right after I make it."

So we started walking towards Lexington, heading for the Number 5 train, which she could take to the Bronx. I thought of giving her the money for a cab, but I only had a few dollars left in my wallet. I thought of stopping at the cash machine on Third Avenue, but then I figured that I had treated her enough.

Still, as we walked to the subway, I kept asking her to take a cab.

"Leave me alone," she said. But I was afraid somebody would attack her. She was wearing a flimsy dress, she had put her lipstick back on, and she had one hundred and fifty dollars in her purse.

At Lexington, I stopped at a cash machine. I didn't want to be cheap, and I had destroyed enough things that night. I gave her twenty dollars. She kissed me on the cheek, and we held each other. She pressed against me like she was my girlfriend. Then a lone late-night taxi came our way.

We kissed good-bye. "I'm sorry about that old man," she said. I closed the door and the taxi took her away.

Russia

I walked east down Eighty-sixth Street towards Carl Schurz Park. I was thinking of this bad spy novel I had read. The hero had been taught that sleep was a weapon. That as long as he slept enough, he had a chance to survive. So I pretended I was a spy in a sleeping city and that things were looking very bad for me. I figured I'd go rest on a bench in Carl Schurz Park and regain my strength.

That was the part of me that wanted to survive. The other part of me hoped that someone would come along and find me on the bench and mug me and kill me.

I made it to the promenade in Carl Schurz and sat on one of the benches that overlooks the East River. The Triborough Bridge was lit up and its lights melted across the water like candles.

I lay down and I had to slip my legs through the circular armrest in the middle of the bench. It was like being strapped to a bed, which was good. I couldn't fall out, and if a mugger did come along it would be hard for me to escape. I rolled my sport coat and put it under my head for a pillow. I held myself; there was a dampness so close to the water. I tried to be a spy and fall asleep, but I thought of Henry screaming at me.

But then I did sleep, until a policeman woke me up at dawn. "You have to sit up," he said. For a moment I thought it was the policeman who had come when I wrecked my car, but it wasn't.

I sat there and looked for the sun, but it was hidden behind thick towers of clouds. There was a pinkness to the sky, but no sun. I left the promenade and I walked back to the diner on Eighty-sixth Street. The late-night waiters were gone. No one recognized me as the man who had been in there hours before with a young transsexual.

I had coffee and toast and then I went out and bought a *Times*. I came back in, ordered more coffee, and glanced at everything and then read the whole sports section. I studied the baseball statistics and that kept my mind off of things.

I returned to the apartment around eight-thirty. I had picked up some plastic garbage bags at the supermarket. I figured that several of those and my suitcase could probably handle everything I owned; I'd pack up quietly while Henry slept and then I'd take a taxi to a flop hotel. I was going to end up in a hotel after all. I thought I'd go to the Riverview on Jane Street. I opened the door of the apartment quietly and tiptoed in. Henry was dressed and standing at the end of his bed fanning out his blanket before laying it down.

He looked at me for a second and said, "Do we have to keep doing this?"

"Doing what?" I asked. I was defensive. I braced myself for him to attack me verbally.

"Going to bed. Getting up. Going to bed. Getting up." He lay his blanket down and patted it.

"Do you have any alternatives?" I asked.

"None that I can afford," he said, and then he walked past me and went into the bathroom. I went and sat on my bed still holding the garbage bags. I listened to Henry urinate. He waited till he was finished and then flushed. The first time ever. He came out and said, "Let's go to the beach in Brooklyn."

"Don't you want me to move out?"

"I'm not as old-fashioned as you think . . . We can go to Brighton Beach. They have Russian cafés on the boardwalk."

He was pretending that nothing of consequence had occurred. I started to say, "I'm sorry," but he walked out of my room. I had a feeling that he thought that any words of apology would be inadequate.

I was really too tired to go to the beach, but of course I would do whatever he said, and so we left the apartment and we got coffee-to-go at The Salt of the Earth. When we were in the Eldorado, speeding down the FDR Drive, spilling and sipping our coffees,

I tried to play along like nothing had happened, and so I asked, "How was the wedding?"

"Too silly for words. They had a renegade divorced priestess with rings on her fingers, showing a lot of leg. She knew I didn't approve of her and she didn't like the way I read from the King James."

"Did Bellman wear a suit?"

"Yes, they found something respectable. And there was a quiver of feeling from him when he said, 'I vill.' And Gershon was happy. He may have proposed to the woman he brought. She's slightly mad. She's in her forties and still a graduate student, but she wouldn't say where. If she's smart she'll say yes."

I wanted to ask him why he came back early, but if I did that would bring what had happened too close to the surface. I did ask, "Lagerfeld enjoyed herself?"

"Of course. Free food. But it won't please her to take the train today. She won't like paying for a ticket. But I had to leave. I was sharing a room with Gershon and he can hardly breathe, he makes an incredible racket. And I didn't have plugs or my eye mask. I put tissue in my ears, but that doesn't work. So I came home. Also I didn't want to see Bellman in the morning; it would have been too much."

I was quiet, but then I said, "Henry, I'm so sorry about . . . when you came home," and then I added weakly, "I was drunk . . ."

"Stop saying you're sorry. Don't be so obsequious."

"Aren't you angry?"

"Yes. But I'm also fond of you."

"You kicked Bellman out for doing less."

"It would be sad to lose you."

"I was with a transsexual."

"Nobody's perfect . . . I thought it was a hermaphrodite. That would have been more interesting."

"No, a transsexual. She takes female hormones, that's why she's like that."

"You're always talking about transvestites, transsexuals. I went through that in Paris in the fifties. Maybe you can go to the American Legion for counseling."

"The American Legion?"

"Oh, yes, they'll straighten you out . . . Or maybe analysis, that might be what you need."

"I've thought of it," I said, to show him that I wanted to change. "Have you ever tried analysis?"

"In college. When my aunt died. I was depressed. I saw the analyst once and he gave up immediately. He told my mother, 'He's going to do what he wants, there's nothing we can do for him.' He was right."

"Do *you* have any advice for me?"

"Don't sin anymore. Don't sin against your body. Follow the Bible. Work. Work on your soul. And pray for enlightenment. Maybe I'll get some too, enlightenment, since we're in the same apartment."

I stared at Henry. His hands were on the wheel. His eyes were on the road ahead. He was fond of me. He would be sad to lose me.

We parked near the boardwalk in Brighton Beach. It was a perfect Sunday in May: hot, but not sweltering; cloudless skies. The beach was already starting to fill up with people lying on towels and blankets. The ocean was calm and blue like the sky above.

We walked down the boardwalk and there were lots of old people walking or sitting on the benches: stooped-over men with ancient, resigned faces, not intelligent faces really, but beautiful for their weathering; old women in peasant dresses with thick arms that had cooked thousands of meals. Brighton Beach felt like Europe, but in the far distance I could see the Cyclone of Coney Island.

We sat at a table at an outdoor café. I looked at the menu and it was written in Russian and English. Henry had said that they had Russian cafés in Brighton Beach, but I hadn't fully grasped what he meant. He was always talking about Russia and I had half-ignored him. I listened to the people around me; no one was speaking English.

I said to Henry, "It really is Russian here."

"Oh, yes. They call this Little Odessa. It's all Russian."

It was probably Russian-Jewish, half my heritage, but for Henry this was the closest to Russia he could get. The sun was bright;

we squinted at the menus. A pretty, dark-haired Russian waitress came and we ordered caviar and blinis and lemonade. It wasn't very expensive—Russian prices, only about six dollars. But caviar! We were living it up.

Some seagulls were poking around on the boardwalk just a few feet from us. Henry said, "Look at them. They walk around like they own the place and they're totally dependent. They don't have a pot to pee in!"

"They do look proud with their chests puffed out," I said.

"Yes."

The waitress brought our lemonades. Henry stared at the ocean. I stared at him.

"I guess we're not like the three sisters anymore," I said.

"How?"

"Well, we finally made it to Russia."

Henry thought about this a moment, then he said, "Yes, but we should go to the real Russia in August. Two can operate very well over there. And you need two. It's safer. Think about it . . . I'll hold off the IRS and you can save some money. We won't need much. It's only three dollars for a bottle of champagne in Riga."

Also available from Pushkin Press

"The word 'hilarious' seems inadequate. The novel is extremely
funny but it is also sad and poignant, and almost incredibly clever"

Guardian

AN IMPRINT OF PUSHKIN PRESS

ONE – an imprint of Pushkin Press – is the home of our contemporary, original English language publishing. The list is as varied as it is distinct, encompassing new voices and established names, fiction and non-fiction. Our stories range from dystopian tales to comic ones, prize-winning novels to memoirs. We select only a small handful of titles each year, and publish them with particular care and attention, which means that every book is a gem. And what makes them ONE? Compelling writing, unique voices, great stories.

THE BEAUTIFUL BUREAUCRAT
Helen Phillips

ONLY KILLERS AND THIEVES
Paul Howarth

AMONG THE LIVING AND THE DEAD
Inara Verzemnieks

SYMPATHY
Olivia Sudjic

SCHOOL OF VELOCITY
Eric Beck Rubin

DON'T LET MY BABY DO RODEO
Boris Fishman

DAREDEVILS
Shawn Vestal

THE MINOR OUTSIDER
Ted McDermott